Prologue

Tim trudged along the rain-soake
busy road. His dark blue anorak was zipp
December drizzle and he clasped a sheet of paper, on which was
printed an outline street map, in his hand, at which he would glance
from time to time, trying to pinpoint his location according to the
names of the side streets that he passed one by one. He didn't
know this city and he had never had to find his way around a
strange place by himself before. He certainly didn't want to be late.

Tim had arrived, after a long train journey that had lasted all
day and had involved crossing London on the underground, late the
previous evening. He had found the guest house that his mother
had booked for him close to the station and had checked in without
any problem. His subsequent search for something to eat for supper
had been less successful and he had ended up sitting on a garden
wall in the cold December darkness eating some nondescript
Chinese take away food from a yellow polystyrene box. He had
almost wished that he was back in the warmth and familiarity of the
school Dining Hall where he at least felt that he belonged and had
friends. Tim had never been totally alone before in his life.

When he awoke to the unfamiliar sound of heavy morning
traffic crawling through a large city centre, he had stood looking out
of his bedroom window at buildings of yellowy white bricks and the
junction of two wide, red coloured roads. To Tim it had felt as if he
was on the other side of the world rather than merely the other end
of the country.

After breakfast he had thought it best to set off on foot for
his destination immediately as he had no idea how long it would
take him to get there. He was certain that it was better to find the
place and then hang around to be sure that he would not be late.

Tim turned left at the junction with another main road. This
was the one! Starting to feel more positive because of his success in
navigating he began to look eagerly around him for likely buildings.
After about another half a mile a group of large red brick buildings

and modern grey concrete buildings of strange shapes came into view, set within bleak, winter dead, gardens. This must be it.

Tim crossed the road and stood on the pavement outside the main entrance to the campus. It appeared huge. Tim turned his printed map over to look at the other side, on which a detailed map of the campus was printed. He felt excited, as if he was standing on the edge of his future and intimidated because he had no idea what to expect from the afternoon ahead. Was he allowed to simply walk into the campus? He half expected, as he headed up the entrance road, to be shouted at or to be stopped and asked who he was and why he was there. Nothing happened. Tim walked past a continuous stream of young men and women, all cheerful in groups of friends, all knowing where they were going and what they were doing. Tim remembered again how alone he was.

Since he had arrived some two hours before his appointment Tim set about exploring the campus with the aid of his map. It proved to be surprisingly easy once he got the hang of it and he soon discovered the tower block that contained the library, the wave shaped concrete building which contained the Economics department where he was due at an open afternoon later and the brick and wood Union building in which Tim sought refuge in the "Main Refectory" where he bought a cup of coffee and sat under a powerful fan heater set into the ceiling in an effort to get his anorak and trousers dry and his body comfortably warm once again. He watched the continued flow of young men and women coming in, eating and drinking alone or in groups and going out again. They all looked very grown up and sophisticated to Tim. They must, he assumed, be very intelligent and hurrying to lessons or to do some incredibly difficult practical work or to write intimidatingly long and complicated essays. He doubted that he would even be able to do well enough at his "A" levels to get a place here, let alone manage the work if he did.

At one thirty Tim found his way to the Economics department and reported to a desk at which sat a number of people who turned out to be existing students. He ticked his name off on a printed list and went to stand round the edge of the room with other visitors. Nobody knew anybody else so there was little conversation and only the occasional nervous laughter. At last they were all called into a huge lecture theatre where they were welcomed to the department, told a bit about the kinds of work that went on and were then handed over to the students who had been sitting at the welcome desk. They introduced themselves and talked a bit about where they had come from and what it was like to be at the university. Tim assumed that they had only been chosen to do this because they had good things to say.

Next the group was given a quick guided tour of the campus, most of which Tim had already found for himself. After that they got into two minibuses and were driven around the local area, looking at student houses and large halls of residence. Finally, they went to a large new "Student Village" three miles away from the main campus which, they were told, was the most popular choice for new students. They got off the buses and were shown round the facilities and a study. It looked surprisingly similar to a study at school to Tim.

Back at the Economics faculty they were offered tea and biscuits and were free to ask any questions or to go when they wanted to. Tim was tired and had seen enough. He headed alone back to the guest house beside the station, found himself a better meal in a Pizza restaurant in which he could sit and eat in the comfort of the restaurant and then spent a bit of time exploring the city centre since the rain had finally stopped. Tomorrow he would embark on the long journey back to school.

Getting In

Tim sat alone in his bedroom looking at the hand written, self-addressed envelope. Obviously, he knew perfectly well what was inside it. His "A" level results. It wasn't really trepidation that was stopping him from opening the envelope, he was going to have to do so and put up with whatever the news turned out to be. He was just feeling a kind of disinterest, an antipathy towards what he saw as his old school's final effort to make a claim upon him, to influence and alter the course of his life remotely, and he didn't like the idea that Barforth School could still exert life changing power over him even after he had officially left.

Tim stuck his finger under the corner of the flap and ripped the top of the blue envelope open. Taking a deep breath to steady his nerves, which despite his best efforts were causing his heart to pound, he extracted the small, type written slip of paper.

A Level Grades : Timothy Croy

Geography : A

Economics : A

Biology : C

Tim stared at the slip, seeing yet uncomprehending. Reading those three life changing letters again and again. Was this correct? Did it really refer to him? So far removed were these grades from those that the school had grudgingly predicted, that they had repeatedly, disparagingly, told him were the best that he could hope for, if he was lucky, that he found himself struggling to comprehend the simple message that he found before his eyes. This meant that he had safely secured his provisional offer of a place at his first choice of university. So successfully had five years of struggle against the might of a great English Public-School ground down upon the confidence and self-esteem of Tim Croy that he had barely bothered to even go through the motions of applying for a place at university almost a year earlier. The school had not been encouraging, only allowing him to do so at the insistence of his parents, and Tim had not really thought about university as a realistic option for him. He had spent a lot of time seeking other options that were open to the less academic school leaver. An apprenticeship to train as a gardener with the Royal Horticultural Society, suggested to him by a friendly man for whom he had gardened successfully during many recent school holidays or joining the Royal Air Force, which seemed to Tim to offer a kind of security of belonging to something together with the possibility of the excitement of learning to fly fighter jets. But now it seemed that he had an academic career ahead of him. Tim knew that, with these results, his parents would expect him to take up his place at university. There could, *would* be no discussion.

Tim stood up, feeling, to his surprise, slightly shaky. He headed down stairs, across the polished wooden floor of the large, rectangular hall and into the oversized stone floored kitchen in which the family spent most of their time. Mrs. Croy was standing at the sink, trying hard to appear engrossed in cleaning the salad vegetables that she had just picked from the vegetable garden but, Tim knew very well, actually on tenterhooks to find out what news the long-expected letter had contained.

"I passed them all!"

"Really dear. *All* of them?"

"Yeah. Two "A's" and a "C"."

"Oh Tim. That's fantastic. Well done! Go and tell your father. I think he's doing something in the garage."

Tim sloped off to the old coach house that now saw duty as a garage and workshop. Mr. Croy was dressed in a dark blue boiler suit and was lying on his back underneath the miniature tractor with which they cut the grass.

"What are you doing?"

"I'm tightening the drive belt. It was starting to slip when the blades were under load. Come and see how it's done."

Tim lay on his back and slid expertly under the machine beside his father. He liked tinkering with machines and enjoyed the peaceful masculine environment of the garage.

"I got two "A's" and a "C"" he told his father.

"Only a "C"?"

As ever, Mr. Croy put the emphasis on the least good part of the equation. Tim didn't care. That was just how his father was. He always had been and always would be like that. There was no ulterior meaning to be taken from it. The two men settled into silent tinkering with spanners, bolts and toothed rubber belts.

"Tim, *Tim* "

"Yeah"

"Telephone for you dear. One of your friends I think."

Tim thumped down the polished wooden stairs to the telephone in the hall.

"Hello"

"Hi Tim, it's Anthony. You alright?"

"Yeah. You?"

"Yeah. I got into university. Did you?"

"Yep. Just shows, doesn't it?"

"Yeah. Mike passed too. I've just been talking to him."

"Great!"

"Listen Tim, my parents said we can use their cottage in Devon for a celebration party if we want. Next week. Can you come?"

"Oh cool. Yeah I don't see why not."

"Great. It'll be you, me and Mike, I think. Can we go in your car Tim?

"Yeah, of course. Can you come down here on the train because you live half way up to Scotland, don't you?"

" Yeah, OK, can I stay at yours the night before?"

"I'll check with mum. It should be OK. We can pick up Mike on our way, he must be in the same kind of direction as Devon!"

Tim waited at the station for Anthony. He had had to negotiate quite persistently with his parents to gain permission to go away with a group of boys for a holiday in his car. He had had to endure a long diatribe from mother and father about the dangers of young men who might try to show off by taking risks while driving. They had reminded him of the terrible fate of Mike earlier in the summer. Tim had reacted furiously, pointing out that they had no idea if he had been doing anything wrong or not and that, surely, they trusted their own son. But now it was all sorted. A week of unsupervised fun stretched before the three friends. Life felt good!

The roar and rattle of the slow and ancient country train pulling into the station interrupted Tim's thoughts. There was Anthony jumping on to the platform, his face, as always, split in half by his wicked grin.

"Hi mate!"

"Mate! Hi!"

Tim grabbed his friend's bag and they headed out of the station to the gravelled car park.

"Oh cool! I wish I'd taken my test. Trouble is I didn't get my act together quick enough to send off for my licence. I had the forms at school but well, you know what I'm like!"

Tim drove through the town, out on to the main road and then off into the maze of single-track lanes that lead to his house. They met a tractor coming in the opposite direction which necessitated Tim reversing for nearly half a mile to a passing place.

"Do you have to do that often?"

"Every time I go out, yeah."

"I'm surprised you ever get anywhere."

"Well that's just how it is round here mate."

First thing the next morning the boys dumped their bags in the boot of Tim's car, together with two big cardboard boxes of provisions that Mrs. Croy insisted that they would need. With a final appeal from her to Anthony to encourage Tim to drive safely Tim let in the clutch and the car crunched along the gravel drive and out into the lane. Tim knew the way to Mike's house, having driven there several times before, and they arrived a little earlier than they had anticipated. Mike came out to greet them and ushered them inside for a cup of coffee and biscuits. Mike's mother knew both the visitors, and Tim had become almost a second son to her over the past three months so the atmosphere was relaxed and easy. At last the three boys got into Tim's car and they set off on the long drive to Devon.

"Your mum's really decent Mike!" Anthony commented.

"No fussing about boys and girls or drinking too much or the dangers of driving. You should have heard mine! It was her who suggested we might like to use her cottage but when I said yes, she started shitting it!"

Tim laughed.

"I had the drive safely lecture and the don't drink too much one too. She didn't do the sex one though – you couldn't imagine my mum talking about that sort of thing, could you Anthony?"

Anthony laughed.

"Well, mine already knows about car accidents, obviously," said Mike "but she's not at all embarrassed to go on and on about sex and babies and things. I don't know what she thinks I do all day but she's got a really dirty mind for a middle-aged mum!"

They all laughed

"Seriously though Mike, your folks always seem well cool to me. Mine are so old fashioned and up tight". Tim turned on the radio and the boys settled into their journey.

By the time they were in the middle of Somerset Tim needed to buy petrol and they all wanted lunch so they pulled into a Happy Eater. Mike got an envelope out of the back pocket of his jeans.

"Mum gave us the money for all the petrol so I'll pay for this."

When they had refuelled the car and themselves, they set off once more, looking forward now to getting there and starting the holiday properly.

"Where, exactly, are we going Anthony?" Tim asked. I need you to direct me.

"*Me?*"

"Well yes, obviously. It's your house and you know where it is."

"Well I know the name of the village but I've no idea how to get there".

"You plonker! There's a map in the back of the AA handbook in the glove box. Use that to navigate."

When the holiday makers finally found their destination Anthony and Tim unloaded the car and Anthony showed them round the tiny cottage.

"The good thing is there's a pub in the village and you can easily walk to the beach.

"Will you be OK on the beach Mike?"

Anthony suddenly sounded concerned for his friend, considering, too late, the problems that he might face doing the kinds of things about which neither of the other boys had to think twice.

"I'll be fine. I've done so much training this holiday. I can swim easily now and my walking is more or less normal too. Oh, and I've almost got the hang of driving with hand controls now too. So really please don't treat me any different to how you used to."

"Yeah, we went for a long walk around the town a couple of weeks ago. You'd never know there was anything wrong"

Tim interjected to avoid any sensitivities getting out of hand. Tim was, himself, close to being over protective of his friend but he knew that Anthony tended to speak without much thought for other people's feelings.

"Let's get something to eat." He began to unpack one of his mother's cardboard boxes onto the kitchen table. Mike started on the other box.

"Decent! You should be careful what you say about your mum Tim!"

Tim looked up to see Mike retrieving twelve cans of beer and two bottles of wine from the depths of his box. They had been camouflaged under packets of biscuits, bags of crisps, a huge fruit cake and a jar of coffee granules. Tim was truly surprised and felt quite gratified. His mother often did come up trumps in completely unexpected ways.

The weather was very hot and heavily humid, as late August in the West Country so often is and this made the boys feel lazy, spending the main part of the day either lying on the beach or loafing around in the dark coolness of the cottage, enjoying themselves doing nothing of any significance.

"What are you going to do about your Army sponsorship?" Tim asked Anthony one afternoon as the boys lay on the beach.

"I've already turned it down. It felt quite good being able to reject an offer. My dad said that it wasn't a good idea to tie myself into sixteen years of commitment at this stage of my life and I decided he's probably right."

"Mmm yeah, I've got to make a decision by next week about my offer from the RAF. I like the idea of flying fast fighter jets and £100 a week would be brilliant. I could have loads of fun with that at university."

"Don't do it!" Mike interjected. "You'll end up spending all your time marching around and having orders shouted at you. I bet you won't get near a fighter jet for years."

"I agree with Mike. You can't bear doing as you're told Tim". Anthony pointed out.

"I've spent most of my life doing as I'm told. How can you say that?"

"Oh, come on mate. You've never really been like that. Yeah, you're good at looking like you are but really you always do what you want. I used to envy the way you could get away with doing exactly what you wanted without anybody realising, even in the Third Form. I always ended up in trouble when I tried."

Tim thought about these comments. He trusted his friends and was secretly rather flattered with their perception of him. He resolved that he would turn down the offer of sponsorship as soon as he got home. Like Anthony, he relished the idea of being in the position of power over authority.

With incredible speed the week had come to an end. Everyone had had a brilliant time doing nothing at all. Each young man felt thoroughly refreshed and inspired to face his new life at university, confident of the friendships from his past and excited by the untold possibilities that the next chapter of his life held.

In the first week of September a large, fat, brown envelope from the university arrived for Tim, in which were forms to be filled in, information about where to be met at the station, when to register and how to collect the student grant. He had been given a shared room in a large student house about two miles from the main campus. Tim had hoped to secure a place in the new student village as this offered single rooms but that was obviously not to be. There was a big booklet containing information about special activities that were being arranged by the student union for "Freshers" during the first week of term and information about all the sports and special interest clubs that were available to join. The opportunities seemed quite endless to Tim who had been used to the strictly controlled and supervised limited choices of a boarding school. He couldn't help wondering what the catch was. This wealth of information and form filling served to confirm the impending start of a new phase of life. Combined with the weird feeling of still being at home in September, when for the past thirteen years, most of his life, the start of the month had heralded a return to school, Tim began to feel a sense of some trepidation. Most of Tim's experiences at different schools had been unpleasant, usually involving being bullied, abused or forcibly repressed by the weight of "the system". It was only natural that he should assume that university would prove to follow a similar pattern and he began to feel that, now that he had a choice for the first time in his life, he really didn't want to take that risk. Tim didn't want to disappoint his parents and his relationship with them had become rather remote and formal, probably as a result of years of separation enforced upon them by boarding school. Tim had nobody with whom to talk about his fears and concerns so he simply buried them in the back of his mind, as he had learned to do with most of the problems that he had had to face in his life so far. He had long ago learned that he had to work his way through life alone. "Make lots of friends and have lots of fun and the rest will fall into place." Had been the advice of one of the men for whom he worked as a gardener in the holidays and Tim liked and trusted him. He hoped that he would be able to follow such cheering advice but somehow doubted that anything could be that easy.

Tim had taken a job working on a stall at the Southampton Boat Show in the third week of September and the daily commute across the New Forest to Southampton and the frantic environment of the show provided a welcome and lucrative diversion from worries about the future. Tim realised that, whatever happened, he was ready and capable to meet the needs of the world of adulthood and commerce head on and he began to feel enthused and stimulated by the prospects that life seemed to hold.

Before they had left school in July Tim had arranged with his parents to take the role of guardian to his friend Usman who had joined the school from Saudi Arabia in the Sixth Form and with whom Tim had had developed a strong friendship. The Croys' were very happy to do so as Mr. Croy often did business in the Gulf region and his clients and their families had been regular visitors to the Croy household so they were used to welcoming people from overseas into their family. On the first of October Tim and his mother set off to Heathrow Airport to meet Usman. He had got a place at Southampton University to read Biochemistry. Tim grinned and waved as Usman came out of the arrivals gate and made his way through the barriers to the public area. He was pushing a well loaded trolley. The serious looking young man shook hands with Mrs. Croy very formally, as Tim remembered he had done with him in the dormitory at Barforth when they had first met.

"I am very truly pleased to meet you Mrs. Croy."

She smiled. "It's good to meet you. Tim's told us so much about you that I feel as if we know you already. Let's get in the car and go home. You must be tired and hungry."

Back home Tim took Usman to a guest bedroom and showed him round the important parts of the house. "Just make yourself at home mate. People will quickly stop being polite to you so you'll have to fend for yourself."

"It is a very famous house, I think?"

"Famous?" Tim was not sure what Usman meant.

"It is, I understand, historic."

"Oh, no. not really, not the way you're thinking, it's just an old house, like most houses in England."

"Anabelle, **Anabelle!**" Tim bellowed up the stairs from the hall, wanting to introduce his sister to his friend. Anabelle came gliding down the wooden staircase, dressed to kill. She was excited at the opportunity to get friendly with a dark and wealthy Arab. So much more exotic, *enviable,* than any of her friends' boyfriends.

When Tim's father came home from work the boys were relaxing in the television room, slumped comfortably in the deep sofas chatting intermittently. Usman stood up quickly and proffered his hand in his customary formal greeting.

"I am very honoured to meet you sir!"

"Assalamo alaikum! Welcome to our house. I hope Tim's made you comfortable." Mr Croy was adept at making people relax and he understood how alien one could feel when alone in a foreign country.

Mrs Croy called them to get ready for dinner. Tim knew that she would have prepared the dining room for the meal because she felt that that was the polite thing to do with a visitor in the house. Soon she would relax and they would be able to return to eating in the informality of the kitchen, which was what they always did when alone as a family.

"I don't know if you've ever eaten venison before, Usman? It's not really the season for it but I had it in the freezer and I know that it's *halal* so that you can eat it dear."

"You are very kind, Mrs. Croy."

"I bet he doesn't know which animal venison comes from. You'd never be able to work it out from that silly name." Tim laughed. *"I don't know where that name comes from!"*

"It's the meat from a deer. It was shot in the wild, by people who go hunting in the woods around here. That's why it's *halal.* "Mrs Croy explained to her young visitor who was now looking totally confused. She felt sorry for him. He was very courageous, coming alone to a foreign country. She felt sure that Barforth School would not have looked after him well. Why on Earth would a Muslim family send their son to live in such a profoundly Christian school? She remembered the horrific story Tim had told them of the poor boy being forced to shave his beard off in front of all the laughing boys on his first night in the school. She had been proud of Tim for being angry about it and had been close to telephoning the Head Master to complain. Her husband had restrained her, pointing out that it was really none of her business.

"Did they offer you *halal* food at school Usman?"

Both boys laughed. "Mum! I sometimes think you live in another world! Of-course they didn't. They hated him for being foreign. They only had him in the school because they wanted his dads' money."

Mrs. Croy believed Tim. Once again, she felt proud of her son for standing up for what was right, never mind the personal cost. That is what she had hoped he would be like. She resolved that she and her family would make this nastiness up to poor Usman. It was essential that he should see that real English people could and would look after him properly.

Two days later Tim drove Usman to Southampton university. He would be taking the train to Hull a day later. Before they left Mrs Croy insisted on giving Usman a large box of food and their telephone number. She extracted a promise that, if he ever needed anything, he was to telephone her first. Further he was to come to visit them regularly. Her husband worked in Southampton so he could collect him from university on a Friday evening and take him back on the Monday morning. Whether he wanted to or not, Usman had to agree. Nobody ever had a chance against the full force of Mrs. Croys' good intentions!

Getting There

Tim was packing a large new suitcase with the things that he thought he would need for his new life. As he filled it with sweaters, T shirts and jeans he made a pile of tweed jackets, formal trousers and shirts and his suit on the bed. They were school clothes and Tim had no further use for them. Mrs Croy came in to see how he was managing.

"Please, at least keep your suit. You may need it one day and it's a good one dear."

After considerable discussion Tim agreed to take it with him. It wasn't worth arguing about it!

"And you ought to take at least a couple of proper shirts and trousers. You need to be able to look smart if you need to."

"That's a bit of a tautology mum. I don't want any of those school things and I haven't got room for them anyway. Chuck them or burn them or give them to a jumble sale but I won't use them again so I'm not keeping them in here."

Tim was adamant and his mother understood that there was no point in forcing the issue. She went and collected a large plastic bag and folded the pile of unwanted but good quality clothes into it. There would be a church jumble sale soon, she knew, and there were people in the village who would be glad of such nice things, she felt sure.

"You will be careful, won't you Tim. There will be so many new things and there won't be any kind of supervision for you. You have to take responsibility for yourself now."

"Of-course mum."

"I hope you know how to cook safely. It's so easy to fall into eating the wrong sort of things or to make yourself ill by not cooking things properly. I've put a simple cookery book in your bag dear."

" I used to cook things at school mum."

"But you didn't *have* to. There were always three meals a day to help yourself to."

"Three *disgusting* meals a day mum!"

Tim could feel that there was more that his mother really wanted to talk about and he could see from the way that she was moving from one foot to the other that she was feeling uncomfortable. He waited for the sex and drugs talk. As expected, it came, but in such an oblique, indirect and discreet way that it was easy for him both to ignore and agree to at the same time. Mrs Croy had done her duty. Satisfied that she had done her best and that Timothy was now fully equipped for everything that he may face, she gathered up her big carrier bag of jumble and left her son to finish his packing. One had to let children fight their own battles.

First thing on Saturday morning Tim loaded his suitcase and a sports bag stuffed with bits and pieces that he had decided may be useful into his fathers' Ford Granada Estate. Mr. Croy had made the unusual decision to take responsibility for taking his son to the station to begin his journey into student life. Usually he left such things to his wife but he understood that she was feeling rather emotional at finally having to let her first child leave the security of environments that she had selected for him. It would be easier for him to do it. Timothy was a sensible young man and Mr. Croy had no doubt that he would be fine. The two men chatted intermittently on the half hour journey to the station, about the latest cars, the progress that was being made to break the power of the trades' unions by Mrs Thatcher. Father and son were not especially close but their relationship was easier because of that. Tim wasn't in the mood to talk much. He was preoccupied with having to make his way across London from one station to another on the underground. He did not know London and had never been there by himself. Beyond the immediate need to navigate the underground there loomed the uncomfortable uncertainty of what he would face upon his arrival in his new life.

Father and son shook hands beside the car outside the station entrance.

"Good luck." Mr. Croy offered the warmest wish he could think of.

"Cheers dad!" Tim swung his sports bag onto his shoulder, lifted his over laden suitcase with one hand and went into the station.

Mr. Croy drove away without a second glance. He wanted to try to find some cheap paint in the surplus stores on the outskirts of town.

Tim settled himself into a seat on the almost empty train to London. Since it was a Saturday there were none of the usual commuters and those who would later be going up to town to shop or to see a show would not think about setting off for two or three hours yet. Tim took up the whole area of two bench seats and a Formica table with his large suitcase and bag.

When he disembarked at Waterloo Tim took a moment to read the signs directing passengers to different underground lines. He consulted a colour keyed map of the underground that he had picked up at his home station and worked out that he had to go for two stops on one line and then five more on another. Jutting his chin determinedly he heaved his heavy case up once more and began the descent of many stairs to the underground station. When the first tube train arrived, sliding its' doors open to disgorge its' cargo of people, Tim was shocked to see that there was no room in it. He watched, appalled, as dozens of people pushed and shoved their way into the already crowded train. While Tim still politely waited the doors slid shut and the train departed without him. It wasn't until this had happened a second time that Tim realised that there was not only no room on the trains but that there was no room for him to be polite. Tim pushed his way onto the next train like the best of them and then struggled to keep hold of his case and look out for his stop through the thick wall of humanity that blocked both the windows and the maps that hung on the walls of the train.

At last Tim reached Kings Cross. By now both his arms ached from carrying his over full suitcase. He wished that his mother had bought one with wheels that enabled it to be pulled along. He had noticed, with envy, that lots of people had these. Really it was typical of his parents to have no idea about the latest good ideas and to end up buying outdated and less than useful stuff. It obviously wasn't because they couldn't afford it, just that they didn't bother to investigate the possibilities properly. Tim's thoughts were interrupted by the sight of a queue. What seemed to be an endless line of boys and girls, all of about his age, all with a few weighty bags and cases and all waiting for the train to Hull. Could all of these people be students like him?

"Holy shit!" he heard another young man exclaim as he too comprehended the length of wait that he could look forward to.

Tim was shocked at the crudeness, the blasphemy indeed, of such language. He wondered if everyone would be as rough and common as that. Tim began to worry once again about exactly what he might be getting himself into.

Getting onto the train at last, Tim walked down the central aisle of several carriages before finding an empty seat opposite an old lady.

"Is this free?" "

Yes, I suppose so".

Tim heaved his case up into the rack above him, it barely fitted. He pushed his bag beside it and took the seat next to the dirty window. A girl came and asked if she could sit beside the lady. She could and did.

"This is the train for Hull, isn't it?"

She asked the question that Tim had wanted to ask but hadn't, not wanting to appear as stupid as he was now starting to feel. Another young man asked to sit beside Tim. Tim helped him to manoeuvre his huge bags onto the luggage rack.

"Thanks mate. I'm Lee."

"I'm Tim."

"Are you a student Tim?"

"Yep. Just starting."

"Me too."

The conversation petered out. Tim wasn't sure that Lee was his type. He had yellow highlights in his dark hair and he wore an earring. A yob, in Tim's Public-School parlance. The train started to move with a slight jerk, accompanied by much loud whistling from the guard and the slamming of doors.

As the journey progressed the four strangers began to talk. The girl, who introduced herself as Fiona, asked the lady if she lived in Hull. She did. She had been visiting her son in Devon and she found it easier and cheaper to use the train than to drive. Fiona also was starting at the university. Lee and Tim said that they were starting too. Fiona asked if they were living in the student village. She was. Tim said that he'd applied to but had been put in a student house instead. Lee was in a student house too. He had applied to be in one but was disappointed that he had not got one close to the university. The lady told them that she lived quite near the student village. She had heard that life there was great fun. The conversation moved on to what they were studying, where they lived, whether or not they had liked their schools. The old lady was a retired school teacher.

"We will be arriving at Kingston Upon Hull Paragon in about five minutes. On behalf of British Rail, we hope you have enjoyed your journey with us" the loudspeaker crackled to the carriage.

People began to reach for luggage, fold up newspapers, shake themselves awake.

"Where's your house Tim?" Lee asked.

"Hold on." Tim fished a piece of paper from his pocket. "73, Cowper Road. I think it's near the student village."

"That's fucking incredible mate. I'm in that house too!"

"That really is amazing" agreed Tim.

"I wonder what the odds of that happening are?"

They were still laughing about the coincidence as they struggled off the train with their luggage and found the promised welcome team arranged behind trestle tables on the platform. Soon they were being bundled into a university mini bus and were on the way to their new home.

The minibus began stopping at addresses to enable people to get off. One boy got out at a big, impressive looking house. Three girls got out at the gates to a girls' hall of residence. Two more girls were dropped outside a row of small terraced houses.

"This is 73, Cowper. The one with the grey door."

Lee and Tim heaved their bags out of a vehicle for the last time. They stood for a moment in the street, looking at a large three-story semidetached house that must once have been quite grand but now purveyed a sense of gentle decline. The boys ambled up the short path and Lee rang the bell. Tim felt that he was very confident. He squared his shoulders and forced a grin in an effort to appear similarly sure of himself. The door was opened by a tall, dark haired, rather serious looking man.

"Hi, I'm Alex. I'm Senior resident. Come in."

Lee and Tim introduced themselves. Alex was consulting a sheet of paper.

"Lee, you're in here." He showed him into the room beside the front door, which obviously would once have been the sitting room.

He led Tim upstairs and then to the left and into a large room overlooking a long garden.

"This is Bill. Bill this is Tim."

The two boys greeted each other.

"Come with me Tim and I'll show you around the house." Bill followed the two out of the room and back downstairs, collecting Lee on the way, along the hall and into a huge room full of arm chairs and a few large tables with plastic, school style chairs.

"There are seventeen of us here, mainly Freshers like you but a few second years and three Finalists. You all share a bedroom except us Finalists. And through here is the kitchen." They followed him into a huge room, with two more Formica topped tables, some wooden lockers, a row of three kitchen sinks, a large fridge and three gas cookers.

"You each find a locker to keep your food in. There are pots and pans and things under the sinks. Please make sure you wash up after yourselves because otherwise the cleaning ladies will give me hell."

With that Alex left them. They wondered into the common room and sat down. They introduced themselves. Two more boys came in and sat down. More introductions. Conversation was awkward and sparse.

"Hi folks!" A tall, fair-haired young man came in. "I'm Mark. I'm a second year and I lived here last year too. You'll love it! I'm making a cup of tea. Are you all having one with me?"

Everyone accepted the welcome offer, glad to have a catalyst around which to gather.

As the afternoon merged into evening the house filled steadily with new boys and a few returning residents. It seemed that the time was filled with constant introductions and repeated potted histories, where they were from, what they were studying, what their journey had been like. Eventually, when everyone was safely installed and they were all lounging aimlessly in the common room Mark came back in again.

"Come on everyone! Let's go up the village to get our tea. I bet your all hungry and it's a good way to get to know your way around. The food's good and it's cheaper than getting it in the pub. There's a decent bar there too so we can socialise a bit after."

There followed a general exodus, grabbing of coats and jackets and cash, and everyone assembled in the hall ready to explore.

Mark was joined by Andy, another second year. Also fair haired, but less lanky than Mark, Andy was similarly cheerful and welcoming but rather less talkative. Mark was giving the Freshers a running commentary as they walked along the main street towards the student village.

" That's a good pub, we often end up there but mostly we go to the one in the other direction because it's nearer. That supermarket is the best in the area but it's not that big. That's a men's hall of residence and there's another beside the student village."

Tim recognised the student village from his visit to his department back in December the previous year. It seemed strange to be here again, buying a meal in the modern self- service restaurant. Now he was a part of this huge new world. A student. He had come a long way. When they had all eaten, chatting amongst themselves easily now, they headed for the bar. They decided to buy each other drinks in pairs. Tim went to buy a pint of Bitter for Bill and himself. He felt rather self-conscious, half expecting to be caught and "busted" for contravening school rules. Tim and Bill drank their pint and Bill went to replenish them. He came back with some dry roasted peanuts. They tasted good with the beer.

Back at the house everyone was in cheerful high spirits now and Mark and Andy set about making tea for everyone. Somebody produced some packets of biscuits and everyone enjoyed the remainder of the evening.

In bed at last, Bill and Tim talked into the night. Bill was from Devon and was into surfing. He had grown up in a tiny village beside the sea and had been to school locally and then done "A" levels at college in Exeter. He hadn't had, or much wanted, a wide group of friends. Tim understood that emotion well. He talked of his life at boarding school and the many harsh discomforts and restrictions. Bill was shocked that places could still be like that. The two boys began, separately, to feel that they would get on well. It was evident that neither was especially gregarious and that both could be described as definitely individual.

Monday October Sixth 1980

Tim woke from a deep sleep and, for a moment, he wasn't sure where he was or what he was supposed to be doing. He looked at his watch. Just past eight. He jumped quietly out of bed, grabbed his tooth brush and paste and headed out to the shower room. When he returned Bill was stirring and mumbling in his bed in the corner of the large room.

"Wake up mate. Busy day for us all today!" Tim grinned at his sleepy room-mate. Dressing quickly Tim went down to the untidy kitchen. Mark Kaye was already there, chatting to two middle aged ladies.

"This is Tim. Tim that's Louise and that's Brenda. They look after us as if we were their own family."

"Hello. Welcome to Hull" the ladies smiled.

Tim thanked them, unsure of how to continue the conversation. He busied himself making some toast from two pieces of the sliced white loaf that he had bought with him. There was no toaster so he lit the gas grill and had to stand watching as the fierce flame singed the bread on one side. He took it out and turned it over. This was the first new experience of the day. He made some instant coffee from the boiling water in the large kettle that was already bubbling on a gas ring. He sat at one of the two large tables in the kitchen, listening to Mark and the two ladies chatting and joking.

Peter French, another Fresher, came in and grabbed some cornflakes and milk from the fridge. Tim offered him coffee and he accepted with a grin of thanks. The two young men sat together.

"Are you going to catch the bus in to university Tim?"

"I suppose so yes. You?"

"Yep. Might as well go together then. See you in five."

They hurried off to collect bags and the papers that would be needed for the registration process.

Bill joined them in the hall and the three set off for the bus stop, looking forward to finally beginning the latest exciting chapter of their lives.

"I'm supposed to register at ten, being early in the alphabet". Tim volunteered. "Twenty past ten for me" Peter replied.

"I'm not until the afternoon" Bill said, "but I'm down for a Library tour at nine thirty. Then I'm off to the Physics department to sort things out there."

"I'm not bothering with a library tour. I can find my way around it when I need to." Peter seemed to be one who liked to do things on his own terms. Tim liked that.

When they disembarked at the university the three bid each other a cheerful farewell and went their separate ways. It was a bit early but Tim decided to make his way to the sports centre to do his registration anyway. He liked to be punctual, and he had nothing better to do. As he approached the sports-centre he could see a long queue of students snaking out of the main entrance and into the car park. This was evidently going to be a lengthy process. Tim joined the back of the line and soon there were many others behind him. As they got into the building people started to separate as they had to collect their grant cheque from their home local authority which were arranged alphabetically. From there Tim got his Student Union card laminated and then paid a large chunk of his grant to the university for his accommodation. Finally, he had to collect another large envelope of information from his department. At last he was finished. Looking at his watch Tim realised that he was due at the Library in ten minutes so he headed directly there.

"Tim Croy!"

Tim turned, surprised to hear his name being called, when he had expected to know no one.

"What are you doing here?"

Tim grinned. It was Richard Norton, a boy from the year above him at his old school.

"I could ask you that too, but I think it's pretty obvious!" Tim laughed.

"I'm in my second year now."

"What's it like?"

"It's great! You'll find it easy after Barforth."

"Good!" Tim had not enjoyed school but he knew that Richard had.

"I'd better rush. See you around!" He was gone.

Tim rather hoped that he wouldn't see him around. He didn't really see why he should be expected to be friends with somebody just because they found themselves in the same university, having been at the same school. He didn't much relish the concept of his new life becoming contaminated by his old one.

As Peter had so pithily suggested, the library tour was pretty much a waste of time, not that Tim had had anything else to do. He didn't learn much that he couldn't have worked out for himself but at least he had taken the opportunity that he had been offered.

Tim went into the student's union building to get something to eat. He grabbed a tray in the main refectory and helped himself to a large plate of chilli con carne and rice. He sat and ate alone at a small table, contemplating the constant comings and goings of the busy room. He remembered sitting there, alone, drinking coffee, nearly a year earlier. Again, he reflected with surprise that he had earned his place at university now, against all expectations. He couldn't help feeling pleased with himself. He had broken free of the tyranny of his old school. In an instant Tim understood why he had not felt pleased to have met Richard earlier. He and Richard had got on quite well at school, despite being in different year groups. Tim had been cox to the First eight in which Richard had been stroke so they had worked and played hard together and had enjoyed considerable success and many good times. Tim had not been happy at school, had never really fitted in. He wanted only to forget the place, put the nightmare five years behind him, to build a solid barrier between him and his past. Meeting someone from school was not a possibility that Tim had considered and he resented the intrusion, the shadow of fear that Richard seemed to Tim to represent.

After lunch and some time spent mooching around looking at the facilities of the Student Union and the University book shop, Tim made his way to the Faculty of Social Sciences in which was located the Economics department, where Tim would be studying. He recognised the grey concrete wave shaped building from his previous visit and quickly found his way into the glass atrium with shiny steel seats and polished black marble floors. It looked for all the world like an airport departure lounge. He headed up the wide spiral staircase to the second floor where his department was.

There were several other Freshers standing nervously, some chatting, others in lonely silence. The room began to fill and Tim found himself engaged in conversation with another boy who introduced himself as Neil

Blashford. He seemed like a cheerful kind of guy and Tim found him easy to talk to.

"Looks like there are about twice as many girls as blokes on this course" he observed.

"That'll be fun for us then." Tim responded, laughing.

Soon the group were shepherded into a lecture theatre where their lecturers and tutors introduced themselves and their specialist topics one by one. Everyone was surprised to discover that they would be required to study Philosophy as one of their units for the entire year, the lecture for which would be at nine fifteen every Monday morning, in the faculty of Perceptive Sciences. There was also to be a unit of Statistics in the Faculty of Mathematics, something that appeared to instil everyone in the room with gloom and dread.

The group were instructed to collect a booklet from the back of the room and that they were invited to a tea party in Staff House in half an hour. The bluntly spoken Northern accented lecturer in public finance advised them to come "because it's the only time you'll be given free cakes here in your life!" Tim remembered, wryly, his first day at school when new boys and their parents had been offered an impressive selection of cakes for the one and only time. Maybe university was going to be just like school after all.

Everyone gathered in the large room in Staff House, helping themselves to a plate of cakes and a cup of tea. Tim started talking to two girls who evidently knew each other.

"We're living in the same hall" explained the girl called Penny.

Her friend, Vicky, seemed very shy but very attractive to Tim. Neil came to join them together with another boy called Michael. Soon they were all chatting and laughing as if they had known each other for ages. The boys helped themselves to two more plates of cakes, keen, as they said, not to waste them. There was lots of food and, because the majority of the group were girls, it was not being eaten very fast. Eventually the party began to disperse as people made their way back to their new homes. Neil walked with Tim to catch the bus. He was living in the Hall near the student village.

"I liked the idea of having all my meals provided. Makes it easier and that way I know how much money I've got to spend on beer!"

"I definitely didn't want institutional food forced on me. I had enough of that at school" Tim responded. There was an easy banter developing between the two boys, both were feeling that they were making a good friend.

Back home in number seventy-three Tim realised that he needed to go shopping if he was to be able to cook himself supper and make breakfast the next morning. Dumping his sports bag of university stuff in his room Tim went straight back out and found his way to the supermarket that Mark had said was the better of the two. Wondering along the aisles Tim realised that he didn't know much about coking at all. He had often "cooked" at school, but always from packets of dried ingredients that only required the addition of water and to be boiled to form an adequate meal. He had recently been frying bacon and sausages for breakfast too but that wasn't exactly going to help him to make sufficient different meals to keep him satisfied. He would start experimenting once he had settled in. He bought milk, bread, cereal and some biscuits. For security he picked up two of his familiar dried ready meals and then, on a whim, a bag of potatoes. He knew you could do lots of different things with potatoes. Emboldened he grabbed a can of baked beans and a piece of cheddar cheese. Thus equipped, Tim went to the checkout, paid and returned to the house with his rather random selection of provisions.

Drinking a cup of tea in the common room Tim was pleased to be able to tell Peter that his prediction about the pointlessness of the library tour had been absolutely right. Peter laughed.

"I spent so long in the sports centre trying to jump through all their hoops that I wouldn't have had time for the Library even if I had wanted to."

"By the time I got there this afternoon it was almost impossible to get everything done" Bill complained as he sat down with his own mug of tea.

Later, when everyone had cooked and eaten some kind of food, leaving the kitchen looking as if it had been the site of a Saturday food market, most of the housemates decided to go for a pint or two in the nearest pub. The Lookers was a large, nondescript pub that looked as if had been built in the nineteen fifties. It contained one large bar and many tables of beaten copper surrounded with stools. The inevitable Juke box sat in one corner and blared the latest top twenty and a selection of more classic songs from the sixties together with a couple of fruit machines to entertain those who didn't want to play darts or watch football on the wall mounted television. To the eye of somebody looking for a nice evening out The Lookers had little to offer but, to the many students who lived within the locality, it was the closest and easiest choice and the pub had responded readily to the dependable student market. Tim and his house mates pulled several of the tables close together in the corner under the television and Lee and Andy went to buy twelve pints of Bitter. The conversation was lively and cheerful, more pints of beer followed, together with several large baskets of chips which the boys devoured enthusiastically.

Life felt good and Tim began to feel positive about his new adventure. Nights at The Lookers would become a recurring theme for Tim for the next three years.

Routine!

Tim slipped into the regular rhythm of university life almost without noticing that he was doing so. What he had seen as daunting before he started proved, in reality, to be little different from that which he had experienced at school. Most days consisted of two or three one-hour long lectures, with a large number of students in a lecture theatre, often from different faculties, listening to a lecturer who may or may not offer much in the way of inspiration or even interest. Tim was used to writing notes as he listened so had little difficulty in recording all the salient points in a clear and succinct manner from which he would be able to revise at some time in the future. Often there would also be a tutorial, with a maximum of eight students gathered in the small, comfortable office of a professor or a research student in which everyone would be expected to have read some set texts and to have prepared to speak about their understanding and what they had learnt from the work. These sessions were often very interesting to Tim and he felt confident and comfortable in articulating his opinions. The rest of the day was unstructured and it was up to the individual student to work in the library, making sure that they were prepared for tutorials or that they got essays written in time for the specified submission date. Tim had been expected to regulate his own working patterns for the last two years in the Sixth form at school so he had no difficulty in keeping up to date with his work without having to let it spill over into his evenings or weekends.

What was exercising Tim's mind was the growing realization that his education at Barforth School really had prepared him well for the university experience. That this was the case was clear for Tim to see, when he talked to his fellow students and heard how they had forgotten to read a required text before a tutorial or had not realised that they were supposed to have handed in an essay because "Nobody told me that I was meant to". All of these things that seemed second nature to Tim seemed to offer endless scope for trouble for most of his friends. Obviously, Tim was glad that he found the methodologies of university work undaunting, but he found it well nigh impossible to accept that he had his old school to thank for this happy state of affairs. Tim had hated school with a passion and the possibility that it may have imparted anything of any good to him was so at odds with everything that he believed and felt that he found his mind completely closed to the notion.

On the third evening of term Tim returned to his house and was surprised, when he went into the common room, to find a large television in the corner, with the selection of arm chairs rearranged in a semicircle in front of it. From this point on the television would dominate the room from the lunch time news until broadcasting ended at midnight. It seemed that someone always wanted to watch something, even if it was just children's programmes to rip apart mercilessly. This surprised Tim as he had been brought up to only turn on the television if there was something specific that he wanted to watch and then to turn it off afterwards. At first, he found the constant, high volume noise an irritating intrusion, but he soon got used to it and settled into talking over the sound. At least there remained no possible requirement to make or sustain awkward conversation when a group of boys were in the room. Everyone could slouch mindlessly in front of the television while chatting, drinking tea, eating or recovering from a session down the Lookers. Life became deliciously lazy and unregulated.

Socially Tim was, as he had always tended to be, lazy. He had spent the first evening of term, like everyone else, traipsing around the Freshers Bazar in which every club, society and sports club in the university had a stall which was actively trying to recruit new members, together with their subscription payment. Tim had not really found any of them very interesting and he had ended up joining the Car Club because it offered access to workshops and training in such skills as welding and electrical repairs and Tim was interested in cars and mechanics and intended to bring his car with him when he returned after Christmas so he thought it may be a good way to keep it going cheaply. He joined the Social Services group because he had enjoyed helping an old lady in the community service group at school and thought that he might benefit from a constant supply of tea and cakes in return for a little bit of help to someone less fortunate than himself. Tim may not have easily articulated the idea but he had a strong sense of his own good fortune and believed that it was incumbent upon those who are more fortunate to help those who are less so.

Faced with line upon line of sports club stands in the second hall of the bazar Tim had opted out completely. He had spent years and years at school being forced to take part in unending formal sports and he had no intention of deliberately setting out to subject himself to the demands of training and fitting in with a team of people that he probably didn't want to spend time with anyway. Tim had been very successful in the school boat club but he felt that he had done enough of that and he guessed that Richard Norton would probably be in the boat club here and he didn't want to have to meet him again so soon.

In consequence Tim's social life revolved around the occupants of his student house and whatever any of them might have thought of doing. The surprising fact was that most of them didn't seem to be exerting much effort when it came to sport or other organised activities with the result that a lot of evenings were spent in front of the television or in the pub.

Bill was studying computer sciences and spent a lot of time in their room with a soldering iron and a box of electronic components trying to build a robot. Tim was fascinated by his efforts and was delighted to learn about a whole new world of electronics that had, so far, passed him by. Bill was happy to instruct him and was glad of Tim's practical understanding and experience of mechanical engineering for the development of the moving parts of his project. The largely silent friendship between the two boys developed well, offering both a kind of easy going and undemanding bond that suited them.

Tim had taken to walking the mile and a half to and from the campus each day, not liking to be tied to bus times and enjoying the solitude of the walk as a time to formulate his own thoughts about whatever subjects he was studying that day. He found that the motion of walking, together with the gentle exercise and fresh air, somehow caused ideas and information to blend and sort themselves out within his head in a very satisfactory way. A nice, easy, passive way of preparing for tutorials or working out the general direction of an essay without feeling as if any serious work had been done.

On the morning of the first Saturday in November the boys were waking up and starting to make themselves breakfast or lunch and gathering round the television in the common room to watch the afternoon sport. Mark and Andy came in in great excitement.

"Come on lads, we all need to get out and collect wood to build the bonfire for Wednesday. We're going to have a firework party!"

With only a very few exceptions everyone became galvanised into action. Meals were finished hastily or postponed completely, clothes put on and plans made as to the best places to find wood. Tim, Bill, Peter and Lee were sent off to the university Botanical Garden, about a mile away, to see what could be found in the woodland there. One group went to a nearby building site and another went in Andy's Vauxhall Viva to scavenge in the forested area of countryside just outside the city.

The Botanical gardens were very interesting to Tim and he had already visited them several times. The woodland area was, however, not very fruitful when it came to searching for bonfire material and after much kicking through drifts of dead leaves and chucking armfuls of them over one another they returned home with only a few moderate sized sticks. Those who had been to the building site had returned with several wooden pallets, lots of short lengths of timber and had gone back for more. A couple of hours later the forest team returned triumphantly with a boot full of sticks and a huge tree trunk poking out of the back window of the car.

Everyone began to excitedly chuck the assorted pieces of wood randomly into a pile in the middle of the lawn.

Tim started to laugh. "It's no use doing it like that! It'll be impossible to light and it won't burn well if you do get it lit."

The house mates were surprised to hear Tim taking control of things in that way. They had always seen him as rather quiet and mild mannered.

"OK! We need to dig a bit of a hole so that we can stand that tree trunk upright and then lean all the other wood around it to look like a kind of solid wigwam"

A couple of boys set about gouging a hole in the lawn with pieces of wood while Tim and some others started to prize the wooden pallets apart into their separate planks so that they could be piled up in the way in which he had instructed. Once the basic fire had been built out of the larger pieces, they stuffed all the remaining smaller bits into the centre to make what Tim described as a "hot core".

As it grew dark everyone went in to make themselves tea and toast and their thoughts turned to the need to make a guy. There was already a generous pile of old newspapers stacked on one of the tables in the common room and Mark set about persuading people to donate shirt, trousers and socks to stuff. By the time everyone was ready to go to the Lookers they had a new, silent, house mate sitting in the corner. Several boys had claimed that it was intended to look like the Vice Chancellor. Tim had no idea what the Vice Chancellor looked like or what he might have done to deserve this treatment but it wasn't really of any concern to him.

Alex collected a donation of five pounds from each house mate with which to buy a worthwhile collection of fireworks and another group of boys took charge of buying and preparing potatoes and sausages to cook in the bonfire. The next three days were filled with excited activity and anticipation. At the last minute it was decided that it would be fun to invite the occupants of a nearby girls' house to the party. That would add another level of interest for the boys and they could be asked to bring a bottle of something each to liven things up.

There were no lectures on a Wednesday afternoon, the time being dedicated to sporting activities and other club events. Consequently, most of the house mates were at home by the early afternoon. The cooks were busy washing potatoes and frying onions to serve with the sausages in hot dog rolls of which they had purchased mountains. Andy announced that he was going to buy a can of petrol to pour over the fire to be sure it started well. Tim advised him to buy paraffin instead because petrol was too volatile. Andy wasn't sure but Alex, who was studying chemistry, intervened to convince him that Tim was correct in his assertion.

Soon after six the girls arrived, excitedly brandishing a large selection of drinks.

Alex and Lee collected them all and decanted everything into one large bucket to concoct what they called a "Lucky Cocktail". Bill and Tim stuffed lots of screwed up newspaper into the cavity of the bonfire and Andy doused it in paraffin.

"You were in charge of building it so you can have the honour of lighting it" Alex told Tim.

Tim was rather less enthusiastic because he could smell paraffin everywhere and he didn't want to be incinerated with the guy, who was now tied to the central tree trunk in the fire. In the end he agreed and, with a powerful roar of igniting vapour, the fire burst into life. There was much merriment, drinks were passed round, scooped out of the bucket with a hastily washed coffee mug and the cooks were keen to put the potatoes and sausages into the fire. Tim tried to point out that they would burn, that you had to wait until there was a deep pile of hot ash to cook in but to no avail.

When at last, the fire began to die down to a hot glow the Fire Works Committee began to ignite the rockets, Roman candles and Catherine wheels. There were many to light and the show lasted for more than half an hour. The cooks began the difficult process of retrieving their sausages and potatoes from the still hugely hot fire. Many of the sausages were burnt beyond edibility and some potatoes were still uncooked but there was sufficient to feed everyone and, cheered by the potent cocktail of drinks, a great time was had by all. As the event drew to a natural close the girls and boys spilled out of the house and into the pub to end the evening riotously there.

Christmas!

Tim's first term at university sped by joyfully and successfully. Looking back, he could hardly believe how good it had proved to be. He had feared that it would turn out to be as uncomfortable and inconvenient as school and that he would, for some reason or another, not fit in. This had very much not proved to be the case and Tim had enjoyed every minute of it. Work wise he found it easy to keep up to date with everything that he was required to do and the content of the work was mostly interesting and stimulating. The exception to this were the Monday morning Philosophy lectures which Tim and just about all of his group found more or less beyond their comprehension. The lecturer himself was weird. He would sit, cross legged, on a table on the lecture stage and, during the course of his lecture, he would gradually remove a selection of his clothes. The group waited weekly with bated breath for him to remove *all* his clothes but, mercifully, this had not yet happened. The subjects that he addressed seemed both irrelevant and quite unnecessary and Tim could see no real use for any of the things about which he found himself dutifully writing notes.

Socially Tim had never enjoyed life more, meeting and mixing with a wider range of people of his own age and similar intellect but from a vast range of backgrounds than he had thought possible. For Tim it was the opportunity to enjoy the things that other people did and to learn from conversations about different points of view about anything and everything that was the most exciting and beneficial kind of experience.

In no time after the Bonfire party it seemed that the Christmas party season was starting. The boys were planning a big house party to which friends and girlfriends would be invited as well as a house Christmas Dinner. There were, of course, also departmental parties and dinners as well as those at halls and houses of friends, so life was evidently going to be busy.

The house party was carefully planned during the course of several evenings in the common room and the Lookers. The main theme was evidently going to be the consumption of alcohol and the opportunity to dance to loud music. A fund was set up to pay for the purchase of copious bottles of wine and spirits with which to start a bucket of "Lucky Cocktail" and a keg of beer was ordered from the bar man at the Lookers. Visitors would be required to bring a bottle as a prerequisite to gaining entry to number 73. They toyed with the idea of fancy dress but the collective decision was that that would entail too much hassle for each individual so that was the end of that.

The Saturday of the party dawned and the house mates all got up well before lunch time, as if by a massive collective effort. Tables and chairs were stacked in a corner of the common room and then moved into the kitchen instead. A powerful music system had been rented from the Students' Union and Andy's Vauxhall was pressed into service first to fill the boot with the cheapest booze that the boys could locate and then to collect the shiny aluminium keg of beer from the Lookers. Luckily the pub was not far from the house because the barrel was too big to allow the boot lid to be shut so the car had to be driven slowly back home with the boot lid flapping dangerously with every bump in the road.

As dusk fell boys were engaged with setting up the music system and sorting out a suitable pile of cassettes to be played throughout the night. Others excitedly opened bottles and tipped the contents into two buckets to create the lethal cocktail that would fuel the night. Someone was trying, without success, to get the beer to come out of the barrel so a contingent was sent hurriedly back to the pub to ask how it worked.

The first rush of guests arrived with their bottles that were collected and stored under the table so that the cocktail buckets could be replenished as they were emptied.

At last the pub boys returned with a small canister of carbon dioxide which needed to be inserted into the top of the keg in order to pressurise it so that the beer could come out of the tap in the base. Success! In a hissing rush the first glass of house beer was served.

The large house was heaving with young men and women trying to dance, swilling drinks of indeterminate origin and being blasted deaf by immensely amplified music. As the night wore on the house became unbearably hot and full of cigarette smoke and windows, the back door and finally the front door were flung open in attempts to bring in fresh air. By now nobody seemed to know anybody and total strangers were walking in off the street. By about three O'clock on Sunday morning all the drinks had run out and all the visitors had left. The house mates, in various states of inebriation, set about closing windows, locking doors and going to bed.

When Tim awoke later on Sunday, he realised that the "Lucky Cocktail" had been anything but lucky for his insides.

Monday evening was the night of Tim's departmental Christmas Dinner, held in Staff House and formal dress was expected. Most of the First Years had planned not to go until they were informed, in very plain terms, that they were *expected* to attend without fail. This displeased everybody because they were required to pay for the privilege of attending an event that was, in effect, compulsory.

Neil Blashford called round to number 73 to collect Tim so that they could walk in to the campus together. Both young men felt uncomfortable wearing a suit and tie for the first time in many months. It felt even stranger, upon arrival, meeting their new friends, all of whom they had only ever seen wearing the standard student dress of jeans and sweaters, now forced into suits and ties or evening dresses for the women. Nobody felt physically comfortable thus dressed and the social atmosphere was similarly false and strained. Even the conversation, as the students stood around in small groups, with staff trying to appear relaxed and friendly, was forced and stilted. The food was fine and there was plenty of wine to drink, but the meal never became a relaxed or enjoyable occasion.

As they walked home together the two friends grumbled.

"I don't get why, just because it's Christmas, people think that it should be fun to behave in a really formal way like that." Neil stated. "I mean, I'm Christian and I like to celebrate Christmas but this sort of thing doesn't have anything to do with it as far as I can see."

"I suppose it's to do with Peace and Goodwill to all men." Tim suggested, cynically.

"If they meant that sincerely then they wouldn't have forced us to pay and then dress like old people."

"It's hard to argue with that. I feel just like I used to feel every Sunday at school when we had to spend an hour or more in Chapel. That was all forced. They tried very hard to force me to get confirmed when I was in the fourth form. I was the only one to refuse and they held it against me for the rest of my time there."

"You're not confirmed? I'm really surprised Tim. I thought someone like you would be sure to have done that."

Tim laughed. "You don't know much about my past Neil. I think I was born a rebel. I just never feel like I can do anything that people say I should, just because convention expects it of me."

"I usually do things just because it's easier than fighting the system."

"Well that's why everyone thinks you're such a nice guy. I bet your parents, your school and the post man all think you know how to do the right thing! People *think* that I'm like that because I'm quiet and I seem posh and I don't look like I'm a rebel but then they get a nasty surprise when they find that I've done what I wanted anyway without them noticing."

They were outside Tim's house now. "Are you coming in for tea or something Neil?"

"No, not tonight thanks. See you tomorrow."

The boys thumped each other between the shoulder blades, a mark of friendship that Tim had brought with him from school and that had been adopted by his new mates, Tim went in and Neil continued his journey to his hall of residence at the end of the road.

The long-awaited House Christmas Dinner was planned for Wednesday night. The customary collection of money had been made and the three Finalists took it upon themselves to buy the food and drink and do all the preparation. The rest of the house mates were totally banned from the kitchen from lunch time onwards. Tim stayed on the campus, which was unusual on a Wednesday, having lunch in the refectory and then doing some reading in the Short Loan Library in his department, an activity that he never enjoyed and avoided as much as he could, since it forced him to remain in the library, under the supervision of the staff, making him feel uncomfortably like he used to feel at school. Neil, Mike and a couple of other boys found him there and had no difficulty persuading him to join them in the Union Bar for end of term drinks. By the Time Tim and Neil were walking home again, five pints of beer happier, a very fine, powdery, snow was starting to fall. It was not settling on the ground but it did make the air feel very cold and raw and the chill stung their hands and faces.

"I suppose this is what I came to the North looking for!" laughed Tim.

"Just wait 'til it gets really bad in February. You'll not be laughing then" warned Neil.

Back home Tim joined his house mates in front of the television in the common room. The smell of roasting turkey was already wafting under the kitchen door and the boys were all in high spirits. Later Alex came out to banish them from the common room also so that it could be transformed into a Grand Dining Hall. Everybody retreated to their bedrooms to lie in wait for the start of frivolities.

When they all returned the room was scarcely recognisable. Every corner was filled with branches of holly, the ceiling was hidden completely by a mass of paper chains and a tape of mixed Christmas music was playing cheerfully. Everyone was impressed at the high quality of the food, the Finalists were all clearly talented cooks, and there were different wines with each of the three courses with brandy to round the meal off. The whole occasion managed to be light hearted, great fun but simultaneously surprisingly civilised.

At the end Tim, who was feeling decidedly headachy after drinking continuously since lunch time, was happy to volunteer to tackle the vast mounds of washing up with Bill and Peter. Since they were all in high spirits, even this monumental task, carried out while everyone else was finishing the evening in the Lookers, was completed in the best of humour. Good Will to All Men!

The next day Tim went to the final tutorial of the term. He was well prepared and looked forward to having his intellect stretched by the ideas and observations of others. He was really enjoying this way of learning. This tutorial turned out to be more of a party than a time for work. Once he had ascertained that the students had properly prepared their work Steve Hockwell, who had often talked about his collection of fine wines in previous tutorials, produced several bottles and glasses together with crisps.

The rest of the session consisted of a chance to taste and rate various wines and to talk about how the place in which the grapes had grown gave the wine it's distinctiveness. Most students were not great wine drinkers and all learnt new information, even if it had little to do with Social Economics.

Vacation

Tim felt growing excitement as the train approached his destination. He hadn't been home for ten weeks, by far the longest uninterrupted time away in his life so far and definitely the most formative. Tim felt more like a man and no longer at all like the school boy that he had still been when he left home in October. He wondered how he would fit back in to his family life. For sure his mother would find fault with his ear covering hair length!

The train rattled to a halt. Tim heaved his bag and suitcase from the luggage rack and struggled with them off the train and onto the platform.

"Tim!"

Usman hurried towards him. The two friends shook hands in the way that Usman always expected to do. He sported a stubbly black beard now, just as he had done when Tim had first met him two years earlier at school. It made him look very adult. Usman took Tim's suitcase from him and they went out to the small car park. Mrs. Croy was standing beside the car. Mother and son hugged briefly while Usman loaded the bags into the boot of her car. They drove home, Tim in the front passenger seat. The conversation moved between the two young men, recounting some of the highlights of their respective first terms at university. Tim was pleased to find that his friend was safely installed with his parents. It would be great to have a friend of his own age with him for the holidays.

Sitting in Tim's bedroom later that evening, after his mothers' formal welcome home dinner in the dining room, the two boys were talking more freely now that they were alone.

"Tim, your parents are very kind to me. I need to say thank you to them properly but I don't know how to in a good way."

"You don't need to think like that mate. They always enjoy having visitors and anyway mum told me that she's started to think of you as her second son. You make them feel very happy just by wanting to visit them."

Tim reflected for a moment. It *was* strange, the way that sometimes you could feel closer to someone else's parents than your own. He supposed that the feeling could work the other way around too. He knew that Mike's mother felt a special relationship to him and he greatly appreciated the welcome that he always enjoyed from that family. Maybe all kids should swap parents in their late teens as a way of side stepping the angst that so often clouds the relationship between parents and children at that very difficult stage.

"Mike's mum feels like that about me." Tim volunteered.

"I think it will be very difficult for me to live in Saudi again. It worries me sometimes."

"What makes you feel like that man?"

"Well, now I'm not at school I am free to do the things that I used to do back home and I can do other things that I can't do there."

"Do you still smoke?"

"Yes, all the time now. I know it's bad but I like it."

"What do you do when you're staying here?"

"Your mum and dad are really cool about it! They told me off at first, said that they couldn't approve of me hurting myself like that and then they told me I could have the sitting room of the flat in your coach house to smoke in."

Tim had trouble taking that information in. His parents, *cool*? Tim had never thought of them like that. It just confirmed that his earlier thoughts had some sense in them.

"I'm really glad they're OK with that mate. I hope it kind of makes up for the way that you kept getting busted at school."

"Something else I've started doing is drinking. The first time I did it I hated it. It tasted horrible and I felt so fucking guilty. Then I went to a party and I had a few small drinks and then lots more. Shit! I did get drunk that night. Luckily my friend took me back to my room because I couldn't walk properly. When I woke up in the morning, I found that I had vomited all over my bed and on the floor. I felt so sick Tim! I had to clean my room and I kept on vomiting and vomiting. I thought I would die. But now I can handle it, like everyone else does."

Tim laughed. "I puked my guts up the first time I got drunk. It was the first term in the Sixth Forms. The term before you came. I puked all over the grass beside the Chapel and then in a bucket in the dorm. I was incredibly lucky to have friends who stopped me getting caught."

Each boy laughed at the others' experience.

"But you know that it is forbidden for a Muslim to drink any alcohol," Usman continued. "I know that my dad does drink when he is abroad and I think he does sometimes in Jeddah. But If he knew I was doing that he would beat me."

"Would he beat you even now, at your age?"

"Yes, for sure." Tim was shocked. The conversation moved on to lighter topics.

The next few days were spent introducing Usman to some of the winter pass times that had been a part of Tim's life for as long as he could remember. As can often be the case, what was mundane to Tim was an exciting new experience for Usman. The two boys split logs and brought them into the house, stacking them in the huge inglenook to dry ready for burning on the log fire or in the wood burning stoves in the hall and the dining room. Tim taught Usman how to use the chainsaw and they spent a day felling and chopping up an ancient apple tree that had started to die. Tim explained how apple wood smelt amazing when it burnt. One morning they dug potatoes, carrots and parsnips from the vegetable garden and took them into the old pantry for Mrs Croy. They went to the woods behind the garden armed with secateurs to cut armfuls of holly for the house.

"We've been invited to Anthony's New Years' Party! We're going to stay the night so we can drink safely."

Tim announced as he came into the sitting room from the telephone in the hall. The warmth of the room enveloped him in welcome comfort after the chill of the draughty hall.

"It'll be nice for you both to have a party. It's always exciting for visitors to have a taste of real life in the country that they're visiting."

Mrs Croy was unusually positive, it seemed to Tim.

"Talking of tradition", she continued. "Obviously, we can't have turkey for Christmas Dinner because it won't be *halal,* so I thought we'd have pheasant."

She smiled broadly at Usman.

"You're the perfect excuse for me to buy more game and fish dear! Maybe I can ask you to keep an eye on it for me while we all go to church."

"Actually, Mrs Croy, do you think they would allow me to come to the church with you? I would really like to join in with your family properly."

"Well, of course, dear, if you'd like that we'd be delighted."

Thus, Christmas Day was arranged.

Early on the thirty-first of December Tim and Usman set off in Tim's car for the Midlands. Tim hadn't been to Anthony's house before but he had experienced, first hand, his inadequate directions! He armed Usman with his road atlas and showed him where he thought they needed to go. They stopped for lunch at the service station on the M1 and then continued determinedly to their destination. It was definitely further than Tim had expected and dusk was falling by the time they found the house. Surprisingly Anthony's instructions had proved to be accurate. It was a very large house, set back from the main road into the town. While obviously not a Stately Home it certainly was a stately house.

"Does everyone live in such big houses" Usman laughed.

There were several older cars parked untidily on the wide sweep of gravel in front of the house. Tim parked where he could and the boys entered the deep, arched porch and knocked firmly on the huge, arched, green painted door with a very traditional looking black painted door knocker in the shape of a lion's head. A beaming Anthony flung open the door. Like Tim he sported shaggily long hair, in tribute to his freedom from the strictures of school rules.

"Tim! Usman! Welcome to William's Towers! Lots of guys are here already and the folks have just left so the party's kind of just starting anyway. Have fun!"

They stepped down into a huge, stone floored hall and were led through to the largest room that Tim had ever seen in a private house. A huge fire burned fiercely in an arched stone grate, guarded by more lions' heads, at the far end of the room. There were lots of people, none of whom Tim knew. Anthony made no effort to make formal introductions so the two new arrivals simply helped themselves to drinks and some sausage rolls and blended in to the growing party.

Tim felt a firm tap between his shoulder blades. Turning he was confronted with the familiar grin of Mike. The friends hugged. There was, between them, a very special bond that never failed to make each young man feel quite emotional.

"You remember Sarah, my sister, obviously."

Tim did remember her, but not the young lady who stood before him now. Tim felt simultaneously excited and shy. Mike had already turned to greet Usman so Tim was forced to say something.

"Hi. Long time no see! How's things?"

"All good! I'm in my last year at school now. Can't wait to get out! Girls' schools are so deadly dull!"

"Mike and I know that it's not just girls' schools." Tim laughed, relaxing as he realised that this goddess really was still Mike's friendly sister.

As the evening got going seriously the room was filled with loud music and the dining room across the hall was opened up and illuminated, revealing a massive polished dining table laden with endless dishes of delicacies. Tim was catching up on news with Anthony. He, too, was really enjoying the freedom of university. Lancaster was, he said, about as far from anywhere else as it was possible to get.

"Just like Hull, but the opposite side of the country!" Tim laughed. "Are you still into Rugby?" "No, I'm not doing any sport to be honest. I needed some time off from that kind of thing after school. How about you? I bet you're rowing again."

"Nope. Same as you really. I'm just enjoying not being made to do anything at the moment."

Anthony drifted away to socialise with his other guests and Tim found himself alone for a moment. He went to the table and heaped his plate once more with cold meat, rice salad, some kind of pie and assorted pickles.

"I'm glad I'm not the only hungry person!" The large room seemed suddenly to over flow with Sarah's cheerfulness.

"Maybe you're thinking that I'm a greedy slob." Tim suggested between mouthfuls.

"Well, if it's here then they want us to eat it. That's how I see it."

Tim felt pleased to be with Sarah again. As they finished eating another wave of hungry party goers' came in, rather pushing them into a corner.

"Let's go and dance" Sarah suggested.

"I'm not much good at that kind of thing. I'll tread on your toes." Tim demurred.

"I'll teach you. No room for discussion."

Sarah grabbed Tim by the wrist with unexpected strength and propelled him across the hall and back into the main room. She proved to be a good tutor and Tim found himself enjoying the experience.

There was more to it than that. Tim was feeling something that he had felt only once before. The slightly light headed, weak kneed physical pleasure of being close to a beautiful girl. He tried to think about other things. This was Mike's sister, not just some girl. He shouldn't be feeling like that about her. Tim was aware of another, more acutely embarrassing physical response as they held each other closely, moving to the music. He tried to adjust his position, to ensure that Sarah would not feel his uncontrollable attraction to her. He hoped that she would attribute his blushes to the heat from the fire.

"I'm hot and thirsty" Tim announced. "I'm going to grab a cold beer. What shall I get you?"

Tim was relieved to be free from dancing. Thrusting his hand in his pocket, to make sure that nothing looked out of place, he headed to the drinks table at the back of the room.

The party began to break up at about one O'clock, after the count down to the New Year had been riotously sung and several celebratory drinks consumed. Those who lived within reach walked or got lifts home, leaving those who were going to stay the night to help Anthony get the house into some semblance of order before they all retired, thankfully, to bed.

Usman and Tim were given a large, chilly, room containing two rather creaky single beds. Anthony apologised as he showed them in.

"They're a bit like school beds I'm afraid. Must have been here since before the war I should think. We don't use the room much though so we've never done it up."

The boys chatted for a while before falling silent, each wanting to sleep but finding himself unable to do so. Inevitably sleep overtook both eventually.

Sarah lay awake in her room. She felt cold and uncomfortable and she was trying to analyse her thoughts. Tim was a strange boy. She found him very difficult to read. She had liked him since the first time that she had met him, when she was just fifteen. He had impressed her and her parents by the way in which he had dedicated his time to helping and supporting Michael after his accident. None of his other friends had even bothered to visit him. Tim was obviously a really kind and loyal person. She could tell that he was shy and yet, in some ways, he appeared incredibly confident. But he was so hard to understand. She had been sure that he fancied her when they were dancing and then, suddenly, he had become cold and distant. That should have made her angry. It had *upset* her. But somehow it had made her fancy him more and had increased her resolve to find out everything that there was to know about Tim. She had to think how she could get Michael's help without making him or her mum think that that was what she was doing. Sarah enjoyed a challenge!

Sleep was escaping Anthony too. He felt pleased that the party had been a success and he was glad that nobody had embarrassed him about the size of his parents' house. He had always avoided inviting his friend's home before because he had felt sure that he would be teased mercilessly about it. It had been great to catch up with his old school mates again, especially Tim. It was strange because, when they had first started at Barforth together he had thought that Tim was rather pathetic and he had often bullied him in his usual rough and thoughtless way. But things had changed, suddenly, and they had become increasingly close friends, often helping each other in various disruptive pranks around the school.

Since leaving school Anthony had started to think about Tim quite often and being with him again tonight had confirmed that they had what he felt to be a very special kind of relationship. He wondered if, no *hoped* that, Tim felt the same way. He had no idea how to find out and he felt rather afraid of the feeling anyway. Despite his often over exuberant behaviour Anthony was very unsure of himself indeed, a result of the constant barrage of reprimands and put-downs that he had suffered throughout the last five years at school. He loved university but it had served to teach him that he really had little idea about who or what he really was.

Boating Again!

At the end of the holiday Tim drove back to Hull in his car. He had been surprised at the ease with which he had been able to convince his parents to let him take it. It was obviously much easier to take all the things that he wanted to take by simply stuffing them carelessly in the boot rather than having to lug them in over weight bags and cases. The car would also offer him status and convenience in his daily life and, having gone to the expense of buying it, it was only sensible to use it rather than leave it deteriorating unused on the drive way at home.

Tim had never driven so far before so that would be an adventure and there was always the possibility that something would go wrong with such an old car. He had spent the last few days tinkering with it, changing the engine oil, testing the antifreeze, cleaning the points and sparking plugs. Usman watched and learnt. In Saudi he had had a new car to drive. Nobody there would ever try to look after a car in that way. He resolved to try to get his UK driving licence so that he could gain the freedom that it would certainly impart. He had only ever driven an automatic car and had no idea what to do with a gear lever. Tim laughed a lot to hear that. It was weird how people lived such different lives in different parts of the world. Mr. Croys' Granada was automatic and Tim knew that he didn't think it was that good. He told Usman that you could get just an automatic licence but that then he wouldn't be able to drive a manual car, the problem being that most cars in England were not automatic.

Tim was glad to be back. It had been great to go home for a while but he felt that his life was now based at the university, with his new friends. There was always something interesting to do and somebody to do it with. He could relax and be himself without any expectations or demands to control him. In essence, for the first time in his life, he was free. Free to find out who he was and free to do as he saw fit. Tim had never been so happy.

Peter French had also returned driving his car, an old Fiat 850. The two young men spent many happy hours tinkering with their cars in the street outside number 73. Each had had to learn quite a lot about cars in order to keep his elderly pride and joy running and each had learnt different things and was happy to help the other when needed. This shared enthusiasm caused a new level of friendship to develop between them which both found unexpectedly pleasing.

One evening, about a week after the beginning of term, Tim was lazing in the common room in front of the television. He heard the doorbell ring and somebody else answer it. The common room door opened to reveal two tall young men who Tim did not recognise.

"We're looking for Tim Croy" the fair-haired guy said.

"That's me"

Tim turned towards them, wondering how they knew him and what they wanted. They walked across the room to him. The dark-haired boy sat in the chair beside him and the taller guy knelt on the floor opposite him. He was incredibly tall, probably the proverbial six foot six, Tim guessed.

"Hi, I'm Kevin"

"And I'm Mark" the dark-haired boy added.

"We've set up a crew in the boat club but we can't get on properly because we don't have a cox. Richard Norton told us that he knew you were in Hull and that you were the best cox that your old school had had for years. We've been trying to find you since November and now we have!" Kevin continued.

He looked very sincere, kneeling on the floor, almost as if he was praying, Tim thought.

"We've come to ask you, *please* will you come and be our cox." Mark put the request directly.

"I did used to cox, and I did do it for Richards' crew but, to be honest, I feel like I've done that enough now. I'm taking a rest from serious sport, and I'm enjoying the freedom."

"Please, Tim! We've heard so many good things about you and we've worked so hard to train as a crew and we've searched for you for so long and now we've finally found you, you *can't* seriously say no."

Kevin sounded as if he might cry at the end of his emotional speech. It had been worth it. Tim was caught. How could he possibly say no to such a heartfelt, and hard worked for request?

"OK. I'll give it a go. But it's nearly two years since I last coxed a boat so I've probably forgotten how to do it and I'm much bigger than I ought to be to make a good cox."

A huge, genuine, grin spread across the faces of both visitors. As one they got to their feet, grasped each of Tim's arms and propelled him up out of his seat.

"Now you're coming to the pub to celebrate and sort everything out properly."

Gripped thus by two of the biggest men that he had ever seen, Tim was in no position to disagree!

Arriving in the Lookers, Kevin and Mark lead Tim to a table at which two more giants were sitting.

"We did it!" Mark bragged.

"Told you we know how to negotiate professionally!" Kevin laughed.

"This is Tom and he's Dave. May I present to you the legendary and elusive Tim Croy".

The young men shook hands in an uncharacteristically formal manner and, before he had a chance to refuse, Mark was placing a frothing pint of bitter on the copper topped table in front of Tim.

"You were at school with Richard? He's a brilliant oarsman, taught us everything about rowing. He really rates you." Tom enthused.

"Trouble is it's been really, really, difficult to find you. It was only by chance that I was complaining to Peter French about not being able to find the only cox in Hull, in the refectory this morning, and he told me that he lived with you!"

Tim laughed. He felt secretly quite pleased that so much importance had become attached to him but, again, he felt the chilling claws of Barforth catching him, evidently unwilling to let him go, forever finding him, reminding him of the life that he so much wanted to discard forever. He had known that meeting Richard Norton on that first morning would lead to this moment.

"Well, like I said to the other two, I'm definitely going to be out of practice so don't get too excited just yet!"

They began talking about where the boat club was and arranged to meet there the next day, Wednesday, at two O'clock. Dave refilled everyone's glass and the newly formed crew began to talk of other things.

As Tim sat eating a pizza in the Union at lunch time the next day, he was feeling uncomfortable. He'd got his tracksuit in a bag in the car and he would keep his word and be at the boat club at the agreed time. Somehow, though, his heart wasn't in it. He had mentally ended his career as a cox at Henley in 1979, on a wonderful winning streak. He had not expected or planned for this and he felt that he had been tricked or forced into it, which was sufficient to spoil anything for Tim. He liked to do as he pleased.

And it was true that he knew that he was too big now to comfortably fit into the cox's diminutive seat at the back of a boat and that he was too heavy to be of real value to them. Too late to think like that now. He had promised and he would do his best. They seemed like a nice bunch of guys and their sheer size suggested that they may make a great crew. Tim had never raced a four before so that also would be a new challenge. It couldn't really be such a bad thing.

Having changed his mind set into positive mode Tim set off to find the Boat Club and start another adventure.

"Left at the end of Cottingham Road, onto Beverley Road. First right then into the park and down the muddy track to the righthand boathouse." Tim followed Mark's directions, feeling increasingly tense and, inexplicably, shy. He parked his car inside the boat house enclosure and, as he got out, the four boys from his new crew came bounding out of the building with all the enthusiasm of a litter of puppies. Tim felt better at once. He had done the right thing.

They took Tim inside and showed him round the boat house. Downstairs were a large bar and club room and shower and changing rooms for men and women. Steps led up to the boat house. Tim was surprised at how few boats there were. He went to change and joined his crew up in the boat house. Richard Norton was waiting for him.

"Welcome Tim! I had a feeling we'd get you here sooner or later."

Tim smiled. He would have to make the best of this relationship, despite his fears.

"I guess there was no escape! It's very small, isn't it?"

"It's all very different to Barforth, Tim. The river's tidal so we have to clear heaps of mud off the steps every time we come here before we can launch the boats. The crew are doing that now. The river has very strong currents in places and that feels weird sometimes too. The most difficult thing is getting the crew to take things seriously. There aren't any Masters to force them to do things so it's down to us and it's not easy."

They wondered over to the edge of the embankment and Tim saw his four crew members busily shovelling mud off the wooden steps that were set into the river bank. The river and its' banks all looked cold, muddy and grey. Tim pictured the lush green beauty of the River Barr with a sudden wave of nostalgia. He really hadn't known how fortunate he was. The lads came up to put away their shovels.

"Are you ready to show Tim what you can do?" asked Richard.

"Come on. Let's do it!" Tim tried to sound keen. "Which is our boat?"

The crew dutifully took Tim to a four named "Fellows". Tim felt excited to be looking at the beauty of a sleek racing boat once again. Despite his doubts about the whole situation he felt a kind of thrill, a challenge, reawakening his competitive spirit. He *would* make a success of this unlikely set up.

"Lift her up Stroke side, ease under when you can Bow side" Tim commanded.

The crew seemed a little uncertain. Tim felt sure that Richard would have taught them properly. They must just be nervous.

"Shoulder height" he commanded as they lifted the vessel free of the storage rack. They carried the small boat carefully down the muddy steps and lowered it into the grey water. Tim squatted to hold it while the crew fetched their blades. He could feel that the current really was strong. The crew returned and began fastening their oars into the gaiters. Kevin was Stroke. Tim guessed that this was the result of Richard's instruction. He was the obvious choice.

"Hands across Bow Side" The two bow siders got themselves settled into their seats and put their blades on the water to balance the boat.

"Hands across Stroke side" The remaining two got in. Tim eased himself in and pushed the boat away from the step with his foot as he did so. He found the steering ropes.

"Come forward, are you ready? Row!"

The boat moved forward. The current was powerful. Tim struggled at first to get a feel for the level of rudder compensation that was needed to steer a straight course. Richard was coaching from the bank. It felt very strange to Tim, who had been used to Richard sitting in front of him as Stroke. He realised how close their sporting relationship had become. He would have to work hard to build as good a one with Kevin.

The crew were very inexperienced and evidently a bit nervous with Tim commanding them. Richard kept on reminding and encouraging them from the bank. Tim wanted to watch and analyse the actions of each individual so that he understood their needs for future training.

"This is as far as you can go in this direction Tim"

"Easy all!" The boat drifted to a halt.

"Cary on Stroke side, back her down Bow side" The boat turned slowly.

They rowed up and down the river twice more before they decided that it was time to stop. Tim had surprised himself at the ease with which he had been able to start coxing again. His skills really had become second nature to him. He now knew that he had only to worry about training his novice crew. They got the boat out of the water and onto trestles on the embankment. Tim located the hose and some cloths. The boat really needed cleaning when it had been on the River Hull! Tim was very surprised when his crew took the cloths and started cheerfully cleaning the boat, leaving him only to direct the hose. That was a real bonus!

"How did we do?" Kevin interrupted Tim's thoughts.

"You're a very powerful crew. Obviously, you need lots of training and we need to do regular sessions in the sports centre too."

"Do you think we can win races Tim?" Mark sounded almost like a hopeful child.

"I'm sure you can, but it will be really hard work at first."

They carried the boat back in and set it back on the rack. Everyone went down to shower and change. Afterwards they regrouped in the club room for a drink.

"Thanks for coming Tim. Now you've seen us, will you join our crew?" Kevin asked.

"PLEASE" Tom added.

"I'm really looking forward to being part of a winning crew again. So yes! Thank you for asking me."

Tim gave Richard a lift back to the campus.

"Why aren't you rowing?"

"I did start last year but there was nobody to coach us so I started to be a coach instead. You can't do both!"

"They don't seem very skilled yet, as if they haven't really jelled as a crew."

"It's difficult Tim. The biggest problem is getting a commitment from everyone all of the time. It's not like school."

"So, you and I are going to have to make it like a Barforth takeover of the club."

Tim hated saying that. But if he was to make a success of it, he had to enlist Richard's help.

"Let's do it!" Richard thumped Tim between the shoulder blades and got out of the car.

Tim drove home deep in thought.

Little by Little!

Tim only had to wait until the next evening to experience the difficulty of controlling his crew within the freer university environment.

The crew were scheduled to meet for an hour of training at seven O'clock in the sports centre. Tim arrived, dressed in shorts and tea shirt, ready to lead an hour of intensive circuit training. Kevin met Tim as they walked into the entrance foyer. Tom and Mark were already waiting.

"Great punctuality. I'm impressed" Tim laughed. "Let's go and set up the circuits while we wait for Dave."

Tim instructed them to get out benches and mats and some dumb bells.

"What are we going to do cox?" Mark was enthusiastic as he always appeared to be.

"We're going to spend an hour repeating this circuit flat out. Let me show you how I want it done." Tim proceeded to demonstrate how he wanted each exercise to be done.

"You're good!" Kevin sounded genuinely impressed.

"I'm out of practice. It must be nearly a year since I last did that." Tim laughed. "I thought I'd retired!" "Does anyone know where Dave is?" Nobody did.

Tom volunteered to go and telephone his house. He returned despondently.

"He's not coming."

"Why?"

"He's gone to play darts."

"DARTS!" Tim couldn't believe his ears. "He did know about this evening?"

"Yeah, he knew. Just got a better offer I guess."

"OK. Crew, please listen to me carefully".

They gathered around Tim obediently. Tim spoke very quietly. Deliberately. He was working hard to control his anger and that was his way of showing it.

"We are a crew. There are only five of us. We have to trust, rely and depend upon each other. It is essential that we can work as one, on and off the water. If we are serious about achieving some wins, we must all agree to this prerequisite. If one of us isn't here or is not doing his best we will not succeed. If anybody isn't up for total commitment then please quit now. Who is going to pass this message on to Dave?"

Kevin volunteered.

"Let's get going!"

Tim set each boy up in his starting place and told them to follow him round. After half an hour, timed from the enormous clock on the wall, Tim called a halt. He could feel that they were tiring. Tim was tiring too.

"OK! Five minutes break. I feel you're getting tired and we're only half way through. We need much better stamina than this."

The crew started again. Tim began to push them and himself harder. At last the end came. Mark lay on the mat. Tom sat with his head in his hands. Kevin sat and looked at Tim.

"Fuck! How did you do that?"

"Not as well as I will with a couple more weeks' practice!"

"Are we going to do this twice a week?"

"Yep, and then we're going to start serious training on the river. You haven't seen Richard when he gets going yet!"

"You haven't set him up against us too?" Mark sat up, sweat dripping from his face.

"Yep! He and I are a team. Have been for nearly three years. We won't compromise and you will have to reach our standards or quit. No other choices."

They cleared away the equipment and went to shower. Everyone was on time for training on the river on Sunday morning. Dave sidled up to Tim to apologise for Thursday evening.

"You've upset Tim already! I did warn you not to." Richard teased.

At seven O'clock on Monday Tim arrived at the sports centre to find not only the entire crew waiting for him but the circuit set up ready as well. Tim very seriously shook hands with each young man in turn.

"That's how we want it. Well done!"

They worked hard, Tim leading and gradually building up the pace. They managed to complete the hour without a break this time. Tim began to believe that there was hope after all.

The following Sunday they met at the boat house as usual. The crew cleared the steps of mud. Richard gave them instructions about the program ahead. They went to get the boat out.

"Where's Mark?" Tim was irritated.

"He's got a hangover. He had to go to the toilet." Tom was looking down at the floor, dejectedly, as if he was at fault.

"Right!"

Tim headed down stairs to the changing rooms. He was about to shout Mark's name but he heard the sound of vomiting coming from the toilet. Tim sat on a bench and waited in silent fury. He heard Mark being sick a couple more times. There was a long silence. The toilet flushed and an ashen faced Mark appeared. He looked sheepish when he clocked Tim waiting for him.

"Sorry"

"You will be sorry when you get on the water!"

"I can't row now mate. I'm really ill."

"You can row, and you're going to row. You're not ill, it's self-inflicted. Everyone else got here in time and managed not to drink too much last night. It was *you* who came to ask, no beg, *me* to cox for you and now you let me down. So, it might be you who causes me to quit. Now, up those stairs and onto the river!"

Much to Tim's surprise Mark complied without further comment.

Neither Richard nor Tim showed any mercy to poor Mark during the two long, cold, hours of training.

In the changing room afterwards, Mark sat huddled and silent. He remained there after everyone had showered and dressed. The three remaining oarsmen headed for the bar. Tim felt suddenly sorry for Mark. He sat next to him on the bench.

"Mark"

Silence.

"Mark, are you OK mate?"

Mark turned slowly to face Tim. He really did look ill now.

"I'm so ashamed. I feel like I can't face any of you again."

"You've made a big mistake Mark. All of us cock up sometimes. We are a crew. All for one and one for all! You've impressed me this morning on the river. You must have been feeling like shit and yet you rowed better than I've ever seen you row before. Go and warm yourself up in the shower and I'll drive you home."

Tim went to join the others in the bar.

"What did you say to Mark?" Kevin wanted to know.

"I told him the truth. Like I told you lot the other day."

When Mark came out from the changing room Tim excused himself to take him home. He knew that he certainly wouldn't be wanting a drink. They drove in silence. Tim felt truly sorry for Mark. He wished he hadn't had to treat him like that. When he was getting out of the car outside his house Tim called him.

"Look at me Mark. No, look me in my eyes."

Mark looked Tim in the eyes for the first time that day.

"Learn from this Mark, but don't beat yourself up. I'm proud to know such a brave guy as you. Smile!"

Mark managed a watery smile.

"Thanks Tim." He whispered.

"See you at the sports hall tomorrow."

Tim was worried. It was going to be very difficult to get every individual to put in the constant, consistent, effort that had to be maintained if the crew was to succeed. There was, as Richard had quite rightly pointed out to him, no structure of external authority that could be invoked to enforce discipline. Neither Richard nor Tim had any intrinsic authority over the crew members. Somehow, they had to build a kind of obligation upon each crew member to regulate themselves and each other. Tim had seen that in Mark's reaction to his mistake that morning. Maybe he could seek Mark's help.

Tim was glad when Peter asked him to go to the scrap yard with him to look for a tail lamp lens for his car. He liked scrap yards and the two mates enjoyed an oily afternoon climbing in and out of old cars, some of which appeared to be better than their own ones.

Once again Tim arrived at the sports centre to find his entire crew waiting dutifully for him with their circuit of equipment all set up and ready to go. The training was the most successful yet. Everyone even seemed quite pleased with themselves at the end. After they had showered Tim suggested that they go to the Union bar for a drink. As he had hoped, nobody refused. Once they were settled with their beers Tim spoke.

"That was a real success tonight. Well done all of us! We need to be disciplined and committed like we were tonight all of the time. We've just demonstrated to ourselves that we can do it when we want to. The problem comes when one of us doesn't feel like it or thinks that he's got something better to do. Remember this slogan, all for one and one for all. We all depend on each other. If one of us fails it ruins it for everyone else. I think that we are all becoming mates. We care about each other. So, each of us owes it to everyone else to be dedicated. I promise that, when we start winning some races, it will all seem worth the small sacrifices that I'm asking you to make right now."

Everyone was looking at Tim.

"You didn't seem to care very much about poor Mark yesterday." The voice of dissent from Kevin.

All eyes on Tim.

"That's not fair Kevin. It was me who hadn't bothered to care about the effort that all of you made to turn up early on a Sunday morning. Tim was exactly right." Mark surprised and impressed Tim with his robust support.

"He's right Kevin" Tom agreed.

"You're out of order Kevin." Dave confirmed his support.

"Kevin, listen, please. If Mark had been ill, had caught some nasty bug or something, I'd have been trying to look after him and helping him to get better. But he wasn't ill in the way that needed sympathy. So, I was tough. What's important though, is that he was brave enough to fight through his hangover and he gave us his best performance ever. That's the kind of courage and determination that we all have to offer each other, all of the time."

Tim saw that Mark was blushing.

"I didn't mean to embarrass you mate." Tim apologised.

"I think that means I should get the next round in" Kevin stood up. The evening seemed to end happily enough.

A week passed and things at the Boat Club and in the Sports Centre were definitely improving. On Sunday morning Richard joined the crew in the clubroom bar.

"That was an impressive outing! You must have felt the boat going smoothly and how much easier rowing gets when it is. The timing was perfect all of the time and the balance was too. If it's as good again on Wednesday I think we'll be ready to start practicing racing techniques."

"Is racing different from normal rowing then?" Mark sought clarification.

"Not really, just like any kind of race, you just need to do the normal thing but faster and with full power."

"I'm tired now!" Tom stated bluntly.

"Yes, but we've been rowing, steadily for two hours, non-stop. In a race it's a maximum of ten minutes, but at full power. It does hurt but your recovery time is much faster." Richard explained.

"Tim will be shouting at you regularly in a race to keep you at maximum effort."

Richard began to laugh. "They'll love you when you get going, won't they Tim?"

"I can't possibly imagine what you mean!"

"Well how about when you started calling me the laziest fucker you'd ever seen with a blade in his hand?"

"Oh yeah. And he was two years older than me and a prefect. But you have to take risks in a race!"

The crew watched the two old friends reminiscing. They were beginning to understand what these experienced friends meant when they talked about unity.

"You must have had some great times" Dave reflected.

"We did, but it was very, very high pressure too. And I was terrified when I first started with the First Eight. I was afraid of the much older boys and even more afraid of cocking up." Tim laughed at the distant memory of his younger self. "Richard, I'd really appreciate it if you'd come to training in the Sports Centre tomorrow at seven. Things have got much better and it'd be great to get some input from you about how to move things on to the next level."

Tim asked, partly with the intention of encouraging his crew to prepare to push themselves harder still. They were all big, powerful young men and he doubted that they had really reached much more than half their true capacity. Richard readily agreed.

As they trained on Monday evening, Tim saw Richard taking out each individual, one by one, and talking earnestly with him. Then it was Tim's turn.

"They all need to double their efforts in my opinion. I've given Kevin the responsibility of building up the pace, because he's Stroke. I'm not certain that he's completely comfortable with the responsibility of being Stroke. He will need a lot of support. You will have to help me there, Tim, because you obviously know him better than me."

"No Richard. You were my Stroke and you know from experience what it takes. You have to do that."

"I just don't feel that we get on with each other that well, to be honest."

"I don't think we do either" retorted Tim. "To be honest he worries me a bit. Like he's not really with us one hundred percent. Kind of holding something important back all the time."

Wednesday was bright, sunny and very windy. Tim arrived to find his crew already changing. He joined them and they had a quick briefing about their aim to have another good outing so that they could start to focus on racing as from Sunday.

The crew went to clean the muddy steps. Tim went to find Richard but was waylaid when he saw only three men on the launching steps. He went to look. There was no Kevin. Tim went back to the changing room and the club room. He wasn't there. Feeling increasingly vexed Tim went out to the car park and was about to climb the steps to the embankment again when, out of the corner of his eye, he saw movement in the shelter of the building. He turned to see Kevin sunning himself, sheltered from the wind, smoking a cigarette. Tim strode over to him.

"What are you doing? You're supposed to be helping to get things ready."

Kevin stared at Tim defiantly. He hadn't noticed how piercingly blue his eyes were.

"You mean you think I should be shovelling shit." He said flatly, almost menacingly.

"I mean you should be working with the rest of the crew. All for one and one for all!"

"Don't patronise me with your poncey public school crap. I don't have to listen to little rich boys like you and your friend. You're no better than me."

"You have chosen to be part of this crew and you need to act as part of it."

Tim spoke slowly and quietly, controlling himself. Suddenly he felt his tracksuit tighten painfully around his neck and Kevin was dragging him up close to his angry face.

"I hate spoilt public-school shits like you. You don't know anything about real life and you just think that it's your birth right to order everyone around."

Kevin could not have known that the mere act of grabbing Tim and pulling him threateningly close to him in that way had unleashed something that Tim could scarcely control. Tim felt his heart racing, heard a roaring, pounding of his pulse in his ears, began to feel a kind of dizziness, a blinding anger, borne of events far away in place and time. He took deep, slow, controlling breaths. He had to be cool.

"You don't know anything about me or my past. You think you're big and tough and you evidently are a thug and a bully. I don't like people like you. But that doesn't mean we can't work together. Let go of me **now** or you will regret it for the rest of your life."

Tim had spoken very quietly but with an intensity, a force, that had evidently had the intended effect. He didn't know what it was but something in the look, the demeanour, of this young man, so much smaller than him, had made Kevin feel very uncomfortable, possibly even afraid. He sensed that Tim really could do anything at that moment and he realised that he may already have pushed him too far.

Kevin let go of Tim's tracksuit and pushed him away roughly.

"Don't try to tell me when I can or can't have a fag" Kevin growled.

"I shall do whatever I see fit to do."

The two young men tried, angrily, to outstare each other. Neither managed to make the other concede. The moment passed.

"Come on, they'll be waiting for us." Kevin sounded like his usual self once more.

The outing went much better than Tim had dared to expect after their stressful altercation. Kevin had been unexpectedly shaken by the encounter and had dreaded having to sit directly in front of Tim, with no chance of escape, for two hours of training. He was surprised and quite grateful that Tim showed no indication of what had passed between them only moments earlier. Maybe he had misjudged him.

When the boat had been washed and put away and everyone had showered and changed the crew and their coach met in the club room. Richard shook hands with each boy in turn.

"That was another all time best! Well done! Now we're ready to prepare to race. We're going to develop ourselves into a race winning machine."

Tim shook each of his crew's hands in turn, holding Kevin's for a fraction of a second longer and looking him in the eye.

"I'm feeling really proud to be part of this crew now. We've come so far in such a short time. We're really going places!"

When Tim got home, he felt strangely weary. His whole body ached. The exchange between him and Kevin had upset him. He had not been frightened of Kevin but the way in which his unknowing behaviour had triggered that reaction in him had really shaken him. Would he never recover?

Tim went and had a very deep, very hot bath for a very long time. He needed to loosen up his tense muscles, to soak away the adrenaline and to forget frightening memories that had been reawakened from deep in his subconsciousness.

Tim was in the common room after supper, watching Nationwide disinterestedly with a number of others when he heard the doorbell ring. Nobody stirred to get it, it had become an expectation that somebody from one of the two downstairs bedrooms would always be there for door duties! Lee stuck his head round the common room door.

"It's for you Tim."

Tim stretched, got up and headed out to the hall. Kevin was standing there, tall and gangling as always. He looked surprisingly shy as Tim came into view.

"Hi Tim, I hoped you'd join me for a pint or two."

"Sounds good to me. Let me go get my jacket."

Tim thumped up the stairs and then back down again. He opened the front door for Kevin and they were out in the chilly night.

"Do you like the Lionheart?"

"I've only been there a couple of times."

"It's quite good, the beers' better kept than at the Lookers."

They walked to the Lionheart in silence. Kevin insisted, despite Tim's protestations, that he was buying. They sat down in a bay window. Kevin tipped out some crisps onto a paper serviette. Both boys took a swig of beer and crunched some crisps.

The silence was becoming awkward.

"Tim, what I really came for was to apologise." Kevin began talking fast, with a slight clicking undertone to his words that suggested a dry mouth.

"I was well out of order, what I said, it wasn't fair and I don't even think it was true and as for roughing you up like that, I don't know what came over me." He fell silent, lowering his eyes, seeming to focus on the foam on the top of his beer.

"Well I'm sorry too. I said plenty that I shouldn't have said and plenty that I didn't really mean. What I think I really want to say is that, while we're obviously very different, I actually rather like you and I enjoy your company."

Tim spoke from his heart. He hoped he hadn't sounded stupid.

Kevin stretched his hand out to Tim, across the table. They shook hands. They shook hands again and then a third time. Both young men began to laugh.

"If anyone noticed us doing this, they'd get the men in white coats!" They laughed some more, the tension of earlier now totally forgotten.

After Tim had got the second pint in, he began to talk about the vital leadership role of Stroke in a crew.

"You're the perfect Stroke physically because of your size and you really have worked hard at your skill as an oarsman. Obviously, as Stroke, you set the pace, the speed and the power output of the other three. You have to lead. But I need you to work closely with me, in the boat so that we begin to think as one, and out of the boat to help to build cohesion, a close-knit team, unity and fun between us all. It's a difficult task, Kevin, but we've got to nail it."

"I've never done anything like that before to be honest. I don't know how to start."

"Richard has. He was Stroke for the top crew for nearly two seasons. He did a great job. If you can bear it, he can teach you a lot."

"What do you mean if I can bear it?" Kevin's eyes flashed.

"Well, Richard can get a bit heavy, in my experience." Tim smiled.

"You do know him well!"

"I lived with him for four years. He was my senior and, at the end, he was in authority over me. So, I know how difficult it can be."

Kevin laughed. "If you can put up with that. I can listen to him for five minutes twice a week!"

"Great!"

As two beers increased to three and then four, conversation became freer and easier. There was much laughter and both young men began to feel as if they had been friends for a very long time. They discovered that they shared a common fascination with people and their behaviours and a cynicism about most things that went on in their worlds. Both had a strong conviction about what constituted right and wrong and neither was afraid to stand up for his beliefs. Loyalty mattered a lot to each of them. When they finally parted outside number 73, they shook hands again. Kevin put his arm over Tim's shoulder.

"Thanks for making it easy for me this evening Tim."

"Thank you for being so brave to come around."

Tim went into his house and Kevin went on his way. Both felt sincere relief.

Elections

As the Spring term progressed the quantity of academic work required of the students began to increase markedly. Many of Tim's cohort began to grumble about having too many things to get done at once and a few began to fall behind with their assignments. One boy complained that the pressure was making him ill and left. Tim found that hard to believe. Tim continued to experience little difficulty. He was self-disciplined and found it easy to take effective notes during lectures which meant that he didn't need to do excessive amounts of reading. He tried always to complete assignments and essays as soon as possible after they were set and he did most of this written work in the library during the day when he was not attending some formal learning. As a result, he never needed to stay up all night to achieve a deadline and always had time to be able to join his friends in some spontaneous activity. All this gave the impression that Tim never did any work. He wasn't at all concerned if that was what people wanted to think and quite enjoyed the cool and carefree image.

The rhythm of his social life had changed considerably as a result of his recruitment to the Boat Club and, on balance, Tim enjoyed the greater structure to his week. Wednesday afternoons and Sunday mornings were spent on the river while Monday and Thursday evenings were spent training in the sports centre. These sessions would often be followed, rather counter productively, by drinks in the union bar. The crew justified this arrangement in the name of team building and it was true that it was bringing about an increased sense of unity, friendship and common purpose which, in turn, paid off in terms of commitment and responsibility.

Tim still had plenty of time to do little or nothing with his house mates and he was starting to enjoy the evening ritual of cooking supper. Visits to the Lookers became less frequent but he was, now, a regular user of the facilities of the Car Club, enthusiastically learning to use an ARC welder and stripping and rebuilding an old Austin engine with Peter. Tim had black engine oil permanently under his fingernails!

One Monday evening, after training, Richard raised the issue of the upcoming boat club elections. He was hoping to be elected as Captain and asked for the support of the crew. They were happy to offer it. Tom asked what other positions there were and Richard said that there were Secretary and Treasurer.

"What are the benefits of doing those things" Mark wanted to know.

"Not very much, beyond being able to influence the way in which the club is managed and having something to put on your CV." Was Richard's answer.

"Do you get keys to the bar?" Kevin had his eye on the practical possibilities.

"Probably, yes. But obviously then you have to be there to open the bar every club night."

The following Wednesday Dave, Kevin and Mark asked Tim if they could nominate him as Treasurer.

"It would give our crew an advantage in deciding what events we can enter." Mark reasoned.

"I don't know anything about keeping accounts. I can't think of anything more boring to be honest. I don't think I'm the right man for that job."

Tim really didn't want this responsibility thrust upon him. The discussion continued, Tim rebuffing all attempts to convince him and his crew trying to persuade him. Eventually Tim agreed to be nominated, on the condition that Tom stood for the post of Secretary. It was agreed. The elections were to be held at the boat house on Saturday at two O'clock. Tim thought nothing more of it.

Tim drove around collecting his crew on Saturday because it was raining heavily. He also collected Richard and his Avenger was very full with five lanky young passengers crammed inside it. The windows steamed up but everyone was in high spirits except for Tim, who would have preferred to have been helping Bill with developing his latest robotic arm.

Tim had never seen the club room so full of people before. He knew one or two of the men, each of whom he had seen sculling, and he recognised the members of the girls' crew, who came down to the river occasionally. The retiring Captain was a tall, quiet Chinese man who Tim had not seen before. He called silence and announced the names of those standing for election.

"For Captain it's Richard Norton, Treasurer, Tim Croy, Secretary Tom Elkins. There are no opposing nominations. Does anybody want to add any nominations at this late stage?"

Nobody did. Tim realised, to his dismay, that he was going to be elected. Two minutes later the unopposed new committee were confirmed.

The club house emptied fast, it was a miserable place on a cold, wet Saturday and everyone seemed to have better things to do than drink in a cold, damp bar. The Crew and Richard remained, with a pile of documents, an accounts file, cheque book and three bunches of keys on the table in front of them.

"Might as well Christen these keys then!" Dave laughed.

He tried several before he found the right key for the bar and then he served everybody a pint. Crisps and peanuts followed.

"It's almost a crew buy out" observed Tim.

"I think this is a real opportunity for us to revitalise this club. You see how disinterested most of the members are." Richard suggested. "Nobody's won any event for more than ten years, as far as I have been able to find out. If we can start to get some trophies coming in, make a bit of successful publicity around the union, we can really get some enthusiastic new recruits in October at the Freshers fair."

"We can start by making the bar better stocked and getting some regular events set up here so we can make some money." Mark sounded suddenly enthusiastic.

"There's a cash and carry card here." Kevin observed. "We should be able to buy some good stuff there. Be useful for all of us personally too I expect."

After a few more drinks, the boys began to sort through the entire contents of the bar. There were several boxes of long out of date crisps and Mars Bars which they piled up ready to take away with them, and they found lots of unused beer and wine glasses. Several unopened bottles of wine and spirits were locked in a cupboard under the far end of the bar.

"I think we can make this quite a fun place. Especially if we got that fire stove working and set up a television and video. I used to work in the kitchens of a pub so I've got a pretty good idea of what it takes." Tom volunteered.

The boys locked up and left the boat house with lots of ideas running around in their heads. They would talk more the next day after their outing.

After the outing on Sunday they decided that the most pressing need was to find out exactly what the Boat Club possessed. They divided themselves up to audit the boat house, the store under the stairs, the bar and to gather up all the sundry items that were scattered around or dumped, forgotten, in corners. Richard and Kevin went upstairs to check all the boats, blades, spares and tools in the boathouse. Tom and Mark set about emptying the huge under stairs store room. Dave was pleased to finish his previous days' work behind the bar. Tim wondered around the changing rooms, club house and the car park, stacking anything that he found in a pile of rubbish or a pile of useful things in the centre of the club room. He then set about clearing out the ancient wood burning stove to see if he could get it working. The room always seemed to be cold.

"What the hell's this for?" Tom shouted from the hall.

"That's an official Cox's outfit." Tim heard Richard shout from upstairs.

Tom and Mark came bounding excitedly into the club room.

"Look Tim! This is for you." They laughed.

Tim saw them carrying a crumpled, cobweb covered white braided blazer and trousers on a coat hanger. It reminded him of the one that he had been so proud to wear at school. Tim laughed

"I had to dress like that when I coxed the school First Eight at official races."

"Cool! You can wear it for us now Tim." Tim realised that Mark wasn't joking.

"No way, man! It made me look stupid at school but I had no choice. I do have a choice now and I'm not dressing like that in public again."

"Come on Tim!" Dave joined in "It looks really posh and distinctive, just like you. It would really help to raise the profile of the club."

"Raise a laugh, more like. No, I can't do that."

"I'm going to take it and get it cleaned" Mark stated obstinately "Then at least you can see if it fits you."

Richard and Kevin came down stairs. "I think we can do up a couple of the old boats and sell them so that we can try to buy one new one. There are stacks of unused oars that we could flog too."

They all settled down to a drink and a discussion about the future of the Boat Club. Richard said that he was going to apply to the union for a grant to buy some new kit because it was clear that there had been no investment in the club for years. They would sell a couple of older boats and blades to add the money to the grant fund. Kevin promised to take charge of that. He would put an advertisement in Exchange and Mart and see what the response was. Tim said that he would get the ancient boat trailer that was rusting away in the car park repaired in the Car Club. It would be good practice for his newly honed welding skills. Dave and Mark were keen to build up the bar and market the club as a good place to come on a Friday night. They would introduce a few river side barbeque nights in the Summer term. There was a feeling of cheerful optimism as they left the club, promising to meet at the Sports Centre as usual the following evening.

Tuesday was Tim's nineteenth birthday. It wasn't the kind of celebration that he liked, hating, as he did, to be the centre of attention. He had never mentioned it to anyone and had no reason to think that anyone would know. He received a card in the post from his parents but stuffed it into his cupboard in the bedroom. He was washing up his supper things when Kevin appeared in the kitchen.

"Hi mate! How did you get here?"

"I rang the bell and he told me you were in here so I came to get you."

"Get me?"

"Yeah. Come on."

Tim followed Kevin through the common room to the hall where he was surprised to find Tom, Mark and Dave waiting. Mark was holding a large white carrier bag.

"Happy birthday Tim!" He laughed, handing him the bag.

"How do you know it's my birthday?"

"Kevin saw your date of birth on a list in the Economics department."

Tim opened the bag. There was the dry cleaned and pressed cox's outfit. He laughed.

"Very fortuitous! Very funny too!"

"We knew you'd like it. You can try it on another time. We've got some celebrating to do!" Tom was in unusually talkative mood.

Tim went upstairs to get his jacket and dump his present on his bed. He would deal with that one another time!

The crew took Tim to the Lionheart. They propelled him to a large table in the corner and Kevin got in five pints of bitter and a large packet of dry roasted peanuts.

"Happy birthday Tim!" he proposed a toast to which everyone swigged their beer.

"Thanks." Tim was rather overwhelmed and very embarrassed. "Why were you looking for my date of birth Kevin?" Tim was sure that it couldn't have been purely accidental.

"Well Richard said he thought it was your birthday soon and we thought a party would really help with crew cohesion. Then I had the idea of looking in the department. You can usually find what you want if you know where to look!"

"Well thanks everyone. It's a really nice thought."

They drank in silence for a few minutes. Tom got in another round and said he'd ordered chips to go with it. Kevin said he'd already advertised the boats and blades in Exchange and Mart. Tim had arranged to get the boat trailer towed to the Car Club workshop. Everyone wanted to know about welding.

"I didn't think you'd be into that kind of thing Tim"

Dave was surprised to hear that he liked nothing better than practical, manual tasks.

"It just shows how much we all rely on stereotypes to form impressions about people. I was reading about that in Sociology." Kevin sounded genuinely animated.

"You could write a thesis about Tim!" Tom suggested, grinning.

"I might do that. There's far more to Tim than any of us know. I think he might be a bank robber in his spare time!" Kevin was laughing now, and Tim couldn't help himself from joining in.

"Please, don't tell me that Richard told you my dark secret from school Kevin. He promised he'd never tell."

"How much did you make Tim?"

"So much that I lost count Dave."

Tim thought for a moment. "What exactly do you two study?" He was referring to Kevin and Mark, who he knew were on the same course. "I seem to meet the two of you in every department I go to!"

"EPS" Mark replied.

"EPS?"

"Yep. Economics, Politics and Sociology."

"I understand the first two, but what do you do in Sociology?"

"I just told you Tim. Kevin's going to start a thesis about you. That's the kind of thing Sociologists do." Tom was laughing. "They should try some real work like me."

Tim knew that he was studying some kind of Mathematics. It sounded incredibly difficult, intelligent sort of stuff to him.

"What do you do Dave?" "Japanese."

"How did you even think about studying that? Do you have to learn to read and write it?"

Dave laughed. "Yeah I can just about read and write it now, about the level that a five year old can do English."

"What about you Tim?" "Economics and Geography, joint."

"That explains why we keep meeting then. I'm off to get my round in!" Mark headed to the bar.

The conversation moved back to the Boat Club. Richard had suggested entering two Head of River races near the end of term, by way of preparation for the Regatta season in the summer.

"What's the difference between a Head of River race and a Regatta Tim?"

"Well a Regatta is a series of races, heats if you like, between two or more boats at a time. You keep going through quarter finals and semi-finals until you get a winner in the final. Head of river is just a series of timed rows over a set distance. Boats do it one at a time, in quick succession, and the one to do it in the least time is awarded Head of River. There's a kind of hybrid thing too, called "Bumps" races, in which all the boats set off in a timed sequence, one after another, and try to bump into the one in front while avoiding being bumped from behind. They can get quite dangerous."

Tim's crew were listening intently, looking at him as if he was some kind of lecturer. It made him laugh.

"You're better at explaining than Richard is. At least we know what we're going to be trying to do now."

Kevin was thinking out loud. "So that's why you keep on pushing us in the sports hall, we obviously need strength. Maybe we should start eating a special diet of steak and bananas or something, like the footballers do."

"Or stop drinking beer!" They all laughed.

"Talking of which, it's my round." Dave got up to buy in.

"How many races did you do at school Tim?"

"Umm well, I was coxing for about seven terms, so I guess I've done between forty and fifty. I'd never really thought about it before."

"No wonder you're so confident. That's a lot of experience mate."

Kevin went to put some music on the juke box and came back with the fifth round of beers. Tim didn't want any more but struggled manfully to keep up with the group. The conversation was becoming more excitable but steadily less coherent. By the time it was Tom's turn to buy his second round of beers Tim was barely half way through his previous pint.

"Come on man! You haven't had five yet. I thought you lot knew how to put it away." Kevin teased Tim.

"Down it in one Tim!" Dave joined in the banter.

Tim, now definitely the worse for wear but considerably emboldened by four and a half pints of Best Bitter, got unsteadily to his feet, lifted his glass and took up the challenge. "One Two Three Four Five..............Yeah!"

The crew chanted and cheered their encouragement.

Tim sat down, still gulping in an effort to contain the drink that he could now feel foaming inside him. He focussed his bleary eyes on Tom and Mark who were building a tower with the contents of Kevin's matchbox.

Tim realised that he hadn't started on his sixth pint and he could see that the others were half way down theirs. He picked up his full glass and forced down a couple of the largest gulps that he could manage.

He sat, breathing heavily. That had been a mistake. He felt the burning acidity of vomit in the back of his throat. He needed the toilet. He stood up clumsily and stumbled his way out of the bar. He felt as if his feet were sinking into the floor with every step. He leaned against the heavy door of the gents to open it and staggered into a cubicle. There was no time to close the door. With a volcanic burp Tim sent a tsunami of sick into the bowl. He did it again and then again. The cold air of the gents, coupled to the relief of an empty stomach, was having a sobering effect on the ill young man. He straightened up, shivering. He took a couple of deep breaths then spat into the toilet.

"Are you OK Tim?" Mark's voice broke into Tim's introverted world.

"I think so yes." Tim emerged from his cubicle and went to a basin to splash water over his face and rinse out his mouth. Mark was beside him, offering a steadying hand.

"Are you ready to go back? Or do you need to stay here for a bit?" Mark seemed to Tim to be very kind and gentle.

"I'm OK" Tim assured him determinedly.

Back at his table in the bar Tim was confused to find three full pints, each arranged neatly on a beer mat, in his place. His friends were looking at him.

"You found him then Mark? He hadn't run away from us." Tom asked.

"Come on mate, you've got to finish off the night properly. Make it the gallon!" Dave encouraged.

"No. I can't."

"Don't be harsh Dave. He's not feeling well. Let him take it slowly." Mark spoke gently.

"He needs a bit of help." Kevin got up and disappeared. He returned with a glass of golden liquid. "Swig that Tim. It'll settle your tummy and make it easier to finish your challenge."

"What's that?"

"Whisky"

"I can't."

"'Course you can! On the count of three. One, Two Three!"

Tim swigged the whole glass. He remembered the pavilion at Barforth where he had first drunk Whisky. It burned his mouth and his throat but he felt it spreading its' warming fingers rapidly through his upset stomach. Tim lifted his beer glass and took a sip. It made him shiver with distaste. He *would* drink it. He knew that this evening had somehow been turned into a challenge for him and, being a stubborn and wilful youth, he was not going to concede defeat. He took a couple more proper gulps of beer. It was fine now!

The others were drinking and chatting again now and Tim joined in as and when he knew what was being talked about. He was just starting on his eighth pint when the bar man called time.

"Come on Tim, get that down you!" Kevin was encouraging him again.

"Drink it with us mate, One for all and all for one!"

The five boys finished their beer in unison.

As they all stood up to leave, Tim stumbled and leant heavily against the table.

"I think we'd better get him home. We can't just leave him by himself in his state."

Mark was talking to his friends, trying to pull them out of their own drunken worlds. The five intoxicated young men weaved their erratic way across the car park and out onto the pavement. It seemed to Tim that the pavement was tipping and tilting up at forty-five degrees, like a mountain in front of him. He couldn't work out why his feet kept sinking through it.

"You got your keys Tim" They were outside number 73.

"Don't need key." Tim reached to turn the door handle but missed and nearly fell onto the path. He was sure the door had moved away from him.

Amidst much laughter the group fell into the house, spilled down the hall, through the common room and into the kitchen.

"Make him some coffee" Kevin suggested.

Tom set about doing so, hampered by his own inebriation as well as being in a strange kitchen. The other boys drew plastic chairs up to one of the tables and sat, sprawled and happy. Peter and Lee came in.

"What's up?"

"We're having a birthday party for Tim. Come and join us."

"Is it your birthday Tim? You kept that quiet."

"Let's have a chips party. Give us a hand peeling and chopping." Dave and Mark started to help.

Tim sat, trying hard to focus on his surroundings, which were blurred and moving in strange jumping patterns. The whole room was kind of swimming in front of his eyes. He felt ill. He stood up unsteadily, lurching towards the back door. Somehow opening it he staggered outside and started vomiting again. When he'd finished the initial bout, he sat on the concrete door step with his spinning head in his hands. From time to time he would heave and wretch into the drain in front of him. He had never felt so horrible.

Lee came out to check on him.

"What have they done to you Tim? Come on, you need to get inside now." He hooked his hands under Tim's arms and lifted him to his unsteady feet.

Tim flopped into a plastic chair.

"Eat some chips. They'll soak up the beer."

Tim could see a huge pile of steaming chips on a newspaper in the middle of the table. Kevin was sprinkling them liberally with salt and vinegar. Everyone began eating. They were good.

When the chips were finished the crew got up to go.

"Can you make sure Tim gets' to bed OK. I don't think he'll get upstairs by himself." Mark was still concerned for his friend.

"Come on mate. Bed for you!"

Peter and Lee helped Tim up from his seat and led him through the common room and upstairs.

"Get your jacket and jeans off and into bed." Lee knew what needed to be done.

"Bill, keep an eye on him. He's in a bad way but I think he'll just sleep it off now."

"What have you been doing Tim?" Bill grinned hazily down at Tim. He just shook his head, rolled over and was asleep.

When Tim woke up, he wished that he had not. His head was thumping, his mouth tasted foul and his stomach was churning queasily. He lay, not daring to move, hoping that things would settle down if he was gentle enough with himself.

He remembered the events of the previous evening. It had been kind of his friends and they had had fun. Tim assumed that they had had even more fun than him, at his expense. Such was life.

He knew that he had to be at a tutorial at eleven fifteen. He would miss his only lecture. It wasn't important.

Presently he got up, brushing his teeth twice in an effort to remove the foul taste that was plastering his mouth. He dressed and went down to the kitchen with the intention of making coffee.

The room was full of the cheerful chatter of cleaners and boys. Tim put a kettle on. Someone began cooking some bacon. The large kitchen filled with the greasy smell of frying. Tim could almost taste the smell. It pushed him over the edge.

He hurried out of the kitchen and back upstairs as fast as his thumping head would allow him. He shut himself in the bathroom where he sat on the edge of the bath, beside the wash basin. His stomach lurched and he spat a mouthful of half-digested chips into the basin. He heaved and deposited another substantial load into the sink. He dribbled miserably. He'd never been so sick, so many times, before in his life.

As he began to feel marginally better, he had to clean up the basin. He cleaned himself up and slunk back to bed for an hour.

Tim drove gently into the university and sat, feeling fragile, through his tutorial. The subject, looking at the cost benefit analysis of the soon to be opened Humber Bridge, was interesting and Tim found it easy to contribute several well formulated ideas to the discussion.

After the tutorial, knowing that he was expected for training at the Boat House as usual, he thought it might be a good idea to get something to eat. He was feeling weak and shaky now, on top of his still serious hangover. He headed for the refectory but, as his senses were assailed by the smell of coffee, fish and chips, pizza and burgers, he decided that he simply wasn't up to eating yet.

He sat quietly in the library for an hour, bracing himself for the inevitable meeting with his crew. He felt embarrassed and ashamed of himself.

Tim pulled on the hand brake, turned off the engine and swung himself out of his car. He could see Tom's motorbike parked beside the building. Tim went in and straight into the changing room. All his crew were there already, in various stages of undress.

"We weren't sure that you'd make it Tim." Kevin grinned.

"It would be pretty sad if I didn't".

"You were in a pretty sad state!" Mark commented.

"I told you that Public School makes them tough. Tim would die before letting us down just because of a hangover. Not like you Mark."

Tim was amused by Kevin's robust certainty in the benefits of Public School. As he had done several times in the recent past, he wondered exactly what Kevin's background was. For sure there was more to find than he let people see.

The outing went well and Richard said that he was going to send in the entries for two Head of River races.

"Are you feeling better Tim" Mark and Dave asked after they'd all showered.

"Buy him a beer!" Tom joked.

"I am feeling better than I did when I got here. But **no!** definitely no beer. Not for at least a week."

Everyone laughed. Kevin admitted to having been in a "bad way" that morning and Tom and Dave agreed that they, too, had been rough. Tim felt less ashamed.

Who Are You Anyway?

The tutorial group were sitting in the sun filled room on orange and green armchairs. The tutor, Steve Hockwell, always tried to set challenging and stimulating topics for his students and he rarely disappointed. Today they were considering the practical consequences of location on personal Economics.

"Obviously this is the fundamental reason why, as a country becomes more economically developed the population becomes increasingly urbanised."

He set the challenge and waited for the students to respond.

"Do you mean that people like us are pushed to live in towns to make money for the rich ruling classes?"

Belinda, a girl who Tim had always thought of as being rather silly asked.

"Of course not." Tim replied. "You live in a town because life there is so much easier and more convenient."

"How can someone like *you* say that? Everything's always easy for posh people."

"Oh, just think for a minute. If you'd wanted to you could have got a paper round when you were fourteen and earned some money easily just by walking around a few streets near your house. If I'd wanted to do the same thing, I'd have had to cycle for about five miles before I could earn the same amount. Much more difficult."

Tim was very sure of his facts because he had actually tried to get a paper round once, to no avail.

"Yes, but I bet you live in a beautiful place. We have to pay to go on holiday to places like that while you just live on holiday all the time. It's not fair!"

Tim snorted with mirth.

"It's true though, Tim. You don't know how lucky you are." Another girl joined in. "You probably live in a great big house with a huge garden. We live in a fourth floor flat with a balcony."

"OK, but your flat probably costs the same as our house. And that's because of economics. Everybody wants to live in the convenient town and nobody wants to live miles from everything like I have to. It's simple supply and demand. That proves my case really neatly."

"You obviously live a better life than us though." The silly girl joined in again, looking sulky.

"I dispute that. Life for us is much more expensive and hard work than it is for you. If my mum wants to go to the super market she has to drive about a twelve miles round trip. That costs money before you start. Your mum can probably just walk there."

"You're lucky to have a car and to be able to drive. My mum can't drive." Mike Leighton joined in.

Tim was beginning to feel beleaguered. He was evidently in a minority in this room and that made him more determined to prove that he was right.

"My poor mum *has to be able to drive.* We couldn't manage if she couldn't. If she had to catch the bus to go to the shops, she would be out all day because the bus only goes at about eight in the morning and doesn't come back until about six at night. She'd be out all day and then there'd be nobody to collect my sister from school. Nobody subsidises our car like the government does to your bus. If I'd gone to my local school, I'd have had to walk nearly three miles there and back each day down muddy, unlit country lanes without a pavement. Because it's less than three miles the County Council don't have to provide a bus."

"Well that's not fair either." The silly girl swapped her side of the discussion to join Tim's.

This went on, moving back and forth without achieving any consensus, for the whole hour. By the end the exercise had achieved its' goal of opening minds and causing long held beliefs and prejudices to be challenged. Steve Hockwell had done a good Job!

Tim lay in bed that night considering the earlier tutorial. He knew and accepted that he was privileged and advantaged. No doubt about that. But it wasn't all good. Most people, he felt, simply envied his parents large house and garden, his private education, without any thought for the down sides, the impossibility of finding holiday work, the loneliness and isolation throughout the teenage years, having to rely on ones parents to go anywhere until you were forced to learn to drive and get a car of your own, if you could earn the money to do so. And what about the "privilege" of boarding school? The forced separation from the love of parents, the constant bullying, the inability to get away from the school, night after day, week after week, month to month. He wondered how that group would have reacted if he had told them of the life changing event that had happened to him, aged just fourteen. Would they still think he was "lucky"? It hurt, really. But Tim did not consider himself to be a victim. It was clear that Belinda, in particular, did think of herself as being one. It must all be to do with one's mind set.

Anthony was also lying awake, alone in his bed in Lancaster. He had been watching a film with some friends about an American boy who was trying to come to terms with being "Gay" and his struggles for acceptance by parents, family and friends. It had affected Anthony badly. He had been wrestling with strange feelings that he couldn't understand and didn't want, for some time. Certainly, since before he left school. He didn't think he was queer, or "gay" as the Americans seemed to call it. He had been with girls before and he had liked it. But he knew that he had emotional feelings about boys as well. He was trying to work out how and why. To apply logic to the problem, as he had always been taught to do.

He had not been popular at school, ever. He had been bullied constantly at prep school and had decided that the new start at Senior School was the opportunity he needed to change things. He had set about making himself a bit of a bully from the start, to try to avoid becoming the victim again. He had succeeded but, far from helping him, it had just made his peers dislike and avoid him and had given the Masters the impression that he was a trouble maker.

At first, he had picked most of all on Tim, who had appeared gentle to the point of weakness. But later the two had become the very best of friends, both living on the fringes of the school society and both being high spirited and lovers of practical jokes.

Somehow, for Anthony, this bond had moved further than mere friendship. He was certain that he didn't *fancy* Tim and he knew for a fact that Tim hated queers with a burning passion, with very good reason. He thought that maybe he *loved* Tim, as a friend, in a completely platonic kind of way. He wondered if Tim felt like that about him. He would like to find a way to talk to him about all this but he didn't know how to begin without sounding stupid or making Tim think that he was queer. Why couldn't everything just be normal, easy and simple?

"You alright Tim?" Tom shouted across the carpark as Tim was getting in to his car on Tuesday afternoon.

"Yeah, fine thanks. I'm just off to get on with the trailer. Do you want to come and give me a hand?"

"Can I?"

"Get in the car man."

The two young men set off for the garages that contained the car club. Tom was telling Tim that he had just started driving lessons and that he knew nothing about cars, driving or engineering.

Tim laughed "My dad's an engineer and I've spent my life watching and helping him with projects around the house. I like cars and, now I've got this one, I've had to learn how to fix it and look after it."

Tim set about getting the ARC welder out and set up.

"Can you measure and mark up the right lengths of that square section steel to replace the missing pieces on the trailer?"

Tom worked diligently. Tim showed him how to use the electric angle grinder to cut the steel into the right lengths. He jumped as the shower of sparks plumed out of the machine.

"It's OK. They're cold!" Tim laughed.

They looked at the sorry, rusting trailer.

"Is it worth bothering Tim? It's well far gone!"

"It looks worse than it is. By the time we've fixed these bars on you'll be able to see its' shape again. Then we can sand blast it to get the old paint and rust off and then we'll paint it. It'll look as good as new."

Tim showed Tom how to clamp the new bars in place, checking that they were level.

"Now for the fun! My latest bit of training."

Tim connected the Earth to the frame.

"Stand back and pull your helmet's visor down."

Tim pulled his visor down and made contact between the electrode and the bars. The fiery metal spread around the joint, showering plumes of sparks and smoke around Tim. He really enjoyed doing it, now that he was gaining experience and confidence.

"That's impressive Tim! When did you learn to do that?"

"Just this term, here. It's cool isn't it?"

Tim was pleased with the result. When they had put the equipment away, giving the newly welded rods the chance to cool, Tim told Tom to pull on them, test them with his weight, to see if they were fixed properly. To his relief they were.

On the river things were progressing well. The crew had started to work as one unit and Tim could feel the result in the way in which the boat moved cleanly away and made smooth progress. Most of all he felt it in his back, which no longer hurt at the end of every outing as a result of being banged against the wooden back of the boat as the crew took each stroke.

Richard had started timing them over set routes and the times were dropping steadily, indicating the crew's increased stamina and strength. They had no way of knowing what kind of speed their competitors might be able to achieve but the statistics that they could find indicated that they were pleasingly better than average. They began to feel optimistic about their first Head of River race in York. Tim and Richard called a crew meeting after training on Monday.

"Our first race is on Saturday. I know that we all know that already. But we need to keep that in mind throughout this week. Everything you do this week can have an effect on what happens on Saturday." Richard was earnest and serious.

Tim understood, obviously, but he could see that the crew were looking sceptical.

"What do you mean by everything we do?" Kevin voiced the thoughts of the crew, in a slightly challenging tone of voice. Tim knew that Richard would be angered by this attitude.

"It's not a big deal Kevin. Just simple things like making sure that none of us gets drunk like I did the other week and that we eat properly so that we are at peak performance and energy levels." The crew laughed.

"Poor Tim. He *hurt* that night!" Mark smiled.

"Did *you* get drunk Tim?" Richard looked angry.

"Yes, I did. But it didn't affect anything and it's definitely not your concern mate. We're not at school now!"

Tim was not going to take Richard's "holier than thou" attitude.

"Now, now!" Mark intervened with a smile before things could go further. He really was quite the diplomat, Tim thought to himself.

Tom and Tim collected their newly finished trailer from the Car Club on the Friday afternoon and delivered it to the Boat Club. They were justifiably proud of their work, which shimmered in its' two coats of deep blue enamel.

"It really does look like new Tim" Tom was impressed.

"Well you did the painting mate and that's what looks so good. Without your help I wouldn't have got it finished in time." They pushed it into the garage and locked up.

The crew assembled in the early morning mist. There was frost on the ground but the day promised to be sunny once the mist had lifted. Tim and Richard showed the crew how to dismantle the boat and fix it securely to the trailer. Everyone had been impressed as Tim and Tom proudly pulled it out of the garage into the car park. The headlights of the Union minibus appeared, crawling down the muddy track. Richard had had to persuade a friend to drive it for them because you had to be twenty-one to do so. Tim showed Tom how to hook the trailer to the tow bar and lock it in place. They locked up the boat house and they were off.

York University Boat Club looked very impressive after their own one. It was situated just outside the city centre in a large green field and the river itself was wide, shallow and clean looking, set amongst green banks with weeping willows whose buds were just beginning to burst with light green leaves. It made Tim and Richard remember the River Barr with some emotion. The other crews were starting to arrive and the field was busy with people reassembling boats and checking programs. Tim remembered races past. He felt very comfortable with what was to come. Once they had got the

Fellows assembled and thoroughly checked Tim took the crew for a walk along the river bank to see the course for themselves.

Tim had already searched out a map of the river in the Library and had enlisted Kevin to study it with him to try to predict the nature of currents and the best way to navigate it. They had not known the exact course but Tim had been able to gain a useful insight. Kevin had been surprised and impressed at Tim's diligence.

"The current is much, much gentler than we're used to. We'll move faster than usual. I think you'll be surprised." Tim talked his crew through what lay ahead.

He could hear the Tannoy starting to explain what was going to happen. Hull knew that they were racing quite late in the event so they had plenty of time to see what other crews were doing. Tim was pleased because he knew that it often helped a crew to have a target time from a competing crew.

"Why is that boat grey?" Tom was commenting about a boat belonging to Newcastle.

"It's made of Carbon Fibre. That's the latest material, it's only been available for a couple of years. It costs a lot but it's lighter than wood though if you break it, it can't be repaired." Tim was glad to share his knowledge with his friends.

"I need another piss. I'm well nervous!" Dave laughed.

The other three decided they should join him. When they returned Tim offered each boy an energy drink. It will give you that extra boost. We'll be racing in about half an hour.

"I'd rather have something to eat!" Mark stated wistfully.

"You can eat after the last race. That really is the golden rule. If you eat before a race it can really hurt you. Terrible stomach cramps that will stop you from rowing. It's the end for us all if that happens." Tim spoke very firmly, knowing that he depended on the self-control of each individual.

"Yes Cox!" The united reply of his crew made him feel confident. They had come a very long way.

Crew after crew set off on the timed course. As the results began to be displayed on a large board it became clear that most were completing it in between seven and nine minutes. The best so far was seven minutes fifty-one seconds. They knew that, in recent training, they had been achieving about eight and a half minutes. They would need to work very hard in this race.

Tim reminded Kevin that he would start really pushing him towards the end of the course and that he and the crew simply had to push themselves beyond what they could bear. They would hurt by the time they had completed the course! The crew gathered round their boat.

"This is it guys!" Richard smiled. "Just remember that whatever happens it's in your hands. Nobody can do it for you."

"OK let's get going." Tim got the crew in position beside the Fellows.

"Hands on. Shoulder height. Right up!" the crew lifted their boat off the trestles and carried down to the pontoon from which they would launch it. Tim squatted, holding the Fellows while his crew fetched their blades.

"Hands across Bow side" Tim commanded. The two young men got in and put their blades flat on the water to balance the boat.

"Hands across Stroke side" Tim got in and pushed the boat away from the pontoon and into the river. Stroke side pushed against the pontoon with their blades until they were far enough away from it to be able to row.

"Come forward. Are you ready? Row!"

They set off to find the starting position. The race master was in his motor launch, issuing instructions as each crew arrived to start the course. Tim positioned the Fellows as he was instructed.

"Come forward to row. I'll ask you once. Are you ready? Row!"

The boat powered through the water with a satisfying swishing sound. There were no wasteful splashing sounds from the blades. Tim felt immense pleasure from racing again, and enjoyment from being on a beautiful river once more. He surveyed his four strong oarsmen with a feeling of benevolent pride. "In out, in out, in out" Tim began to increase the frequency of their strokes. They were already approaching the half way point of the course. "Stride it out!" Kevin stretched himself further forward, making his back almost horizontal with the boat, as Tim had regularly described to them.

"Good man!" Tim spoke quietly, especially for Kevin.

"In, out, in out, in out." About one kilometre to go now. This was the point at which they would start to win.

"Stride it out! Come on you lazy bastards. You're not out for a Sunday afternoon pick nick now. S-t-r-e-t-c-h those arms! Find that power!"

Tim was pushing them. He could feel their growing pain. He hadn't raced with these men before and he wasn't certain what their limit was.

"We're nearly there. Last push. Kill yourselves!".

They were past the red buoys. The finish line motor launch had clocked them.

"Easy All!"

The crew held their feathered blades above the surface of the water. The boat glided gradually to a standstill.

"Well done! That was a real race!" Tim was proud of them.

"I thought I really was going to die!" Dave called from Bow.

"It was impressive work from you all." Tim grinned. Let's get back and see what we've done.

Richard was waiting for them on the pontoon.

"Fucking fantastic!"

Tim knew that the news must be good, Richard never used that word!

"Seven forty-eight. Best time so far!"

The crew were exhausted. They did not respond. Obediently they removed their oars and took them back to the trailer. They returned and lifted the boat from the water and took it back to the trestles. Tim called them together.

"Did you hear our time?" They all shook their heads, dully. "Seven minutes forty-eight seconds. The best so far. We're in with a good chance."

"It feels like it, mate." Kevin sounded dead pan.

The crew lay on the cool green grass. They really were exhausted. They hadn't been prepared for the emotional and physical effort that a real race demanded. Tim felt very sorry for them.

"What shall I get them to eat Richard?" Tim asked. "I mean, what would you have really, *really* wanted if you were feeling like they are?"

"Energy! See if you can find some doughnuts or something."

Tim set off on his mission. He was on his way back, laden with a dozen warm jam doughnuts, when he heard that racing was over. Results would be confirmed shortly. Tim fund his crew sitting up now, looking more normal. They were well pleased to see Tim and some food.

"It seems we've done it" Kevin spoke in an unusually stilted manner. "Richard just went to look. But we'll have to wait to hear it officially."

They ate their doughnuts silently.

"It's official!" Richard bounced up to the group.

"Kevin, as Stroke it's your privilege to go up to the podium to collect the trophy. You need to be ready, near the podium. Let's head over that way".

Kevin leapt up to the podium to receive the York Head of River trophy as if he was a seasoned professional. He held it up, high above his head, to massive applause. When he returned to his crew everybody was keen to touch, to feel their prize.

"I must admit I didn't expect that, not on our first try" Richard was laughing.

"I'm insulted! You know me and my crews better than anyone." Tim retorted. "Anyway, I think you and I should share the Barforth tradition of the coach buying a meal for the winning crew."

"We're buying dinner for us all down the Lookers tonight." Tim told everyone before Richard could think of any reason not to.

"Actually, Tim, there's another tradition that your crew don't know about."

"What?"

"Think about it, Tim, I know you know!"

Richard called the oarsmen over to him, indicating that Tim was not included. Tim realised what he was referring to. He watched him demonstrating actions to the lads.

The four young men sauntered over to Tim, looking very serious.

"It's my solemn duty to carry out one final act as Stroke before we leave the river." Kevin was an impressive actor.

"On the count of three, crew! One, two, three!" Each boy gripped one of Tim's ankles or wrists, the tall crew lifted Tim high above their heads, carrying him horizontally towards the river bank. They began to swing him backwards and forwards, in a motion that Tim had long associated with race winning. Suddenly they released him, he flew through the air and sploshed into the water. Tim righted himself and waded out of the river, his clenched fist raised in victory salute above his head, to the applause of his waiting crew.

The joyful crew and their coach assembled in the pub as soon as they had put away the boat and trailer. Kevin bought a round of beers and then Tom got in another. Tim and Richard ordered Chilli Con Carne and rice with four extra portions of chips and House Special ice cream for everyone.

The party lasted long into the evening until Richard reminded them that they really needed to train again the next morning if they wanted to secure a second victory the following Saturday. Not a man objected!

Next morning everyone was at the Boat House punctually. Each oarsman was complaining of stiff, aching muscles.

Tim took them all out to the Rugby pitches beyond the car park.

"OK! We're going to jog around a bit and try to loosen up. Really, we should all have gone home to have a long, hot bath before we went to the pub. Learn from that!"

Tim began to jog around the perimeter and his crew followed. After a few circuits he was suddenly sent sprawling to the ground by a Rugby tackle.

"What was that for?"

"We've had enough. I thought it would be a fun way to stop you." Kevin was looking too sincere for Tim to believe him.

"Good move mate! Let's get the boat out."

The Invincible

The Summer term began badly for Tim. As he was driving back to Hull, soon after he had joined the M1, he noticed the temperature gage moving higher up its' scale. He hoped that the higher, steady speed of motorway driving would cool it down again so he pressed on with his journey. At one point he felt the engine stutter but then it seemed to be OK again. Then, minutes later, the whole car was enveloped in a cloud of steam. The gage was as far up the scale, coloured red, as it could go.

Tim turned onto the hard shoulder and stopped the engine. He sat for a few moments, listening to hissing, bubbling sounds coming from under the bonnet. When things seemed to have settled down a little he got out, lifted the bonnet and took a look. His nose was filled with the smell of antifreeze and hot engine oil. Very quickly he clocked blue liquid dribbling out from the water pump. He doubted that the AA would be able to fix it. Tim retrieved his yellow hand book from the glove box and walked up to the emergency telephone. They would be with him within an hour.

After nearly two hours Tim called them again. They claimed that he was not where he said he was. Tim explained patiently that he was exactly under the sign for junction sixteen, Northbound. They told him that they knew, from the telephone, that he was somewhere else. Tim pointed out to them that he was standing under the sign. He was not stupid. He went back to wait in his dead car. He was very bored and now not a little displeased. He saw an AA van drive straight past him. Then another. Were they really so stupid? He paid plenty to belong to this organization and now, the first time that he needed them, they were making things more difficult for him. At last a yellow van pulled in in front of him and put on its' yellow flashing roof lights. Tim got out. He told the man that he thought the water pump had gone. The man took a cursory glance and agreed with him.

"I'll have to get a tow truck. Can't fix that here."

Tim gave him his membership certificate and the man radioed for a tow truck.

"Should be with you in thirty minutes. I'll be off now."

Tim returned to sit in his silent car. At last the tow truck arrived and winched Tim's yellow car onto the back. Tim got into the passenger seat of the cab and they began the long journey to Hull. The driver was a cheerful guy and the two men talked about cars, mechanics and other such boys talk for the entire journey.

By the time they finally got to his house in Hull it was past ten O'clock. Tim was tired, stressed and tetchy. He was very hungry but, by the time he had unloaded his things from the car he hardly felt like eating. In the end he went down the fish and chip shop and scoffed his meal out of the newspaper, slouching in an arm chair in the common room.

It was three days before Tim got around to taking his car to the Car Club where he could strip out the water pump and fit the expensive new replacement that he had purchased from Halfords. The task proved to be more fiddly than he had anticipated and he had to enlist the help of Peter to lift and pull the alternator out of the way while he slid the pump on to the mounting bolts on the engine block. After that it took some considerable time to fill the system with new water and antifreeze and bleed it of airlocks. Peter had done a similar job before and his experience proved invaluable to Tim. That evening Tim was glad to take his friend out for food and drinks by way of thanks.

On the river things were more positive. Tim and his crew had returned for the Summer Regatta season eagerly, with very high hopes after their two Head of River awards at the end of the last term. They all believed that they could achieve anything, that they worked well together and they were certain that if they made the effort, they would achieve their aims. That was exactly the attitude that Richard and Tim knew that they needed to foster and they were relieved to have achieved it, despite their initial reservations. Each of the oarsmen were proud to tell each other of the exercise and fitness regime that each had imposed upon himself, during the month long holiday.

For the Boat Club, the committee devised a programme of events to try to raise the awareness of the very existence of the club and to make some much needed money to improve the facilities. There would be two barbecues and they planned to try to borrow some normal rowing boats so that they could hold a "Novices" race safely to try to get people interested in river sports prior to the new academic year in October.

Academically the assignments and tutorial preparations were coming thick and fast and Tim was kept busy during most of each day to keep up to date with his work. There was increasing talk about the "Part One" exams which would happen in the first two weeks of June. Each exam would last for three hours. There would be six in total. Tim struggled to imagine what an exam that lasted three hours must be like. The very toughest of his "A" levels had been only two hours. He began to have feelings of unease and self-doubt. Maybe he really wasn't up to university level study, as Barforth had repeatedly told him. He really didn't want to fail now that he had started and was enjoying the experience so much.

The first of the Summer Regattas was approaching fast. The weather was warm and sunny day after day and Tim suggested fitting in an extra practice on the river each Tuesday evening at seven, now that it stayed light so long. The crew had gladly agreed, the added incentive being to take advantage of the cheap beer in the club bar afterwards. As they sat enjoying their beer outside on the grassy playing field Tom raised something that Tim had hoped had been long forgotten.

"I hope you've kept that Cox's outfit we got cleaned for you Tim"

"Yeah, you ought to try it on for us tomorrow so we've got time to get it altered if we need to." Dave added.

"I said I wasn't prepared to wear it." Tim tried to make it clear, from the tone of his voice, that that was the end of it.

"But Tim, you're part of the Boat Club Committee now, and that brings responsibility and obligation to do what's best for the Club." Kevin looked very serious and sincere.

Tim never felt sure if that look of his was genuine or if he was taking the micky.

"Come on man! I thought you were braver than that. Don't let us down." Mark added gently.

Tim liked Mark, very much. He always seemed to offer the voice of reason in a really kind way.

"OK, but only if it fits properly."

"You hero!"

"Well done mate"

The boys finished their beer and Tom went into the club house to refill their glasses. The down side of drinking at the club was that the boys had to wash up their own glasses afterwards!

The next day, as he prepared to drive into the university, Tim took the white carrier bag containing the contentious suit with him. He had not looked at it or taken it out of the bag since he had been handed it as a present on the night of his birthday.

Tim gave a lift to Kevin from the campus to the club. In the changing room Tim laughed.

"The moment you've all been waiting for!"

He pulled on the white trousers, which were just about ok, if a little too wide around the waist, and shrugged the jacket on over his T shirt. It fitted fine.

"That looks so cool!"

Tim would not have used the word cool himself, he felt just as stupid as he had at school.

"You'll have to wear a proper white shirt and a tie" observed Kevin.

"I've got a shirt. But, really, I should have a Boat Club tie."

"Someone didn't open his birthday present properly!" Mark laughed.

"What do you mean Mark?"

Tom felt into the bottom of the bag and retrieved a moss green tie, wrapped in plastic. Removing it from its' wrapping for him he unfolded it, revealing an embroidered crest. On closer inspection Tim could see it read HUBC under the emblem.

"We found a whole box of them in the store room. They'll last us for years!" Kevin explained.

"Well that's me sorted then." Tim knew when he was beaten.

The crew assembled excitedly at the Boat House early on Saturday morning. The oarsmen looked resplendent in their dark green shorts and white vests with moss green hoops round them. Tim felt silly in his white braided blazer and trousers, fastened safely by a belt. He had his tracksuit in a bag with him, in the hope that he would need a change of clothes after a win.

With the Fellows dismantled and secured on the trailer and the trailer attached to the minibus the crew set off for their first Regatta, in Bradford. They were surprised to find the host club located in a beautifully green, wooded location outside the city. It was not at all what Tim and his crew had pictured and the diagram of the river that Tim and Kevin had studied, in the library, two days earlier had given them little indication of what it would be like. They busied themselves assembling the Fellows and then took their customary walk along the bank to see the course for themselves.

"If we get into either of the outside lanes, I will use the current to help you" Tim explained.

"Kevin and I checked it out in the library and now you can see the way the water is moving in the bends. Just be ready because it will tend to snatch your blades out of your hands. I will warn you by shouting "current."

Richard told them that they had been drawn against Bradford and Sheffield. Kevin said he was going to try to get a look at the opposition. He returned grinning.

"Sheffield's crew made me feel like a pygmy!" Everyone felt immediately threatened and determined to show them what for anyway.

Their race was the second of three so, after the first race had been started Tim got his crew onto the river and steered them to the start line. They were in the middle lane so there would be little opportunity to benefit from changes in the current or their position in a corner. Tim stole a glance at the giants of Sheffield. He wasn't at all convinced that Kevin's observations had been accurate.

"Come forward to row" The start steward called over the Tannoy. "I'll ask you once. Are you ready? Row!" Tim felt the Fellows surge forward smoothly and powerfully. He felt a corresponding surge of pride in his crew and their boat. Almost immediately they were pulling ahead of Bradford. Sheffield were definitely holding their own against them. Tim waited patiently, enjoying seeing his boat pull clear of Bradford and wanting his oarsmen to benefit from the psychological advantage of seeing themselves pass one opponent.

"In, out! In, out! In, out!" "S-t-r-i-d-e i t o-u-t!" Kevin stretched himself forward, his back horizontal. Tim could feel the extra power being translated slowly into speed. The white ball on the bow of the Fellows began to move clear of that on the Sheffield boat.

"Come on Hull! We're gaining advantage. Push yourselves! Let's get a full bows' length between us."

The Fellows continued to inch forward. It wasn't enough. At any time, the Sheffield cox might demand, and get, more from his crew. Tim knew from experience that this was now critical.

"Get those asses in gear! Use those slides. What's all that training been for?".

Kevin was glowing red, his cropped fair hair beaded with sweat. Tim could see that he was giving it everything he had. "Please don't stop Kev" Tim spoke quietly, especially for his friend and Stroke. "E-a-s-y a-l-l!" They were past the red finish buoys. Kevin looked at Tim, his eyebrows raised in question.

"We did it! It was close but we definitely did it. Well done!"

Tim knew how much his exhausted crew needed to be praised, a comfort for their suffering. They rowed slowly back. There was a long break now for the last race and then lunch. After lunch there would be the final. Richard told them that one of their opponents was going to be Newcastle.

"They're the crew with the carbon fibre boat!" Tom remembered. "They must be a wealthy club. Probably got a proper coach too."

"Who cares? We've got the benefit of a long-established leadership team in Richard and Tim! You can't better them!" Tim was surprised to hear Kevin trumpet their praises.

The crew drank two energy drinks during the long rest period. It was time to launch the Fellows once again. Their other opponent was Birmingham. This time they were in the left-hand lane. Tim had calculated that that was the lane with the most potential advantage. It must be a good omen!

"Come forward to row. I'll ask you once. Are you ready? Row!" The Hull boat took off beautifully, Tim was certain that they had just achieved their best start ever. The crews proved stubbornly well matched. They were still about level as Tim realised that they were nearly at the half way point. He remembered that there was a sharp meander in the river at this point. He would use the current.

"Current, lads."

He steered as close to the bank as he dared and felt the river take a grip on the boat. He steered immediately away from the bank to allow the Fellows to be washed back on course for the second bend. He glanced over at his opponents. Yes! They were clearly ahead of both boats. "Stride it out!" Tim watched his oarsmen bravely rise to the challenge once again. They were nearly there. Newcastle's Cox was bellowing at his crew. They were gaining lost ground. "Last ounces boys!" Tim called. Twenty seconds passed. "Easy all!" The Fellows glided to a gentle halt.

" We've done it!" Tim raised his fist in a salute to his crew.

The crew saluted Tim.

"Did you feel that current."

"Yes. It was STRONG"

"That's what did it for us – that's where my skills and experience really can make all the difference" Tim explained.

They paddled gently back.

Kevin was on the podium, raising a large silver trophy. To Tim's surprise he was presented with a bottle of Champagne which he fumbled to open and then sprayed around excitedly. The crew then drank the remains from their silver cup. When the Fellows was safely washed, dismantled and attached to the trailer Kevin came to chat to Tim.

"You were very gentle to us in that race Tim."

"I didn't want to be nasty to you if I didn't need to. You are my friends after all!"

"I was expecting some insults." Tom joined in.

"Like I said, you're my mates and I know that you hurt yourselves in every race. I only try the insults trick if I know I have to. As a last resort."

As Tim was talking, he was aware of the crew positioning themselves around him. Very subtly and with no obvious signal they closed in. Tim felt his ankles and wrists being gripped. He was swung aloft by his powerful friends. They ran, shouting, with him held high above their shoulders and then, with consummate ease, they tossed him into the river. The river was deep and Tim had to swim, with some difficulty in his heavy suit, to the bank. Mark lay on the grass to help him out.

"You're our friend too Tim. But some things simply can't be avoided." Kevin was laughing.

Tim squelched his way to the changing rooms to shower and get dry. He could not have felt more content.

Tim and Richard bought the crew their now traditional meal and they drank several pints. They would train on Sunday afternoon instead of the morning, to allow a well-deserved lie in.

Richard and Kevin would compose an article about their first trophy for the Boat Club in seventeen years. It was a seriously big break through!

Part Ones

As the Summer term progressed Tim and the crew continued to clock up win after win in the Regatta scene. Nobody was more surprised than the crew themselves who still regarded themselves as novices. Tim's take on the situation was that probably most university crews were novices but that they had not had the benefit of two experienced people to force a tough regime upon them. He regularly praised the courage and determination of his crew because he knew very well that they had had to make compromises and sacrifices to adhere to the strict demands of Richard and Tim. The crew knew that this was the case but they were more than pleased to reap the rewards of their efforts. Success really was making everybody happy and the crew cohesion that they had thought would be so elusive had become a crew friendship that meant more to each individual than he could articulate.

Their efforts to revitalise the club were proving more difficult than expected. The Union agreed to award them an extra grant with which to purchase a new boat, but it would not become available until the new academic year in October. Kevin had managed to sell the two old boats, each with a set of four oars, but not for as much money as they had hoped for. Richard had sanctioned the sale after much discussion because they decided that any money was better than none and there was no point in keeping two old boats that were never going to be used until they rotted away.

Trying to make the Boat Club bar a venue of choice on a Friday night, or a Tuesday night or, indeed, on any night had proved impossible. It was too far off the beaten track, too poorly stocked and too unattractive a location so they cut their losses and stopped wasting their time coming to open it in the hope of somebody visiting.

The first barbecue night had not gone well either. It had taken place on what turned out to be the only wet evening of the term which made it difficult to make it the enjoyable and attractive event that it needed to be. Tim and Kevin had struggled to even get the large barrel barbecue lit, so damp had the charcoal become. Kevin went to get some paraffin to pour over it and that had at least got it burning but then they had to wait for ages before the smell of paraffin subsided sufficiently to allow cooking to begin. Both boys enjoyed the process of cooking burgers, sausages and chicken drumsticks but they soon realised that they were cooking more food than the small number of people who had actually come merited.

Behind the bar, Tom and Dave were having better luck and they sold more drinks, nuts and crisps than they had hoped, largely because everybody who had come had nothing better to do than huddle in the club room. Mark spent his time good naturedly carrying trays of barbecued food from the increasingly wet and bedraggled chefs to the hungry visitors.

At the end of it all they had made a fairly good profit because a lot of people who had bought tickets hadn't come. There was a lot of uncooked food that was shared between the committee for personal consumption and wet, smutty faced Kevin and Tim had learnt, finally, that it would be better to light the barbecue earlier and to cook on demand.

Before Tim could really worry about them the dreaded "Part One" exams were upon him. He did spend the Sunday afternoon flicking through the ring file of notes that he had taken during the course of the year, sitting in the sun in the back garden of number 73 with several of his house mates and a glass of cider. He believed that he had a good understanding of the concepts and that he would be able to adapt and apply his knowledge to the specific demands of the question. Whatever was going to happen would happen. Tim had never been one to lose sleep over revision and he wasn't planning to start now. He was still uncertain as to how he was expected to fill three hours with written answers but he would find out soon enough!

The first exam was "Understanding and interpreting statistics." This, with the possible exception of Philosophy, was likely to be Tim's worst exam so it was good to get it out of the way first. Once he had overcome the chilling dread of finding his seat in the main Sports Hall and waiting for the exam to be officially started Tim was surprised, both at the ease with which he found he could craft an essay answer from a series of dry looking statistics and at the speed with which three hours drained away to the warning of the last ten minutes. Five more similar exams followed in quick succession and then it was over. There would be a two week wait, a kind of limbo, during which exams were marked and results collated and then the students would know if they had passed or would be required to re-sit the exams in September. The sun was shining and the demands of academic work had reduced hugely so there was plenty of time for everyone to have fun.

Peter and Tim joined a day long "treasure hunt" with the car club. Being a student event, it inevitably involved lots of historic information about the pubs of East Yorkshire together with a visit to two sea side locations and a sewerage works. Peter was driving because his car was probably more economical and, he claimed, that Tim was certain to be better at navigating than he would. By the time they had ticked off all the questions on their four-page task sheet they had driven more than one hundred miles and walked several more miles along perilous cliff tops, muddy drainage ditches and desolate moorlands. It had been a nice, gentle kind of adventure and both boys were happy to have completed it. Everybody met in a large pub on the main road beside the campus and celebrated their mishaps and successes. Students do not need very much from which to create a big celebration.

The occupants of number 73 decided that they were going to have a summer house party, which would celebrate the end of the academic year and the start of three months of holiday. Tim had never had such a long period of complete freedom before and it was likely to be even better than he might have expected because he was entitled to claim unemployment benefit during the long summer break. He would have money to spend on having a good time. The house mates collected donations of the customary five pounds per person to fund drinks and a few snacks and this time the fancy-dress faction won the day. Everybody would have to dress up! Tim was unconcerned because he wore fancy dress at the Boat Club nearly every Saturday and he planned to wear the same things for the party. Take it easy!

The day of the party coincided with the penultimate regatta of the season so Tim invited the entire crew to come and celebrate at the house instead of the usual pub. They were happy to agree because it would make an interesting change to the routine. It began to exercise Tim's mind that his fancy dress outfit was, judged by past performances, likely to be soaking wet. He decided that, if he wore it wet, on the minibus all the way home from the race it would be just about dry in time for the party.

On Thursday the results of the exams were to be published at two O'clock, on the main departmental notice board. Tim drove into the university with Neil Blashford in time to get some lunch in the Union to fortify themselves before the moment of truth had to be faced. Both young men appeared to be in high spirits.

"Obviously they want us to pass so they get money from us again next year." Neil sounded confident of his logic.

"Well it's too late to worry now anyway. Whatever's happened it's all settled now." Tim shrugged away any concern.

After a cheerful lunch the two friends headed over to the department. There was a small crowd of students milling around in the foyer waiting for the results to be pinned up on the board. The secretary appeared and did the honours. The students thronged around the board, following their name across the matrix of six subject columns. Tim had scraped a pass in Statistics and Philosophy and had done really rather well in the other four. He was safe for another year. Neil was similarly satisfied.

Most of the group headed straight off to the union bar to celebrate. They had all been more stressed by the waiting than they had realised. The mood was buoyant and soon the bar was full, as students from other departments received their results, and the glass doors were opened onto the lawn so that people could spill out into the sunshine and settle in groups to enjoy an afternoon of nothingness. Tim, sitting with a large throng from his department reflected that this kind of relaxed and happy occasion really was what student life was all about. He had never felt more relaxed and carefree than he had over the past year. It had all been such a contrast to the restrictive, oppressive, controlling regime at school.

After the long, hot, afternoon of steady drinking Tim was definitely past his peak as he drove home. He had a shower to try to revitalise himself, heated up some chilli con carne and rice that he had left in the fridge from two nights earlier and packed his sports kit into his bag. He decided he would walk back to the sports centre in an effort to finish off the process of sobering up before he was expected to train with the crew. When he met his friends, it became clear that none of them were in the best state to train. All had been celebrating their success at "Part Ones".

Saturday dawned bright and sunny as everyone had begun to expect from that Summer. The crew assembled at the Boat House and carried out their well-rehearsed routine of loading the boat trailer and collecting spares and tools to ensure a successful day's racing. The drive to Rotherham was not too long and they arrived in plenty of time to find their designated location, assemble the Fellows and check out the course from the bank. They had no reason to feel daunted and everyone was relaxed and cheerful.

The day passed without incident and Hull University Men's Four won the event. The usual Podium based celebration took place with Kevin collecting the cup and spraying his crew with Champaign before sharing a drink of the remainder from the silver tankard. Once the spoils of success were safely stowed in the minibus the crew caught their cox and man handled him, high above their shoulders for all to see, into the river.

The river was not a nice clear one and Tim came sploshing out covered in streaks of foul-smelling mud. Nobody wanted to sit near poor Tim on the minibus as the heat and evaporating river water made him smell like a sewerage works. It became obvious that he would not be able to wear this outfit to his party. No problem! He would dress in his normal training outfit and borrow an oarsman's vest from the club. There would be five oarsmen at the party that night.

By the time that they reached the Boat Club Tim was, as he had hoped, nearly dry but his clothes had become stiff with dried river slime. He could barely move out of his seat. Once the kit was all put safely to rest the crew assembled in the changing rooms to shower and prepare to party. All were going dressed in rowing kit, as a kind of living advert for the Boat Club. Tim borrowed a set of kit from the store room. They had a few "warm up" celebration drinks in the bar before piling into Tim's Avenger to drive to number 73. It would be a good night!

The following Saturday was the final regatta of the season. Possibly because there was so much self-imposed pressure on the crew to maintain their unbroken chain of wins everyone felt as nervous as they had done before their first Head of River race back in March. They need not have worried. Hull University Men's Four became the unchallenged winner of every race that they had entered. As soon as they had unloaded the trailer and added the cup to the impressive display behind the bar, they locked up the Boat Club for the last time that term and headed to their respective homes to change. They were to meet again at seven at the Lionheart. There was some very serious celebrating to do!

Long Vacation

Tim arrived home in the middle of Saturday afternoon. He had had an easy drive and was pleased to have successfully completed his first year at university. It had gone so quickly. Now three long months stretched before him. Some of his friends had taken holiday jobs but he had decided that he would rather enjoy the freedom to do as he pleased. He was going to sign on to claim the dole on Monday, when the office opened again. That would give him enough money to keep him in beer and petrol!

It took Tim a while to acclimatise to the tranquillity of solitude. It felt strange to be at home without the responsibility and companionship of Usman. He really had become like a twin brother to him. Tim's sister and parents were going to go away for three weeks camping in Germany. Tim had said that he didn't want to join them, for the first time.

Mrs. Croy had tried hard to persuade him but to no avail. She understood that Tim had his own interests, his own life to lead and that he didn't want to be at the mercy of his family controlling what he did on a holiday. But it had made her feel sad, as if her role as a mother was being curtailed. What would happen when Annabelle also decided not to join them on a family holiday? It wouldn't really *be* a family holiday if there was no family on it. It was better not to think that far ahead. Tim had promised to look after the house and garden, which would be nice, on the condition that he could invite friends to stay with him. While Mrs. Croy *thought* that she could trust Tim to be responsible, she couldn't help imagining the kind of things that could go wrong. She must be getting old!

Tim drove into the city on Monday morning to "Sign On". He had never done that before and was not sure what it would entail. First, he had to locate the Benefit Office which turned out to be a rundown red brick building in a back street not far from the station. There was a long queue of young people, mainly students like Tim, snaking round between roped off barriers, waiting to be seen at the counter which had a "New Claimants" sign above it. When it was Tim's turn, he marched up to the counter.

"Yes?"

"I want to sign on as unemployed please."

"You a student in full time education?"

"Yes."

"Got your National Insurance card?"

Tim handed it to her. She filled in some forms.

"Sign there and there, love."

Tim signed.

"You'll get your claim book in the post in seven working days. You have to get it signed fortnightly on a Thursday between nine and ten in the morning at that counter over there. OK?"

"Yes. Thanks."

Tim left, his days' work completed.

The next week, before the schools finished for the summer, Tim spent time checking and servicing the mechanical and electrical parts of the caravan. He had learnt to carry out these tasks over many years of helping his father and he enjoyed the methodical, logical processes involved. It was not arduous work but very satisfying. It was from doing this that Tim had known how to restore the Boat Club trailer to good working order. When he wasn't working on the caravan Tim was undertaking the many varied tasks associated with a large garden in mid-summer. Weeding, mowing, clipping hedges, picking raspberries.

Tim had hoped to get together an exclusive house party of his two best friends from school but this proved impossible because of their differing commitments to family events. So, each friend would come for a separate week. It would still be a great way to enjoy the freedom of having the house to himself.

Watching his parents and sister pack the caravan and car for their long holiday made Tim feel a little left out. He didn't mind, was, indeed, looking forward to having the freedom, but he did feel a bit strange. He imagined that Usman must feel like that quite often when he was staying with them.

When they finally departed Tim had a few days to himself. The large house felt very strange with nobody in it but him. He started hearing sounds that he hadn't noticed before. The click from down in the cellar when the boiler ignited to heat the water, the occasional creak from the roof as it heated up in the morning sun or cooled down again in the evening. He began to be a bit nervous about checking that everything was locked up before he went to bed at night or before he went out. He did not want to be responsible for letting the house be burgled.

Tim knew perfectly well that his parents almost never locked anything. One afternoon while he was in the local town buying some food, he remembered to his horror that his dad usually left his car unlocked in the coach house *with the key in the ignition!* As soon as he got back, he went to check and, sure enough, there was the key in the car. Tim removed it, and closed the drivers' door. He sighed and opened it again, inserted the key, turned on the ignition and closed the electric window. He then locked the car with a loud clunk from the central locking system. He shut the key in the desk in the study. Really his parents were so obtuse sometimes!

Tim was also exercised by the daily requirements of the swimming pool. It needed to be cleaned with the brush and sucking device each day, which Tim was used to doing. It also needed to have the water tested for chemical concentrations and to have sufficient chlorine and algicide added according to the results. Tim was no chemist and felt permanently confused about exactly how much he should or should not add. He hoped that his assessment of the doses required was not as critical as his father had suggested would prove to be the case.

Tim was sitting on the terrace reading bits of the previous days Sunday Times and enjoying the sun. Anthony was due to arrive at some point in the afternoon so he couldn't really stray too far from the house or use any noisy machinery. He was feeling very pleased with himself, having spent the morning concocting a large meal of chili con carne. He would only need to reheat it and boil some rice to have a suitably large supper for the two of them. It would be great having a good friend with him for a few days. He hadn't made any particular plans for the week ahead, they were on holiday after all, and it was much easier to simply let things happen spontaneously. Both boys were always full of fun ideas and neither ever had enough time to do all of them. Tim smiled. He liked Anthony's easy going, boisterous and cheerful personality. He always made Tim feel better about life. Tim knew that he really needed to teach himself to think and worry about things less, he could learn a lot from his friend's happy go lucky attitude.

Tim's thoughts were interrupted by the sound of crunching gravel on the driveway at the front of the house. It must be Anthony. Tim walked quickly through the orchard at the side of the house, emerging onto the sweep of gravel just as Anthony was swinging open the door of his Austin Maxi.

"Anthony!" Tim shouted.

The friends shook hands and then began to laugh at the unnecessary formality of their greeting.

"Come around the back mate and let me get you something cold to drink."

Tim led his friend to the terrace and went to collect two cans of lager from the fridge. He returned with a bowl of cashew nuts as well. It was always nice to graze things while socialising.

"This is a nice place Tim! And what a fine swimming pool. I don't feel so embarrassed by my folks' house now."

"Like I said, we can have a fun time holiday here without bothering to go anywhere if we want."

"That's cool by me man, but I have got one or two ideas that we might think about sometime."

They drank their beers and finished the nuts as the conversation moved from one thing to another.

"Let's get your things in and then we can hit the water before the day starts to cool off."

Anthony was sitting at the scrubbed wood kitchen table watching Tim boil the rice and heat his chilli con carne. He had found that he had to stand stirring it or the bubbles would build up in the thick sauce and explode, splashing glutinous red mess all over the cooker and the tiles behind it. It didn't matter in his student house but here he would have to waste his time cleaning up. As they ate their supper the talk turned to news of shared friends.

"I've ended up under the authority of Richard Norton again. Can you believe it?"

"I bet that means that you ended up going to the boat club after all."

Tim laughed and told him the long story. "I really didn't choose to, it just kind of happened. I've quite enjoyed it really, but Richard is still Richard, I can't really enjoy his company, it always feels as if he's watching me on behalf of Barforth. It sounds really paranoid saying it out loud but, for example, we were all chatting one evening and one of my mates mentioned a time when I got well pissed and Richard suddenly stuck his nose in and tried to tell me off."

"Yeah I can imagine. He always was a bit of a prat!" They both laughed. "Simon Huband was just like him too. All nice smiles and a forked tongue behind your back. Do you remember how the bastard kept on busting Usman? He used to follow him if he thought he was off for a fag. You'd have thought he would have had better things to do."

"I think he might have fancied him and that was his perverted way of getting pleasure from him. I'm sure he was queer!"

"He was, definitely."

They finished their meal and Tim loaded the dirty dishes into the washing up machine. He scooped two bowls full of ice cream from the freezer and they went out to the terrace to eat it. They sat there as the evening turned to night, enjoying the warm darkness as they consumed several more cans of beer and a large pack of dry roast peanuts.

The days passed, filled only with banter, swimming and food. Anthony suggested driving to Lyme Regis one day so that he could collect some fossils. He was studying Geography and would be doing a specialist area of study in Geology for his final two years. Tim was enthusiastic about the idea and disappeared into the coach house. He returned after some time bearing a number of hammers, chisels and a miniature pick axe.

"Just what we need to be Geologists for the day!"

They piled the things into Anthony's Maxi that evening so that they could set off at first light the next morning.

Tim enjoyed being driven by somebody else. It was good not to have the responsibility of having to park the car or plan the journey. He laughed.

"How do you navigate mate? Last summer when we went to your cottage you didn't have a clue!"

"I still don't really. I just set off and hope to find signs to tell me."

"And you're studying for a degree in Geography?"

"It's not that kind of Geography."

"That's lucky then mate!"

The roads were beautifully clear at that time in the morning and the friends arrived at their destination just after seven. They decided that they would go straight down to the beach and poke around in the base of the crumbly cliffs to see what they could unearth. As the morning grew hotter their bag became fuller of interesting looking fossils. At length Anthony declared that he had got enough so they carried the heavy bag between them back to the car and deposited all their things in the boot.

Running excitedly back to the beach they pulled off their shorts and shirts and splashed their way into the chilly sea. An exhilarating hour ensued, at the end of which they sat shivering on the stony beach, letting the hot midday sun dry them off and warm them up.

They headed into the village where they bought a ploughman's lunch and two pints of bitter in one of the three pubs.

"I still feel as if I need to be careful not to get busted Tim!"

"Yeah, I do too, sometimes. It's crazy how a place like Barforth can affect you for so long after you've left."

After lunch they walked along the green cliff top for miles, marvelling at the stunning views of Durdle Door. They stopped, took their shirts off and lay sunning themselves on the short grass.

"How are things going with you and Sarah?" Anthony broke the silence with a bomb shell.

"What do you mean" Tim asked, sounding rather too defensive.

"Well you spent almost the whole night with her at my party, and then the two of you were making eyes at each other all through breakfast. You can't convince me that there's nothing going on."

"Really there isn't Anthony."

"And my dad's the Prime Minister!"

"You've got an over active imagination mate."

"Not just me mate. Usman was asking me about her. Who she was, and how you two had met. It's obvious you're an item."

"I promise we're not Anthony. She's Mikes' sister for God's sake!"

"She's a beautiful girl who fancies you rotten Tim. It's got nothing to do with Mike."

Tim felt himself blushing and he knew that Anthony had seen him.

"OK mate, I know you'll tell me all about it one day, when you're ready. But please Tim, relax and enjoy it. She's a super girl, perfect for you I'd say!"

They talked late into the night. The week was over and Anthony would be driving home the next morning. They still thrived on each-others' company and there was a wonderful depth to their friendship, one that both felt but neither could adequately define.

Two days later Tim was waiting for Mike, sitting on the terrace once again, listening to the swallows swooping and calling in the air above and around the house. That sight and sound was, for Tim, the very essence of summer. He had tried his hand at roasting a big piece of ham, which was now cooling in the pantry. It was much bigger than Tim had realised and he guessed that they would be able to eat it for days.

He heard the insistent jangling of the telephone in the hall and he decided that he had better answer it in case it was Mike who had got lost or broken down or something. It was the Vicar's wife wanting to speak to his mother. Tim explained that she wouldn't be back for another ten days. Yes, he would leave her a message. He was writing the message on the pad on the hall table when the crunching of gravel under tyres heralded Mike's arrival.

Tim burst, beaming, out of the front door onto the drive way. Mike swung himself out of his Ford Escort, his face split in two by his customary huge grin. They hugged, neither feeling the need to use words by way of greeting.

"Impressive directions Tim! I could have left my map at home."

"You know me mate, always fussing about details! Come on let's get us a cool beer. You must be hot after a long drive on a day like this."

They settled themselves on the terrace.

"How've you been man? It's been much too long. I'd meant to get you over here last holidays but Usman got ill and I didn't want you to catch it."

"What was wrong with him? I never saw him ill before."

"He got the mumps, poor guy. They don't have it in Saudi so he wasn't immune."

"I heard that's nasty when you're grown up."

"It was. He's fine now though. Safely in Saudi for the summer. It's 44 Centigrade there now."

"I'm all good, how about you?"

"Good too. Enjoying dossing now."

" Yeah, me too."

"How's the new car Mike? I haven't seen you driving with hand controls yet. You'll have to take me out sometime."

"I don't think about it now I've got the hang of it. Mum was fussing about me coming here. She only let me because it's you. She's still over protective of me."

"I'm not surprised mate. She wouldn't be able to get it out of her mind, you know, what happened."

"Yeah, I guess. She and dad send you their best and say that you've got to come to visit us this summer or else! Sarah asked me to remember her to you too."

Tim thought that he detected a strange look on Mike's face as he said that. He dismissed the idea. He hadn't done anything wrong, though he *had* wanted to!

"Come on Mike, you've got to help me get supper!" Tim led his friend to the vegetable garden and handed him a fork and a bucket.

"Dig up some of those potatoes while I pick some beans."

"This is incredible Tim! I thought they only had gardens like this on those TV shows."

"My dad likes gardening. I do too, in fact. If I hadn't got to university, I was set to do a gardening apprenticeship."

"You're a dark horse Tim!"

In the kitchen Tim instructed Mike on how to wash the potatoes by rubbing them under the tap between his finger and thumb.

"They're new potatoes so you don't need to peel them."

"How did you learn to cook?"

"I've been living in a student house so I've been self-catering for a year. It's not difficult you just need to try things out, or maybe read a recipe."

"I've been in Hall so I was fed. But It wasn't that good so next year I'm in a student house too. I need to learn fast."

Tim showed Mike how to make parsley sauce and then showed him his roast ham. "That's impressive Tim."

"Tell you what, we can cook together this week. You decide what you fancy and we will try to make it. Should be fun!"

They sat finishing the bottle of white wine that Tim had opened with supper. The warm evening closed in around them as they caught up with their news.

"How's your sex life Tim?" Mike grinned, flashing his teeth in the gathering gloom.

"What's one of those Mike?" Tim laughed. "What about yours Mike?"

"It's been a good year actually. I've got lucky a few times. Nothing serious though."

"Good man!" Tim thumped him between his shoulder blades.

Lying in bed that night Mike reflected on life, and upon Tim in particular. Sarah had been asking him lots of questions about Tim. Not all at once, she knew how to be discreet, but still too many questions for them to be entirely innocent. Tim had clammed up when he had enquired, under cover of a joke, about his sex life. But he had seen how much time Sarah and Tim had spent together at Anthony's New Year Party. There was, he was certain, something between them. He hoped that there was. Mike liked Tim and knew that he was honest, dependable and decent. Just the kind of guy who he would want for his sister. He would get them together again soon and see what happened.

The boys fell into an easy going routine of swimming, planning their menu for the evening, cooking together and talking late into the night. They spent one day walking in the depths of the New Forest, where they had a long lunch in one of the fine pubs that thrive there. On another afternoon Tim took Mike to a trout farm on the edge of the River Avon. They spent hours looking at tanks full of sploshing, flapping trout of different sizes and then seeing how they hung gutted fish in a wide chimney with smouldering wood chips beneath it to produce smoked trout. The boys returned home with several fresh and smoked fish to play with in the kitchen. Mike was becoming more confident and adventurous in what he felt able to cook and each meal became something of a competition between them.

Things fell back into normality when Tim's parents returned. Freed of responsibility for looking after the house Tim regressed to a lazy student approach to life. He did lots of work around the house and garden and he went to garden for his two long term clients to supplement his dole money.

Mike telephoned to invite him to stay with his family for a few days. Tim fancied a change and was glad to accept the offer. He liked the Andrews family and he knew that they liked him. He felt especially excited at the prospect of seeing Sarah again, though he knew that there would be little chance to be alone with her, which was what he would really have liked, despite the prospect filling him with trepidation.

The drive to Mike's house took only an hour and Tim was there before lunch. Mike met him before he could get out of the car.

"It's so good to see you here man! Come in."

"Tim! The stranger returns! Where have you been? I thought we'd upset you."

"Well I know that you're always too nice to me. I did intend to come with Usman at Easter but he caught the mumps and was really ill with it and Mum said that we couldn't risk spreading it around."

"Poor Usman! It can be very nasty in a young man."

Tim grinned. "It was!"

"Help Tim get his things in Michael and by then lunch will be ready. It's nothing special I'm afraid Tim but it will be nice to eat together again."

As Tim heaved his bag upstairs to Mike's room, he met Sarah on the landing.

"Hi" they greeted each other, both feeling joyful excitement and both trying to sound casual.

Tim felt Mike watching them intently. But no. That was paranoia again. There was nothing for Mike to be watching.

Over Lunch Mrs. Andrews had a theme to follow.

"What have you been doing to Michael Tim?"

"Sorry?" Tim was genuinely lost.

"He went to stay with you for one week and when he came back, he was a good cook. You must have worked some kind of miracle on him."

Tim laughed. "My parents were away so we had to cook for ourselves. I didn't see why I should do all the hard work so I made Mike help me."

"But how did you learn Tim?"

"I was in a self-catering student house. After a couple of weeks living off fried eggs and chips or Vesta meals, I started to feel sick. Mum had given me a simple cookery book and I started playing around with things from there and then I decided I could try things by myself. I find cooking quite fun now really."

"Well you've certainly got Michael cooking well. It's a big worry off my mind, knowing that he won't starve next year!"

That evening, after supper with Mr. Andrews, who was as ebullient as ever and kept on quizzing Tim about university and his sporting life, the boys went off to enjoy a few country pubs. Sarah came with them and Mike drove. Tim was fascinated to watch him driving using a hand control for the brakes and accelerator.

"If I couldn't see you doing that, I'd never guess you weren't driving normally."

"Really, Tim, you don't think about it once you get used to it. It doesn't make any difference to me now. I've been incredibly lucky in fact. It could all have worked out so much worse."

When they were sitting in the first pub, each of them sipping a Coke and ice, wanting to keep Mike company on an alcohol-free night, Tim asked Sarah where she would be going to university.

"Warwick. I'm going to do Psychology."

"That's interesting. I've got a friend who's doing that. He locked me in a dark cellar and asked me lots of questions one day. Something to do with the way our perceptions change in different circumstances."

"I hope it will be interesting. I got so bored in the last year at school. I need a change!"

Tim smiled at her, looking deep into her very blue eyes. He did fancy her! She smiled back, the look between them lasting dangerously long.

"The most important thing about university is to make lots of friends and have lots of fun. The work will just kind of happen in between."

"You always make things sound so easy Tim." Mike was laughing now. "What he says is true though Sarah, the most important thing is to enjoy yourself. Just don't let mum hear you saying I told you that!" They all laughed.

On the last day of Tim's visit Mike had to go to the hospital for a check up on his leg. Mrs. Andrews wanted to go with him so that she could understand for herself how he was healing. Tim would stay at home with Sarah. Sarah had said that she would make supper for everyone. After lazing around reading the paper Tim sauntered into the kitchen.

"Do you want a hand?"

"Please! I thought I'd make a trifle for pudding. Do you want to do that? Look there's jelly there, sponges there and a tin of fruit in the cupboard".

Tim got on efficiently, moving around the kitchen confidently. Sarah thought how cheerful and calm he was. No wonder Mike liked him so much.

Once the jelly was setting on the fruit and sponge Tim headed over to join Sarah at the sink. They were close now and both could feel something like electricity crackling between them. Tim knew he ought to move away but he didn't. Instead he moved towards her and kissed her, very lightly, on her cheek. It felt soft and warm and it did things to Tim that he had not expected. Sarah blushed a little and turned to face him. Their lips met in a proper, full kiss. And another. Tim hugged her close to him. He had a hard on and he knew that she would be able to feel it. He wanted her to feel it. They moved, together, into the sitting room, the sofa. Tim felt slightly light headed. He knew now, for certain, what was going to happen.

They kissed some more and Tim moved his hands under her top, fingering her firm, full breasts. He felt as if his whole body was boiling over. Somehow both of them rid themselves, or each other, of clothes. Tim felt momentarily shy about his nakedness, his rigid cock. For a second he felt extreme self-doubt, fear of the unknown, of making a mistake. But then everything came together, as nature intended. Tim loved Sarah and Sarah loved Tim. When they were finished, much faster than Tim would have hoped, Tim lay, relaxed, naked and hugely relieved.

"I love you Sarah. I've wanted that to happen since that party. I expect you think I'm some kind of pervert."

"I think you're a great guy Tim. I was afraid that you didn't like me, after I felt you were horny but you just left me at that party."

"I was afraid, to be honest. I felt ashamed for wanting to take advantage of you, as if I was trying to steal something from Mike and his family. I can't really explain properly but I know what I mean!"

Sarah giggled. "Tim you really do think too much."

They decided they had better get dressed and finish their cooking. The others would be back soon.

"Do you mind if we don't tell anyone about that yet?"

"I'd be much happier if we didn't Sarah. I feel shy about having to tell Mike that I love you. We can put it off for as long as we can, as far as I'm concerned."

Tim felt as if his relationship with Mike had changed, though, obviously, it hadn't, it couldn't have because Mike knew nothing. But Tim felt a kind of guilt, holding a secret back from his best friend, one that, of all secrets, he probably had the most right to know about. He was also feeling outrageously pleased with himself, proud of himself, he felt as if now he really was a man, once and for all.

Back to The Boat Club

The first evening of term was the Freshers' Bazar and Tim and his crew were in charge of running the Boat Club stand. They had every reason to be optimistic of their chances of recruiting plenty of new students and thus generating a more solid income from subscriptions which would, in turn, cause them to get a larger injection of money from the Students' Union. They set up their stand, displaying their impressive selection of trophies from the last season together with a number of action photographs, blown up to a large A3 size, at considerable expense. They would be used to decorate the club room after the bazar. Tim had agreed, rather reluctantly, to dress not only in his swanky Cox's outfit but to sport a straw boater too, sourced mysteriously by Tom. The other young men wore their rowing kit, shivering in their shorts in the chilly October night. The event lasted a long time and kept everyone very busy but they were attracting plenty of attention and getting a decent number of people to join and pay their membership fees. They were making a list of the names of everyone who joined, their contact details and what, if any, experience they had had. Richard was in charge of making this list because he had not wanted to be actively involved in the process of attracting people to the stand. Tim found it to be unexpectedly good fun and it was, in general, a light hearted occasion.

The committee were excitedly anticipating the arrival of the Union grant with which they would be able to buy their new boat. They had many discussions, supported by catalogues from boat builders and professional reviews in sports magazines, about the benefits or demerits of going for carbon fibre, which would cost more but would, most likely, give them a competitive advantage. Tim had concerns about the durability of carbon fibre and the fact that he had heard that it became brittle with age, meaning that it could easily be broken. Kevin and Richard joined forces to point out that carbon fibre was the future and that, as it would be the top crew's boat, it was unlikely that it would be misused to the extent of becoming damaged. Mark had a kind of romantic, artistic attachment to the compelling beauty of a wooden shell, a sentiment that Tim tended to share. Eventually it was voted, four to two, that they should go for carbon fibre. Once the decision had been made it was easy for the two dissenters to become enthused about the possibilities that the new boat would offer.

Richard was very busy teaching the new recruits to the Boat Club how to row and he soon enlisted Kevin to sit in the clinker and lead each novice crew in the skills of an oarsman. Tim found himself coxing these crews regularly and he was impressed by Kevin's patient and gentle method of teaching. As Tim's crew had found the previous year there was a total absence of volunteers to train to be a cox. Tim spent many hours extolling the virtues of the role to anyone who would listen and, eventually, he succeeded in convincing two brave guys to train in his specialism. The crew, now officially known as Hull University First Four, were building up their strength and stamina in the Sports Centre each Monday and Thursday and got on the river every Wednesday and Sunday. There would be no competitions until the Head of River races which would not begin until February.

Socially Tim was enjoying life in number 73 and the new faces of the first-year students with their different characters and interests making for a different dynamic in the house. He and Bill had changed bedrooms to one of the larger top floor rooms where they felt more independent from the main house. Bill had returned with a new motorcycle and he spent a lot of time with two new residents who were also bikers.

Tim's heart and mind were often drifting towards Warwick to which he made long telephone calls and wrote heart felt letters. He would go there for a weekend at the end of October, when Sarah had had a chance to settle in to her new life. Tim felt as if something inside him had shifted in some way, causing him to feel more in need of one persons' company than he ever had before. He found the feeling rather uncomfortable and unsettling. He talked to Bill about it one night as they lay in bed.

"They call it love sick where I come from Tim" Bill laughed.

"But it's so powerful. I can't get her out of my mind."

"How long have you fancied her Tim?"

Tim thought." Well I've known about her for four or five years. I first talked to her three years ago and I really got to know her, started to fancy her, a year ago. Then, at the end of the holidays, I finally got her into bed. Just once, but it's done something to me Bill."

"I'm really pleased for you Tim. Just enjoy it, take it as it comes." Tim thought about the advice as he drifted off to sleep.

"I have to go away for the weekend so I'll miss training on Sunday. I'm really, really sorry but it just can't be avoided." Tim lied to his crew.

"That's fine Tim, it's not the racing season so no harm will be done. Have a good time mate." Mark, as always, was easy going about it.

"Is everything OK Tim?" Kevin was concerned. He knew that it was not like Tim to suddenly go away.

"I'm fine mate, I just need to do something." That, at least, *was* true!

Tim skipped his afternoon lecture on Friday and, after a hasty lunch in the Union he jumped eagerly into his car and set off for Warwick. He had stowed his bag in the boot that morning. He felt free and joyful as he drove through the Autumn sunshine and he put the radio on loudly to enhance the holiday feeling. He made good progress, missing, as he had intended, any rush hour traffic. Sarah's directions proved to be completely accurate and he found himself driving into the car park of her student village half an hour earlier than he had anticipated. He hoped that she had got back from the campus early.

Tim wondered about for a while, his bag over his shoulder, unsure how the numbering of the blocks and rooms was arranged. At last he was certain that he had located her room. Grinning from ear to ear Tim knocked. Sarah flung her door open and fell into his open arms. They stood, embracing, half in and half out of her room for ages. Neither could believe how wonderful it felt to be together.

"Let's at least get inside!" Sarah suggested eventually, ever practical.

She made a mug of tea for them both and opened some biscuits. Tim realised that he was hungry.

"How's it going here? Are you settled Ok and pleased with the course?"

"It's good. I'm still not used to the freedom though."

"I felt like that. But you'll find that you are much better at using your time than most of the other people. Boarding school certainly teaches you how to get the work done!"

Tea finished Tim hugged Sarah to him.

"I've missed you so much. I had no idea how that morning kind of cemented our relationship, made it so important for us to be together. I haven't been able to get you out of my mind ever since. I love you so much, I think I had since that party last New Year, but I didn't know how much."

"I know. I feel like that too. You're so good with words Tim."

They kissed and kissed some more. Twenty minutes later they lay in bed together, their desire fulfilled. They talked intermittently for a while, lazily relaxed.

They made love again, gently, passionately and long lastingly. Tim felt pleased with his performance for the first time, more under his control now than the initial, explosive urgency. They dressed and went to buy supper in the food hall on site. Tim judged it to be pretty much the same kind of food as he got in the union. They shared horror stories about the food at their respective schools.

The weekend sped by. They did little, spending most of the time in Sarah's room, either making love or talking, eagerly learning every detail of one another's lives. Both wanted to know, to understand each other as perfectly as any couple can do. They seemed to have so many things in common, to share similar points of view about so much, both felt that they must have been made to be together. Tim's heart was heavy as they ate a sumptuous Sunday lunch in a fine old pub in the centre of town. He knew that, while he might delay his departure by an hour or two, depart he must. He felt every bit as despondent as he used to when he had to return to Barforth after the holidays.

The crew detected his mood almost at once when they congregated at the Sports Centre for their training session.

"Come on mate! It's never that bad." Dave tried to draw Tim out.

"I think he's in love. You can see it in his eyes." Tom joked, much too close to the truth than Tim felt comfortable with.

As they trained and became steadily more tired and sweaty Tim thought about what Tom had said. He had nothing to hide from his friends and he would probably find them encouraging and supportive. They deserved to know his good fortune. They always shared their girlfriend experiences, good and bad, so why was he being so secretive?

After they'd showered and settled themselves into the Union bar Tim got in the first round.

"Actually" Tim broke into the conversation, needing now to go through with his admission, "Tom, you were just about right, what you said earlier. I am in love. And it hurts. And I'm finding it really hard not being with her. I'm sorry for not telling you all before but I felt shy."

The four men looked at Tim. Kevin broke the silence.

"I bet it's even harder when you *are* with her mate!"

Everyone laughed. Trust Kevin to bring things down to basics! Tim blushed.

"You've embarrassed him now Kev." Mark rebuked him.

"Well it's sure to be true. Nothing wrong with it either. I'm really pleased for you man. Let's drink to Tim!" They drank.

"What's her name"

Tim told them. They partied into the night, genuinely pleased for him and always glad of an excuse for a celebration.

Tim finished wiping down the Fellows and put away the leather, folded into a plastic bag so that it didn't dry out and become like cardboard by the following outing. He walked the length of the boat house to go to close and lock the double wooden doors that opened out onto the river bank. He was surprised to see Kevin leaning against the wall.

"Kevin?" The young man looked at Tim, seeming surprised. "I thought you were showering with the others. Are you OK?"

"I felt a bit rough after we put the boat away. I just came out here to get some fresh air. I thought I might be going to puke but I didn't. I'm OK now."

The friends went back inside and joined the others in the showers.

"Come forward to row. I'll ask you once. Are you ready? Row"

The crew were practicing racing starts, getting back into practice in preparation for the Head of River season in the Easter term. They had not been pushing themselves so far this term, their minds being on enjoyment and the wider administrative side of the Boat Club and getting new crews together and trained.

"That wasn't bad, but try to focus on slicing cleanly into the water, your blade should be vertical to the water before entry and remain so until you lift it out and feather it. That maximises power transmission and minimises drag. Makes it more comfortable for me too!"

"I'll remember that, next time you piss me off!" Kevin grinned at his friend from his position at Stroke.

"Let's do it again." They continued starting imaginary races for half an hour.

"OK, we'll turn her round and then complete a two-kilometre race, get the feel of racing back to the front of our minds."

Towards the end of the race Tim became aware that Kevin was looking redder than he remembered him doing before. He could see him perspiring profusely and he had a pained look on his face. When they'd finished and were resting Tim spoke quietly to Kevin.

"Are you OK man? You looked well knackered by half way through."

"I was. I didn't realise I'd got so unfit in the holidays. I'll try and do some extra weight training. Maybe go in the Sports Centre at lunchtimes or something."

"Good man!"

The crew were training on Monday evening as usual. Tim called out to change activity for the next five-minute slot. Everyone stopped what they were doing and began to shuffle round to the next activity. Tim saw Kevin appear to stumble and then sit down very heavily on the bench that he was supposed to be using for step ups. Tim and Mark hurried over to him.

"What's up mate?" Mark was sitting by his side, supporting his back with his arm. Kevin was red and dripping sweat.

"I felt a bit dizzy. I'm OK now." Tim listened to the conversation, recognising the use of words.

"I don't think you should do the next couple of rounds Kev. Take a rest for a bit mate." To his surprise Kevin didn't argue. That *was* worrying!

When they were clearing away the kit Tim took Mark aside.

"I'm worried about Kevin Mark. I feel there's something wrong. This is the third time, to my knowledge, that he's felt ill in training in the past two weeks."

"Yeah I'd noticed that too Tim. But he always says he's OK."

"I know. But that doesn't mean he *is* OK. Do you think you can get him to get himself checked out at the Health Centre? He's closer to you and I think he might listen to you more than he would to me."

"I don't think that's true Tim. He always does as you instruct us because he accepts that you have power over him in the crew."

"OK, let's do it together. Catch him with me after we shower. We need to really coerce him!"

Kevin was sitting on the bench, rubbing his hair dry with his towel when Mark and Tim sat down each side of him.

"We need to talk, seriously, man to man Kevin." Tim opened the conversation bluntly.

"We've both noticed that you're not feeling well lately and that your performance is definitely getting worse. We're worried about you mate and we want to get you checked out."

Mark spoke to Kevin gently, sounding sincere and caring in the way that Tim knew he was so good at. Kevin looked down at the floor. He looked up again and sighed.

"I think you're right. I don't know what's happened to me."

"Mark and I are going to take you to the Health Centre tomorrow morning. We'll be at your place in the car at nine."

Tim made the arrangement bossily, giving nobody any chance to discuss the idea.

Kevin laughed. "That's Tim! You can't argue with him when he makes a decision, even if it is about you. I ought to punch you for that mate!"

The three friends laughed, relieved to see Kevin as they knew and loved him best. The crew headed for the Union Bar.

Next morning Tim collected Mark and then Kevin and drove to the Health Centre, opposite the campus. Tim had never been there before and the hospital smell made him feel uneasy. Kevin went to the reception desk and booked himself in. The three waited for nearly an hour while other students went in, seeking solutions for hangovers or fearful of having contracted some kind of sexually transmitted disease.

"Mr. Dunn?" Tim didn't realise that it was Kevin being called, hardly ever having used his sir name.

Kevin went in. Twenty minutes later he returned.

"All OK?" Mark asked.

"I've got to wait to see the nurse for some blood tests. You two go and get on with your days."

"We'll wait" both boys replied in unison.

At last Kevin was called into the nurse's room. He returned looking very white.

"Shit! Did she try to murder you?" Tim laughed.

Kevin grinned weakly. "I hate needles."

Mark looked very sympathetic. "I do too. I fainted in the queue for a flu jab at school once. Miles before I got anywhere near a needle!"

Kevin looked better at that news.

"When will you get the results?" Tim enquired.

"Dunno"

They left the Health Centre with some relief.

They cancelled their outing on the river on Wednesday. Tim and the remaining three oarsmen spent the afternoon training new members. Richard was planning on setting up three crews, based on ability, in the next few weeks so there was a feeling or urgency and excitement amongst the young men and women.

Tim was watching television in the common room at number 73 on Thursday evening when Tom appeared.

"Tom! What brings you here? Do you want tea or coffee with my biscuits?"

Tim was programmed to offer guests a hot drink. That had something to do with the status of increasing seniority at boarding school, where to be able to offer it immediately told a visitor that you had achieved position and importance within the school.

"Not for me thanks mate. Listen I've got bad news. Kevin's got some serious illness. He's gone back home for the rest of term."

Tim felt shaken. "When did this happen?"

"His parents were just collecting him when I got back from lectures. He apologises to all of you for not coming to see you but he didn't have time and I know that he didn't want any kind of fuss."

"Do you know what's wrong with him?"

"It's serious. Leukaemia."

"Oh my God! I knew somebody who died of that a few years ago. Are they sure?"

"I think so yes."

"Have you told the others yet?"

"I'm on my way to now. I'm going to get Richard to meet us all tomorrow so we can plan what to do about getting someone in his place in the crew. Temporarily obviously."

"Good thinking. Can we meet at lunch time do you think?"

"I'll let you know when I've fixed things."

Tim led Tom out to the door. "Thanks for coming to tell me."

Tom grinned and thumped Tim between the shoulder blades. "See you tomorrow!"

Tim closed the front door and went up to his room where he sat at his desk and thought about the news. He felt shaky, almost ill himself. Poor Kevin. How must he be feeling? Why? How? These things weren't supposed to happen in real life.

Next day Tim, Richard and the remaining oarsmen met over coffee in the Union. All were feeling shocked and upset by the news. Obviously, if they were to continue as a crew and keep ready for when Kevin got back to good health, they had to find somebody to temporarily take Kevin's place at Stroke. Nobody really felt like talking about it, let alone making a decision. Everybody was glad when Richard, as their coach and Captain of the Boat Club, took charge of the situation.

"I've been looking at the lists of new club members and their details about past experience. There's one guy who stands out as being the best candidate, on paper at least, to step straight in to Kevin's place without causing too much difficulty for the rest of you. Have any of you come across Ed in training?"

Nobody had.

"Well he's a tall guy, so physically he'd fit in with your reach as a crew. Best of all he's got years of rowing experience, as Stroke. He was at Gainswell School Tim. We used to race against them sometimes. Do you remember?"

"Yes, I do remember Gainswell. They were quite good."

"Exactly, so he should be quite good too. Shall I get him to come down to join us on Sunday? Then you can meet him and row with him and see how you get on."

Nobody dissented so the arrangement was agreed by default.

When Tim arrived at the Boat Club on Sunday, he found the remainder of his crew waiting for him.

"I'm not really feeling like doing this." Dave spoke for everyone.

"Well, we don't have a choice. And If we really want to stay at the top of our game, so that we can start winning again when Kevin can join us, we have to keep on rowing and training. I don't feel like it, but I do think that we owe it to Kevin to keep things going for him." Tom was very forceful in his speech and he succeeded in motivating everyone.

They could see a bicycle bouncing its' way along the rough track.

"This might be Ed." Tim suggested.

The bike arrived and a very tall Asian lad dismounted. He smiled shyly at the crew.

"Hi, I'm Ed. Richard told me that you wanted to test me out as your temporary Stroke."

"Brilliant, great to see you. I'm Tim, the cox."

Each of the others introduced themselves and welcomed Ed to the crew.

"Let's get going" Tim rallied them all.

They went to change.

Tim could tell that Ed was experienced from the first command that he gave to lift the boat. As the time passed on the water, he began to see that Ed would, indeed, make a good caretaker Stroke. He was the right size to be able to lead the rest of the crew in terms of reach and he appeared to be fairly fit. As Tim watched him row and respond to his different commands, he understood that the young man had been well trained at Gainswell. When the crew had cleaned the boat and put it away in the Boathouse they went to change. Tim went to chat with Richard.

"What do you think Tim?"

"I think he's our man. He obviously knows his stuff and he's the right size. I just hope that he can fit in socially, we were so well integrated last year and it will be difficult for us if it doesn't work well."

"It is a risk, but I don't see much choice, Ed makes most sense to me."

"I agree Richard. Let's let him and the crew talk over a drink or two."

"I doubt he drinks. I think he's a Muslim."

Tim went to change and suggested that they interview Ed over a drink. Everyone agreed. Mark got in the beers, without asking Ed.

"I like what I've seen on the water Ed. Now I want the crew to chat to you and kind of interrogate you to see how you will fit with us socially. I think you understand how vital cohesion is within a crew".

"That's fine. Fire away!" Ed spoke gently with a big smile. Tim warmed to him.

"How much rowing have you done Ed?" Dave started the interview.

"Five years. I started rowing when I went to school at Gainswell. I was lucky enough to be selected to stroke the top crew in my year and, in the end, I stroked for the First Eight."

"That's impressive mate. Tim used to cox his First Eight. He's been really good for us. He's a demanding man though, really forces us to train hard. Are you up for near death training sessions?"

"I'm used to that."

"What's your real name? I don't believe it's Ed."

Tim winced at the directness of Tom's question. Ed grinned.

"You're right. My real name's Mohammed. Ed is the last syllable. It makes it easier for people."

"So, you're a Muslim then. But you're drinking beer?"

Tim wished Tom would be a little gentler. This really was becoming an inquisition!

"I am a Muslim, but I don't practice it much. I think of myself as more English than Muslim."

"That's very honest Ed" Mark always acted as the appeaser.

"I just don't want him to get upset or feel left out when we celebrate our wins or have our cohesion meetings after training."

"Don't worry about that. I can party as well as anyone!"

"Have you all talked as much as you need?" Tim was glad to see Richard coming over to the group.

"Anyone got any more for this poor guy?" Nobody had.

"Tim and I were really impressed by your style and experience. We both feel that you'd fit well into the crew. You do understand, though, that it is only temporary, until Kevin gets better."

"Yes."

"So, will you join us Ed?" Tim asked.

"Is that an offer Tim?"

"Yes, I guess so."

"I'd be really happy to join your great crew."

"That's settled then mate. Welcome to the Hull University First Four!"

Richard went and got six more pints from behind the bar.

"To Ed!" Everyone toasted the new recruit.

Ed was very amused when he discovered that they had to wash up the beer glasses.

Get Through It!

Ed proved to be a good choice to cover for the absence of Kevin. He was polite, calm and an excellent oarsman. He understood the difficult circumstances under which he found himself in his new position and he remained patient when one or another of the crew lamented Kevin or expressed irritation that things were no longer the same. Ed did not possess, never could have matched, the style of charisma that Kevin brought to the crew but, as Tim once pointed out, it was his very blandness by comparison that had enabled him to fit in so seamlessly.

In fact, the crew began to go from strength to strength. The confidence that they had derived from the previous seasons' unbeaten record proved to be sufficient to carry them over the upset caused be the loss of their stroke and leader. Ed felt, as he regularly expressed to the others, very fortunate to have the opportunity to work with such a successful group of people and the crew appreciated his kind and sincere comments. They were all impressed by his evident skill and experience, both technical and in his role as the leader of the crew. He had very quickly set about getting to know and understand each individual so that he could get the very best out of them and work effectively with them. In short, he had put each man at ease. Socially there had been no problems and the crew soon felt unified once more.

"Hey Ed!" Tim called across the quadrangle between the Students' Union and the Chemistry department.

The tall young man turned and then beamed in recognition.

"Have you got time to join me for lunch mate?" Tim hurried to catch up with his new friend. "I've been wanting to catch you for ages, just so we can kind of get to know each other beyond the Boat Club."

"That'd be good. I was just on my way to get lunch anyway. Do you do Chemistry Tim?"

"No, I'm doing Geography and Economics. I just cut through that way to save time. What do you do?"

"Management and accounting. I'm expecting to see you pull a face now!"

"No. It sounds very serious. Sure, to lead you to a good job, too."

Tim led them to a smaller restaurant upstairs. "Take what you want Ed. I'm paying."

The boys found themselves a table and balanced their laden trays on it.

"How did you find life at Gainswell"

"It was OK really. I did quite well there, once I'd got myself accepted. Obviously, I look different and you know how difference is ridiculed at those places."

"Yeah I do. Did they treat you badly at first then?"

"A bit. But that's in the past now. I just worked and played hard to show them what for!"

"Yeah, I can imagine."

"How about you Tim? You were at Barforth, with Richard, weren't you?"

"Yeah. He was in the year above me. I used to cox him since we were in the Under Sixteens." Tim avoided the intended question about how he had liked school. Some things are best left in the past!

"How are you settling in here?"

"Great! I really appreciate the freedom and you guys have made me so welcome in your crew, I feel like I belong in it!"

"I'm glad about that Ed. It's not easy to fit in suddenly like you have. The other guys are finding that they can learn new things from you. None of them had so much as sat in a boat until this time last year."

"Really? They got to a high level really fast then."

"Yeah. They're good guys. The biggest problem I had last year was getting them to work as a crew, seriously, on and off the river. That's why we were so interested in you, socially, when we were "interviewing" you."

"Yeah I got that. And I understood completely."

The boys went their separate ways and Tim reflected that, while they had barely stopped talking, he still felt that he knew nothing about Ed. Either he really was as bland as he seemed or he was very secretive. At least he had tried.

"Tim, do you feel like taking us to see Kevin on Saturday?" Mark asked at their training in the Sports Hall on Monday.

"Oh yes! Are we all going?"

"All the old crew, so the four of us. I've explained to Ed, don't worry!" Dave was quick to pre-empt any concern that Tim might raise about cohesion.

"Let's do it. It might cheer him up to catch up on all the gossip."

Tim set off at nine on Saturday morning, collecting the other three before heading out to the main road that follows the Humber estuary until it joins the motorway. He estimated that the journey would take about two hours. They were in high spirits at the prospect of seeing Kevin and looking forward to seeing how he was doing. Mark said that he thought he would have lost his hair because of the chemotherapy.

Tom began to laugh. "We probably won't see much difference then. He shaves his hair so short and it's so blond that it always looked like he was bald anyway!"

Tim had to join him in the laughter because it was true. They stopped at the service station before the exit for Nottingham to have a piss and buy some sweets and a book for Kevin.

"Are you OK to navigate for me to Kevin's house Tom, I know you've been there before?"

"Ummmm OK, I'll try but you'll have to be patient with me Tim, I'm not that certain."

Tim was taken aback when they arrived at the Dunn's large detached house in a tree lined road. He had somehow had the impression, supported by constant hints from Kevin, that he lived in a tiny, run down terrace in a poor part of town. He remembered thinking to himself that there was more to Kevin than met the eye.

Dave rang the bell and the door was opened almost at once by Kevin. There were immediate, effusive, greetings between the five friends. Kevin was blushing with excitement to have his crew around him again and the laughing, joking and inuendo were as they always had been.

Kevin introduced everyone to his parents and younger brother. Mrs Dunn told them that lunch would be ready in an hour or so. She knew that big young men needed feeding and she was keen to make Kevin's friends welcome. Kevin had become so much more animated and cheerful when he had heard of the planned visit. It had done him more visible good than any of the extensive range of medicines that he had to take on a daily basis.

Kevin led his friends to the sitting room and then went to get mugs of coffee for everyone. When he returned the excited banter resumed, everyone wanting to talk at once. Tim sat watching and listening, trying to ascertain how well Kevin was recovering. It felt really good to be all together again.

"How are you doing Kev?" Mark eventually asked, daring to voice the question the needed to be faced but that nobody wanted to ask.

"I'm Ok most of the time. The chemo makes me feel like shit though. I usually spend the next two days puking my guts up. But most of the time I'm fine. Very bored though and I miss the Boat Club loads. I'd hardly believe how much I've grown to like it, or maybe it's just you lot I miss."

"We miss you too Kev. We got a new guy to sit in your seat in the boat, just so as we can keep on training while you're getting better. But man! He isn't a shadow of you Kev." Tim spoke, certain that his friends wouldn't disagree.

"I bet you really mean that he's not a stroppy sod like me!" They all laughed.

After lunch, much to their surprise, Kevin suggested a visit to the pub for a lunch time drink.

"Remember that you shouldn't have more than one pint dear. You're not up to it yet." Kevin's mother fussed, causing her son to turn a fine shade of pink.

Tom bought in the beers and they sat together at a copper topped table.

"Does this table full of beer remind you of anything Tim?" Kevin was mocking his friend now, as he loved to do.

Tim grinned. "That was the biggest birthday of my life. I will never, ever, forget it. My stomach can still *feel* it!"

"Well next time we'll make it even more fun!" Kevin vowed.

"I'm going to 'phone your doctor Kev and beg him to put in writing that you cannot return to Hull until mid- February at the earliest, even if he declares you fit tomorrow!"

After just one round, the boys headed back to Kevin's house. His mother insisted that they all stay for tea, after which they bade their farewells and promised to return before the Christmas holidays. Each boy hugged Kevin, thumping him heartily between the shoulders.

They completed the return journey quietly, each young man deep in his own thoughts.

"Seeing Kev again made me realise what a big hole he has left in the crew." Tim said as they approached Hull.

"It has. Like we've lost our soul," Tom agreed, sounding morose.

"Just focus on how lucky we are to have Ed to fill his seat. It's better that Ed isn't as strong a character as Kevin or it would be harder to accept him." Mark spoke wise words.

The following Friday afternoon Tim set off once again for Warwick. He would return on Saturday night to be back in time for the Sunday outing. It was great to be with Sarah, even for just a short while. It felt to Tim as if they became closer, more special to each other, each time they were together. He told her about Kevin, about what a hole his absence had left within the crew. Sarah loved Tim's sensitivity for other people and his evident concern for their wellbeing. She thought that it was probably that, which she had first seen when Michael had been in hospital, that had made him so attractive to her.

The crew began to settle once again. Ed was not Kevin and never could, would or should be Kevin. He was, however, an excellent oarsman and very willing to fit with the established routines of the crew. The crew had always appreciated his abilities but began, now, to accept Ed as one of them, to feel relaxed in his company and to allow him to get to know them fully. One by one they began to probe Ed, wanting to know and understand him so that they could better integrate him within the close-knit group. Slowly Ed began to relax and open up to his new friends, feeling the growing warmth and welcome that the young men were extending to him.

Ed was a naturally shy person and he had often been rejected by groups of people with whom he had been placed in the past. Hidden deep inside him, so deeply that even Ed did not know it, he had developed a protection mechanism that caused him to give nothing of his true self away so that it could not be used to hurt him in the future. It was this subconscious need to protect himself from the nastiness that he knew could be unleashed upon him at any time that made him appear remote and noncommittal and bland. Ed needed simple, uncomplicated friendship which is exactly what the Hull University First Four were offering.

"Come forward to row. I'll ask you once. Are you ready? Row!"

Tim had been putting the crew through their racing paces for the whole outing. The river was swollen from the recent persistent rain and the currents were powerful, providing the perfect opportunity for training against adverse conditions and simultaneous building of strength and stamina amongst the oarsmen. Tim could see that they were becoming tired now and they would finish soon. He wanted to see how far he could push Ed and how well Ed would respond in his leadership of the crew's response to Tim's increasingly impossible demands.

"You're doing a great job Ed." Tim spoke quietly, only to Ed. "I'm going to give you all one last push. I know that you can do it."

"Come on you lazy bastards! Move those oars! You're all slacking! We've got to get past those bastards from Gainswell!"

To Tim's immense pleasure he felt the boat accelerate, sensed the air rushing past his cold face at a faster rate and was aware of the ropes twitching in his hand as the currents played with the rudder. "E-a-s-y a-l-l. We beat the bastards! Just half a length but we've done it!" The boat glided to a halt and the oarsmen dropped their feathered blades onto the surface of the water.

Tim let the current move the Fellows into the side of the landing stage. He jumped out skilfully and squatted down, holding the boat steady as the oarsmen removed their blades from the gaiters and disembarked. They took their blades into the boat house and returned to lift the Fellows out of the water and onto the trestles for cleaning.

"Who are Gainswell?" Tom enquired as they were dressing after their showers.

"They're my old school." Ed grinned. "I'd love to beat them into the river bank!"

"My school crew did beat them into the river bank. Three times successively!" Tim boasted, goading Ed.

"I obviously wasn't in the crew then. It couldn't have happened if I had been!"

"Oooh! We're going to see public school boy fistycuffs!" Dave was laughing.

"Ed and I are best friends now. One for all and all for one!" Tim was quick to put the fun into perspective.

Laughing, they went to the club room and Tom took his favourite position behind the bar to fill five beer glasses.

"Tim was showing you how he bullies us in a race Ed." Mark warned.

"I'm used to that. Our cox at school used to get really personal when he wanted to get us going. I can handle anything that Tim might chuck our way."

"You do seem very calm and relaxed. I can learn from you."

"You Mark? You're the calmest guy I know." Tom sounded surprised.

The conversation moved on to the plans for the forthcoming Boat Club Christmas party. Plans were well advanced and it seemed that more than half the tickets had been sold.

"That's good." Tim pointed out. "At the last barbeque we did we sold loads of tickets and most people didn't bother coming in the end so we made money for nothing. Quite literally!"

"The very best accountancy practice!" Ed laughed.

"Talking of which, I got pushed in to standing for Club accountant last year. I think you would be the ideal candidate to take over from me in February when the elections come around again Ed. Since you are studying Management and Accountancy."

"I second that." Dave hurried to respond.

"Tim's being put forward as Captain" Tom dropped a bombshell.

"*Who told you that?*" Tim was not delighted. "It should be Kevin if anyone. I don't think I'm up to that task."

"Well I second that idea." Mark and Dave responded together.

"Hopefully some other nominations will come forward nearer the time. I shall try to stir people up so we have properly contested elections this time. It's much healthier that way." Tim resolved.

Mark went to refill everyone's glass and returned with a double portion of dry roasted nuts in a blue glass bowl.

"This is really feeling like old times. I think Ed's starting to feel at home with us." Dave announced.

"I think you're right." Agreed Tom.

"I am feeling really welcome. I do tend to take time to feel settled. Not just with you lot, with being at university too. I don't feel like a new boy so much now in general."

Drinks finished, the boys washed up, locked the bar and headed home. Tim gave Dave a lift back to the campus. They discussed the way forward for the crew.

"I feel better about things than I have since Kev got ill."

"Yeah, I agree. I do think that Ed just needs time to get to know us all. I bet we'll see things in him that will surprise us."

"I still hope that Kev will be fit to join us again soon."

"I doubt that will happen before the Summer term, to be honest. I think we have to assume that Ed will be leading the crew through the Head of River races."

"I was thinking that we should try to get into some Bumps Races this year. They're more exciting than Head of Rivers." Tim was keen to widen the experience of his fun-loving crew.

"We'd better talk about it with the others next time. At the crew cohesion session after training tomorrow evening."

"OK, let's do it!"

Parties and Love

The last couple of weeks of term were to be, as always, very busy with parties and other seasonal celebrations. Tim found himself with a number of near obligations, the Boat Club party, for which he was partly responsible, the Departmental Dinner, which he knew would be no fun but that all students were expected to attend, the house party, which he would attend by default, Sarah's party, which was on the Friday night before his house party and the crew had arranged to visit Kevin again.

The committee had deliberately scheduled the Boat Club Christmas party to be held on a Thursday evening, just before the main party season got underway. They had marketed it as being the first of the season and, much to their surprise, they had managed to sell all of the tickets. The week before they set off in Tim's car to visit the cash and carry to stock up the bar and buy plenty of crisps, nuts and other things to eat that could be served as and when they were needed or could be kept for use in future events. They had set out with a basic shopping list that they had decided upon in the club room after their Sunday outing. Once in the huge warehouse like place they all began to see things that might be nice or which they fancied. Their cart very quickly became full of lots of unplanned purchases which they agreed, on the spur of the moment, would add to the party experience. Back at the Boat Club they had some difficulty stowing all their goodies behind the bar. Tim was taking charge of decorating the room, with help from Tom and Mark. Dave was to be responsible for keeping the food flowing and they would all take turns behind the bar, making sure that there were always at least two of them there.

On the day of the party Tim collected his three friends at midday and they set about transforming the Club room and the wider Boat House. Tim lit the wood burning stove to be sure that the rooms would be warm and welcoming. While he did that Tom and Mark strung up several sets of coloured lights around the room, together with a set of outside ones around the front of the building. That proved to be harder than expected because they needed to drill holes and screw in hanging brackets, using the elderly tools that had once been used for boat maintenance. Dave was cleaning and arranging the bar and finding as many suitable bowls and dishes as he could. Tom had to tinker with one of the speakers for the stereo which had started to make only a miserable crackling sound. When everything was finally prepared, they had about an hour to go before anybody would come. Tim trundled off in his car to buy four helpings of fish and chips to sustain them all. They washed their meal down with a couple of pints of beer to get them into the party mood.

The next afternoon Tim set off at lunch time to go to Warwick. Sarah's party was to be fancy dress so Tim had taken his cox's outfit, with the addition of a straw boater, to suggest something from the Victorian age. The journey, in pouring rain, took longer than he had hoped and, by the time Tim arrived at the student village he was tired and starting to get a headache. The sight and feel of Sarah soon put him in good spirits and, after a cup of coffee, they decided that there was plenty of time to go to bed before they needed to get dressed for the party.

Sarah laughed when she saw Tim dressed in his white outfit with green crested tie.

" I remember seeing something a bit like that in your study at school once, when I went to collect Mike."

Tim grinned. "Yeah It was pretty much the same."

"I didn't know you then but I thought you must be very cool and sophisticated."

"And I am!" Sarah pushed Tim hard onto the bed and smothered him with her pillow.

"No!" she laughed.

The party was fun and Tim got a lot of comments about his outfit. He found it especially funny when he came face to face with a near clone.

"Are you really a cox?" Tim asked the young man.

"Yes I am. I'm really surprised to find another one. We're a rare breed!"

Tim told him that he was from Hull. They were unlikely to meet at any races as they were part of different "Circuits".

Sarah was keen to introduce Tim to her wide circle of friends and soon his head was spinning with names and faces, not to mention beer. By the time the party was coming to an end Tim was glad to look forward to bed. The two lovers woke up late the next day and made love slowly, deeply, wonderfully twice. Then they had to hurry to dress in order to get lunch before the restaurant shut.

"Are we going to meet in the holidays Tim?"

"I hope so. Certainly, I shall visit Mike a couple of times, but I'm not sure how we can fix it to be *together!* "

"We will find a way."

"Hopefully. I think we should tell Mike about us. I feel kind of guilty, having such a big secret."

"Ok, but not mum and dad yet Tim."

"OK."

Soon after lunch Tim was back in his car to return to Hull just in time for his house party. By the time he got there he was even more tired. He had a shower to try to wake up but with little real effect. There wasn't time to cook any supper, and he was very hungry so Tim went into the town to get himself fish and chips for the second time in almost as many days.

As the boisterous evening progressed Tim consumed more and more of the traditional "Magic Cocktail". By the time the party drew to a close in the early hours of Sunday morning Tim was much the worse for wear. He knew that he was expected at the Boat Club for training later in the morning and he felt certain that he would not be fit to do much. He crawled upstairs and found his bed and the world turned a dizzy black.

Tim awoke to the persistent buzzing of his alarm clock. Bill stirred and grumbled in his bed on the other side of the room. Tim reached out and banged the stop button on top of the clock. Somehow, he managed to hit it with the side of his little finger, sending a shock wave of agony up his arm.

"Fuck"

He got out of bed, stumbled to the bathroom, returned to pull on his tracksuit and let himself out of the house. Tim wondered, as he pulled out the choke and turned the key, if he was in a fit state to drive. Come to think of it, he probably shouldn't be coxing a boat either! When he went into the changing rooms Tim found Ed sitting looking miserable.

"I had a heavy night man! Shit Tim, you obviously did too. You look rougher than I feel."

Tim sat heavily on the wooden bench. The three other crew members turned up one by one, each complaining about their state of health.

"Maybe we should all just agree to cancel this session." Tim suggested hopefully.

"*Tim!* I can't believe I heard you say that." Mark sounded genuinely shocked. "A good old session in the fresh air will make us all feel better." As always, his wise words proved to be true.

The following Saturday the friends set off to visit Kevin. They were excited to be seeing him again and had filled the car with presents for him. When he answered the door, everyone could see that things were not going well. He had visibly lost weight and had a translucent quality to his complexion that shouted "Illness" to the world.

He put on a very brave attempt to appear his normal self but it was evident that he could barely muster the energy to keep up the banter that played between them. He hardly touched the delicious lunch that Mrs. Dunn served and by the middle of the afternoon the boys could sense that he had had enough. Tom reminded them all that they needed to get him back for his departmental party.

"That'll be fun! I remember last year's one well. Half cold soup, that crazy professor making a fool of himself doing magic tricks and only one glass of cheap wine each the whole evening."

The memory appeared to bring back some of the Kevin that they all knew and loved and that raised their spirits slightly.

"I really don't think it's looking good." Mark said as Tim was joining the motorway.

"It seemed bad to my mind too, though I'm no doctor, obviously. Did you see his colour?" Dave added gloomily.

"He did look a bit better when you were talking about last years' dinner. It must have amused him a lot." Tim wanted to cheer the mood up.

At last Tim found himself turning off the A 303 and heading across a frozen Salisbury Plain towards a dead and equally frozen New Forest. He was pleased to see Usman's Citroen already parked outside the house, its' windows covered in the intricate patterns of frost that suggested that it hadn't been moved that day. Yanking his bag out of the boot, Tim strode over to the front door and let himself in.

"Tim!" His mother came out of the kitchen, drying her hands on a tea towel. Mother and son hugged.

Usman appeared from the sitting room and shook Tim's hand

"Alhamdulillah! You are safe after such a long cold journey. Let me make you some tea."

They went into the warm kitchen where Mrs. Croy already had the kettle on. She arranged some mince pies on a plate, knowing that they were a long-standing favourite of her sons'.

Later that evening the friends sat talking in Tim's room. Tim had told Usman all about Kevin and how ill he had seemed when he last saw him.

"It is not a good thing when someone is very sick like that Tim. In Islam we would make many prayers for him."

"Yes, Christians do that too. I have been. But I just wish I could actually *do* something about it."

"It is only Allah, God, who can do that kind of thing Tim."

"But what about doctors Usman? I mean it's their job and they know about diseases and medicines and things. Are you saying that they're no good?"

"No Tim, not like you think. But they can only do as much as human knowledge allows them to do. It is only with Allah to make somebody live or die or get well again. I know that that is difficult to understand but, if you think about it enough Tim, you will see what I mean. If it wasn't true, then, if you take the right medicine you would be certain to get better and that is not the case, is it?"

Tim had to agree that it wasn't. He had never considered these kinds of questions before. It was an interesting challenge.

"How's Jane mate? You've not mentioned her yet. Is everything good between you?"

"Yes. Everything is good. I love her more and more Tim."

"I'm glad about that." Tim thought for a moment, remembering his conversation in the Summer with Anthony. He took a deep breath.

"Actually, Usman, I've got some news on the girl friend front too. But you've got to promise not to breath a word to anyone."

"Of-course Tim."

"Well I've started going out with Sarah. You know, Mike's sister. You met her at Anthony's party last year."

"I do remember her. You spent all the evening with her. I thought you were getting off with her then."

"No, I wasn't then, well not really, not seriously, I did fancy her but it didn't seem right, with her being Mike's sister."

"She is very nice Tim."

"I haven't told Mike yet Usman. That's why it's a secret. I'm a bit afraid of telling him to be honest."

"I think he would be pleased Tim. You are for sure his best friend."

"I know, but I'm frightened that this might spoil our friendship."

"Never! You looked after him like a brother when he was hurt Tim. He would not forget that. It even made me like you more because it showed me what a good guy you were."

"How's the car Usman?" Tim moved the subject on.

"I like it very much. Your father was very wise in his advice. Now I find driving here easy and normal. Just like you!"

"Hi Mike! It's Tim. How's it hanging?"

"Good thanks Tim. You?"

"Yeah, never better! Do you want to come over to see us, before Christmas? Stay the night so you can have a decent meal."

"OK, I'd like that."

"Brilliant. How about Thursday?"

"See you then."

The weather remained clear, crisp, blue skied, and sub-zero, more like January than December. After Mike, Usman and Tim had eaten lunch with Mrs. Croy and enjoyed coffee and polite conversation afterwards, Tim suggested that the three of them went outside to have a bonfire. Tim knew that there was a large pile of pruned sticks, too small for the indoor fires, waiting to be burned and that there was a pile of weeds to incinerate on top of them. His dad would be pleased to find the job done and it would be good to have a healthy outdoor task to complete together. Tim had always loved bonfires and assumed that the others would too.

"OK Usman, it's exam time for you! Remember how Dad showed you how to light a successful bonfire? Here're the matches and some newspaper. Show us how it's done."

Usman grinned confidently. He really did enjoy learning these skills of English country living and was glad to demonstrate them.

Tim led Mike off to get the hand cart and pitch forks to load the pile of weeds from the kitchen garden. Tim demonstrated the easy way to use a pitch fork.

"This is the back end of vegetable gardening Mike. After you've enjoyed the vegetables you have to dig it all over ready for planting again in the Spring and burn the weeds."

"You really like gardening don't you Tim?"

"Yes. I wouldn't mind being a gardener to be honest."

The boys began to work up a sweat. They paused when the first cart load of weeds was ready.

"Mike, I need to talk to you but I'm not sure how to go about it."

"You're making me worry Tim. It sounds well serious."

Tim looked Mike in the eyes. "I'm just going to say it directly. Sarah and I have started going out with each other. I wanted to tell you myself before you just find out. I'm sorry."

Mike looked at Tim strangely. His face broke into the grin that Tim knew so well.

"Why did you say sorry? I kind of felt that there was something between you. I'm so pleased Tim." Mike strode over to him and hugged him. "You're my best mate Tim. I couldn't want a nicer guy for my sister."

"She doesn't want to tell your parents yet Mike."

"No worries!"

They began to drag the heavy cart towards the plumes of hot blue wood smoke. Usman had done a great job with the pile of sticks.

After dinner they walked through a swirling mist to the village pub. There were two large wood fires in the bar and it felt welcomingly warm and cheerful after the cold, dank night outside. Tim bought the first round, together with the customary dry roasted nuts and the friends settled at a table within range of the warm glow of the fire.

"My brother is thinking of coming to school in England. Your mum is looking at different schools for him."

"Isn't he going to go to Barforth?" Mike looked serious.

"Well it wasn't that good for me really. If I had not found such good friends as you two, I could not have stayed there, Mike."

Mike burst into roars of laughter. "Your face Usman! You look so serious. Did you think I was serious?"

Usman started to laugh too. "You have always been the one to joke. Many times, I did not understand that something you said was a joke. I used to be confused with my understanding often with you. And still you can trick me!"

"And me mate." Tim interjected.

Mike suddenly became crest fallen. "Actually, Tim, I need to put a very old joke right. It was the worst joke and the biggest mistake I ever made. I just want to apologise to you Tim."

"I don't understand"

"Well you remember that time in the shower?"

Tim blushed. "Yes."

"That was supposed to be a joke. I had read all about what Lucas did to you in the Head of House Diary in Top Study One. I thought it would be funny to pretend that I was queer too, just to see how you'd react. I was so stupid Tim. If I had thought at all I would have known it wasn't a funny thing and that it would frighten you really, really badly." Mike looked Tim in the eyes. "Can you, will you forgive me?"

Tim stood up and shook Mike's hand. Then they hugged. Both felt a little overwhelmed. "I thought we'd sorted that in hospital that time."

"We did. Or rather you did. But I wanted to sort out my part of it properly too Tim."

Darkness

Tim turned off the motorway on his way back to Hull. He was going to drop in to see Kevin. He had 'phoned the day before to check that it was OK and Kevin's mum had told him that he was going through a bit of a bad patch but that she knew it would cheer him up to see Tim. He rang the doo bell and Mrs. Dunn answered.

"Kevin's upstairs Tim. Straight up and then second door on the left. I'll have lunch ready in about half an hour."

Tim climbed the stairs, feeling rather shy. It never felt right wondering about in someone else's house. He tapped quietly on Kevin's door and pushed it open. Kevin was lying flat on the bed. Tim thought he was asleep but then he saw a big smile spread over his pale face. Kevin struggled to sit up.

"Tim! Where did you come from?"

"Surprise visit mate. Happy New Year!"

They shook hands. Tim rearranged the pillows behind Kevin, wanting to make him more comfortable.

"Silly question, I know, but how are you feeling mate?"

"Ten times better for seeing you man! I get so fucking bored, stuck inside with nothing to do."

"I can kind of imagine that feeling. I get bored at home in the holidays sometimes to be honest."

"Me too!" They both laughed, guilty for being so ungrateful about holiday times. "So, tell me about your girlfriend. Sarah wasn't it? Do you still claim that it's harder when you're not with her?"

"I never said that Kev. That was your clever twist of my words. That's what we miss most about not having you in the crew with us."

"You don't get away with it that easily Tim. How's it going with Sarah?"

"It's great, actually. She's the sister of my best mate from school, so I've known her for several years but things turned serious between us last Summer. I felt bad about it at first, as if I was taking advantage of my friend."

"You think too much Tim. Thinking's good but not if you let it stop you from doing perfectly normal things."

Mrs. Dunn appeared. "Do you feel up to joining Tim and me at the table dear or shall I bring you something on a tray?"

"I'm coming down thanks. Is it ready?" The boys followed her down to the warm kitchen where the table was covered in a feast.

"That looks fantastic Mrs. Dunn. I didn't realise I was so hungry!"

"It's not often we have a visitor on a week day so it's fun to have a reason to do some proper cooking."

Tim filled them in about the Boat Club and wider university gossip as they ate. "The new boat will be delivered next week Kevin.

I hope you will be able to come to the naming ceremony later in the term. It wouldn't feel right if you're not with us, since you spent so much time choosing it."

"Wild horses won't keep me away mate. I really need to be there again."

"I might ask you to shovel the landing stage clear for us Kev." Tim provoked.

Kevin blushed, making him look more as he should. "In that case I might lift you off the ground again, Cox!" Both boys laughed until they could hardly breath.

"Something very funny there that I missed" Mrs. Dunn observed.

"It was just a crazy argument that we had, which was the moment that we both realised that we'd found a friend for life." Kevin grinned.

"It does sound crazy, but we both know what we mean." Tim began to chuckle again. "Nearly a year ago."

"Yep. Amazing what's happened in a year. I didn't think we'd ever even get on the river since we couldn't get a cox. And then look what we achieved!"

"Come on Tim, you're not eating. There's so much here. Kevin's not got much of an apatite and middle-aged ladies never eat! But you need to Tim."

"That's very kind Mrs Dunn." Tim filled his plate again.

After lunch the three went to the sitting room with mugs of coffee. Kevin began to visibly tire and eventually apologised and said he was going to have to go to sleep. Tim stood up.

"I'd better be making my way now anyway. Thanks for your brilliant lunch. Kevin, I'll bring the crew to see you soon, maybe the Saturday after next, once everyone's settled back in to Hull.

Remember I need you fit by the beginning of March so you can shovel those steps for me!"

Kevin grinned. "Thanks for coming mate. It means a lot. Especially from a posh public-school slob like you!"

In the hall they shook hands, then, both boys filled with sudden emotion, they hugged briefly, as men sometimes do, sharing a bond to which mere words could never do justice. Kevin walked slowly upstairs, and, with another "thank you" to Mrs Dunn, Tim let himself out of the front door.

On the morning of the first Thursday of term the new carbon fibre boat was due to be delivered. Richard, as Captain of the Boat Club, took responsibility for awaiting delivery and getting it put safely away in the Boat House. At lunch time Tim collected the crew to go and inspect it. Like young children beside the Christmas Tree they stood and stared, wide eyed, almost reverently, at the dull sheen of the dark grey hull. One by one they reached out to touch it, checking if it was real. Tom dropped to his hands and knees to look under the rack, to check out the interior.

"Come on, let's get it the right way up on the trestles to have a good look." Tim suggested. Ed and Tom fetched the new trestles, which Kevin had negotiated as part of the deal. "Hands across, lift! Ease her out. Gently please!" The boys lifted her off the rack, turned her over and rested her on the trestles. Eagerly they moved their seats to and froe, checked out the gaiter mechanisms. Tim tried the rudder ropes, noticing with approval the padding against the stern, a token gesture towards the comfort of his back.

"Shit! I can't believe this is for us." Dave articulated everyone's thoughts.

"It's amazing! The best there is." Mark had a dreamy look in his eyes.

"Is there any chance of a quick outing right now?" Tom suggested.

"I'm up for it" Ed enthused.

"I can't mate. Got a tutorial to lead. Sorry." Dave spoiled the idea.

"It wouldn't be a good idea anyway. I bet nobody's got their kit here." Tim tried to reduce the disappointment. Regretfully they lifted the boat back onto the rack, locked up and hurried back to the campus.

At the training session in the Sports Centre that evening everyone was in high spirits. The start of the Easter term heralded the start of the racing season which gave an added impetus to the need for each person to achieve his personal peak of fitness. The arrival of the new boat really was the icing on the proverbial cake. At the cohesion meeting in the Union Bar afterwards they agreed that, as Tim had suggested, they would arrange to visit Kevin a week on Saturday. Mark would 'phone to confirm it on Monday.

When Tim arrived at the Boat Club on Sunday morning, he found everyone arriving on their bicycles at about the same time. Tim drove gently round them on the muddy field, winding down his window to greet them as he did so. Tom's motorcycle was already parked. It's bright blue petrol tank gleaming in the low January sunshine. The crew hurried to clean the steps of tidal mud deposits with unheard of enthusiasm. Richard arrived to coach them from the bank. With uncharacteristic caution they carried the boat out and launched it onto the swirling, muddy water. Tim squatted to hold it while the oarsmen collected their blades. The following two hours were spent getting a feel for their new toy. Tim found it beautifully responsive to his steering inputs but the oarsmen took a bit of time to get their balance right. The hull seemed to want to roll around on the water more than the old wooden one had done. Tim began to worry that, instead of giving them a competitive advantage, it may cost them some success. He need not have done. Within an hour they were gliding through the water as smoothly as ever, beginning to enjoy the silent operation of slides and gaiters, the slippery ease with which the vessel seemed to cut through the water. This was the culmination of almost a year of their dreams.

On Tuesday evening Tim was sitting in the common room after supper. Coronation Street was on the television but he wasn't really watching. He heard the doorbell ring but did not respond. It wasn't his responsibility. Lee stuck his head round the common room door.

"It's for you Tim."

Tim got up and sauntered out to the hall. Tom was standing there, in his black motorcycling leathers. His face was pale and drawn. Almost blue. Tim noticed, for the first time, that he had pale freckles.

"Tim!"

Tim felt, with a sudden tidal wave of horror, that something was badly wrong.

"Tim. I'm sorry mate. Kevin's died."

Tom took a step towards Tim and Tim took one towards Tom. Tim's head was spinning, he felt remote, distant, surreal.

"Come upstairs mate." Tim led Tom up the two long flights of stairs to his room. He sat heavily on his chair beside his desk. He indicated his bed as a seat for Tom.

"This is shit Tim!"

Tim nodded, unable to trust himself to speak. He saw his strong, tall, friends' body shudder. Tears began cascading down the young man's cheeks, silently.

"Tom!" Tim moved across to his bed and sat next to him. He pulled him to him an urgent hug and thumped him gently on his back. Tom was crying unashamedly now. Tim began to feel his tears soaking wetly through his sweater and shirt. He wondered, remotely, why he wasn't crying too. At length Tom began to calm down. He pulled away from Tim and sat up straight.

"God I'm so sorry Tim. I've never felt like that before."

"Do the others know?"

"Yeah. Mark came to tell me and I went to tell Dave and you, because I've got the bike."

"How did they take it?"

"I think Mark had been crying before he came to see me. I was like you Tim, just shocked. Kind of frozen. Dave took it really badly. I had to stay with him for more than an hour. I was afraid he'd hurt himself or something. I got his house mates to keep with him for the night. And then I told you and it set me off. Shit, I am sorry mate."

"No worries! I'm going to go make us some hot, very sweet tea. It's meant to make you feel better at times like this."

When he returned Tom was looking composed. They sipped their tea in silence, neither able to think of anything to say.

"I'd better go mate" Tom was getting to his feet, needing space, feeling ashamed. Tim went down to the hall with him. "Are we going to train as normal tomorrow?"

"Unless you hear otherwise yes. I think it's best if we do."

Everyone was feeling numbed with shock and grief the next afternoon when they met. Ed, who hadn't known Kevin, felt guilty for not being able to share his crew's grief and had no idea how to behave towards them. He felt shut out, excluded. Nobody had the emotional capacity to reach out to him. They cut the outing down to one hour, and it was not really a success. Tim steered the boat and commanded his crew like an automaton. He found himself resenting seeing Ed's brown face sliding towards and away from him. It should have been Kevin sitting in Stroke's seat. Tim hated himself for feeling that way. He knew that it was neither fair nor reasonable and, anyway, he had started to like Ed. When they had returned the carefully cleaned boat to its' rack, they went down stairs to change.

Tim walked down the embankment to the carpark and to the field beyond. He remembered a day, almost exactly a year earlier, when he had found Kevin smoking a cigarette there before their outing, when he should have been with the crew cleaning the steps. He could still feel the anger that had flared up between them.

"Oh, fuck I'm so sorry Kev!" Tim dropped to his knees onto the soggy field, crying freely at last. He wept and wept and wept some more. He cried for Kevin, for Kevin's parents, for the crew and he cried for his own loss. How could such a fit, strong, powerful young man die at the age of nineteen? It wasn't meant to be like that.

"Come on mate." Tim felt strong arms enveloping his chest from behind, lifting him to his feet. He turned, unseeing, to find Mark. Tim leant on his shoulder, overwhelmed by grief again.

"It's OK mate. We've all been like this on and off. But you've got to share it with us. None of us is alone. One for all and all for one, remember?" Mark guided Tim back to the Boat House where Tom handed him a glass of brandy. He didn't speak. There was no need.

Tim was lying on his stomach on his bed, his face buried in his pillow. He had remained there since he got back from rowing. He hadn't felt like eating and didn't know really what to do with himself. Bill had come in to the room to do some work and had tried hard to engage Tim in conversation. But Bill was not naturally a talkative person and he had no idea how to reach out and help his friend in his grief.

There was a gentle tap on the door. Tim ignored it. Another tap. "Yeah?" he called dully. He raised his head from the pillow slightly to see who it was that demanded his attention.

"Ed!" Tim turned over and sat up, suddenly apologetic. "I'm sorry mate. If I'd known it was you, I'd never have ignored you like that. Shame on me!"

"No problem Man!" Ed walked in to the room, rather shyly Tim felt. "I wanted to come to see you Tim. Just to tell you that I'm your friend and that I want to share your grief as much as I can. I've been to see the other three already for the same reason."

Tim managed a weak smile. "That means a lot Ed. I need to apologise to you actually."

"Why?"

"Because, when we were in the boat, I kept on feeling kind of angry that you were there when it should have been Kevin. And I'm ashamed."

"I'd never have known Tim. And I understand that completely. That's why I wanted to spend a bit of time with each of you."

"You going to have tea or coffee?"

"Coffee please Tim."

Tim set off to the kitchen. As he boiled the kettle, he began to feel a bit better. Ed was a really good guy, spending his evening in that way. Not many people would have tried to understand the situation like that. When he returned with a steaming mug in each hand and a packet of biscuits lodged under his arm, he found Ed inspecting his book shelf.

"Are you into welding Tim?"

"Yes, I learnt at the car club last year. I welded up the boat trailer."

"Cool. Can you show me how to do it sometime?"

"Sure."

"Tim, can I ask you something a bit private?"

"You can try."

"Are you religious?"

Tim thought carefully. "Not properly no. I do believe in God but I don't go to church. I had too much of that stuffed down my throat at Barforth."

"OK, because, for me, I know that my religion would really help me at a time like this, even though I don't practice and I know I'm a really bad Muslim."

"I just can't get my head around why God would want somebody young like Kevin to die like that, for no reason."

"Yeah, it's a tough one to try to understand. At times like this I wish I had spent more time learning about it. Like you, though, school got in the way. Obviously, they stopped me doing anything to do with Islam from the word go."

Tim grinned. "I can well imagine." He told the story of Usman being forced to shave in public on his first night at the school. Tim put his empty mug down.

"Ed, please come out to get something to eat with me."

"I didn't come to trouble you Tim."

"I know. But I'm hungry. I haven't eaten since last night. And you've been working hard going around to see everyone. I bet you haven't eaten either, have you?"

Ed had to admit that he hadn't.

At the Sports Centre on Thursday evening Tom told them that Kevin's funeral was to be on Tuesday. They would all go. The prospect of actually doing something about the situation, even if it would change nothing, made everyone feel a little more positive and gave a kind of impetus to their training.

Tim drove around collecting his three friends early on Tuesday morning. Everyone was trying bravely to make bland conversation as they drove. They got stuck in a long tail back on the M1, adding nearly an hour to the journey. Tim started to feel stressed from the constant inching forward and stopping. At last they turned off for Nottingham. Mark had worked out directions to get them to the crematorium. They arrived twenty minutes early and had time to visit the toilets and walk around a bit, collecting their thoughts. The service was short, much to the boy's relief. It ended with the hymn "Fight the good fight" which made Tim remember again his fight with Kevin, and then how they had laughed about it with his mum just two weeks ago. Tim felt tears burning the back of his eyes and swallowed hard several times to gain control.

As everyone left each of the crew shook hands solemnly with Kevin's father, mother and brother. None of them could think of anything suitable to say. They were invited back for tea but declined, knowing that they would not know how best to behave in such circumstances. They began the long drive back to Hull, in heavy hearted silence.

"Do you all feel up to making a statement of crew intent to get an unbroken record of wins again this season, in memory of Kev?" Tom broke the silence, his voice sounding somehow constricted.

"Definitely" the other three agreed.

"I'm going to suggest to Richard that we could name the boat Kevin Dunn. Does anyone object?" Mark asked.

Nobody did.

"And I suggest, if it's OK with all of you, that tomorrow after the outing we confirm to Ed his permanent position in the crew, and try to give him a proper welcome."

"Definitely yes Tim" Dave replied.

"Yeah. We should try to make just a little bit of a party of it, you know Kev would have." Tom sounded a little better.

"Actually, I think Ed's been a bit of a hero this last week. He's been incredibly kind and considerate and thoughtful, sort of tried to look after us all." Dave voiced the thoughts of them all.

"Does anyone else want to get something to eat? I'm starving!" Tim changed the topic of conversation.

Tim pulled into the next service station and the boys headed hungrily for the main restaurant. When they'd all got a tray full of food and settled at a table with a fine view of the rushing motorway traffic, they began to feel a little better. Their spirits began to lift further with the warming, fortifying food.

"Ed is a nice guy. I'm not sure I'd want to have put up with what he's put up with us being like this." Tom was trying to articulate something that each of them had been feeling.

"Yep. He must have been feeling really left out of it. And he worked like a slave to keep us all going. Real cohesion!" Mark thought out loud.

"I think, if we let ourselves accept the idea, that Ed has a lot more to him than he seems to." Tim heard himself standing up for his new friend. He realised that Ed really had become a friend.

"I think you're right, mate." Dave agreed.

"So, let's stand together at this moment, in this place and pledge that we are going to move forward, together, from now on. Kevin would expect nothing less of us!" Mark captured the mood and made it official for them all. They returned to the car feeling almost buoyant.

The crew settled themselves into the Club House after their outing on Wednesday. Tim tried his hand behind the bar filling beer glasses for everyone for the first time. He caused riotous amusement when he pulled the handle of the beer pump and sent a loudly hissing gush of brown beer foam spraying all over himself and the bar.

"Tim! If you don't know how to do something, ask someone who does." Tom was the first to stop laughing enough to be able to speak.

"OK, I give up. Come and teach me Tom." Eventually Tim got five, pint glasses filled successfully. "I'm a qualified bar tender at last!"

"Don't go asking for a job at the Lookers just yet mate" Mark advised.

"Well I can open a packet of nuts at least." Tim retorted, doing just that and joining his friends at the table. They drank and crunched nuts for a few moments.

"I think that, as cox, it falls to me to ask you if you will agree to join our crew on a permanent basis Ed."

" You've been doing a brilliant job and you've taught all of us new things already. We've all grown to think of you as a friend too." Dave spoke confidently.

"I've really been enjoying it. So yes! I'd be pleased to join you permanently."

"To Ed!" Tom was always quick to raise a toast for any reason and this was an especially good one. Each young man shook Ed's hand in turn to formally welcome him.

"Are you going to refill us all Tim?" Mark teased.

After supper Tim set off on foot for the student village. He grumbled to himself, as he always did when he went there, unable to quickly locate the block and the room for which he was looking. At last! Tim knocked on Ed's door.

"Yeah!"

Tim opened the door gently and went in. Ed was lying on his bed reading Motor magazine.

"Tim! What's up?"

"*You're getting up!* Come on, the others are waiting for us."

"What for?"

"It's the Hull University First Men's Crew welcome party for a Mr. Mohammed Choudhury." Ed looked bemused.

"Just come with me and enjoy!"

Ed grabbed his jacket and keys and followed Tim. It wasn't far to the Lionheart and they reached it in time to see Mark going in. The other two were already installed at a big table and Tom was bringing over the first round of beers and a large bag of dry roasted nuts. Tim let Ed go ahead of him to get a seat. Mark remained standing.

"I'd like to take this opportunity to formally celebrate Ed becoming Stroke to the First Men's crew." Everyone stood and swigged their beer. Ed looked shy.

"Seriously, mate, we all really want you to feel completely part of us now, relax, be yourself and say whatever you need to say to make us a better crew and have lots of fun together." Tom said it straight, in his inimitable way.

"Stop being polite! None of us are polite to each other, as you must have noticed." Dave encouraged.

"To be honest I'm feeling really embarrassed now. It's such a nice surprise and it means a lot to me. Thanks!" They all drank again and started crunching nuts.

"We want to make this an even better season than last year. We're going to enter more events and we've got a brilliant new boat. All we need now is your expertise as an experienced

Stroke. We're all looking to you as the Crew's leader." Tim handed the position over to Ed decisively.

He knew that Ed understood the significance of his role and was certain that he would have lots of new initiatives to contribute. Dave got in the next round. Conversation turned to the coming Head of River events, the first of which would be in two weeks. As the evening wore on the party became rowdier and Ed visibly relaxed and started to join in with the group as they had never seen him do before. When Tim got in the final round Tom had an announcement to make.

"It's become a tradition, Ed, that the newest member of the crew has to down his last pint in one."

"I can't Tom."

"Try man!"

Ed was, by now, sufficiently intoxicated to be easily induced to throw caution to the wind. "I can't fight tradition either!" Ed stood up and began to gulp his beer. The crew began counting. "One, Two, Three...." Ed finished and sat down heavily. As the others finished their beer Tim could see Ed was very drunk.

"Do you remember Tim's birthday?" Dave started laughing.

Tim felt himself blushing. "Ed and I will find out one of your birthdays soon and then you'll be sorry!" He resolved.

As they left the pub they needed to go in different directions. Tim decided that he would have to accompany Ed back to his room. He was evidently not in a fit state to be left alone.

"Give me your key Ed" Ed fumbled in his pocket and retrieved it. Tim opened the door and Ed stumbled into his room. He slumped on to his bed. "Come on man, I think you need to go for a piss before you sleep." Tim hoisted him off the bed and he lurched his way across the landing to the bathroom. Tim looked around Ed's room. He tipped the screwed up balls of paper out of his rubbish bin, and placed it beside his bed. Ed was back, laughing.

"Get you things off Ed and into bed. Tim turned away for Ed to change and suddenly felt himself being pelted with paper balls. He turned and retaliated. The two friends fought excitedly for ten minutes. "Come on mate, time for bed!" Once he was safely in bed Tim was ready to go. "I put your bin right beside you Ed, just in case you feel sick in the night. You've had a serious skin full!" Tim hoped Ed had understood. "Sleep well!" He turned out the light and closed the door behind him.

Spain

The first race that the crew entered was something new for the original three oarsmen. The Bradford Bumps was to be held at the same venue as their Summer Regatta so Tim had a good knowledge of the river. That was of great significance in a Bumps race because one had to be aware of what was happening at both ends of the boat. Tim felt under pressure because of the newness and high value of their boat. Ed spent a lot of time explaining the techniques and processes of taking part in bumps races. Unfortunately, there were still insufficient crews at the university club for them to be able to practice the real thing. Never the less the crew set off on the frosty morning with high hopes. They all knew what their aims for this season were and why they had set them.

"I can feel Kev looking down on us" declared Tom. Nobody disagreed with his sentiment.

They put their boat together and then walked around assessing the competition. They all felt proud to know that theirs was the only carbon fibre boat there. Newcastle had not entered this competition. They took a brusque walk along the river bank to keep warm. There was a bitterly cold edge to the powerful breeze and there were threatening yellowish grey clouds building up rapidly. Tim recognised the land marks along the course but the river appeared much less attractive in the stark, leafless winter.

It was time to launch the nameless boat.

"Let's just call it Incognito for the time being!" Tim suggested.

The idea caused a ripple of appreciative laughter.

"It will be less humiliating for the other crews than being beaten by nothing." Observed Mark quietly.

The crew got their blades as Tim squatted holding the Incognito. He was, once again, being tormented by the feeling that Kevin should, by rights, be with them. He shook his head vigorously, hoping to somehow rid himself of the unwelcome thought. They rowed gently to the start line. They were in fourth place to start the race. Tim smiled at Ed, sitting relaxed in front of him.

"I bet you're looking forward to starting your career with Hull properly at last."

"Yes. I am. But I do feel very responsible, trying to do Kevin's job."

"You're not trying to do Kevin's job and you're not trying to be Kevin. You're Ed and we are all looking forward to being a new crew. We all meant what we said."

Tim spoke with a conviction that he hoped he would start to feel.

"Hull University. Come forward to row." The marshal interrupted any more morose thoughts. The crew slid forward to their front stops, their blades poised to cut into the water. "I'll ask you once. Are you ready? Row!" The Incognito shot forward with a power that took Tim by surprise. Was this really his crew? No time for musing! Tim was aiming his bow for the stern of the boat ahead. He turned to glance over his shoulder as he heard the following boat being started. "In, out, in, out, in, out" Tim realised that his intervention was not needed. The Incognito made contact with the boat in front, her cox conceded and Hull moved past them. Tim glanced over his shoulder again and could see the following boat challenging the boat that they had just passed. They must be a strong crew too, he thought.

Suddenly his face was stung by a flurry of snow, hurled at him by a sudden gust of bitingly cold wind. Shit! Screwing up his eyes against what was becoming a positive blizzard, Tim focussed on the need to make contact with the next boat. "Stride it out!" He encouraged his crew, as much to cheer them up against the horrible conditions as for any technical need. Contact at last! The opposing cox conceded and let the Incognito past.

"One more to go! Keep it up. You're doing great!"

Tim felt a real pride in his crew, it seemed to physically warm his entire body. They were strong and brave. He could see the leading boat visibly struggling in the terrible weather. Hull men were made of sterner stuff!

"We've got them in our sights! Reach for that final ounce of energy." The Incognito ploughed powerfully forwards through the choppy grey river. "Yes! Yes! Yes! Final push!" Glancing over his shoulder once again Tim was horrified to find a boat just metres behind him. "In, Out, In Out, In Out! Come on you plonkers! You can see the danger behind us!"

Contact! The incognito touched the leading boats stern. The cox conceded and steered to the side to allow the Incognito to pass. Tim knew that the boat that had been threatening them would have to take some time to connect with the boat that they had just passed. There was only another one hundred metres. The first win of the year was within their grasp. "E-a-s-y A-l-l!" The Incognito continued to glide through the water, seemingly frictionless. Tim grinned at his crew, their hooped vests slowly becoming frosted with glistening snow.

"We've done it! That was amazing boys."

They rather struggled to dismantle the boat and tie it securely to the trailer because their fingers were becoming numb and clumsy with cold. The crew were becoming cold now, as the heat of exertion was rapidly dissipated. Tim saw the crew huddled in conversation. He dreaded what he now knew was to come. They approached him, Ed looking especially serious. Tim felt his wrists and ankles gripped by eight cold hands. He was lifted high by four strong young men and tossed with disdainful ease into the cold grey water. Tim struggled to get out, his mind suddenly filled with the memory of a similarly cold experience in the brook at Barforth when he was just thirteen. Friendly arms reached down to help him. He clambered out, dripping and shaking.

"Come on! Let's go get showered." Tom spoke good sense.

As they stood drying themselves, feeling the blood circulating once again after very hot showers, Ed came up to Tim.

"I felt really bad doing that Tim. I could see how cold you were already. Are you OK now?"

"No worries. It was great to feel you leading the crew Ed. Now go and get us the cup!"

The customary pub celebration that night was more heart felt than ever before. It was as if each of the five friends were feeling released from some kind of pent up fear. All were glad that the first test of the new crew and boat had been a success. Tom proposed a toast to Ed. Ed bought in the next round and insisted on toasting the crew for making him so welcome. Tim asked Ed if he wanted to down his pint in one. Ed screwed up a crisp packet and lobbed it at Tim.

"Don't forget which of us is bigger!"

"Now you're even sounding like Kevin." Tim laughed.

That was the first time that the original crew members had been able to mention Kevin in a happy way. That, too, was a milestone in the recovery process. When they eventually emerged from the Lionheart, they found the world covered in a crystalline white blanket. The snow was still falling heavily.

"Shit!"

The friends started scraping up handfuls of snow from the car park and enjoying an impromptu snow ball fight. When everyone was wet, thoroughly cold and unexpectedly sober they called it quits.

"I vote we cancel rowing tomorrow. If it goes on like this, we won't be able to get there anyway." Dave suggested. They were all happy to agree.

"See you all on Monday evening then."

Tim woke up on Sunday morning soaked in a cold sweat. He lay shivering miserably in his bed. His head and body ached. He remembered feeling like that once before at school, when he had had the flu.

"You look rough Tim." Bill observed helpfully.

A little later Tim struggled dizzily out of bed and hurried to the bathroom where he was violently sick. He hid in his bed for the whole day, emerging only to be sick again at unpleasantly regular intervals. Surely, he hadn't drunk that much? It must be the dirty river water or was it just because he'd got too cold?

By Monday morning Tim was feeling better. He ate his breakfast and went into the university. He headed straight for the refectory where he drank coffee and ate a double round of toast. By midmorning he needed more food. He noticed, with irritation, that something had stung him on his leg and arm.

" There must have been a fucking gnat in bed with me "he grumbled to his friend.

When he got changed at the Sports Centre for the crew training session, he counted no less than six gnat bites. He told Mark all about it.

"That's too bad mate. It's horrible when you're sick like that."

Ed was truly remorseful. "We shouldn't throw you in when it's that cold. I certainly won't do it again if the weather's like it was on Saturday" he vowed.

When he woke up on Tuesday Tim was covered in red gnat bites.

"You need to go to the Health Centre mate." Bill recommended.

When he went down to get breakfast one of the cleaning ladies took one look at him and told him that he'd got chicken pox. Tim laughed.

"I had that when I was eight."

"Go and ask at the Health Centre love. They'll tell you!"

Tim went and waited patiently in the Health Centre. He remembered waiting there with Kevin. He worried that he might be seriously ill. The lady doctor saw him.

"Chicken Pox" she said. "I hope you haven't been walking around like that, spreading it everywhere."

Tim told her the story. "Oh! You poor boy! Go home and stay away from the university until the spots stop itching."

Tim went home. He telephoned Ed to tell him the bad news. He would come to the Boat House on Wednesday.

The weather remained sub-zero for the following two weeks and, despite two more wins, Tim did not get thrown in. Ed had, at least in Tim's opinion, made his first seriously positive impact on the workings of the crew.

Tim was ready for his holiday. He drove home and felt an immediate kind of relief from the incredibly stressful term. The familiar surroundings of the house in which he had grown up with his parents and sister, still following the same routines that they always had, offered him a calming atmosphere, safe from the still raw reminders of Kevin that seemed to lurk behind every corner of his life in Hull. Usman returned two days after Tim and the joy that he felt to be with him again was amazing. His mother insisted that Usman should guide Tim in his purchase of suitable clothes for the impending holiday in Spain and Tim was more than happy to comply. Usman seemed to have an instinctive understanding of fashion and the right combinations of things that he had never possessed.

The next day Tim went to visit Mike and Sarah at their house.

"Welcome Stranger!" Mrs. Andrews laughed.

Tim and Mike had much to catch up on and they went out for a long walk together, laughing and enjoying each others' company.

"I'm sorry Mike! Maybe a long walk isn't the nicest activity for you. It's just that you're so fit now I forget about your leg."

"No problem! If I didn't have to take it off, along with my clothes, when I go to bed I would forget too. The physiotherapist was right when she promised me that it wouldn't affect my life badly if I didn't let it. It's quite incredible actually."

"I'm so glad about that mate."

"I didn't tell you that I've started playing hockey again, did I? I actually made it into a team this year. It felt really good to be doing it seriously again."

"I understand that. I think competitive sport kind of gets into your blood once you've got used to it. I really thought that I didn't want to bother with it anymore when I went to Hull but now, I'm in it up to my eyeballs and I love it."

"Yeah, I'm in it up to my balls too. Talking of balls, how's things with you and Sarah?"

"Brilliant thanks Mike. And thanks again for being so understanding."

"No worries. Obviously, my girlfriend, Liz is somebody's sister and her brother doesn't poke his nose into our lives so I wouldn't either."

"I know mate. I just didn't like keeping it secret from you. I respect you too much Mike."

They returned to Mike's house in time for lunch with Mrs. Andrews and Sarah.

"Michael told me that one of your friends died Tim. That must have been so upsetting for you all."

"It was. It still is, sometimes. I find it really hard to understand and accept it. It sounds silly, trying to explain it, but I just can't kind of believe that it really did happen. I still expect to meet Kevin at any moment. To be honest it's a relief to have got away from Hull so that I don't have to feel that anymore."

"I understand that Tim." Sarah smiled.

Tim knew very well that she did. He had spent many hours crying and talking to her about it and she had taken a large share of the responsibility for helping him to get over the experience.

"It is hard to imagine someone of our age being dead. It just doesn't feel normal." Mike thought out loud.

"Well these tragedies do happen dear and, as you get older and older, they happen more often." Mrs Andrews joined in.

The conversation moved on to happier things. Mike lamented the fact that he was going to have to spend six weeks of the summer holidays at university writing a dissertation. Tim laughed.

"I've got to too mate. And poor old Anthony's got to spend six weeks on the Isle of Skye doing field work, so that's even worse."

"Yeah, I suppose I'm not alone." Mike conceded grudgingly.

"Usman's got six weeks practical to do too, so that means he can't go back to his home for half the holiday. He's much more patient about it than I would be though. I think he quite likes the idea of living with his girlfriend all that time, which makes it much less of a torture!" They all laughed.

After lunch Mike considerately orchestrated the opportunity for Tim and Sarah to spend a couple of hours unnoticed in her room together. Tim lay on his back smiling after they had made love, as quietly as possible, for the second time. There weren't many friends who would be as good as Mike in these circumstances.

As the 'plane began its' descent towards Valencia Tim began to suffer discomfort in his ears. It always seemed to happen to him when he travelled by air and he didn't like it.

He and Usman went to extricate all their bags and cases from the carousel. The young men soon had everything piled on a trolley and cooperated to try to move it smoothly despite its' evident bad temperament.

Usman introduced Tim to his father and younger brother Ali. Tim thought how shy Ali appeared. When they arrived at the villa, after what seemed to be a very long and difficult drive, Usman began another series of introductions to his mother and sisters. Tim was impressed at the size and beauty of the villa that Mr. Albad had rented.

When they began to explore both he and Usman were even more excited as they discovered the large blue swimming pool, the sauna set within a jungle of bamboo plants, the massive basement that contained snooker and table tennis tables as well as a small bar and kitchen that could be opened up to join seamlessly with the swimming pool area.

"I could live in a house like this Tim!" Usman was wide eyed.

"You bet mate. But you can't find places like this in England. Most of the posh houses there are all old. Like Anthony's. You remember that don't you?"

"Yes, that was very big and very old. And your house is old too Tim. In Jeddah all the houses are new. And you can build whatever kind of house you want. Your dad told me that In England you have to get special permission to build anything."

"Yep. And usually they won't let you build anything strange or different. It has to look like all the other things near it."

The boys started to explore the nearby coast line. They became interested in finding remote and isolated beaches where they could enjoy themselves without disturbance. Ali and Usman told Tim how they liked to dive on the coral reef to catch conches to cook on a fire. They considered doing similarly there, with the alteration of catching muscles and sea urchins from rock pools. Tim pointed out that it would be difficult to catch sea urchins because of their spines.

"And we don't know if they are safe to eat." He warned, not feeling comfortable with the idea at all.

A couple of evenings later, when the families were out at a restaurant, Usman pointed excitedly at the sea food counter, where there were sea urchins.

"See Tim, I told you, all things from the sea are halal for us to eat. Tomorrow we will make a barbecue, inshaAllah."

Tim was coerced into collecting a pile of drift wood while the brothers collected a bag full of black muscles and then tried to devise a way of prizing the sea urchins off the rocks without impaling their fingers on the spines. Ali showed Tim how to pile the wood over a shallow pit so that it would fill with hot ash in which they could cook. Usman produced a small kettle of water into which he poured lots of tea leaves and nearly half a bag of sugar.

"Egyptian tea." He grinned in response to Tim's look of surprise. "Our house keeper was Egyptian and he taught us to make it like this. It is a drink for energy when you want to play and swim."

Tim had always been a cautious eater, easily suspicious of anything that he had not eaten before. He was sure that he had heard of terrible cases of food poisoning from sea food and he was not at all keen to hurt himself thus. After a long session of beach football and then swimming in the chilly sea he was, however, glad to drink from the jet black, almost syrupy, tea. To his surprise the shell fish was good too.

"You see!" The Saudis laughed "All food from the sea is good to eat. Allah told us so. It is written in the noble Qu'ran Tim. You told us that you found the Qu'ran to be a good and powerful book. So, trust the words of Allah."

Tim had to concede that point. He was enjoying experiencing so many new things, despite his natural caution.

One afternoon they went to the marina and rented a small boat with an outboard engine and several fishing lines and nets. Tim was going to show the brothers how to fish. He knew how to handle a power boat, having learnt to drive the motor launch at school.

"Somethings at Barforth were useful!" He laughed with Usman.

Tim demonstrated how the engine was controlled and how to swing it from side to side on its' mounting to change the direction of travel of the boat. Each brother had a go. At length Tim judged that they were far enough out to sea to try fishing. Everyone was surprised at the quantity of fish that they were soon landing.

"We will take it home and eat it for our dinner inshaAllah." Ali was excited at the prospect.

"We'll make dinner with it. Give our mothers a rest!" Tim said.

"I do not think that they would like us to do that Tim. I cannot cook." Usman was adamant.

"You cook on a fire on the beach very deliciously Usman. We'll do it together. I'm good at cooking. I will teach you something new tonight!"

In the kitchen Tim began to instruct the Saudi boys how to chop vegetables, peel potatoes and make white sauce.

"Ali, you must stir it all the time until it becomes thick. If you stop stirring it will all just become one big lump like a rock!"

"Usman, you're going to make a cake. Here's a recipe, read it and do as it says. It's all just Chemistry mate, which is what you do best, so for sure you can do this well too. And you can't eat what you do in the lab!"

Tim sent Ali to set up the barbecue so that it would be hot and glowing by the time they were ready to cook the fishes. He started chopping up lots of fresh herbs that he had collected from the garden around the pool. It smelled good and Usman commented, impressed, that Tim could become a chef.

"Not quite, but I have started to like cooking. When I first went to Hull, I couldn't do it at all but I soon had to learn. Now I just think of it as if I'm messing about in a lab like my clever mate Usman."

Usman thumped his friend hard. "You laugh about me Tim!"

"Yes!"

Ali returned, wanting to know what the commotion was about. Tim showed Ali how to spread the chopped herbs on the inside of the fish, after Usman had gutted them.

Everyone was impressed as they watched the boys set out their feast and cook the freshly caught fish.

"Tomorrow or the next day it will be the girls turn to make us all dinner." Mrs. Albad declared. "I did not know that my sons could cook like a professional. Now I know that England is good for them!"

The Search

"Ed, I'm going to do some welding on a friend's car tonight. Do you feel like coming and learning how it's done?"

"Oh yes please!" Ed's enthusiasm made Tim want to laugh.

"Ok. I'll pick you up at about half six."

Tim was driving his friends' car, on to which he was going to weld two new front wings. He had become very confident at the task and enjoyed helping people. He was also secretly pleased to be able to demonstrate his skill.

Tim talked Ed through the different components of the welding kit and how they were used. They set about removing the headlamp from the drivers' side wing and then Tim showed Ed how to use the welder to remove the old metal joins. He gave Ed some scrap pieces of steel to try welding on to the old wing. Ed was, understandably, nervous when the first plume of sparks spurted from the metal as he made contact with the electrode. He quickly got the hang of it though and soon sported a big, satisfied grin as he realised that he was doing it all by himself. Tim was man handling the new, black primed wing into position. He set up the welding equipment and set about fixing it to the car. He asked Ed to replace the headlamp as he tidied up the work shop. He would do the other wing another time.

"That was brilliant Tim. Thanks mate. I think I could really get into that. I want to buy a car this summer. Do you know about cars?"

"Yes. I know a fair bit. I'd be happy to teach you if you want."

"I do want!"

"Have you got time for a coffee Ed? I'd really like to pick your brain for a bit mate." "Yeah that's cool by me."

Tim made the coffee and grabbed a packet of chocolate Digestives.

"let's go up to my room Ed. It's easier to talk there." Tim grabbed Bill's chair and they sat at Tim's desk.

"This sounds a bit serious Tim. Are you OK?"

"Yes. Well no actually. No! That's not right either. I've got a really big rattle in my brain Ed and I'm hoping you can help me with it."

"What's going on Tim?"

Tim took a deep breath. He really wasn't sure where or how to start this conversation. He wasn't even certain that he wanted to start it at all because he had a sinking feeling inside him that, once started, it was one of those things that would not stop, that may grow beyond his control. Tim was truly frightened and very, very confused.

"I've got a friend from school who came from Saudi. We became really good mates and, since we left school, he's started staying at our house in the short holidays from university. We get on really well and have lots in common. Last summer he gave me a Qu'ran in English and I promised to look at it. He'd marked some parts that he thought I would find most interesting. I did look at it but I didn't think much of it. I was just being polite in case he asked me about it to be honest."

Tim looked at Ed, who was listening to him carefully, his head tilted to his left.

"Then, when I was in a real state after Kev died, I started looking at it again. One night especially, I couldn't sleep and I was incredibly unhappy. I couldn't actually read it because it was dark and Bill was asleep. But I just got it off the shelf and held it and it did something to me Ed. I felt like a surge of power, like an electric shock except nice, not painful, and I felt calm straight away. It sounds crazy saying it out loud, but it's true. I didn't even open it or read it, just held it and it made me feel better."

Tim realised that he had been talking rapidly, probably sounding like a mad man. Ed was still looking at him.

"I haven't been able to get it out of my mind and now I'm starting, only starting though, to think that maybe I want to become a Muslim. And that frightens and confuses me Ed. And that's where you come in. Will you let me ask you things sometimes and help me to think this through properly?"

Ed remained quiet for a painfully long time. When, at last, he did speak his voice had a strange, kind of strangulated quality to it.

"Tim, what you've just been saying, it's really got to me. I saw your Qu'ran on the shelf when I was looking at your books that time when I asked you about welding. I'm not sure how to respond to be honest, because I'm not a good example of a Muslim and I don't have much real knowledge. I don't know how to help you Tim, though I'd love to."

"Please Ed. You're my friend, I trust you and I like you. You're easy for me to talk to. And I specifically don't want some religious freak to start cramming me with difficult details. That's what turned me off Christianity for ever."

"It's a big deal Tim. It's obvious that you've experienced the power of Allah, God. And I know that Allah guides people when He wants to. And I guess he is guiding you. You are very lucky. And I can see that it must be very scary for you Tim."

"I am frightened Ed. Not about the religion exactly, but about having to change everything about my life. And losing my friends. And my family. I don't know what to do with myself."

"Listen Tim. You are my friend and you have been a really good friend to me. Obviously, I will talk with you any time you need to and I will try to find answers to your questions. I promise I won't abandon you Tim. Just don't imagine that I am the sort of guy that you ought to be learning from, because I'm ashamed to admit that I'm not."

The boys drank their tea quietly for a few minutes. Both felt rather drained.

After rowing on Sunday morning followed by the customary social in the club house, Ed caught up with Tim.

"Have you got a minute mate?"

"Yeah sure."

"Let's go for a walk along the river bank." They set off, enjoying the warm spring sunshine.

"Tim, I want to apologise for the other evening. I'm so ashamed of myself. I didn't help you at all and that was unforgiveable. It just took me by surprise and I really didn't know what to do. But I should have been more positive at least. I am very, very happy that you're interested in Islam, I hoped that something like this might happen to you when I saw that you'd got a copy of the Qu'ran. I just didn't think that it would suddenly become my responsibility and I wasn't prepared for it."

Tim smiled. "No worries Ed. I shouldn't have sprung it on you like that but I'm confused in my own mind, like I said."

"Well I've thought about it a lot Tim. In fact, I haven't been able to think about anything else because it's made me think about my life too. What a mess!"

"I wanted to say that I think that you are a brilliant example of a Muslim Ed. The way you went around visiting each of us, trying to help us and cheer us up when Kevin died. That was the behaviour of a good, kind, considerate person who thinks of other people and how he can help them. That must be good Ed."

Ed stopped walking. He turned to Tim with a strange look. He moved towards him and suddenly Tim was enveloped in a powerful bear hug.

"Sorry Tim. I'm not queer or anything. That's what Muslims do to each other when they meet. And I feel like I might be meeting a Muslim in you."

"Thanks Ed. Please don't talk about this to any of the others. I'm not sure what will happen yet or what I will do about it all. But I do know that I will need to talk to you more."

"And I'm going to start learning with you Tim. I think that this could be the reminder that I need to sort myself out. I've got a guilty feeling that maybe you already know more about Islam than I do."

They both laughed. Each young man felt that he had got an even more special friend than he had realised.

Tim was driving to Warwick for a long awaited weekend with Sarah. The sun was shining and he had the window wound down, warm wind ruffling his shoulder length hair. The radio was on and he was thoroughly enjoying the drive. He realised that he had not felt so completely relaxed, happy and at peace with the world for ages.

Sarah and Tim embraced, both overjoyed to be together again. After they had made love, they lay together with evening sun rays warming their bed.

"I think we ought to tell mum and dad about us soon Tim. Then we will be able to spend time together in the long holidays without having to pretend that you're visiting Mike all the time. I love you Tim and I've got a feeling that we will be together for a long time. What do you think?"

"I guess you're right but it does make me feel a bit nervous. Very nervous in fact!"

"They don't bite! You know them and they like you. You're almost like part of the family Tim."

"That makes it look even more like I've used my position to steal you from under their noses."

"Tim! I am not a piece of jewellery or something. I can't just get stolen. That's really insulting."

"You're more beautiful than a piece of jewellery. That's what I meant. And it's because I want to treat you and your family fairly and properly that I feel worried."

"Then let's tell them Tim."

"Yes let's."

The drive, the very next day, to the Andrews' house, was filled with downright fear for Tim. He had pictures in his imagination of Mr. Andrews shouting and man handling him out of his house. He knew that was absolutely stupid but he couldn't help it. Obviously, they would be wondering whatever was going on. Why would Tim be bringing Sarah to them for lunch? Tim was Mike's friend and Mike wasn't there. That was pretty much a giveaway. Sarah agreed.

"We'd better explain straight away. That will clear the air. Plus, if we do that, you'll feel better and be able to eat lunch. If you stay like this, you'll be sick."

"This is a real surprise Tim." Mrs. Andrews laughed when they got there. "Let's have our coffee."

Tim shook hands with Mr. Andrews and sat talking, in a rather contrived way, about the display of flowers in the front garden. Mr. Andrew's had not known that Tim was so interested and knowledgeable about gardening. It just showed that he did have hidden depths, as Michael had often told them.

"Tim wanted to talk to you" Sarah announced when everyone was sitting, nursing mugs of coffee. Immediately Tim felt himself blushing, his mouth drying out, making his tongue feel too large for his mouth. Why had he ever got himself into this situation? Mr. and Mrs. Andrews were looking at him. Sarah smiled encouragingly. Tim forced a deep breath. He swallowed hard.

"I, no Sarah and I wanted to tell you that we, we"

What was he trying to say? He felt humiliated, ashamed, guilty, shy, afraid. He could have been a boy of thirteen in a Latin lesson again, forced to try to answer a difficult question when he had been caught day dreaming. He gulped another deep breath, realising that he probably looked like a fish out of water.

"I've fallen in love with Sarah and we want to go out with each other."

Tim hung his head, drained from the pressure and emotion of the experience. There was a short silence. Tim braced himself for the anger, the refusal, to be forcibly removed from the house.

"About time too!" Mr. Andrews knew how to relax the poor young man.

It was not a surprise to either parent. They had seen the looks, watched Michael making it easy for them to be together.

"That's wonderful Tim. You looked so frightened. I thought we were friends already." Mrs Andrews was concerned for Tim, he looked so disturbed. Were she and her husband really so frightening?

Tim's head was spinning now. From fear to relief in thirty seconds. It was not good for him. Sarah was hugging her mother then her father.

"Poor Tim was terrified the whole way here! I thought he might crash the car."

Mr. Andrews stood, moved towards Tim and shook his hand.

"Sarah couldn't have found herself a better boyfriend. And we couldn't have wanted better for her." He poured a glass of brandy for everyone. "I think you need this Tim!" he laughed, pouring a second measure into Tim's glass.

Lunch was a very excited occasion. Afterwards Mrs. Andrews wanted to 'phone Michael.

"He already knows dear. We guessed as much, didn't we? No point in embarrassing poor Tim any more. Don't you think he's suffered enough over this today already?"

"Why don't the two of you stay the night? You can drive back tomorrow. That way we can go out for a meal to celebrate properly."

"You don't need to make a big deal of it mum."

"No, but we want to make a special occasion of it. We are so pleased and we want to welcome Tim closer to the family." The matter was settled.

"I was going to make up Michael's bed for you Tim but I guessed you'd want to sleep with Sarah."

"Mum!"

Tim blushed, so deeply that he began to sweat visibly as well. He looked away, looked down, wished the floor would swallow him.

"Oh, I'm so sorry! I knew it was coming out wrongly as I said it. I don't get any better at being diplomatic as I get older. Poor Tim. You must hate me now. A dragon of a mother in law before we get to that stage!"

"No worries Mrs Andrews."

When Tim got back to Hull, late on Sunday evening, he was tired but incredibly happy. Life was sometimes strange, he reflected. He looked forward to inviting Sarah to visit him and his parents. He hoped that they would like her. His mum at least knew Mrs. Andrews which might help, he supposed.

His time began to be consumed by lots of serious work in the Boat Club and preparation for exams. He was not as concerned about them this year because he knew what to expect and was much more confident of his own abilities.

The crew achieved their first regatta win on the first Saturday in May and Tim was duly dispatched into the lake, Ed having decided that a sunny day of 23 degrees definitely was not too cold to risk harming him. Tim, in turn, took some pleasure when Ed, who had never done it before, had most of the contents of the champagne bottle spurt all over him when he tried to open it with the usual celebratory flourish.

"Silly idiot!" He laughed with him as he passed the remnants between the crew in their trophy.

"I've got two things that are worrying me at the moment."

Ed and Tim were lying on the grass near the Boat club, purportedly revising but mainly enjoying the weather and access to their exclusive club bar.

"Go on then mate."

"If I did become a Muslim, would I have to change my name?"

Ed thought about it. "I don't know. I suppose you'd probably want to, as a kind of public declaration of what you'd done. I know a lot of people who do change their religion change their name too."

"Do you know anyone who changed to being a Muslim?"

"Not personally, but there are quite a few in the Islamic Society here at the university. I can find some of them for you if you want Tim."

"No. I'm not up for that yet Ed. I'm not nearly ready to make a decision yet. It's a big deal and, and well I'm not ready yet."

"That's cool. What's the other thing?"

"I'm frightened that I might lose all my friends and that none of the people who are already Muslims will accept me."

"I accept you and I'm a Muslim."

"That's different. You're my friend already."

"I'm your friend because I like you, you're a decent guy and you accepted me. It'll be just the same as making new friends when you came to Hull or when you end up getting a job and living in a new place."

Tim laughed. "You make it sound so easy Ed."

"Because it is easy, if you let it be easy."

Tim liked Ed, envied him even, because he lived his life in the way he'd just described. Easy!

End of Term

As the Summer weather became progressively hotter Tim took and passed his second-year exams. The constant sunshine made even the river Hull appear attractive and the Boat Club became increasingly the centre of the lives of the crew. Tim had been elected as Captain of the club, despite his protestations, and Ed had taken over Tim's old role as Treasurer. Once again, the First Men's Four held all the committee positions, which made the club effectively theirs. It had grown in popularity, slightly, with considerably more members than the previous year, though this had not translated into very much more rowing activity, which was a shame but did make it easier to schedule extra outings as and when they wanted to. Competition wise the crew were maintaining their unbeaten record and had become something of a legend within the Northern Universities rowing circuit. Tim was fast becoming a connoisseur of the taste and smell of the different rivers and lakes on which the competitions were held. The Boat Club dry cleaning bill rose steadily and Tim was on first name terms with the girl in the dry-cleaning shop, who awaited his visit with a bag of wet and smelly white jacket and trousers every Monday morning.

Saturday saw the penultimate regatta, at York. The crew assembled early at the Boat House to load the trailer. The drive to York was full of the usual optimism and the sunshine made the venue doubly attractive. There was a real carnival atmosphere with families and picnics and lots of stalls selling food and gifts. Hull University unloaded and assembled Kevin Dunn, as the carbon fibre four had recently been named. The crew romped through the first two races with their now expected ease. There was a long lunch break, during which the crew had only energy drinks. They were well disciplined and Tim felt no need to keep checks on them. It was a great achievement to have reached the stage at which everyone could be trusted like that, Tim reflected.

Just over half way through the final Tim began to sense that Ed was struggling. He could see sweat streaming down his forehead.

"Don't give up mate. We're nearly there. Two more minutes man!" Tim spoke quietly, only for Ed, who seemed to be beyond responding.

The race was over. They had won. Just. "Eeeeeasy All. The boat drifted gently to a halt. The crew relaxed. Tim could see Ed gulping for breath.

"What's up Ed? Are you OK?"

Ed nodded. "Yeah, I will be in a minute." He gasped.

They turned the boat around and paddled gently back to the pontoons. Boat out, dismantled and loaded on to the trailer. Time now to eat, change and then collect the cup. The boys headed off to buy the food that they had been craving for hours. Tim was following slightly behind the others. He saw Ed appear to stumble and then fall. Mark was beside him in an instant. Tim ran to help too. By the time he got there Ed was sitting up, looking dazed.

"What happened?"

"Ed fainted I think."

"Ed? What's going on mate?"

Tim and Mark were both thinking the same terrifying thought. Remembering Kev and the way in which his illness had started. Surely this couldn't be a repeat of that. Neither felt that he could bear it.

"I think I've overdone it. I'm so sorry."

"What do you mean Ed?"

"It's Ramadan and I'm fasting but I think that the heat and three races was just too much."

"When did you last eat and drink mate?" Mark was thinking out loud.

"Three O'clock this morning."

"Shit! You poor man. Why didn't you tell us?"

"I didn't want to let you down. I thought I'd be fine."

"Stay with him Mark. I'll go get some energy drinks and something for him to eat."

Tim set off at a run and returned within a couple of minutes. Ed was sitting up more comfortably now, Mark anxious at his side.

"Get that down you." Tim handed him a bottle. Ed drank, slowly.

"Thanks mate. I'm really sorry."

Tim handed Mark a ten-pound note. "Get the three of us something to eat. Fish and chips if you can find it, for Ed and me." Mark set off.

"I thought that, if you were travelling to another city you could skip your fast?"

"Yes, but I just thought I'd do it anyway. Stupid I know." Ed still sounded very faint and weak.

"Drink the next one." Tim handed him another bottle. Ed drank, slowly again.

Dave and Tom arrived on the scene. "Mark told us what happened. You going to be OK Ed?"

The celebrations were unusually muted. Ed collected the cup but left it to the others to share the bubbly. Tim received his customary dunking but the journey home was less boisterous than usual. Ed was sweating profusely and seemed to be lost in a trance like state. When they'd unloaded the boat and locked up the Boat House, they stood chatting briefly.

"I think you should take Ed to the Health Centre Tim. He needs to get checked out."

Tom sounded unusually serious. Tim guessed that he, too, was making frightening connections with the recent past.

"I think I'll have to miss the pub tonight. I've got such a headache" Ed spoke for the first time.

"No worries. We'll celebrate for you!" Dave promised.

"Come on mate. Get in the car and let's get you sorted." Tim opened the passenger door for his friend. After registering at the desk, they sat in the waiting room.

Ed went to the toilet, saying he was going to be sick. He came back five minutes later, sweating again. He was called in to the surgery. Tim went with him. Ed explained that he had been fasting and then about the race and how ill he felt.

"Classic dehydration. You can't do that level of sport in this heat, if you're not eating and drinking properly." Ed looked guilty. "I've half a mind to admit you and keep you on a saline drip all night."

"I'd rather not."

"Well, if your friend here is willing to take responsibility for keeping an eye on you, you can go home. Bed rest and drink the rehydration powder mixed with a cup of warm water, every hour until it's used up. Come back in the morning for blood tests."

The boys left with a prescription in hand. Tim drove around searching for the twenty-four hour chemist to get the powder. They went back to Eds' room.

"OK mate. I'm going to mix up the first cup of that stuff. You get undressed and into bed. Just do as Doctor Cox tells you!"

When Tim came back Ed was in his bed.

"Good lad. Drink this. It smells horrible I'm afraid."

Ed took a sip. "Shit! It is disgusting."

"That's the punishment for trying to be a hero beyond any sensible limits."

They sat talking.

"I'm going to be sick again." Ed hurried out. He returned looking awful.

"Try to sleep for a bit Ed. I'll come back in a couple of hours. Tim took Ed's keys and drove home. He had a long bath and a mug of tea. He 'phoned Tom to say that he wouldn't make the celebration that night. Ed would be OK. It wasn't anything like they had all feared. Dehydration. Tim put his pillow and a couple of blankets in his car and went back to Ed's. He turned the key in the door as quietly as he could. Ed stirred and then sat up.

"I think I did sleep. I feel much better now."

"Good! Just in time for more of that medicine."

"Oh no. Please Tim. I think that's what made me puke."

"You need it mate. If you puke this time, I won't make you have it again. Deal?"

"Deal doc!" Tim was relieved to feel that Ed evidently was feeling much better. Their conversation was as lively and fun as it usually was.

"How are you getting on with your research?"

"Research?"

"About Islam. You had any more thoughts, now that you've got time to think, with exams finished?"

Tim blushed. "I got rather frightened to be honest Ed. I read that I'd have to get circumcised. I don't think I can go through with that."

"I hadn't thought of that Tim. Obviously I don't remember having it done to me. I can see that it wouldn't be exactly a bundle of fun though."

"It must be so painful, having your nob out all the time, rubbing against your clothes."

"I suppose you just get used to it mate. You don't see me limping around all the time, do you?"

Tim had to concede that that observation was indeed true.

"I just can't imagine going to the doctor, thwacking my meat on the table and asking him to peel it for me."

Ed laughed and laughed and laughed some more. "I don't think you'd get it done like that Tim! But I do understand how it must be incredibly frightening and embarrassing. I doubt I'd be brave enough to do it either, so I can't tell you not to be silly or anything trite like that."

"That's what I like about talking things over with you Ed. You're so nice and truthful." They slapped hands. "But Tim, promise me that you won't let even as big a thing as that stop you from becoming Muslim. It will be a horrible thing to do but it will be over quickly and you will still have the best religion in the world."

Tim hadn't heard Ed talking so fervently about his faith before. It reminded him of Usman. He went to mix up the next cup of powder for him.

"I've got some decent biscuits Tim. Let's eat them. I'm starting to feel hungry now and you must be starving. In fact, you ought to go get something proper to eat, you can't miss your supper just because of me."

Back in Ed's room Tim had things to talk about.

"If you need to fast Ed, tell us. We will understand and we will cancel the last regatta. You are much more important than a race."

"I know and thanks. What you said earlier is right though. If I'm travelling out of the city, I can miss my fast that day and make it up later, so I will be fine to race. I must say I was impressed with your knowledge Tim. You already know more than many Muslims. A very diligent student!"

"It really does excite me Ed. Islam feels so much more real somehow. I know what I mean but it's hard to put it into words. I'm pretty sure I will become one but there are a few things I've got to resolve."

"I feel very privileged to know you and to be watching you learn Tim. You've done me a lot of good. I'm starting to feel interested in my own religion for the first time."

"I'd like to start the evening by saying how amazed I am that we got here, unbeaten, for the second season. I know I didn't think we'd survive at all." Tim was standing at the pint laden table at the final celebration of the year.

"I want to drink to Ed. Without him we wouldn't be here and he is an incredibly special man, not only a brilliant oarsman but a real friend to us all too." Mark voiced the feelings of them all.

Ed looked very shy, avoiding eye contact and fiddling with his glass.

"To Ed and to Us!" Tom raised his glass and the party began in earnest.

Nobody knew it but Tim had decided that this would be the last occasion on which he would drink alcohol.

The end of the term and of Tim's second year was upon them. He felt increasingly uncomfortable as he watched so many of his friends and his house mates packing up and departing for the long Summer vacation. Tim, meanwhile, was staying exactly where he was, with only six weeks of daily work in the library to look forward to. He tried hard to join in with the usual boisterous partying and fun but his heart wasn't in it. Nothing felt right and he could neither enjoy himself nor start to focus on the task ahead of him. He felt as if he was just watching life going on around him without really being a part of it.

Dissertation

Tim lay awake in the silent Sunday morning sunlight. He knew it was late but he didn't care. He had nothing to do and nobody to do it with. Neil Blashford would be moving in to the house later in the day but, apart from him, the large house, which Tim had only ever known full of seventeen lively fellow students, would be empty. Last night, as Tim had cooked his dinner, he had felt weird, almost afraid. So lonely had he been, with only his portable black and white television for company, sitting lost in the corner where the rented twenty six inch colour set had once been, that he had done all the piles of washing up that his house mates had left, abandoned, in sinks, on tables and on the floor. He didn't want the cleaning ladies to have to do it and it felt better to be busy than bored.

At length he got up and walked, naked, to the shower room to wake himself up. He went down to the deserted common room, full of memories and chairs, and then to the abnormally clean kitchen where he made himself coffee and toast. After he'd eaten and washed up, he set about emptying the fridge of stale food, half eaten pies and shrivelled lettuce leaves. He walked to the news agent and bought a copy of the Observer. That occupied him, slouched in an easy chair that he dragged from the common room into the garden, for a couple of hours.

He went back up to his room and read through the booklet that contained the instructions and expectations for his dissertation. He found it difficult to focus on such a lengthy task and he had no idea how he was going to get started the next day. What on earth was he going to do for the coming six weeks? How was he supposed to complete a ten-thousand-word piece of original library-based research? He did not feel equipped with sufficient skills or knowledge to do so. He imagined that everyone else would be feeling similar doubts. That made him feel less inadequate. He knew he would get it done somehow.

Tim went back down to the kitchen, lit the gas under the kettle and made himself a mug of tea. Finding a selection of mugs, clean and ready for use, served to underline that he really was alone in the house. He took his tea into the empty common room, put it down on the floor beside his chair and ripped open a new packet of chocolate Digestives. He was just crunching his way through the second one when the doorbell jangled. There was no one else to open the door so Tim ambled out to the silent hall and welcomed Neil to his new home.

"I've just made a mug of tea. Come and join me. I'm bored stiff already!" Tim led his friend through to the kitchen and made the tea. Sitting back in the common room it felt good to have someone to share his biscuits.

"I stayed in bed all morning" Neil admitted. "Then I hardly had enough time to pack my things before the warden came to boot me out. The place has been let for some conference or other."

Tim talked about his exciting time alone in the house. "At least now we'll be able to encourage each other in this massive task. Did you say you were going to get your girlfriend to come to stay for a bit?"

"Hopefully, yes."

"I think mine will come for a bit. And I've a mate from school coming next weekend. He's at Southampton and doing a dissertation. Biochemistry. We'll be able to grumble together!"

Usman and his friend duly arrived on the following Friday afternoon. The week had passed unexpectedly quickly and both Neil and Tim had managed to make a start on their dissertations. Once he had actually written just the first paragraph Tim found that the paralysis of fear and trepidation had lifted and he realised that a dissertation would be no different to a very long essay. He would be able to complete it in the six weeks quite easily, just so long as he worked steadily, in his usual stoic way. By the time he answered the door to his two visitors Tim was in a buoyant mood. "Usman!"

"Tim! This is Ali. Ali meet Tim." Tim led them into the common room and introduced them to Neil.

The next morning the four men decided to go to Bridlington for the day.

"Maybe we can find some shell fish for you to cook on a fire, like you did in Spain Usman." Tim had been impressed by Usman's relaxed confidence about finding and eating shell fish.

"I did that with Anthony when I went to see him in Lancaster. We dug some shells up from under the beach. There were people digging up truckloads of them for sale. I had never seen that before."

Tim admitted that he hadn't either but Neil had read about it.

"I think they're called cockles."

"Yes, that is right. They are very delicious to eat."

They drove in high spirits over the Wolds towards the coast and stopped to buy lots of other provisions to make a feast on their fire. All of them were excited by the plan to live wild for the day. Fire always seems to unite people in a common purpose.

The main beach was very busy on a sunny Summer Saturday so Tim drove North along the coast road for a few miles until they found an empty stretch of sandy beach, with some rocky areas beside it.

"We should be able to catch something to eat in the rock pools over there."

The lads splashed and played in the chilly water and then set about dislodging and collecting muscles from the rocks. Neil announced that you could eat the long brown strands of seaweed that clung to the rocks. Usman agreed with him while Tim and Ali were less enthusiastic.

"Everything from the sea is halal, Ali" Usman taught him.

"Yes, but that doesn't mean it has to be *nice* to eat. I'm not that keen on normal vegetables and you're trying to convince me to put that stuff in my mouth!"

Tim liked Ali's spirited response. Neil and Usman set about building the fire from driftwood that Tim and Ali collected and soon they were cooking their experimental meal. The muscles were delicious, the seaweed less so. Everyone was glad that they had purchased some more usual things to supplement their foraged foods. Usman told them of his regular camping trips to the remote desert beaches near Jeddah, during which he and his friends would live wild for a week at a time. It sounded very exotic and exciting to the three English men.

That night, sitting in Tim's room and enjoying tea and biscuits, Usman started Tim talking about his current thoughts on Islam.

"Tim, you were very interested when we were talking in the holidays. How have you been thinking since then. Ali is here specially to help you."

Ali blushed. "I'm not sure how helpful I will be, but I am happy to try to help you to understand your feelings. I remember how tough and confusing they can get at your stage."

"To be honest I am almost certain, now, that I will do it. It does feel right and makes a lot of sense to me. But there are some things that do worry me and that I am struggling to sort out."

"There always will be some things that don't seem to fit. Like everything else in the world." Ali seemed very sensible.

"I'm worried about my parents' reaction. I don't want to upset them."

"I think they will be happy Tim. Your mother said that she is pleased with the things I have taught you." Usman was quick to encourage his friend.

"Yes, but that's one thing, me giving up the faith of my parents and becoming something else is something much bigger Usman."

"My parents were upset at first but they're cool about it now. Some of my friends disappeared when I stopped drinking and chasing after girls, but I've got new friends instead."

"I've already stopped drinking. A whole two weeks now! I wanted to see how I'd get on and it's been fine. Neil is the only person who knows so far but he didn't have a problem."

"That's great Tim!"

"Then there's Sarah. I love her, and I have fancied her for years and we've only been officially going out with each other for a year now and I don't want to stop that."

"I split up with Jane. It was very upsetting. I did cry every day for a week." Usman was suddenly intense and serious.

"You should have come to see uncle Tim!"

"I did want to but I knew that you were thinking of becoming Muslim and I did not want to frighten you away by seeing me upset about doing something I did to please Allah. That is why I went to see Anthony. He always knows how to make you laugh."

"Yes, he's a great guy. I've liked his attitude since we were in the Third Form. I was really frightened of him at first but then we started messing around together and we became as thick as thieves. A real disruptive influence at Barforth!"

"Tim, you need to understand that you don't have to change everything all at once. You must take things one step at a time or it will become too much for you. Islam was revealed gradually for a good reason. Just concentrate on praying properly to start with and Allah will make other things come bit by bit. I'm still learning and developing, and it does get easier." Sound, reasoned advice from Ali again.

Tim went quiet, fidgeting, looking embarrassed. Ali, being a kind and sensitive guy, felt pretty certain that the issue of circumcision was in Tim's mind. He decided to put him out of his misery, as another revert had done for him.

"Something that might be worrying you is the thought of getting circumcised." He put it bluntly, there being no delicate way of raising the subject.

"Yes, I'm terrified of that." Tim was blushing seriously now.

Usman looked very uncomfortable. Again, his discomfort made Ali want to laugh.

"I nearly made Usman faint when I explained what that meant. He didn't know about it at all."

"But he must have had it done."

"But I did not remember, because I was a baby, and I never thought about it."

"I just feel so embarrassed. Like you must have felt, Usman, when I had to put ice on you that time. And then there is the fear of pain, having it done and the pain afterwards. It must be uncomfortable all the time."

"It was humiliating. There is no way round that. And it took five weeks to heal fully. A guy who I talked to before I did it told me it would take five weeks so I think that is the standard time. All of that time I was terrified of getting horny in case the wound opened up again. It did feel weird, and uncomfortable for a few days but you get completely used to that. It's not like the feeling that you're thinking of' Tim."

"Thanks for being so honest Ali. Where do you go to get it done?"

"You can go to hospital, but that's really expensive. I went to a GP which was cheaper but however you do it, it will be embarrassing. Usman or I will take you and be with you Tim. You will not be alone I promise you that."

Usman had been listening to this exchange quietly, contemplating. He was amazed at the courage and the sacrifices that these friends of his needed in their search for his religion. It made him feel very humble because Allah had just given him these things without any need for any action on his part. Indeed, he had taken deliberate action to move away from the straight path. He bit his lip, remembering the shame that he had brought upon himself.

They enjoyed a long, late, leisurely breakfast on Sunday morning and then went for a walk around the botanical gardens. Tim always enjoyed the place and Usman was very interested in some of the more exotic plants in the green houses because they were natural sources of some of the organic compounds with which he was working for his extended project. Ali knew little about plants or gardening but was amazed at the diversity of habitat in which plants could live. He told Tim how it was the wonder of living things that had first opened his eyes to Islam. Tim talked about Usman's way of thinking and behaving that had first aroused his interest. Each understood the other's perspective and found it interesting. They would find it easy to become friends. Tim felt sorry when the time came to see the two friends off on their long journey South.

Neil's girlfriend, Annie had arrived and, after introductions, Tim joined them for a dinner that Neil had cooked.

"I thought you told me you couldn't cook." Tim complained as they drank mugs of tea afterwards.

"I didn't say that. I said that I can't be bothered to do it for myself every day. That's different!"

Annie laughed.

"I'll cook for you two soon. Sarah's coming on Tuesday so the house will be fuller. Maybe Neil and I won't get much work done though."

"The girls can cook and clean for us Tim. That way we can concentrate on our serious work better. That's what they're here for anyway!"

Annie jumped up and chased Neil upstairs. Tim didn't see him again that evening.

Sarah arrived three days later, planning to stay for a long weekend. She had taken a holiday job in a photograph processing factory so was unable to spend as much time away as she would have liked. Tim was overjoyed to be with her again and her presence proved, unexpectedly, to be a motivation rather than a distraction from his work. He started working harder and faster to enable him to complete the required quantity of work in just a morning in the library, freeing him to spend the remainder of the day with Sarah. They visited York, enjoying the tiny shopping streets in the old city centre, they spent an evening in Beverly and they walked the coastal path at Scarborough. Most of all they spent time together, each simply enjoying the experience of the others' company. Their love stretched well beyond the merely physical, almost as if they had known each other for years, making for an easy comfort between them.

Tim knew that he needed to talk to Sarah about his intention to change his religion. He hoped that she would be able to understand, that he wouldn't hurt her with his decision. He was so happy when they were together and he couldn't bear to spoil everything just because of a weird idea that he felt the need to chase after. And yet his soul was starting to ache after the fulfilment that a religion, a faith, a way of life would give him and he now knew that that was something that he had to achieve, for his very survival. Tim wondered why life had to be so complicated. Was it like this for everyone? Or did he, Tim Croy, make life difficult for himself simply by thinking himself into impossible situations? "Take things easy." Ed had advised him once. Why was it so impossible for him to do just that?

"You know how I've been interested in Islam as a religion for a long time?"

"Yes, you've often talked about your friend, Usman, isn't he?"

"Yeah. Well I think that I might become Muslim myself quite soon. I've thought about it so much and it feels like the right thing for me to do. I think I've always wanted to be religious, *needed to* probably, but I was completely turned away from Christianity by the difference between what we were taught at Barforth and the way in which they actually behaved. I just couldn't go with it and I got into loads of trouble because of that. Islam is so much clearer, simpler and more real. It is basically similar in its' teachings but explained more accurately and with more clearly defined codes of conduct. It's something that I can understand and comply with."

"I'm sure that that is what you should do then Tim, if you feel that convinced. I think I'm like you, I never got the point of religion at school, but I'm certainly not closed to the need for something bigger than us to help us. I'm just not really bothered about it at the moment."

"The thing is, if I go for it, I have to do it properly and try to follow all the rules. And that means I'm not allowed to have a girlfriend." Tim went straight to the point, not being able to think of a gentle or less direct way to face up to the dilemma that he was bringing into both their lives.

"Does that mean that you want to break up with me?"

"**No!** I want to be with you forever. I'd love to think that we might get married in a year or two, once you finish university and I've had time to get a job and earn a bit of money so I can look after you properly. But, in the meantime, I don't think that we can be more than really special friends. I know that sounds weird but I can't see any other way. I'm sorry."

There was a long silence. Tim felt sick, as if he had broken something that was priceless, through his own selfishness. He remembered Usman saying something along the lines of "If you do something only to please God then, for sure, God will make it work out alright for you, even if it isn't the way you thought you wanted it to be." He hoped that that would prove to be the case now.

"I can live with that! I feel the same about you Tim. I love you and I want you to be happy. The thing I like best about you is how sincere and honest you are, and this is all a part of that, so yes, it's not a problem for me. I can and will wait for as long as it takes."

Tim felt as if he might cry. He had not expected such a supportive reaction. He felt an overpowering emotion towards Sarah. He loved her, more than he could ever have imagined that he could love another person.

"I'm not a Muslim yet!" He laughed, grabbing her and pulling her onto the bed.

"Good afternoon. May I speak to Mohammed please? I'm Tim, from university."

"Hi Tim. How's it going?"

"All the better for being nearly over! Listen, I promised I'd come and look at cars with you. If you'd still like me to let's do it either this weekend or the next, before I disappear down South for the rest of the holiday."

"Brilliant man! That's what's so good about you Tim. You don't forget your promises. You're living in your usual house, aren't you? I will come to you on Friday and we can find something near you. Is that OK?"

"Cool by me. Try to get to Hull by midday. It'll give us more time and I can have an excuse to take time out of the library. Let me know what time your train gets in and I'll be there to meet you mate."

"OK. See you then Tim."

Tim parked his car on the bomb site about half a mile from the station because it was free to do so. He felt happy to be meeting up with Ed again and was looking forward to spending the weekend messing about with second hand cars. He arrived just as the train was pulling in to the platform.

"Tim!" Ed shouted as their eyes met. They shook hands and Tim insisted on taking Eds' bag.

"I've parked half a mile away because I'm too tight to pay for station parking! So, the least I can do is carry this."

Safely back at the house Tim made tea and got out the biscuits.

"I always associate you with these Tim."

"I like them so I just keep on buying them, I guess."

"It seems strange, this house being so empty."

"Yeah, I hated it at first. Made me feel even more pissed off about the dissertation but I've got used to it now." Tea finished they started talking about cars.

"I've got £800 to spend, maximum. I know that I want something economical so that I can use it as much as I want and, hopefully, it will be reliable because I don't know much about them."

"Well that's a start. Let's go get the evening paper, it's always got the motoring section in it on a Friday. Then we can drive around and do some tyre kicking tonight so that we can make a short list for tomorrow."

"Thanks Tim. I don't know anyone else who knows anything about cars. I've never forgotten watching you weld those wings on that car. You're an expert!"

Tim laughed and told him about the time his car had broken down on the motorway and how the free telephones had been connected up wrongly so no one could find him. They returned with the paper and shared out the section with car adverts in it. Tim scanned his pages rapidly, marking possible adverts. Ed was much slower, often becoming excited about things that Tim would quickly dismiss.

"Cool! A Capri 3000. Only £495. I fancy that."

"You won't be able to insure that, Ed, because it's sporty and has a three litre engine. It'd drink petrol too."

"How about a T registration Renault 20?"

"Same problem mate." Tim got his street map from the car and they worked out a journey to visit thirteen garages around the city.

"You can navigate Ed."

"You might regret that Tim. My dad says he can't trust me to get back home if I so much as cross the road."

"If you're going to drive a car you've got to learn."

First stop was to look at a Fiat 127.

"As I thought, it's a rust bucket. Look at the rear of the front wings, the bottom of both doors and that bit below the rear window. Forget this one."

The next Vauxhall Viva was dismissed on similar grounds. A Hillman Hunter caught Tim's eye.

"This looks good Ed. Might be a bit thirsty but it's good condition and only sixty-three thousand miles on it."

"It's like yours isn't it?"

"Mines an avenger, a bit smaller. We're looking at one in a bit."

They started their short list with the Hunter. They added the Austin Maxi that they saw next. The VW Beetle was crossed off because it had been crashed and badly repaired.

"Come over here Ed. How does that car look to you from a distance?"

"It looks kind of too low at the front."

"Exactly. That means that the shock absorbers are shagged or that they've rusted out of their mountings. Forget that one!"

The Avenger was added to the list as was the second Viva. A Datsun Cherry followed and final entry was a Renault 12.

"I'm hungry! Let's get a meal out. My treat Tim."

"Sounds good to me man."

"Do you like Indian?"

"Never really had it to be honest. My mum cooks curry sometimes but I've not had the real thing."

"Let me introduce you to it then. I know a good curry house and I'll help you choose the right things."

They had a brilliant meal. Tim was amazed at the different flavours of the food on offer.

"The meat here is halal Tim so I can eat it and you will be able to too."

"OK."

"Do you know about halal?"

"Yes, it's to do with it being killed in the name of Allah."

"Yes, and it has to be killed quickly and kindly Tim. And it's supposed to have been looked after properly for all of its' life too."

"I like that bit Ed."

Back home Tim introduced Ed to Neil. They drank tea and ate more biscuits together. Neil recommended a Renault Fuego to Ed. Tim laughed.

"You've no idea have you Neil?"

"No but they look well cool. I wanted my dad to get one but he got a Renault 18 instead. Boring!"

"Dream on Neil!" Tim grinned.

Neil excused himself, wanting to catch up with his writing. "I took a whole week out when Annie was here and now, I'm all behind with my schedule. Girls!" He left the room, grinning wickedly.

"How are you getting on with your thoughts about Islam Tim? I've been thinking about you a lot and praying for you too. You've done me a lot of good, made me think about my own religion."

"I'm definitely going to do it Ed. You're the first person I've said that to. I just need to talk it over with my parents."

"Really Tim? Seriously? Shit! That's incredible. It's just amazing Tim. I'm so proud of you man."

Tim felt embarrassed. He'd never seen Ed so emotional and he was surprised at his reaction.

"It's a real privilege Tim, you telling me first. I'm almost crying."

"Well you've been a big part of it, Ed. I know you're going to say you're not a good example, but to me you are. You are just so normal and unintimidating and fundamentally decent."

The next morning the friends set off to check out their shortlist plus a couple of private advertisers. By lunch time they had a shortened shortlist of three. Austin Maxi, Hillman Hunter or Renault 12.

"Really it's down to your preference Ed. The Renault will be the most economical, The Maxi has the most space in it and the Hunter will be the simplest to work on. The other two are front wheel drive which makes them more complicated mechanically but they handle better in snow and ice. The maxi is a hatch back so will be more versatile – you can even turn the seats into a bed!"

"I really don't know Tim. What would you choose?"

"I've been very pleased with my Hillman. The Renault is one year newer and they're supposed to be very strong. I think I'd probably go for the Renault."

"OK. I'll take your advice Tim. Let's do the deal then I can buy tax and insurance before the day's over so I can use it straight away. I'm excited now!"

It didn't prove to be quite as simple as that. The garage man needed to put a new MOT on the car, which couldn't be done until Monday. Tim managed to get him to agree to fit a new battery too, since the one in the car could barely turn the engine over.

"It'll be better to buy your insurance on Monday too Ed because more companies will be open then so you've got a better chance of finding the best deal. It's a real bore but worth 'phoning round loads. I saved nearly seventy quid last time I did it."

"I'll do that Tim. Can I stay with you until Tuesday?"

"Obviously. I'll be glad of your company mate."

A Half Holiday

At last Tim was driving home for what remained of the Summer holiday. In reality he knew that there was still as much remaining as he had had for the whole Summer when he was at school but he still felt rather hard done by. Never mind! He had lots of good things planned and he certainly intended to make the most of it. He had set off at first light so the journey had been an easy one and he arrived home by ten thirty.

His mother was in the sitting room arranging flowers in a blue and brown jug. They hugged.

"Just in time for coffee!"

They went into the kitchen, Mrs. Croy put the filter machine on and then they took their steaming mugs, along with the tin of biscuits, out to the marble topped table on the terrace.

"Usman went to Jeddah yesterday. We took him to the airport and then spent the afternoon at Wisley. You'd have loved it dear."

"And when's Ali coming? I'm guessing about the third week in August?"

"About then yes. I don't think they've booked the flight yet. I think, reading between the lines, that Ali might be having second thoughts."

"Poor him. I think it will be tough for him. There's no getting away from it. I'm sure I couldn't have done it, though I think I'd have liked to try."

"You've made me feel very proud of you Timothy, the way you've taken Usman under your wing, and the way you helped poor Michael. Mrs. Andrews just can't speak highly enough of you. I went for lunch with her last week. She's so pleased that you and Sarah are together. I came away quite pink from hearing so many good things about you."

Tim blushed. "I just like to take care of my friends mum. Whatever they said, Barforth didn't take care of people unless they thought they'd get something extra from them."

"A lot of life is like that Timothy. There aren't enough decent people. That's why it's so important and so difficult to try to treat people properly, wherever you go and whatever you do."

"I'm going to go and stay with Anthony next week. His parents are away and he's alone in the house, like I was here last year. You should see their house, it's *massive!*"

"Well just remember that it is his parents' house, not his!"

"*Mum!*"

Tim drove very gently on the way to Anthony's. He had been reading about how to drive with economy in mind and he wanted to see if he could do it. He enjoyed everything to do with cars and driving and he was starting to wish that he had studied engineering of some kind. He had always like tinkering with machinery and mechanical things always seemed so much less complicated than things to do with people.

He reflected, as he drove, how often he had been hurt by people and, indeed, how often he had hurt people. He remembered, with shame, how he had bullied Mike for several months, all because of a silly joke that Mike, who Tim knew had always been a joker, had tried to play on him. He remembered, too, how insensitive he had been to Rian, making him feel threatened by him as he prepared himself to take Rians' place as cox to the First Eight. His thoughts turned, for the first time in months, to Kevin and how it had been unkindness on each boys' part, followed by repentance, that had made them the closest of friends. Tim wasn't at all certain that he deserved the faith that his mother seemed to have in his good character. It was with surprise that he realised that he was almost at Anthony's house. He indicated, slowed and turned into the great drive way of the grand house.

Anthony was striding across the drive to Tim's car before he had his seatbelt undone.

"Tim am I glad to see you mate!"

"How was Skye?"

"Shit! I'm still covered in gnat bites. I won't be going back there again if I can help it."

"Isn't that where they make the fudge?"

"They don't have anything nice there. Just gnats and bogs and they eat seaweed."

"You obviously had as much fun as I had, stuck in the library tower block for six weeks."

Tim followed Anthony to the large kitchen.

"Tea or coffee?"

"Coffee please, mate. Might wake me up after a slow journey."

"Bad traffic?"

"No, I was trying out driving for economy, just to see if it really works and if it's worth the hassle."

"Of-course it won't save you much, silly plonker!"

"Thanks for the encouragement. It's an interesting idea, intellectually. If you think about it, people are spending a fortune buying new cars with the latest fuel saving devices but, by driving slightly differently you can save just as much plus thousands that you didn't have to spend on a new car. It might prove to be a winner."

"What's this I hear about you and Islam Tim?" Anthony came straight to the point in his usual blunt way.

"I think it's an interesting religion. It's quite like Christianity but easier to understand. Somehow it feels more sincere."

"But you're not religious Tim. You never were. You were the only one of us who refused to get confirmed. Don't you remember the fuss and how old Pullman never forgave you?"

"Yes, but that wasn't because I didn't believe in God. It was because I didn't believe all the crap they pushed down our throats there. I couldn't promise to follow that."

"You always have done your own thing Tim. I admire you for that."

Tim took a deep breath. Time to get some advice.

"Would you still be mates with me if I became a Muslim?"

"Yeah, of course. I'm mates with Tim, not his weird ideas, and your ideas always have been weird!"

"That means a lot Anthony. I would hate to lose a friend like you."

That evening they walked to a pub in a village two miles away.

"I don't like being in a pub with people who all know my folks." Anthony expressed a feeling that Tim shared.

"I get that mate. I always feel like they're watching me, waiting to make nasty comments to my parents about me."

"Yeah, exactly. I don't think parents' friends ever let you grow up!"

"What you having Anthony?" "Pint of Farmers please mate. I deffo recommend it."

Tim found Anthony at a table in the garden and deposited the beer and his Coke with ice and lemon.

"What's that all about?"

"I'm trying life without alcohol, just in case I do become Muslim. It doesn't upset me at all in reality. I was surprised to be honest."

"You really are serious Tim. I think you should just go for it mate."

"I'm just worried about Sarah. I love her so much and she's become so special to me, and her family too. I don't want to hurt her or let her go."

Tim verbalised, with a wave of relief, his one remaining fear. Just saying it out loud, to one of his best friends, seemed to make it less daunting. And Tim hoped that Anthony would come up with some magic solution for him.

"I get that mate. Usman was really cut up when he split with Jane. I'd never seen him like that, not at all his usual cool self."

As the boys sat eating a late breakfast in the ancient kitchen their thoughts turned to what they might do over the coming days.

"Actually Tim, I know you've come here for a holiday, but could I ask you to look at my car sometime? I saw a load of steam coming out yesterday after I'd been in town. I don't know a thing about cars and I know that you're an expert."

Tim laughed. "Flattery will get you everywhere! "

"When did you last check the fluids?"

"I put some washer water in at Easter."

"Oil? Radiator water?"

"Nope."

"Anthony! You've had the car for at least two years to my knowledge. It's an old car and you need to check monthly at least. Look. The oil is below the minimum level. I can't see the water level at all and the battery water is below the plates. I'm amazed you ever get it started at all."

"Shit. I didn't know about that kind of thing."

Tim sent Anthony to get water and to seek oil and deionised water in the garage. He came back with a watering can of water.

"Can you come to look with me in the garage? I don't really know what I need."

They went together and Tim showed his friend the things that they needed.

" Pour some of the antifreeze in here. Now fill it up to that mark with water. Now add oil and keep checking with the dipstick until it shows full. Look! We put deionized water in each cell of the battery until it just covers the plates. Can you see that?"

Tim squeezed the water hoses and looked for any signs of leaks, talking his friend through his actions.

"OK, start it up and put the heater on"

Anthony started his car.

"Let's leave it ticking over while we wash our hands. We need it to get warmed up properly."

When they returned to the car the gage showed that it was at normal temperature. Tim looked for any signs of steam or leaking water, without success.

"Take us for a five-mile drive."

"Tim" Anthony started talking as he drove. "I need to tell you something. You were so honest when we talked about Islam yesterday. And the truth is I'm starting to feel really religious too. Christian, but it's starting to mean more and more to me. That's why I understand your ideas so well."

"That's great news mate. It kind of confirms what a decent man you are. I really am pleased Anthony."

They were back at home again.

"Don't turn off yet. Lift the bonnet and see if there's any steam." There was none. "The battery light doesn't come on any more either Tim."

"That's because the battery can charge properly now it's full of water again."

As Tim drove home, he reflected on Anthony. He had clearly been on a considerable journey of discovery. Tim felt very pleased that he had found comfort in religion but found it quite difficult to imagine him as being religious. He supposed that that was how people felt about him too. Probably it was a basic belief in God and the kind of code of conduct that it brought about that made somebody the kind of person that Tim liked.

"Tim! **Tim**" Mrs Croy was standing in the hall, shouting up the stairs.

Tim, who had been lying on his bed, deep in thought about nothing in particular, opened his door and thumped down the polished wooden stairs.

"I've just had Mrs. Albad on the 'phone. She's very upset. Ali just set off for the airport with his father but he was really unhappy. She's so worried about him. I promised we'd look after him extra carefully. We need to think of ways that we can help him to feel safe and confident to face his new life. It is a big step for anyone and he's obviously feeling very frightened."

"Yeah, it is a big deal, but I think he'll get over the shock as soon as he's alone on the plane."

Mother and son made coffee and took it, together with the tin of biscuits, out to the sunny terrace.

"Poor boy! I'm sure that he felt that he needed to follow in Usman's footsteps but he isn't Usman."

"Usman came here all alone and without anyone to turn to. He managed fine so Ali will too."

"I think that Ali is the baby of the family and that means that he won't be so grown up."

"Well boarding school will soon toughen him up!" Tim sounded bitter.

"You really didn't like Barforth did you dear? I do regret it so much because we only ever wanted what was best for you but it seems that we ended up hurting you badly."

"I know you didn't mean any harm. I was just not cut out for it. It did do me some good, like giving me a head start to life at university and it certainly made me independent and self-reliant and tough."

Mrs. Croy and Tim drove to Heathrow after lunch.

"We simply mustn't be late. It would be terribly frightening for Ali to find nobody waiting for him."

They waited outside the gates in the arrivals' hall. People began to emerge, a few to start with and then in greater numbers. Tim could see the distinctive Saudia emblem on some of their bags. There was Ali. Tim's heart went out to him. He looked so young, nervous, positively frightened. Tim hurried to the edge of the barrier.

"Ali! Welcome to England!"

He took the trolley from the boy and shook his hand. Remembering the Arab culture Tim hugged Ali. He couldn't bring himself to kiss him, as he knew the Arabs did, that was too big a leap of cultural difference for Tim to make.

"Thank you, Tim. You are very kind."

Ali's voice was very quiet and Tim thought he detected a tremble in it. Mrs. Croy was with them now.

"It's so lovely to see you again Ali!" she said, hugging him to her, with not a trace of the awkwardness that Tim knew he had displayed. He pushed the trolley while his mother subjected Ali to a barrage of questions, her way of trying to take his mind off his misery. Tim loaded the luggage into the boot and then got into the back seat next to Ali. He felt that it was the most visible kind of solidarity and friendship that he could show to the nervous boy. Tim and his mother kept up a steady stream of questions and explanations throughout the two-hour journey, trying to encourage a response from their charge. Ali responded politely but minimally. Tim began to feel that he may be more successful when the two of them could be alone together. Less overwhelming.

"Oh my God! You live in a castle!" Ali spoke without prompting for the first time as they arrived at the house.

"It is a big house, but it really isn't a castle dear" Mrs Croy laughed. "This is your home now Ali. I want you to think of yourself as part of our family. We are all so pleased to have you here."

"Thank you. You are very kind. Usman told me that he has two mothers now!"

Tim took Ali's bags upstairs and showed him his room.

"This is your room Ali. Nobody else will use it and you should start to make it how you want it."

He showed Ali round the rest of the house, encouraging him to feel free to go wherever he wanted to.

"Guess who lives in this room!"

Ali laughed for the first time. "Subhaan Allah! Usman always has things like that in his room. I will tell my mother. She will be very angry with him doing that in your house."

Tim laughed. "Ali please, this is your house now. Soon we will stop being polite to you and we will treat you like we treat each other. Then you will have to behave like part of the family." He finished the house tour with the downstairs rooms and then took Ali back upstairs.

"Have a wash and relax for a bit and then I'll come to get you for tea. Remember where the bathroom is?"

Tim stood in his room, looking out of the window across the green of the lawn, striped by the lawn mower. The cedar tree spread its wide, flat branches over the edge of the drive way, brown cones sprouting skywards. He so much wanted to make Ali feel welcome and to help him to face his new school with confidence. Confidence really was the key to success in the brutal machine of a Public School. But what was the best way to achieve this? Tim gave up for the moment, left his room and headed across the landing to Ali's room. He knocked and pushed the door gently open. Ali was taking some things out of a suitcase which lay open on the bed.

"I have some presents for you all."

"Come and get some tea. Let's relax a bit, you must be very tired after your travels."

As they went downstairs Tim turned to Ali and looked him deeply in the eyes.

"Ali, please, always ask for anything that you want or need. We all really do want you to become part of our family, like Usman has. When you see him here you will understand what we mean."

Ali smiled. He had the same smile as Usman and his father. For some reason it made Tim feel certain that he would find his way through this new chapter in his life.

In the kitchen Mrs. Croy had the kettle on.

"Would you like tea or coffee dear?" She started to explain the different possibilities.

Tim laughed to himself. His mother was very good at obliging guests to respond to her. They took the tea and plates of cake and biscuits out to the terrace. Ali walked to the edge of the terrace and looked at the swimming pool.

"That is very good."

"I know you're a great swimmer Ali. The pool is there to be used. Please use it any time you want."

"You're studying the three Sciences and Maths Ali. You must be a very good pupil." Mrs. Croy tried to encourage a response.

"I want to become a doctor. It is a very good career to make."

"It certainly is dear. And I'm sure you will make a super doctor."

Tim took Ali for a walk around the garden and then took him up to the old flat above the coach house.

"This is Usman's smoking room. I know you smoke too so feel free to come here when you need to. But please don't smoke at school too much. I'm sure Usman must have told you how much trouble he got into for doing that!"

"Actually, I think that I need to smoke now."

"Cool. Let's sit and enjoy!"

"Do you smoke Tim?"

"No. I tried one once, when I was fourteen but it just made me sick so I never tried again."

Ali drew deeply on his Rothman's. He exhaled a twisting plume of smoke. Immediately he seemed to relax visibly. Tim began to understand why somebody might get addicted to tobacco. After a few more deep inhalations Ali began to talk.

"Tim, I worry that my English will not be enough to study properly."

"Do you like to worry Ali?"

Ali looked questioningly at Tim.

"I mean you seem to make a worry about everything Ali. I promised you back in the Spring in Spain that your English is very good. When you are at school it will become perfect very fast. By October you will sound like an English man."

"You are kind Tim. And how can I make friends Tim. Usman said that he only got some friends because you made him be your friend."

"Somebody will do the same thing to you, for sure Ali. You're a nice guy and after a week you will have some friends. I know it must feel very frightening right now. That is a normal feeling but everything always feels worse before it starts. As soon as you get there you will find that things just happen."

Ali lit another Rothman's. Tim moved to sit beside him on the sofa. He took hold of his hand and squeezed it.

"Ali, everything will be good. Remember that Allah is close to you always."

"Oh yes Tim! Usman said that maybe you want to be a Muslim. Is that real?"

"Yes."

"My father was so happy that he did cry. He said he had sand in his eyes but we know that was not true because we were in our house."

Tim laughed and blushed.

There were more introductions when first Anabelle and then Mr. Croy returned home. They had dinner, served formally, in the dining room and Annabelle flirted with Ali throughout the meal. Tim could cheerfully have beaten his little sister by the time they all retired to the sitting room for coffee.

At breakfast Mrs. Croy had some news.

"You need to take Ali to the doctor for his MMR jab at ten Tim."

Ali looked questioningly at her. "An injection dear" She mimed a jab in the arm. "Usman got very ill from the Mumps and we don't want that to happen to you."

"It was very nasty Ali" Tim added.

Tim introduced Ali to the doctor who smiled when he remembered Usman.

"You certainly don't want to get mumps Ali."

Ali presented his arm and winced as he was needled.

"All done! You may get a bit feverish. If you do drink lots, rest and take aspirin if you need to. You know the routine Tim."

Back home, as the sun rose higher and hotter in the summer sky Tim suggested a swim. Ali was a competition swimmer, he knew, and he hoped it would help to relax him. It did. Tim was truly impressed at Ali's strength, power and speed and his vast range of strokes and techniques.

"You will impress them at school with that Ali, I bet you're competing for the school in no time."

"Assalamo alaikum! Dr. Chaudhury? Please may I speak to Mohammed? It's Tim from university."

"Hi Ed. Tim. Do you fancy a couple of days in the New Forest? Come and stay at our place. How about Wednesday next week? Cool. Just Head for Brockenhurst and call me when you get there. I'll meet you. See you then. Bye!"

Tim was looking for Ali. After searching the house and garden he went up to the Coach House flat. Ali was sitting smoking.

"I've been looking for you man!" Tim grinned.

"I have a bad feeling Tim. I needed a smoke."

"What kind of bad feeling?"

"My head hurts and I think maybe I will vomit."

"That must be the injection. I can see you're sweating." Tim sat down opposite Ali. He wished this wasn't happening to him. He was uncomfortable enough as it was. They talked intermittently. Ali smoked two more Rothmans. Tim struggled to understand why he'd want to smoke if he was already feeling sick.

Ali suddenly stood up and walked quickly across the room and out to the hall. Tim followed, concerned for him. As he got to the hall, he heard a retch, followed by a splashing sound.

He found Ali leaning over the toilet, a thick rope of mucus hanging from his mouth. He spat. Tim was standing behind him, rubbing his tummy with the palm of his hand. He felt Ali heave and another volley of vomit sploshed into the pan, followed by a loud burp and some more sick. The sharp stink of vomit filled the small room. Ali dribbled and spat a bit then straightened up.

"I am sorry."

"No worries. Do you feel a little bit better now?"

"I think so." He cleaned himself up in the sink and they returned to the sitting room.

"Why don't we go to your bedroom and you can sleep for a bit?"

Ali agreed.

Tim got him two aspirin dissolved in a little water and made him drink it. He sat with him until he fell asleep. At bed time Tim brought Ali two more dissolved aspirin and, at his mothers' suggestion, moved a camp bed into Ali's room to sleep with him for reassurance.

They talked into the night. Ali said he was feeling better and was hungry. Tim advised him not to eat until breakfast.

"Tim, Usman told me that you would be my friend and now I know for sure that this is true. It was not nice for you to see me vomit but you stayed with me and made me feel better. Now you have come to stay in my room with me."

"And I told you that you have become part of our family now Ali."

In the morning, after a hearty breakfast Mrs Croy sent the boys out to the trout farm to buy some fish.

"Ali will find it interesting."

They spent the morning looking at the fish in their tanks, in increasing size. Ali was fascinated and had endless questions, not all of which Tim was able to answer with any authority. He began to understand that Ali was blessed with an immense intelligence. He would be a great success.

When they returned Ali took the fresh fish to Mrs. Croy in the kitchen.

"What did you think of the fish farm?"

Ali spoke animatedly. He would like to make something like that in Jeddah one day.

"I'm glad you enjoyed it. You seem happier than you've been since you arrived."

"I am very happy now. Because you and Tim were so kind to me yesterday. Truly you are like my mother. I know for sure that I will be safe in England, like Usman said."

Mrs. Croy wiped her hands on her apron, strode across to her young charge and hugged him. "Thank you dear. That was such a kind thing to say. I promise that we will all do as much as we can to make things good for you."

The remaining days sped past and soon it was the first day of the new academic year at Somerton School. New boys and their families were invited to a special tea at Three O' Clock. Mrs. Croy insisted that Tim was to come with her and Ali.

Tim felt incredibly nervous and uncomfortable. It had such frightening similarities to his first afternoon at Barforth, seven years ago. He was unable to admit or explain his fears to his mother and he obviously had to appear positive and confident so as to support and encourage Ali. This was Ali's day and it was he who would be feeling fearful. Tim would return safely home after enduring a maximum of two hours discomfort. Even so, as he and Ali, dressed in crisp, uncomfortable uniform, got into the back of the car Tim was feeling as if he might well be sick. Tim and his mother kept up a steady stream of light hearted conversation to which Ali bravely responded. The journey took longer than the one to Barforth and they arrived with little time to spare before tea. They decided to unload the car afterwards.

"We can ask Mr. Boyd, your House Master, where to take your things, it will be better than struggling with them when we don't know where we're going."

The "Welcome Tea Party" was signposted, as it had been at Barforth. The Dining Hall felt uncomfortably similar to Tim, with the stern portraits of past Head Masters scowling down upon the visitors. Tim was feeling more and more uncomfortable. The place even smelt like his old school. "Please God make it easy for Ali and protect him from the horrors that Usman and I experienced," Tim prayed silently.

The Head Master, younger looking than Tim's had been, welcomed and shook hands with each of them. Mrs Croy introduced Tim and explained that he would be visiting Ali quite often.

"Let me find Mr. Boyd. He has everything ready for you Ali" The Head Master strode away, leaving the three nibbling cakes.

"Try to eat plenty Ali." Tim advised. "You probably won't get such nice food again!"

A cheerfully exuberant man with wavy fair hair bounced up and introduced himself as Tim Boyd. They talked for a bit as they finished their tea. Tim introduced himself and explained his role in Ali's guardianship.

"Let's go and find his study. Where are you parked?" Mrs. Croy explained. "If there's room in the car for me I can get you much closer to where we are going."

They all returned to the car and Mr. Boyd sat in the front directing them to the study block where Ali was to be based.

"I asked Dave Brown to come back to school early, on the promise of enjoying the welcome tea party, so he's here, waiting to welcome you Ali. There's nothing worse than being left all alone in a new school. Dave volunteered to share a room with you and I'm sure that he will be a good friend to get you settled."

Tim warmed to this man, remembering the horrible way that Usman had been left, abandoned for hours, until he had found him alone and dejected.

Mr Boyd led them along a wide, light passage to Study ten. He knocked on the door which was flung open by a tall, smiling boy with chestnut brown hair.

"Dave, this is Ali Albad. Would you help him get his things in from the car please?"

Mrs Croy gave Ali the car key. Tim was looking around the large study. There were two beds, built in desks and cupboards and book shelves and even two easy chairs, all in warm brown and orange tones. This was more hotel than school. It made the best that Barforth had had to offer appear inadequate.

"I made sure that Ali got into one of the better blocks. It's so important that he at least feels warm and comfortable, especially in the first few days which will be daunting for him. We will all be keeping a careful eye on him."

He stopped talking as the boys came in with Ali's trunk. They went back to the car for the remaining things.

"I'll keep you posted about his settling in progress. Is there anything that's worrying him especially?"

"He's very worried that his English may not be good enough, but I think he will be fine." Tim felt it best to make things clear. "And he's worried that he won't fit in, being foreign and because all the other boys have been friends for three years already. It can be difficult to break into existing groups." "Oh, and there's the food problem. He has to eat halal meat or vegetarian or fish."

Mr. Boyd smiled. "He's certainly got a great guardian in you! I truly believe that we are a happy and welcoming school. I know that we all say that but I'm happy to let Ali confirm that to you after a week or so. Food is not a problem. There is always a decent vegetarian option, anything made with chicken is halal and we often have fish of some kind. I will explain all this to him and Dave will be with him in the first few days to help him. They are both studying the same subjects so they will be together all the time."

The boys returned.

"Is that everything?"

"Yes sir."

"Well I'll leave you to say your good byes. Dave, bring Ali back to the party when the Croys go, you deserve your tea and I bet Ali hasn't had enough either!" He bounced away.

Tim proffered his hand to Dave, who looked a little surprised.

"Thank you for all your help, and especially for coming back to school early."

He shook Ali's hand. "'Phone us when you can Ali. I'll come to take you out a week on Sunday. Try to have fun!"

Mrs Croy hugged Ali. "I can feel that you're going to have a great time."

Tim and his mother left.

Last of the Summer

"Tim. **Tim!**"

Tim came hurrying in from his seat on the sunny terrace.

"Mohammed's on the 'phone dear."

Tim padded into the hall and picked up the receiver from the cabinet on which sat the telephone.

"Hi Ed! Where are you? "

"Hi Tim. I'm parked on the High Street, beside Barclays bank."

"I'll be with you in ten, mate."

Tim was excited at the prospect of welcoming his friend.

"I'm just off to get him Mum. Should be back in twenty minutes. OK?"

Tim jumped into his Avenger and headed off for the town centre. There was Ed's Renault. Tim parked a few yards up the road and walked over to the car. Ed jumped out, laughing.

"That was quick man!"

"I didn't want you sitting beside the road when you could be having fun! Follow me!"

Tim started his car and waited until he saw the Renault approaching. He indicated and pulled out.

Ed followed Tim, becoming increasingly concerned at the narrowness of the lanes. He had always lived in a town and had never had reason to venture into such remote territory. He was relieved when he saw Tim indicate and swing into a wide gravelled drive. They parked to the left of the imposing house.

"That is some house Tim! You didn't tell me you were aristocracy!"

"That's because I'm not!"

The friends laughed and Tim led Ed inside. They went straight into the kitchen to meet Mrs. Croy.

"Hello!"

"Hello Mrs. Croy. I'm Mohammed. Thank you so much for inviting me."

"We always enjoy meeting Timothy's friends. I think it makes us feel young again! You're just in time for coffee to revive you after the journey. Take him out to the terrace dear, it's a shame to waste the sunshine!"

"*Tim!*"

"What?"

"That pool. Is that yours too?"

Tim blushed, unused to such attention being paid to his parents' success. "Yes. But you should see how much work it takes every day to keep it looking good. We can swim after lunch if you want, it's nice and warm, even by my standards!"

"The garden's superb too man."

Tim laughed. "You can mow the lawn as well if you want!"

Mrs. Croy appeared with mugs of coffee and a plate of biscuits.

"Thank you!" Ed was impressing her.

"What's with introducing yourself as Mohammed?" It was his turn to be knocked off balance.

"It's your fault actually! You've impressed me so much with your decision to become a Muslim Tim that I decided that it's a disgrace that I have been trying to hide my religion for as long as I can remember. So now I am Mohammed and proud of it. I'm trying to pray properly too, but that's not so easy. I *will* do it though."

Tim stood and shook his hand. "I'm proud of you Mohammed! Maybe we can learn together when we get back to Hull. I will need lots of help."

"You're deffo going to do it then?"

"Yes. Parents are OK with it and Sarah says she is too. So, as soon as Usman's back I will take Shahada."

"That is fantastic news Tim." Mohammed pumped Tim's hand.

Just before Dinner the 'phone rang. Tim answered and was delighted to hear Ali's voice.

"How's it going Ali?"

"It is good Tim. I should not have felt so frightened. Dave is helping me so much and everyone is being kind to me."

"Brilliant news. Here's mum."

"Hello Ali dear I gather it is going well for you."

"Yes Mrs. Croy. You have chosen a very good school for me."

"We will be coming to take you out on Sunday. See you then."

"Thank you. Bye."

There was roast chicken for dinner.

"It is halal Mohammed. I'm well used to the needs of Muslims now!"

"That is very kind of you Mrs. Croy. Most people don't know or care."

"Mohammed had a hard time at his school too. It's really disgraceful."

"It is, yes."

"I think you've done well for Ali though. Maybe they will restore our faith!"

Later, sitting in Tim's room, enjoying tea and biscuits, Tim was concerned that Mohammed seemed unusually quiet.

"It's silly really Tim. Just that your mum is so thoughtful, searching for halal food just for me. And then you telling her I had a hard time at school. It reminded me of just how hard it was. I didn't know how bad it had been until I got to Hull and, especially, joined your crew. The four of you just completely accepted me. I was never "Paki" or "Wog" I was just Ed. You all really tried to include me in your fun."

"Did people call you things like that at school?"

"Yes, always. And worse."

"What was worse?"

"People refused to sit near me or to share a room with me." Mohammed went quiet.

Tim could see him swallowing hard.

"Can I tell you something Tim. I've never spoken about it before but I trust you and I think it will help me."

"I won't tell another living soul."

"Well almost as soon as I joined the school, they started teasing me because they said they knew I was circumcised. Then one day a group ambushed me and stripped me to find out."

Tim saw a tear run down Mohammed's cheek. He moved to sit beside him and put his arm round him. He had a dreadful feeling of what was coming next. Mohammed gulped.

"I'm sorry Tim. This is disgusting."

"Go on man, you've nearly done it."

"Yeah. I was trying not to get angry or upset because I didn't want them to find it funny and do it again. So, I just let them do it to me. Two of them started playing with it and made it hard. They all laughed and said that that proved that I liked it so I must be gay. From that day on I was called "Gwog,"an abbreviation for gay wog."

"Oh God!" Tim hugged Mohammed, who was crying properly now. When he finally began to calm down Tim told him about his rape. The two young men cried together some more, almost relieved to know somebody else who had suffered as badly.

"Now I know why you were so cautious and guarded when we first knew you. You felt frightened and threatened by how nasty you know people can be."

"Yes."

"Shit! The tea's gone cold. I'll go get some more. I think we both need some, very warm and sweet!"

When he came back Mohammed was composed.

"I'm sorry about that Tim, and thanks for listening. I kind of feel a weight off me now. And I'm so sorry about what happened to you."

"Bastards the whole lot of them!"

They both laughed and began to enjoy their hot, sweet tea.

"Eat your breakfast fast Mohammed. After last night we both need some fun!"

Tim raided the freezer for some frozen rolls and collected some salad things from the vegetable garden. He searched the coach house and returned with two ancient coal axes and a sturdy leather bag which he put in the boot of the car. He took a box of matches from the kitchen drawer.

"What's the grand plan Tim?" Mohammed asked as they were getting into the car.

"Well I think we need a bit of fun and adventure. We both got really upset last night."

"I actually feel good today Tim. I feel like I've emptied at least part of my head from the pain. And knowing about what happened to you makes it seem less serious too."

"It will never be less serious Mohammad, but a problem shared is a problem halved, or so somebody very wise once said. I just feel so disgusted at the way people like me were so racist to you. For what it's worth I am sorry."

The sun was shining, the country roads were clear and Tim put the radio on. The mood lifted steadily to one of joyful youthfulness. Tim pulled into a garage and bought a disposable barbeque. As they continued their journey the landscape became hillier and more dramatic.

"Look Mohammed. The Sea!"

"It looks fantastic. So blue, almost as if it belongs on a postcard from abroad."

They parked in the grassy field that a farmer had diversified into a summer car park, paid their two pounds and Tim took the bag and coal axes out of the boot.

"What are they for Tim? I've been worried all morning!"

"You'll understand in a minute mate."

They clambered down the steep but well-worn path to the rocky cove. Tim led his friend along the beach to get further away from most of the visitors. He started searching the rocks.

"Look at this!"

Mohammed came over. "A fossil. Cool."

"This is known as the Jurassic Coast for a reason! Do you collect fossils?"

"No"

"Well today you're going to start. We'll stop when we've got twenty in the bag for you."

Tim showed him how, by splitting and chipping the rocks it was easy to remove complete fossils. He handed his friend one of the axes and the boys busied themselves collecting their trophies. When they had achieved their target, Tim stood up straight and laughed.

"These poor things have all been dead and extinct for millions of years Mohammed. But you and I are two great survivors of boarding school!"

Mohammed laughed and thumped Tim on the back. "You can turn anything into fun Tim!"

They lugged the heavy bag up to the car and returned with the barbeque and provisions. Tim took a detour to a small fresh fish stall and bought two fish and a pound of large prawns.

"This is going to be a feast!"

They found a sheltered spot, lit the barbeque and sat waiting for the flames to die down. Tim flipped the two fish on to it and arranged the prawns around them.

"Now we wait ten minutes."

The meal was excellent and left the friends full and lazy, sunning themselves.

"Sarah 'phoned you Tim. I told her you'd call back."

"OK but first we need some tea!"

"I hope Tim hasn't been dragging you too far Mohammed. He does tend to get these wild ideas."

"That's why we all like Tim Mrs. Croy. He encourages us to push ourselves. Especially in rowing!" Mohammed laughed.

The boys took their mugs of tea and the biscuit tin out to the terrace.

"Do you fancy a swim later?"

"I'm not the worlds' best swimmer to be honest Tim."

"Me neither, but it's good to mess about in water. Relaxes you."

"Good evening Mrs. Andrews, it's Tim. Sarah asked me to call back."

"Tim, how are you dear. Are you coming to see us soon? Have you recovered from your dissertation yet? Michael's still sulking about his!"

"I think I'm sulking too, if you ask about it. But mostly I'm trying to pretend it never happened."

"That's an excellent policy Tim. I shall tell Michael to adopt it at once. Here's Sarah."

"Tim! How's it going?"

"Good thanks."

"Have you got a tent?"

"Yes. Why?"

"You're taking me camping next week then. Mike and Liz are going and you and I are joining them."

"Cool! Where are we going?"

"Wales."

"Wales? Can't we go somewhere else?"

"Wales is beautiful Tim."

"I'll believe you, but with difficulty Sarah. I've only ever experienced the dark side of Wales!"

"Well you'd better keep your mind open Tim."

"I'll try. I'll be with you, midmorning on Monday. See you then. Give my best to Mike and ask him about our CCF camping trip in Wales!"

"Did you have to endure the CCF Mohammed?"

"Yeah. I was stupid enough to join the Army section because I didn't have a clue what it would involve. Marching up and down all afternoon being verbally abused by a retired Sargent Major!"

"I was in the RAF section and we had to do that too. And assault courses and camping trips in Wales."

"We had to spend three days camping in the Lake District. It rained and snowed the whole time and, by the time I got back to school, I was so ill I spent a week in the san, which was even worse than the camping had been!"

"That proves what I said about you and me being true survivors!" They laughed at the memory of their past suffering.

Chatting over their mugs of tea and biscuits in Tim's room that night Tim steered their thoughts towards the Boat Club stall at the Freshers Bazaar.

"We've got to make it really attractive. Last year we tried and we got quite a few recruits but most of them never actually turned up. In fact, you're the only real success story. We *must* attract some more experienced oarsmen or at least some guys who seriously want to learn because this time next year you will be the only remaining member of the men's crew."

"Shit!"

"Exactly. Obviously in February you are going to become Captain of the club so you've got to take some responsibility for this recruitment drive."

"Oh, thanks Tim! No pressure on me then."

"We'll all be involved. I'll dress up as a prat like cox again – I'm sure you had a good laugh about me last year, didn't you?"

Mohammed looked sheepish.

"Exactly! I think we should display the Kevin Dunn, try to hang it up above the stand, see if we can find a way of putting the oars in it too, as it looks on the water. Richard took miles of video of us winning races in the Spring and Summer and Tom's going to compile the best of them into a constant play loop. He's good at that kind of thing. But we need to really make the whole stand attractive and tempting. I've heard that you're pretty creative in your spare time so I think you've got a lot to contribute."

"How did you hear that?"

"I have my spies Mohammed." Tim grinned. "And I saw the way you'd decorated your room. It was incredibly skilful."

Mohammed thumped Tim gently. "I think that you are the spy mate!"

Tim set off for Somerton immediately after Sunday breakfast. He arrived early, the school was empty and silent, evidently the church service was still in progress. Tim could hear thunderous singing from the distant church. He sat in the car with the window open and remembered chapel at Barforth. It seemed a long time ago now, though the pain of some events there was as overpowering as ever, evidenced by the recent tears with Mohammed. Tim mouthed a silent prayer that Ali would be saved from any such incidents.

Tim truly believed that, if anybody that he knew and loved had such a thing done to him he would not be able to stop himself from committing murder. Maybe he should just give himself up to the police now, before he did something terrible. He felt horrible, contemplating the damage that that school had inflicted upon him. He knew now that he would never be able to overcome it. He doubted that Mohammed would either. His thoughts were brought to an end by the sound of hundreds of boys streaming through the car park, freed at last from church. He watched for Ali, wondering if he would recognise his car.

There he was! Looking such a grown man in his blue suit, white shirt and school tie. Tim laughed inwardly. Ali came to the car.

"Shall I change here or come in my suit?"

"I think you have to leave school in your suit. You've got casuals at home, so let's roll!"

Tim nosed his car into the stream of Volvos and Jaguars taking boys home for lunch. Tim felt a little inferior in his elderly Avenger. He laughed about it with Ali.

"How's the first two weeks been then Ali?" Tim began the first of the many questions that he knew poor Ali would be subjected to during the day.

"Al hamdulillah! It has been much better than I was afraid it might be. Dave is a very good friend to me and now I am starting to make more real friends."

"Good man! I told you you'd be fine. How are you finding the lessons? Not too difficult to understand the English?"

"The lessons are very good Tim. So much more interesting than in Jeddah. Mostly I do understand the English and if I do not somebody will always help me."

Mrs Croy hugged Ali when they arrived at the house.

"You're looking good! I haven't seen you so relaxed."

"Thank you. I am very happy in fact. I think I will enjoy school in England. Now I am pleased that I did decide to have this adventure."

"Well go and change out of your suit and let's have lunch."

The day passed quickly. Tim and Ali spent a long time putting up scaffolding beside an early apple tree and picking the crisp apples. A large box was put in the boot of Tim's car for Ali to take to school.

"I have never seen apples on a tree before. In Jeddah we have only dates and bananas."

"I've never seen dates or bananas growing." Tim laughed.

First thing on Monday Tim set off for Sarah's house. He had his tent and a camping gas stove together with an airbed and sleeping bag and a few clothes and washing things in his holdall. He was pleased to arrive before eleven. Mike was loading his car with extensive looking kit when he pulled onto the drive way.

"Mike! What's with so much kit?"

"Tim! Long time, no see! Well I don't want it to turn out like that CCF trip to wales!"

Both friends laughed, shared memories of blisters and cold filling each boys mind. Mike took Tim inside where his mother had coffee waiting.

"Why has it been so long Tim?"

"Well I blame the dissertation idea!"

"Don't mention the D word again or you'll set Michael off and then you'll never get away."

Sarah came smiling in. Tim hugged her then pulled away quickly for fear that someone would see that he was hard. He had missed her so much. Now they had a week together in a tent. Tim was looking forward to that at least. He had still not been able to disconnect the words Wales and misery in his mind. Mike came back with Liz. He introduced Tim as his "best mate". Tim felt shy at the description, knowing that he had once let Mike down seriously. He had never stopped beating himself up over that incident.

At last they were getting into Mike's car. Liz was in the front with Mike and Tim and Sarah in the back. It was a nice change for Tim to have neither driving nor navigating responsibilities.

"You're quiet today, Tim" Mike observed.

"I keep remembering our CCF trip to Wales, and that other time when we went on a map reading exercise for Field Day. That was miserable too, all cold and damp and misty. I'm struggling to imagine having a nice time in Wales at all. I hope this is going to change my perception."

"You're such a misery Tim." Sarah poked him in the thigh. "Wales is *beautiful.*"

"Tim's right. If you'd only experienced what we have you'd feel the same. I had a terrible cold, and crippling blisters for two weeks, after our camping trip." Mike willingly supported his friend against his sister.

"Even so he should be in the holiday mood." Sarah persisted.

"The only reason I came is that I know that being with you will make everything nice." Tim grinned. He received the provoked painful poke in the thigh.

Mile after mile of the M4 unfolded like a long grey carpet in front of the car. Tim was surprised that the sun continued to shine and that the sky remained relentlessly blue. That, combined with the joy of sitting so close to Sarah caused even his spirits to lift.

As Mike turned off the motorway at last Tim was surprised to see green hills and stone farm houses bathing peacefully in the late afternoon sunshine. Maybe he had been unjust to Wales after all. After a few more miles the road climbed a long hill and, as they passed the summit there appeared before them the sparkling blue sea, flanked by a wide, white sandy beach. It looked, even Tim was forced to admit, spectacular.

The camp site was right beside the beach and, as soon as they had pitched their tents, the four headed to the beach to feel the sand and sea between their toes.

They decided to celebrate the start of the holiday by eating in the restaurant and they spent two hours enjoying plenty of food and beer.

"Are you still violently opposed to Wales Tim?" Sarah joked.

Tim conceded that he had been unfair to base his judgement on a whole country on two uncomfortable school memories.

"But they were bloody awful!" Mike added, mostly to seek the satisfaction of a reaction from his sister.

As they were preparing for bed, huffing and puffing to inflate recalcitrant air beds, unfurling sleeping bags and grumbling about lack of space in the tiny ridge tents Mike called Tim urgently. Tim emerged, glad to have been released from trying to blow up Sarah's bed, already breathless from his efforts with his own. Mike indicated to him to follow him. Once out of earshot of the girls Mike looked embarrassed.

"I'm sorry Tim, but have you got a couple of condoms I can have. I've got a horrible feeling I left mine in the kitchen. Now I'm going to endure endless lectures from mum when we get back. She's certain to have found them and she will be looking forward to humiliating me."

"No probs mate." Tim got his bag and handed Mike three square foils.

"If you can't be good, at least be careful!" Tim couldn't resist teasing his best friend.

Mike thumped Tim playfully. "Thanks mate!"

The next few days were spent exploring the fantastic coastal scenery of West Wales. Tim's constant sniping about Wales was silenced as he had first to admit that this area was beautiful and then, gradually he began to accept that he needed to rid himself of his prejudice altogether. It really was not fair to pass judgement on a place just because Barforth had caused him to experience the very worst aspects of it.

Sarah began to adopt a very irritating "I told you so" attitude which Tim had to accept he had brought upon himself. Mike was not so generous to his sister and warned Tim that that was what she was like most of the time in real life, when she wasn't trying to impress him.

Tim and Liz couldn't stop themselves from enjoying seeing their lovers descending into their childhood roles in that way. Siblings the world over seem to enjoy the same kind of love hate relationship.

Tim led an expedition to collect cockles and muscles on the beach to cook on a driftwood fire.

"Usman taught me this and, once I had got over my fear of being poisoned, I found it's great fun."

Liz collected some green fronds of seaweed that she assured everyone would be deliciously crispy when cooked. The Andrews sibling were not at all keen on the idea but they had the courage to try the food and, by the time the meal was finished, they too had been converted to the concept of the Saudi beach barbeque. They spent a day exploring the ancient town of St. David's and Tim was taken aback when Mike presented him with a paper bag containing a packet of Durex.

"Why?"

"You gave me some when I was in need so I'm returning them." Mike made everything simple.

"You didn't need to mate. It's hardly a big deal."

"It was a very big deal for me!"

Tim and Sarah lay in their tent, the morning sunshine starting to make it very warm. They were relaxed after making love twice in an hour, both blissfully content. Tim reflected that this would almost certainly be the last time that he had sex for at least a year. He wondered if he could really go through with his wish to become Muslim. If he did, he knew that he had to do it properly and this aspect was going to be very difficult. Out of habit he simply buried the worry in the back of his mind.

The day after he returned from Wales Tim went to meet Usman at Heathrow. It was good to have his friend with him again. Both boys really had become like brothers. Tim's parents also seemed genuinely joyful to have Usman back with them. It was evident to Tim that they, too, had developed a very special relationship with him.

On Sunday Usman drove them to Somerton School. They were going to take Ali and Dave out for a meal. Usman wanted to look round the school too, interested to make comparisons with Barforth.

"You'll be amazed. I couldn't believe how much better it is. Just wait until you see Ali's room. It's better than School Study One, and he's only in the lower sixth."

They sat in the car waiting for the boys to be released from church. Tim wound down the window to let in the distant sounds of hymn singing.

"I bet you miss chapel Usman?"

Usman laughed. "Soon, InshaAllah, you will be coming to the mosque with me."

"Yes, I will. I am looking forward to it now."

The conversation was interrupted as Ali and Dave approached the car.

"I think we should change from our suits first. Nobody will know and it is more comfortable."

Ali introduced Usman to Dave. Usman locked the car.

"I want to see this school Ali. You two can give me a tour, earn your lunch!" The four set off together.

After a very thorough tour of Somerton, which left both Usman and Tim speechless, they got into the car and headed off to the town.

"Are you OK with Pizza Dave?" Tim asked.

"Yes please!" Tim smiled at the boyish enthusiasm. It brought back memories of his first meal out with the Andrews family.

They took a large table and each ordered the pizza of choice. Usman added lots of different side dishes to double the size of the meal. He naturally assumed that both of the guests would be half starved as he and Tim had always been.

"Dave you have been a truly good friend to Ali. I know how important a friend is when you come to a new school from overseas. Tim became my special friend. I would have run away back home if it was not for him. I and my parents want to truly thank you from our hearts."

Dave was blushing. "I wanted to do it. And Ali is a great guy to have as a friend."

The food arrived, thus sparing poor Dave from further embarrassment. Usman told them about being forced to shave in front of the whole house on his first night. Dave was appalled. When they had finished their meal, rounded off with Italian ice creams that Usman insisted they all needed, they explored the town. Dave led them to a fast-flowing brook. Tim recounted the story of being Brook Ball Boy. At length they found a tea shop where Usman once again bought an excess of tempting foods. He broke all English conventions by asking for a paper bag so that the two boys could take the remaining cakes back to school with them.

"When you are foreign you can get away with many things Ali!" Usman explained.

As they drove home, they chatted about the amazing differences between Barforth and Somerton.

"I think all our parents were well cheated. They should complain and get some of their money back. Especially yours Usman. They were ripped off just because they live in another country."

"I am just glad that Ali is happy. He is not as tough as I am. Barforth would have hurt him very badly."

They drove in silence for a while. Tim needed to talk to Usman but he was struggling with the enormity, the finality, of what he was going to say.

Deep breath! "Usman."

"Yes?"

"Would you be able to come up to Hull for the second weekend of term?"

"I guess so. Why?"

"Because I am going to take Shahada and it would mean a lot if you could be with me Usman. It's mainly because of you and Mohammed that I am going to do this."

"Tim! I will be there for sure. And I will bring Ali with me too. He will be so pleased for you. Shit! I feel like I might cry."

Usman reached out his left hand and thumped Tim on the shoulder.

A New Man!

At the end of the Summer term Tim had been voted in to the position of Senior Resident at number 73. It was a useful "position of responsibility" to be able to write on his CV and on job application forms and it meant that he got a large single room for the same price as a shared room. He rather looked forward to organizing and managing the house that he had grown to love during the past two years.

Tim was expected to return two days early to prepare himself and the house. He found a pile of letters on the hall table, all addressed to "The Senior Resident". That was him! He remembered having to write a similar letter himself, two years ago, to confirm when he was expecting to arrive. How fast those two years had passed. Tim thought with a shudder that soon he would be pushed out of university and into the wide world of work. He turned and went out to the car to unload it. He took his things up to the Senior Residents' room. He felt a weird thrill of excitement. The room was large and he was important. A success, as he had never been at school. He went up to his old room and moved the things that he had left there down to his new home.

He went to the kitchen, all clean and empty, to boil some water for tea. He sat, alone in the big common room, drinking his tea and eating biscuits as he opened and read twelve similarly awkward letters to him introducing the name of a new boy and advising him of his time of arrival. Tim smiled, imagining the trepidation that each would be feeling right now. It was his job to help them settle in happily. He would allocate them their rooms on a list soon, so that he would be organised when they began to arrive. First, he would go to the supermarket.

Tim awoke early on Saturday. He showered and breakfasted and cleaned up the kitchen. He went to buy a paper and sat in the common room waiting for the first arrival. He felt strangely nervous, for reasons that he could not understand. At length the doorbell rang. He welcomed the nervous young man to the house and took him to his room. He gave him a brief tour of the house and then made him tea and proffered biscuits. Tim was thus occupied for the next six hours. He was very relieved as some of the second years and then Bill arrived to support him in the task of welcoming the Freshers.

The next few days were spent collecting money from each resident for the communal fund and more money with which to rent a television and buy a licence for it. Tim had to register for his final year and, with the usual documents was a large envelope addressed to "The Graduand" he wasn't sure if that was a real word or a spelling mistake. In either event the documents inside required him to register with the Careers Service and to book an initial interview and a tour of their "extensive facilities". Tim, once again, felt the chill winds of the real adult world reaching out to claim him. It made him feel uneasy, uncomfortable, in a way that he had not felt for two years. He didn't want the happiness that was university to come to an end. He struggled to put these concerns to the back of his mind.

The crew spent ages setting up the Boat Club stand at the Freshers' Bazaar. Tim borrowed two hoists from the Car Club from which they suspended the Kevin Dunn, high above the reach of visitors. Mohammed had had several action shots of their winning races enlarged and he mounted them very professionally. Tom had edited the various film loops that Richard had taken into a continuously running video which was played through a large television. They had decided to sell some of the Boat Club ties, as there were more than one hundred still in the box and it was evident that they would never be used. Any income that they could generate would be welcome. Tim went home and returned dressed in his coxes' outfit and the four oarsmen bravely stood in shorts and hooped vests. In contrast to the previous year they managed to generate a lot of interest and to get nearly forty new recruits. Mohammed had to be given most credit for that. He was a born salesman.

Tim went to see Mohammed. It was strange to think that this time last year they had never met. They were so close now.

"I need your help to arrange things. I hope to do whatever it is I have to do to become Muslim the Saturday after next. Can you talk to the guy for me and see if you can arrange it for then?"

Mohammed leapt to his feet, a huge grin spreading from ear to ear. He moved towards Tim and suddenly he was at the centre of a breath-taking bear hug that lifted him off his feet.

"Oh Tim! That's amazing news. I will sort that for you straight away. Shit I don't know how to say the right thing. No words seem big enough. I feel so proud to know you."

Later that evening Mohammed come to see Tim.

"It's all arranged. Eleven O'clock Saturday after next. You'll say Shahada in front of the Imam and a few witnesses and you will officially be a Muslim."

Tim waited on the telephone, listening to the sounds of student life in Southampton.

"Hello, Tim?"

"Usman. Please can you come the weekend after next. Try to get Ali to come with you. It's all arranged."

"Tim! That's brilliant. I can't wait to tell Ali. I am so pleased for you. It will be the best decision you will ever make in all your life."

Tim returned to the house early on Friday afternoon. He knew that Usman and Ali would be arriving at some point and he wanted to be there to greet them. He had found it difficult to focus on his work anyway, his mind kept leaping to his worries about the massive change that he was about to make to his whole life. The closer he got to the occasion the more he wanted to do it but, simultaneously, the more nervous he became. He heard Nick shout for him. That must be them! He bounded down the stairs to see the open front door and his visitors on the door step.

"Didn't he even invite you in? No manners!" Usman hugged Tim and Ali shook his hand. "Come and get some tea."

Later Mohammed came around. Tim introduced him to Ali and Usman.

"Usman was my first ever Muslim friend."

"I've heard so much about you Usman. Tim really rates you."

"It is only because Tim was so kind and friendly to me on my first day at school that I am here now. He truly changed my life."

"And now you three are about to change mine!" Tim interjected before Usman could embarrass him further.

Most of the house occupants headed off to the pub by about seven and Tim got his three friends to come to the kitchen with him while he cooked dinner.

"I'm going to make Paella. I've tried making it several times so it should work out OK. I got Mohammed to buy me some chicken from the halal shop so it will be good for all of you to eat."

"I'm impressed Tim, I don't think I could boil an egg!" Ali was laughing.

"Tim is a brilliant cook! I often deliberately visit him when he's likely to be cooking so that he has to invite me!" Mohammed joked.

"Tim has taught me to cook too. In Spain he taught me and my brother to make a feast for our families with fish that we caught in the sea. My mother is still talking about it. She even made me cook when I went home for a holiday so Tim has much to answer for!"

Tim was blushing. "When I first came here I could only fry bacon or sausages or boil up a Vesta meal. But I didn't want to starve so I had to learn. I rather enjoy it now."

The finished meal was delicious and everybody ate everything that was served. They had juices to drink and Tim had made an upside-down cake for pudding which he served with cream. Ali insisted on writing down the recipe there and then.

"I want to make this every day!" he declared.

When the drunken boys began to return to the house the four friends decided it was time to move on.

"If it's OK with you Ali, Mohammed has offered to have you stay with him. There isn't really room for three of us in my room."

"That's cool. We'll see you in the morning!"

Usman and Tim made mugs of tea and, armed with the now obligatory packet of chocolate Digestives, they went up to Tim's room.

"I am glad to have some time alone with you Tim."

"I am too. I am feeling rather strange to be honest Usman. Not frightened but kind of apprehensive, like just before you do a big exam or something."

"It is a very big thing that you are doing Tim. I think the biggest thing that you will ever do. But I do promise that I will look after you Tim, as you have looked after me for four years now. I thank Allah for the chance to help you now."

"Please Usman, you're making me feel like I'm going to cry now. You're a great guy and I've loved every minute of knowing you."

"And I feel the same Tim. That is why I said that." "Have you chosen a Muslim name yet?"

"No, I don't really know any."

"I have been thinking about it a lot Tim. I think Ali had a good idea when he said that he had not changed his name much. If you can keep the initial T. you can move between your Arabic and English names easily and just sign things T. Croy."

"Sounds good to me."

"You know that all Arabic names have meanings Tim?"

"I had read that, yes."

"Well one name beginning with T has a very good meaning that is exactly right for you Tim."

"Tell me. It needs to be easy for an English man to say!"

"The name is Tamam. It means generous. And you are the most generous man I have ever met."

"Tamam. I can say that. Cheers Usman! Tamam it is!"

"Thankyou Tim. It is a very big privilege to give a man a new name. I feel a bit emotional."

"Me too Usman. I just want to say that you are an incredibly special friend. I believe that Allah pushed us together to bring me to this point."

"And to make me stay in England Tim. If it was not for you, I was ready to call my dad to take me home on that first day at school. Truly you changed everything for me."

"I still feel terrified of getting circumcised Usman. Please pray for me to have the courage to do it."

"Allah will make it easy for you Tim. Allah promises that he will never test someone beyond what he can bear and that has always been true for me. Like what I was just saying. I was nearly crying when you came to talk to me that first day and suddenly everything became good again."

Tim woke early after a restless night. He had to go to the union to one of the rooms upstairs where he would meet with the Imam and a few Muslim students to witness his shahada. He was feeling queasy with trepidation, more to do with shyness for being the centre of attention than for the enormity of what he was about to do. He crept out of his room to wash. Usman was deeply asleep. He went to the kitchen and boiled a kettle. He needed coffee but was not hungry. He went back to his room to dress. Usman was waking up now.

"I'll be in the kitchen mate" Tim said.

Usman joined Tim in the kitchen as he was slurping his coffee. "Coffee?"

"Yes please Tim."

"What else do you want? There's cornflakes or toast or I can borrow a couple of eggs."

"What are you having?"

"I can't eat."

"Tim you must eat something. I will make some toast for both of us. You do not have a choice!" Tim laughed. It was nice to be looked after, to have decisions made for him.

The doorbell rang. Tim went to get it, knowing who it would be. Mohammed and Ali came in.

"Have you had breakfast?"

"Yes. Mohammed looked after me brilliantly Tim."

"I think we should be going soon Tim. Are you all psyched up?"

"I'm shaking to be honest. Feeling rather shy. I just want to get it done now."

Mohammed put his arm round Tim. "You'll be fine. We're all with you and Allah will make everything easy for you."

They all piled into Mohammed's Renault and headed for the Union.

Mohammed led the way up to the room on the second floor. He introduced them to the Imam who, in turn, introduced the other men in the room. Tim began to feel very out of his depth. It all seemed so alien. Could he ever be accepted by these people? Would he be able to change enough to fit in? A powerful reaction inside him made him want to turn and run away. He didn't have to do this. The others were all talking together. Tim was left out already. This was his chance. He was going to run. He just couldn't do it.

NO! He had been thinking about adopting Islam for a year now. He definitely wanted to. He would regret it forever if he didn't take this opportunity. Tim swallowed hard and forced a smile. Attention was turning to him. He had missed his chance to escape now. Mohammed touched him gently on his back.

"Let's do it Tim. Just repeat the words after the Imam."

Tim listened carefully, the imam spoke slowly, Tim's mouth was dry, his voice had the sound of a sore throat. Suddenly it was done. Tim was a Muslim. He wasn't Tim any more. Meet Tamam!

The Imam hugged him. The witnesses shook his hand. Ali shook his hand. Mohammed gave him a bear hug, almost squeezing the life out of him. Tim realised that he was crying. Usman hugged him

"Now you are truly my brother. I will never leave you Tamam." Tamam realised that Usman was shaking and crying too. Tamam hugged him again. Suddenly the emotion of the occasion overcame him. He began to cry. Mohammed joined them in a tearful trio.

"I'm sorry Tim. It just made me feel so small, watching you do that. I am so proud to know you Tim."

"That is what I wanted to say too. I have never seen this happen before. I am so glad it is you Tamam. Nobody deserves it more than you!"

At last they were getting into the Renault once again.

"Did I hear Usman calling you Tamam?"

"Yes. He suggested it last night. I liked Ali's advice so I thought I could at least keep the same initial so I can sign things T. Croy still. No change is all change!"

"Brilliant!"

"Where are we going Mohammed?"

"We're getting our celebration lunch!"

"This is the biggest day of celebrations that any of us have ever had" Usman was laughing. "Except Ali of course. He has had this celebration before."

"How are you feeling Tamam?" Ali was speaking quietly.

"I don't know. I was ready to run away before I did it, but now it's all done. I think I just feel overwhelmed. I'm shaking."

"It will all calm down very quickly now. You've jumped off the cliff so now you can start to build your new life. We'll all be here to help you. You'll never be alone."

"Thanks Ali. I know that you understand. It's a real comfort to know you at this moment."

Mohammed was parking. They vacated the car and followed him to a brightly painted restaurant. The Star of Asia.

"This is the best halal restaurant in Hull. InshaAllah we can have a great meal here."

Mohammed helped everyone to choose good things that would not be too hot for them and then ordered lots of additional things to turn a meal into a feast. The mood lightened and Tim began to realise that he was very hungry indeed. As they were finishing the food Mohammed went to the counter. He came back grinning.

"The staff want to meet our newest brother in Islam and give him a small surprise."

Three young men appeared carrying a huge cake with sparklers burning in it. They placed it on the table and, one by one, shook Tamams' hand and hugged him. He insisted that the staff come to sit at the table to help to eat the cake. One of them went to get a large jug of black tea. It became Tamams' duty to cut and serve the cake. He felt very shy.

They piled back into Mohammed's car and drove to the student village. In His room each of the boys gave Tamam a present. A fine, silk prayer mat from Usman, A book about the daily routines of Muslim life from Ali, who had written inside it that this book had helped him through the first months of being a Muslim. Mohammed gave him a big book of teachings of the Prophet.

"I want to work through this with you Tamam. I told you I was going to learn with you. You've motivated me like nobody else has ever managed to."

Tamam felt very emotional again. He struggled to hold back more tears.

"We should pray together. It will be Mahgrib soon and we need to pray Asr" Ali reminded them.

" I will teach Tamam to make Wuduh" Mohammed volunteered. "Just copy me"

When they returned to the room Usman stood in front to lead the prayer and the other three stood behind him, Tamam in the middle. Again, he was told to simply copy what the others did.

Later that evening they drove to the university to pray Isha in the Union prayer room. Then they went into the city centre.

"I have booked a table at a famous fish restaurant" Usman told them. "I asked Mohammed to help me because he could check it to be sure it is good."

They all enjoyed another excellent meal. Tamam was able to fully enjoy it this time because he was feeling his usual self again. Towards the end of the meal he stood up.

"I just want to say a big thank you to all of you for the presents and the support today. And most of all I want to say how much all of you have helped me to reach this day. I would never have got here without you three. Really you have become the best, most important friends that I have ever had. Allah knows that I can't find the right words for this but I pray that He rewards you all."

Mohammed Stood. "Tamam I need to tell you, in front of our friends, that you, single handed, saved my religion for me. I was a terrible mess when you first knew Ed and I'm not much better now but seeing you choosing Islam and asking for my help made me face up to my mistakes and I am trying to put things right. I know that we will grow together."

Next Usman stood, "Tamam. You made yourself my friend when I was all alone and very frightened. You shared your friends with me and you protected me from many bad things. Later you shared your family and home with me. You nursed me when I was very sick. And, like Mohammed, your interest in Islam made me understand how bad I had become and made me change. Now you are truly my brother and it is my turn to look after you."

To everyone's surprise Ali Stood. "I have no history with you. But I can talk from experience. There will be many problems for you to face but Allah will make things easy for you. We will all be here for you and you will quickly find many new people to help you too."

On Sunday Tamam and Mohammed had to go to training at the Boat Club. Usman and Ali went with them to see what they did there. Usman remembered watching Tim race at Barforth and would never forget seeing him win the Princess Elizabeth cup at Henley Royal Regatta. He was rather shocked at the contrast between Barforth Boat Club and Hull University Boat Club.

After lunch Usman and Ali had to set off for the long drive back to Southampton.

Usman hugged Tamam tightly. "I am so proud of you. I will call you often. You will be inside my prayers every day. I know that Mohammed will help you all the time."

Ali shook his hand. "You will find things difficult at first. There will be times when you wonder whatever made you do this. Sometimes you will feel despair. But when you feel bad pray to Allah and go to see Mohammed. I know that he will help you no end."

Tamam found Ali's words especially meaningful because he knew that he was speaking from experience. It was a great comfort to know somebody who had been there before.

"Come on Tamam, let's go back to mine for a bit." Mohammed sensed the sudden feeling of isolation that had enveloped him as soon as his old friend had departed.

Mohammed was feeling very, very, responsible for his friend. Ali had warned him that Tamam would experience every kind of emotion in rapid and repeated succession for the next few weeks and that he would need lots of patient support. He prayed that he would be good at this job that Allah had thrust upon him. He remembered how Tim had looked after him when he had been drunk and when he became dehydrated. How gentle and encouraging he had been when he first joined the crew. He *would* make a success of this responsibility.

Days of Difficulty

Tim woke up as usual on Monday morning. He performed the normal routine of washing, dressing, making and eating breakfast, stuffing whatever he needed into his bag and driving to the campus.

It was while driving that it hit him. He wasn't Tim any more. He was Tamam, a Muslim. His life was not, could never be, the same anymore. The magnitude of what he had done hit him in the temple as his heavy boot had once hit his greatest enemy in his temple. He felt a kind of panic, a delayed shock. He had no idea how he was supposed to behave, to live his life, to get through a day. He had reverted to babyhood, totally dependent upon other people to guide him through every aspect of his life.

He had parked the car now, in his habitual place, without noticing what he was doing. He sat in the car in silence, unable to muster the motivation to get out, not wanting or feeling able to face the newness of his ostensibly familiar life. How could everything that had been so ordinary last week have become so daunting now? Tim, or Tamam or whoever he now was had never felt so totally alone, helpless and desolate in his life before. Maybe this was how Usman had felt on his first day at Barforth. He was so glad that he had helped him then. If Allah was just then, for sure, somebody would help him now. He still didn't feel able to get out of the car. He wanted to sit there alone and cry. He simply didn't know what to do or even who he was. He watched, disinterestedly, other cars parking around him, their drivers jumping out enthusiastically to get on with their day. He had been like them just three days earlier but now it was all over.

Someone was tapping on his window. He didn't want to have to interact with anybody. Why did whoever it was have to choose today to irritate him? He looked out into the smiling face of Mohammed. Tim wound down the window.

"Thank God you're here! Please get in the car." He leaned across to unlock the front passenger door.

Mohammed got in. "Assalamo alaikum Tamam!"

"Wa alaikum salam" He managed by way of reply. Then his voice seemed to become choked.

"What's the matter?" Mohammed's voice was thick with concern. He could see that his friend was suffering and it didn't take a genius to guess why.

Tim tried to put the jumble of thoughts and fears into a coherent explanation but he knew, as he spoke, that he just sounded like a mad man.

"I don't know how I'm supposed to live my life, I don't know what is expected of me now, I don't even know who I am anymore. I feel so alone. I can't even get out of the car. I'm just terrified to be honest." He stopped talking as tears began to cascade freely down his cheeks.

Mohammed sat listening, and then thinking. He had not been prepared for this and did not feel equipped to help his friend properly. He had no choice. Ali had warned him that this would happen and he had often promised Tim that he would always be there for him.

He felt embarrassed but leant across the car and put his arm around the shaking shoulders of his friend. He waited without speaking, until he felt him become calmer. Tamam suddenly laughed a little.

"I shouldn't have let myself get in that state. This is my first lesson in trusting Allah. I was crying that I needed someone to help me and within a minute you were tapping on my window. Thanks Mohammed and I'm sorry."

"Ok, here's the plan Tamam. Right now, we're going to go get coffee and cakes. Then some lectures and whatever. We will meet at twelve and go together to pray. Then lunch together and you can tell me how you've got on this morning. More lectures then meet again, pray and go to mine to get supper. Pray together at mine and go to training. After training we have our crew social when you're going to tell them that you're a Muslim now."

"I feel very daunted. I just don't know what's come over me."

"Nothing has. You've made a huge, life changing decision and now you don't know what to expect and you feel frightened and alone. It's normal Tamam. Today you will find that, for ninety percent of your life nothing will be different at all. I will be with you to help with all the difficult new stuff, for as long as it takes. I promised you that before and I won't change my mind now." He wished that he felt as confident as he sounded.

"How's it been then mate?" Mohammed was careful not to use Tim's new name, not wanting to overload his friend with the newness of his life.

"It's been fine. Nothing different, just like you said. I feel really ashamed of myself now."

"Well don't. I don't think I could be as brave as you have been these last two days. Let's go and wash and pray. I need lunch!"

More lectures and a tutorial followed before the friends met once more for prayer.

"Show me how much you remember about wuduh Tamam." He tried hard to remember the confusing ritual.

"Brilliant! I would guess that's about seventy percent right. Let's do it slowly together again. You're a quick learner."

After prayer they went back to Mohammed's room.

"Leave your car here. You can collect it after training."

They ate together in the restaurant in the student village, Mohammed talking Tamam through the ways to be sure that food was halal. They went back to Mohammed's room to pray together. Then they drove to the campus for training, stopping at Tamams' house to collect his kit. He was starting to feel tired after a stressful day but he was determined to make a good showing for his crew.

After they'd showered Mohammed caught up with Tamam. "You ready for the big announcement?"

"I don't want to do that. Can't I go home and let you tell them for me. I'm so afraid that they will hate me for it."

"**No way!** It's your news so you need to share it. And as for hating you, Why? They don't hate me. I will set things up for you but you have to tell them. I know you can do it."

Mohammed bought three pints and two Cokes. As they began to drink, he made his move.

"Tim's got something very exciting to tell you."

All eyes turned to Tim. He felt himself blushing and his mouth went suddenly dry. He looked down at his drink.

"Well, actually, on Saturday I officially became a Muslim." He waited for the reaction. There was a long silence.

Mark stood, walked round the table and grasped his hand.

"That's amazing mate. Well done!"

"So now you won't be getting drunk on your twenty-first. I'm impressed Tim." Dave was thinking through the implications.

Tom surprised everyone. "You've made a very good decision Tim. I've been thinking about doing that too. I was so impressed by Mohammed when he looked after all of us when Kev died, I've been researching Islam ever since. I think I will be following your lead soon."

"Thanks everyone. I was so afraid you'd turn against me or something."

"Never. Why?" Tamam knew that his fears had been groundless.

Mohammed was shocked. Had his normal behaviour really influenced Tom too? He would have to talk with him alone sometime. It seemed that Allah had a mission for him. He *would* rise to it. The conversation turned to more normal things and a happy occasion was enjoyed as usual.

The next couple of weeks were slow moving but much less worrying for Tamam. He began to find it easy to switch between his two names, he mastered wuduh, which became much less time consuming for him and he began to learn some of the Qu'ran so that he could pray by himself when the need arose. He and Mohammed set up a regular study slot together on a Tuesday evening. Mohammed felt more positive and enthusiastic about his own religion than he ever had before. He started to feel a real pride in being a Muslim, in contrast to his previous efforts to hide it from the world.

Mohammed arranged a meeting between him, the Imam and three Muslim converts. He had a promise to fulfil. Later the same afternoon he drove into the city centre to a doctor's surgery. He explained his mission to the receptionist and, after a short wait, was called in to see the doctor.

"Yes, I can certainly do that. Just make an appointment with the receptionist for forty-five minutes. I look forward to meeting your friend next Thursday."

That evening, after the customary crew training and unity meeting Mohammed asked Tim to follow him back to the student village. They settled in to his room with a steaming mug of tea each.

"Tamam there is one more huge hurdle for you to jump, as you know. I think that this is the right time to do it. You are settling into the religion well and you have started to recover from your fears. It would be good to get the greatest fear of all out of the way."

Tamam sighed and swallowed hard. "It's been rattling in the back of my mind for so long. I hate blood and medicine and doctors. I am terrified that it might damage me for ever. I dread the pain and the embarrassment. But I know that it must be done and I do understand now that Allah will help me with it."

"So, shall I arrange it for you? I have found a doctor to do it. Two other guys here have used him in the past year."

"OK."

"Assalamo alaikum Tamam."

"Wa alaikum salam Usman."

"Can I come to visit you the weekend after next. Ali, my brother is on half term and he's really keen to meet Tamam!"

"That would be great. I've got so much to talk about and I've missed you being part of my growing up!"

"I've missed that too. We will probably get to you about lunch time if that's OK." "Yes. I will come home early. Looking forward to it mate."

Tamam awoke with a sick feeling in his stomach on Thursday morning. He hoped he wasn't becoming ill before his best friends' visit. No! Of-course he wasn't. He had a long-dreaded appointment this afternoon. He met up with Mohammed after prayer.

"Come on Tamam. You've been waiting for this moment for a year!

Tamam forced a brave smile that he certainly didn't feel. Sitting in Mohammed's car, being driven through the city centre, he began to feel overwhelmed with fear.

"I really don't want to do this."

"I know you don't. I wouldn't either. I don't think I could ever be as brave as you've been this last few weeks. You're not going to disappoint me now, are you?"

"No. I know I have to do this. I'm not sure if it's the embarrassment or the pain that I fear most."

"I'm going to be your nurse. Just try to be brave and calm for one more hour and then it will be just a case of getting better. Just remember the huge reward that Allah will give you. I was thinking how this really *must* be only for Allah. Nobody would do this for fun!"

Mohammed stayed out of the doctor's surgery while the operation was done. He said, quite honestly, that it was to save Tamam even more embarrassment. But there was the added reason that he was squeamish and knew that, if he watched he would almost certainly faint. He would be no help to his friend then!

At last Tamam emerged, ashen faced.

"All done?"

"Yes."

Mohammed went to him and hugged him, taking care not to make contact with the painful area. "I'm so proud of you. You're the bravest man I know." He whispered.

"I have to get this medicine, if that's OK."

"Sure. Let's get you home. Does it hurt?"

"I can't feel it at all at the moment. It's still numb."

Back at Mohammed's room he indicated his bed.

"That's for you tonight my friend. The doctor said you must lie down for at least four hours so that it can start to heal." He laughed. "You see how just Allah is. You were my doctor in here in the summer, now our roles have reversed. You were so strict Tamam! You made me drink that stuff even when you knew it had made me sick. Now it's my turn."

Tim lay back. His cock was beginning to hurt with a burning sensation. "I trust you Mohammed. I'm at your mercy."

"We ought to pray Tamam. You can pray sitting in a chair when you're hurt. After that we can go and get some supper."

"I'm not hungry really." Tamam needed to rest.

"Can you give me one of those pain killers. It's really hurting like mad now."

"I'm going to get an ice pack. I'm afraid I will have to apply it. I'm really sorry mate."

He returned with water and ice pack. Tamam swallowed the pain killer.

"I'm sorry. I won't look more than I have to."

Mohammed carefully opened Tamams' trousers and eased down his shorts. He took a sharp intake of breath. Poor man! It looked terrible. Mohammed heard a sudden roaring in his ears, he hoped he wouldn't faint. He pressed the ice against the wound and saw Tamam wince.

"This will reduce the swelling they said. You deffo need it."

"It feels bad. The cold really makes it worse. It's making me feel sick."

"I believe you. But it has to be done. Just hang in there."

When he'd finished Mohammed dressed his friend again and took the ice back to the freezer. He returned with a washing up bowl.

"Just in case you actually do need to be sick. I'm going to training now. Be back in an hour and a half. I won't stay for the social."

Tamam lay in pain. He was quite glad to be alone. The medicine did take some of the pain away. He shivered. He could still feel the ice. Presently he eased himself up to a sitting position. He wasn't feeling good. His head was spinning. He reached out to touch the washing up bowl. He had a nasty feeling that he was going to make use of it.

Sitting up helped a lot. He got up to visit the toilet. Pissing did not hurt as he had feared it would but he was shocked to see how swollen his cock was. Just seeing it made him feel a wave of panic. He returned to Mohamed's room and prayed to Allah to make him better quickly. "I did this only for you and to worship you alone. Please reward me by healing me quickly." This was the first time that Tamam had prayed to Allah outside the normal five daily prayers. He was surprised at the way in which it had an immediate calming effect upon him and his pain.

Mohammed came in grinning widely.

"Assalamo alaikum! You've got a visitor!"

Tom came in, all smiles and brandishing a huge pizza box.

"Mohammed told me you couldn't eat so I've come to prove him wrong!"

"I think I can eat now. I was feeling terrible but I prayed for Allah's help and it came immediately."

"That's good news. We want you back for Monday's training. Mohammed's a real bastard when he's in charge!"

"He's a very strict nurse too!"

Mohammed laughed. "Power obviously goes to my head!"

The three friends began to consume the pizza. It became quite a party.

Tamam woke with a start. He wasn't sure where he was. He was just remembering when Mohammed came in with plates of toast and honey and mugs of coffee.

"Breakfast in bed for the invalid!"

"I think I'll be OK today. Maybe use pain killers."

"I'm taking charge of feeding your friends this evening, so you can rest. After breakfast, before university, I'm applying ice again. I promised the doctor." Tamam grimaced.

After a tutorial and a lecture Tamam was ready to go home. While no longer in terrible pain he was feeling considerable discomfort from his wound rubbing against his shorts as he moved. He waited patiently for Mohammed.

"All ready? How did it go? You certainly look happier."

"I am happier, and so glad it's been done finally. I feel like I've had a death sentence lifted."

Tamam cooked baked potatoes served with baked beans and grated cheese, a child hood favourite. Mohammed was impressed that something so easy and simple could taste so good. The doorbell rang.

"This will be them!" Tamam went to answer.

Usman jumped, beaming, over the door step and lifted him up in a powerful embrace. Ali held back, a little shy. Once inside he too hugged Tamam.

"Now we are brothers. I am so pleased for you Tim."

They went through to the common room. Mohammed and Usman greeted each other and Usman introduced Ali.

"You look well Ali. I think Somerton is looking after you."

"Yes, Tim it is. And your family too. I have visited them twice now and they do make me very welcome."

Mohammed went to make mugs of tea for everyone and Tamam found the obligatory chocolate Digestives. The conversation was excited and joyful.

"Tamam is especially happy today." Laughed Mohammed.

"Why?"

"I faced my biggest fear yesterday Usman. I finally had the snip!"

"The snip?"

"He got circumcised." Mohammed explained.

"What does that mean?" Ali replicated Usman's question of a year earlier. Usman explained in Arabic.

"Oh, I am sorry Tamam. I did not understand that word and I thought that all people had that." They all laughed.

Mohammed took them all to his Indian restaurant again.

"This is my treat because I know that Tamam hasn't eaten properly since Wednesday and I want to congratulate him on his courage."

"I will buy the deserts because I love sweet things and they are good for an invalid!" Usman insisted. A wonderful party mood prevailed.

That evening, after Mohammed had taken Ali to stay with him, Usman wanted to talk to Tamam.

"I am proud of you. You are so brave. I am sorry that I am not with you more to help you to grow. But I want to give you a present in the holidays. My father and mother send you their love and they want you to come to Jeddah with Ali and me so that they can take you to Macca. I need your passport to get you your visa."

"That's incredible. They are so kind but I can't accept such an expensive gift Usman."

"To refuse a gift is the most insulting thing that you can do to an Arab. My parents love you and all of your family. You have looked after me and now Ali as if we were your own family. My parents were so excited that you did become Muslim. You cannot say no!"

"In that case YES! Thank you."

"I need your passport."

"My parents have it. They will give it to you when you take Ali back."

The weekend passed all too quickly. The distraction of visitors took Tamams' mind off his pain and it did begin to recede. The weather was miserable so they didn't really do very much. Just relaxing, socialising and catching up on one another's news. The four boys had an easy relationship and shared a joy in practical jokes.

"I've been thinking Tamam." Ali said after lunch on Saturday. "Tim was short for Timothy so I guess you liked a more snappy, one syllable name. Maybe you should call yourself Tam for short. It would sound more English too"

"I do like your thinking Ali. Yes! I shall become Tam from this point forwards."

On Sunday the two Hull boys went to the river and their visitors joined them. Ali had never seen rowing before and he was fascinated.

"Maybe I will do this next term at school. Do you think I can learn quickly?"

"Well these guys became a winning crew from nothing in about ten weeks, so for sure you can." Tam was happy to encourage him and glad to sing the praises of his crew. He was genuinely impressed by each of them.

What Do You Want?

"I just want to try to get to know a bit more about you and what makes you tick in this meeting."

Mrs. Young was a pleasant middle-aged lady who worked in the careers centre. Tam was sitting rather dejectedly on the opposite side of her desk. He had been trying, unsuccessfully, for the past few days to think of careers that might interest him, of what he wanted out of life, of things that he enjoyed doing.

"I like gardening and tinkering with mechanical things. For sport I have been a very successful cox and I'm very efficient and well organized in everything that I do."

Mrs. Young was scribbling on her pad. For some reason Tam felt sure that she was not writing about him.

"What do you like to do socially?"

"Nothing really, sit around or go to the pub. Most of my time is spent running the Boat Club."

"Have you had any official roles?"

"I was Treasurer of the Boat Club and now I am Captain. I'm Senior Resident of a student house too."

"Have you had many thoughts about what kind of career you'd like?"

"No."

"What do you want from life?"

"A decent salary, something I enjoy doing, something I'm good at, I hate doing things badly."

"I think you should do one of our tests. I can book you in tomorrow afternoon if you like."

"OK."

"Now I'll show you round here. You can come in any time to read up on things or to check the latest jobs on the notice board. Take these three books with you. They're free and full of good advice and lots of company adverts. Here we have a fortnightly news sheet with updated job opportunities. It's always worth picking it up."

Tam left, weighed down with the three big glossy books, but none the wiser about his future.

Next afternoon he dutifully reported to the careers centre to do his test. There were a dozen other students there, none of whom he knew. The test lasted fifty minutes and involved loads of questions with tick boxes in which to respond. Tam didn't really see the point of many of the questions, let alone have an unequivocal answer, but he did his best, hoping that "they" would give him the guidance that he definitely needed. By the time he went home he was feeling really disheartened. He had no idea what he wanted to do or what he *could* do and, almost every evening, the news told of factory closures, company bankruptcies, and three million unemployed people all searching for the few remaining dead-end jobs. Tam was glad to go to training with his crew that evening and he worked twice as hard as usual in an attempt to pump the frustration and disappointment out of himself.

"Are you OK mate?" Tom had noticed his unusually urgent exercising.

"Just pissed off!" Tam went on to explain about his two visits to the careers centre.

"I'm going there tomorrow. Thanks for the warning!"

Tam was subdued at their unity meeting, feeling that his happy life would soon be crumbling about him.

After the Sunday training on the river and the traditional drinks in the club house, at which they started to plan the club Christmas event, Tom asked Tam if he was busy.

"No, just going to look at some of those horrible careers books, see if there's anything in the world that I can do and would *like* to do."

"Can I come to see you for a bit?"

"Sure. Why don't you follow me back now? We can make some lunch together too."

In the messy kitchen Tam retrieved two chicken breasts from the fridge and instructed Tom to peel and cut some potatoes into chips. He took a selection of spices and coated the chicken in them. He had to wash up a frying pan, grumbling to himself as he did so. Soon the chicken and chips were frying in separate pans and the boys started to chop vegetables for a salad. Tam was impressed by Tom's culinary skills.

"Like you I've been in a student house for more than two years so I had to learn! I quite enjoy it to be honest."

"Maybe we should open a restaurant together. T&T's Honest Food! "

"It might come to that mate. That careers meeting and test didn't help me at all, I still have no idea about what I can or can't do and they didn't make any useful suggestions. I don't think I really want to do anything!"

Tam laughed. "That could be me talking!"

Once they'd eaten, they headed upstairs carrying mugs of coffee. Tam sat on his swivel chair, leaving the easy chair for Tom. They slurped their coffee and munched some biscuits in contented silence.

"Actually. I wanted to talk to you about how you're feeling now you're a Muslim. Mohammed came to see me the other day and he's promised to arrange things for me when I'm ready. I think I am ready but I'm feeling kind of nervous. I'm certain it's right for me but it feels like a big leap."

"It is a big leap, but it is worth it. If you feel ready, it's better just to get on with it and go for it." Tam looked deeply into Tom's eyes. "I promise that I will be here for you, night and day, whenever you need a friend. There will be times when you wonder whatever you've done, when you feel afraid or confused. The key thing is never stay alone at times like that. Between Mohammed and me you can be sure that you will always have a friend waiting for you."

"What was the hardest time for you?"

Tam told him the story of the first Monday morning, the shock, confusion and fear.

"And then there was getting circumcised. Is that something you're going to have to do?"

"Yep. I'm not going to think about that yet though!"

"Tom, becoming a Muslim has been life changing for me. I'm only just at the start of the process but I do feel pleased with the decision most of the time. Sometimes something feels weird or difficult and occasionally I miss being good old Tim but I guess that's normal. I think, actually, it's like we were talking about earlier, the prospect of changing from being a student to joining the grownup world of work!"

"You're very strong and tough Tam, it must come from your public-school upbringing. I don't think I'm as brave as you."

"I've watched you training and developing yourself for nearly two years. I remember you coming around to each of us to tell us about Kevin. You are brave, strong and decent. Allah guides only the best people to find Islam. He will never let you down."

They finished their coffee in silence.

"I'm going to do it. It's just crazy and painful to put it off, my brain can't think about anything else."

"Shall we go and see Mohammed now?"

"Let's!"

The friends walked brusquely towards the student village. Tam knocked on Mohammed's door.

"Come!"

They walked in.

"Tam! That was good timing!"

Tam could see a Haynes manual open on his desk and guessed that he needed help with his car.

"Before we get dirty with the Renault Tom needs to talk to you."

It was best to give Tom a push, Tam could sense the paralysis of fear taking hold of his friend at this pivotal moment. Mohammed sensed it too and helped him.

"Sit down both of you. Let's chill. Coffee?"

When they all had steaming mugs of coffee in their hands Tam reached across to Tom and placed a reassuring hand firmly on his shoulder. Tom took a deep breath. He looked very pale, like when he had told Tim about Kevin.

"Mohammed I've decided I'm ready to become a Muslim like you two. Please can you arrange things for me as soon as possible?"

Mohammed jumped to his feet, nearly spilling his own coffee and pulled Tom out of his seat to hug him. Both began to laugh.

"Subhan Allah! It was you, Tom, who questioned me really deeply about whether or not I was a Muslim, that first time I came to see your crew. I was afraid that you hated Muslims. Then, when I was made a permanent member of the crew you said to me that you all wanted me to be myself and make whatever changes I felt were best for the crew. I bet you didn't mean this kind of change. Suddenly sixty percent of us will be Muslims!"

Tam was laughing now. "If we had known that then we'd have booted you out!"

Mohammed promised that he would arrange with the Imam for Tom to take shahada as soon as possible.

"I'll meet you for lunch to tell you when we will do it. I think tomorrow evening will probably be fine, so be ready!"

Tom was strangely quiet, Tam understood fully how he must be feeling and went to reassure him with the silent solidarity of sitting beside him.

"What's happened to your car?" Tam prompted Mohammed, who now seemed to be more interested in Tom and making certain that he was ready for his leap of faith.

"When I was coming back from the boat club it said it was getting too hot. Could you show me how to try to find out what might be the matter with it? It's much easier when you show me than trying to read it at the same time as doing it."

"Sure. I haven't got my tools with me but we can take a look."

"Do you mind if I join in? I need to learn that kind of thing too." Tom was always enthusiastic.

The three set off to the car park, Mohammed carrying his Haynes manual.

"lift the bonnet for me but don't start the engine." Tam instructed.

"Look, there is the expansion tank where you put in the water. It links to the radiator, there and you can see the water pump fixed to the engine there. It's got an electric fan and you can see all the hoses. Open the cap on the expansion tank Mohammed, just one turn and you will hear it hiss as the pressure escapes, then open it fully. Look! The water level is low. I bet you've never checked it."

Mohammed conceded that he hadn't. He trudged off to get some water.

"You make it all sound so simple."

"It is simple. And I've watched my dad doing this kind of thing since I could first walk."

"I think I'll have to buy a new car so I don't need to learn." They both laughed.

"OK Mohammed, fill it up until the water touches that thing you can see sticking out from the side of the bottle."

When he had done that Tam showed them how to squeeze the hoses to make the water circulate.

"See now you need to put some more in. Great! Now turn the heater full on and start the engine, but leave the lid off."

When the water had started to circulate Tam showed his two friends how they could see the water moving. "That shows that the pump's working. Put the cap back on tightly now and let it all warm up."

They stood around chatting and laughing.

"What's that?" Tom asked when there was a sudden whirring sound.

"That's the fan cutting in, so we know that's working too. What's the temperature gage saying?"

"Normal."

"Take us for a drive."

They shut the bonnet and piled in. They drove for about five miles out to Skidby and back again. The temperature remained as it should be.

"That should teach you to do as I once told you. Check all the fluids every month."

Mohammed laughed guiltily. "I'm lazy and I'm afraid of breaking something."

"I'm going to do it tomorrow at four thirty. Please can you try to come, it would mean a lot to me." Tom caught Tam after the crew post training drinks on Monday.

"Tom! That's fantastic! Wild horses wouldn't keep me away. I'm so pleased for you mate. I won't pretend that it's all going to be easy because it won't but it is the best decision you will ever make." Tom grinned, part pleased and part embarrassed by the attention.

The ceremony was short and simple, as Tim's had been. After he had officially been welcomed into the fold of Islam Tom, who had now become Kareem, shook hands with the Imam and the witnesses and then Mohammed and Tam hugged their friend. Tam was embarrassed to find himself crying openly.

"I'm so pleased for you. Now you are my brother!" He tried to explain his feelings adequately.

The two friends escorted Kareem away with them for a celebration meal in the halal curry house. The staff there were amused that they were becoming the scene for so many such events. They returned to Mohammed's room to pray together and to give Kareem his presents. By now he was evidently feeling rather overwhelmed. Tam drove him home and promised to collect him in the morning. He had left his motorcycle on the campus.

"I'm so proud of you! If you need anything just call me, even in the middle of the night."

"I'll be fine man! Thanks though, it means a lot."

Saudi Arabia

The three friends were sitting in three adjacent seats on the Saudia 'plane. Each had a small bag in the overhead locker which contained two oversized white bath towels. They had practiced how to wear them, with much laughter, together in Tams' room at home the evening before. Now they would change into them in the toilet when the pilot told them that it was the correct point in the journey to do so.

The Albad brothers were naturally excited to be returning home but Tam was feeling rather shy and nervous. They ate their lunch, which was quite good for prepacked airline food. The pilot made an announcement in Arabic.

"It is time to change." Ali told Tam.

The three got up, retrieved their bags and headed for the front of the cabin. Tam struggled a bit to get the towelling securely fitted to him and then emerged, very shyly, to meet Ali who was looking similarly uncertain of himself. Usman went to change. They returned to their seats, each feeling rather solemn as they reflected upon the religious duty that they were about to perform.

"It is good that we are together because I have never done this in my life." Ali confided.

As they prepared to disembark into the late afternoon of Jeddah Tam was taken by surprise at the huge wave of heat that swept over him as the door was opened.

"Welcome to Saudi!" Laughed Usman.

"And this is the middle of the winter. You can guess what it is like in the summer." Ali grinned.

The two siblings were able to use the security lane dedicated to Saudi citizens. Tam had to use the line for "others". Finally the three were reunited at the slow moving luggage delivery belts. At last they had each collected their bags.

"Now you must be patient while your bag is searched Tam. Let us all join the same queue. We can cheer each other up that way." "This makes me angry every time I come home. It is one reason why I will never come back to live here." Usman already sounded insulted.

Tam found the process interesting and amusing but Usman had clearly been thoroughly ruffled by it. Free at last they gathered together and left the security zone. Tam suddenly felt overwhelmed by his usual shyness. He remembered how Ali had looked when he met him at Heathrow in August. That gave Tam a boost of courage.

"There is our father, look! He also is dressed for Umrah. He does know what to do so that will be useful!"

The brothers greeted their father while Tam hung back shyly.

"Tam! Why are you hiding?" Usman chided him.

He proffered his hand to Mr. Albad. The man shook it, looking deep into Tam's eyes. Suddenly he was hugging him and, to his embarrassment, kissing him on each cheek as an Arab does.

"Now you are my brother in Al Islam. Truly this is a great day for me and all of my family." Tam blushed at the statement and was shocked to see his friends' father crying.

"Dad is very happy for you Tam. I did tell you that he did that when Usman said you might become Muslim." Ali reminded him.

The next shock for Tam was the size of the Albads' GMC Suburban car. He couldn't believe that such huge cars existed. He had never seen anything like it.

"We will go directly to Macca. It is best to perform Umrah in the cool of the evening." Usman explained.

The three friends were sitting together in the back, each brother keen to support their visitor, both remembering the many times that Tim or Tam had done the same thing for them. Tam was shocked at the size of all the cars on the road, the speed at which they moved and the disregard for any rules. How could a child of twelve drive here?

They left the city limits of Jeddah and were driving through the desert. Tam was fascinated by the totally new kind of landscape that he was seeing. Sand and bare black mountains in the distance. Not a sign of any living plants. A total contrast to his native New Forest.

"I think I'm starting to understand why even the simplest things in England are so interesting to you two" he smiled. "I'm amazed at everything I'm seeing."

"Look, there is the city of Macca, can you see that special white archway over the road?"

Mr. Albad was parking the car. Everyone got out. They started walking over a wide expanse of white marble pavement.

"This is the Holy Mosque," Ali told Tam.

They walked through the arched entrance and past vast areas of marble flooring covered in strips of thick red carpet on which people prayed. Down some steps into a wide, white marble circular area in the middle of which stood a black cube shaped building. Tam recognised it at once as the Ka'aba , the centre of the Muslim world and the place to which every Muslim faces to pray at least five times every day. The feeling that Tam experienced at that moment was like no other that he had ever or would ever feel again.

"My dad knows exactly how to perform Umrah correctly. So, we're all going to do it with him. Just do as he does. I've never done it before either so we will be complete beginners together." Ali made Tam feel less confused and concerned.

The small group walked around the ka'aba many times, Tam lost count but he thought he remembered that it should be seven times. Then they moved to a kind of passage way between two rocky outcrops along which they had to walk, with a short section of running in between. Tam felt concerned that his rather insecurely fixed bath towel may come off under the stress of so much exercise but it remained safely in place. At the end Mr. Albad snipped a small piece of hair off each young man's head. Usman performed that duty for his father.

"Some people get all their hair shaved off at this point but it is not essential." Usman explained. "Now we will rest a little, pray Margrihb prayer and then go home to eat."

They found a quiet area to sit on a rug and settled down. Mr. Albad brought each of them a plastic cup of water. "This is called Zam Zam water. It comes from a spring under the ground right here. It is very special and has many healing properties. You will taste that it feels almost like oil rather than ordinary water. Drink it slowly Tam and ask Allah for anything that you want." Usman was a very thorough and gentle teacher.

The drive back to Jeddah was altogether more relaxed for everyone, the serious religious mission having been accomplished successfully. The two brothers were, naturally, excited to be going home to their family. Tam felt a little shy, as he always did in such circumstances, but he knew that they were nice people and he was with Usman who was very keen to show him the delights of Jeddah. It was a real adventure and Tam had always liked adventure.

The car stopped outside a set of large wrought iron gates set into a white painted wall on top of which were brightly shining electric lights at regular intervals. Mr. Albad hooted the horn and a young black boy jumped to attention and opened the gates for them.

"Welcome to my home Tam!"

They got out of the car. Ali told Tam to leave his bags in the car. A servant would bring them in for him. Mr. Albad opened a wide frosted glass door at the top of a semi-circular flight of four steps and they entered a huge hall with sparkly black marble floor and white painted walls and some ornate looking pillars. Tam was amazed.

The brothers hugged their mother and two sisters. Tam knew that he should not shake hands or make any physical contact with a female.

"Assalamo Alaikum!" he said simply.

"Wa alaikum salam! I hope that you had a very good Umrah. We are so happy to welcome you to our home. Usman and Ali, take Tamam up to your rooms and get yourselves washed and dressed. Then we will have our dinner." Mrs. Albad spoke excellent English.

Ali led the way up two flights of curved white marble stairs.

"This floor is only for us Tam so you can move around freely. Please wait for one of us to take you to other floors so that we do not disturb the ladies."

They showed him his room with its' private bathroom. There were three more bedrooms and a large sitting room with television.

"Let us all go shower and change and we'll meet here soon." Usman was feeling tired and was certain that Tam must be feeling thoroughly confused by so many new experiences in such a short time.

The boys went down stairs, Tam and Ali wearing jeans and T shirts while Usman wore a traditional white thobe. Mr. Albad was waiting for them in the dining room in which a feast had been set out on the table. He and Ali sat on one side and Tam and Usman on the other.

"Bismilah!" Mr. Albad blessed the meal. "I thought you boys were not going to come. I am very hungry, even if you are not. Tamam, I hope my sons are looking after you well. Please eat as much as you want. In our culture it is important that a guest eats well."

"Shokran! Anta Kareem!" Tam tried to speak a little Arabic, to demonstrate politeness.

"Very good Tamam! I am so proud to know a man like you. When Usman told us that you became Muslim I had to tell all my friends about it. There are many people who want to meet you now. We are all so happy."

After dinner they moved into a huge sitting room with deep pile red rugs and chairs sofas and tables made of gold painted frames and red velvet upholstery. It looked very exotic to Tam. Mrs. Albad and her two daughters joined them and a maid set out a pot of coffee and some delicious looking pastries.

"You must eat some of these Tam." Usman encouraged, filling his own plate with several.

Tam laughed "You always love sweet things, don't you?"

"Yes" Usman replied, his voice indistinct as his mouth was already full of crumbly pastry.

"We were so excited when Usman told us you had taken Shahada. How did you decide to do that?" Mrs. Albad was speaking.

"I had the best of teachers and examples in Usman."

"We have found it difficult to understand that. We never thought of him as religious." One of the sisters spoke.

"Well it was more the way in which he behaves and the way he understands life and the world around us that interested me at first. He is the first Muslim that I had ever spoken to."

"And what did your family think? It must be difficult and a bit sad for them."

"I think it was difficult for them, but they know and love Usman and they had a wonderful holiday with all of you so they know that Islam makes good people and that made it easier."

"I think that Allah has rewarded you because you have always been so kind to Usman and now to Ali too." The second sister spoke.

Tam blushed, feeling embarrassed.

Later the boys were relaxing upstairs. More relaxed without the formality of all the family, reverting to the banter of young friends. Ali picked up the 'phone and spoke in Arabic.

"Tam always gives us Tea and biscuits at bed time. We must treat him well too Usman."

A maid arrived with tea in a pot, cups and more pastries.

"I am tired. All my body aches." Usman grumbled at their late breakfast the next morning.

"I think you're unfit Usman. I'm fine. I thought you were an archer and a footballer."

"Usman is getting old!" Ali teased.

"Too many Rothmans if you ask me." Tam laughed.

They spent the day relaxing. The brothers made 'phone calls, trying to meet up with old friends.

"We are going to meet Abdul Aziz after Asr Tam. You remember how many times I have talked about him. I think you will become friends very easily."

Tam could feel Usman's tension as he tried to nose the big car into the evening rush hour traffic.

"See how badly people drive here. I cannot believe that I was happy driving here before, even when I was twelve. Now I am nearly pissing myself!"

"I don't think I could do it either."

At last they were in the main flow of traffic.

"All these American cars are so big! Now I understand how difficult it must have been for you to feel happy to buy your little car in England. It must have felt like a toy."

"I love it now. I can get five people in it, which is the same as this, so this must be really badly designed." Usman was parking outside a huge blue glass structure that towered over the city.

Usman bought them both a glass of juice while they waited for Abdul Aziz. It tasted very sweet and was a strange green-brown colour.

"What is this made from?"

"It is sugar cane juice. I think the Egyptians brought it here but now we all like it."

"Usman!" A young man in a white thobe and red and white gutra bounded up to the table. They hugged and kissed.

"Meet Tamam. I have told you about him many times. He was called Tim but now he is a Muslim."

"That is a very wonderful thing" Abdul Aziz said seriously as they shook hands and then hugged. Tam was glad that he deleted the kissing part of the traditional greeting.

"Please call me Tam. All my friends do."

Usman got his friend a juice and soon the three young men were chatting and laughing together as if they had known each other all their lives. Tam reflected, not for the first time, how you could find the same kind of characters in any place in the world and they would become friends.

They wondered around the huge shopping centre, looking at the latest electronic goods and fiddling with those that were most readily accessible. Tam was amazed to see so many shops competing to sell the same goods. Each shop seemed to specialise in one specific brand, Sony, Panasonic or Sharp. The prices displayed were merely a starting point for a long-winded bargaining process. The very concept of negotiating with a shop keeper was incredible to him. That was what you did when buying a second hand car in England!

Suddenly an amplified call to prayer echoed around the mall and the shops began to shut. No business was allowed to stay open in Saudi Arabia during prayer times so that everybody could easily attend a mosque. Tam was impressed by this. The three friends followed a crowd to the mosque that was built within the mall.

When they had finished Abdul Aziz declared that he was hungry.

"Let us take Tam to Al Tazitch. He cannot visit Jeddah without tasting that food."

He turned to Tam, laughing. "Usman has to eat this food as soon as he gets here for his holiday. Last Summer I thought that he might be pregnant because he wanted to eat it every time we met."

The food was delicious, a baby chicken, split in half and barbequed, served on a flat bread with chips and salad. Tam found it a little difficult to eat with his fingers, as is tradition in Saudi.

"You should come to England to do a Masters degree Abdul Aziz" Usman suggested.

"Do you think I would be able to. I do need to do something exciting with my life before I have to settle down."

"Yes, it is easy. They want your money! I am applying to do one so I can stay in England longer."

"Your English is superb so you'd have no problems with that." Tam encouraged.

"I will go to get some forms for you in the British Council." Promised Usman.

Usman and Tam went to do just that the next morning. Tam was interested to see which English schools and universities were seeking students.

"Look Usman a prospectus from Barforth. Let's take a copy. It will give us a laugh."

They chose several postgraduate prospectuses, from Southampton, Cambridge, Manchester and, on Tam's recommendation, Hull. Tam chatted with the man at the reception desk who was interested to know that he was English and helping his friend to study in England.

A couple of days later Abdul Aziz visited the Albad's house and Usman and Tam helped him to complete four extensive application forms.

"My father said he will pay for me to do this. Now I feel real excited. I do hope I can get a place."

"Look, you can put my name and address here, they want to confirm that you have a contact in the UK who will support you if you need it." Tam was glad to offer help.

After they had finished their work, they went out to drink tea from a flask beside the sea in the warm, dark night.

"It's incredible, the way so many people come to eat and drink beside the sea in the night. You live in a very beautiful city."

"Next week we will go camping in the desert beside the sea. You remember I have told you about those adventures many times." Usman sounded enthusiastic.

On Saturday, the first day of the working week in Saudi Arabia, Abdul Aziz arrived at the Albads' house in his fathers' Jeep. Usman had already got a servant to fetch their traditional tent from the garage, together with many cushions and large bottles of drinking water. The Jeep had a fridge built into the boot, much to Tam's interest.

Soon they were on their way. There was some heated discussion between the two Arabs about which direction, North or South, would be most interesting for Tam. In the end they headed

South. The city slowly thinned out and then gave way to open desert. In the distance were black mountains, but mainly they could see only reddish gold coloured sand dunes. The road was covered in a shallow layer of sand which made a hissing sound as the wheels made it hit the underside of the car.

"Look Tam, wild camels." Tam looked at the line of eight proud looking creatures walking majestically over the sand dunes.

"Wow. That is fantastic. I never expected to see such a thing in my life."

"Where Tam lives there are wild horses in the forest. I often stop my car to look at them. They remind me of these camels in a strange kind of way. If you come to England, we will have many good times together."

At length they stopped, checked out the local terrain and decided to pitch camp there. The Saudi boys were both surprised when Tam demonstrated his skills at putting up the tent.

"I did not expect that Tam. You never stop showing me new skills!" Usman was laughing.

"We always used to go camping for our family holidays so I have been learning about tents since I was three."

"You will see this when you come Abdul Aziz. In England people do everything by themselves. I have learnt to drive a tractor and I have climbed with bare feet all over the high roof of the Croys' house and I have looked after the engine of my car."

They settled in to rest and drink cold water in their tent, keeping out of the afternoon heat. Later they prayed and changed into swimming things.

"You will love the sea!"

Tam was shocked at the heat of the sand on his bare feet. It was very white beside the sea.

"The sand here, by the water, is made from crushed up coral. That is why it is different from the desert sand." Abdul Aziz seemed almost to have read Tam's mind.

The water was warm. Bath temperature! The boys spent a happy hour swimming, chasing each other and splashing in the warm, very salty water.

"Let us show Tam the reef and catch our supper."

"The water will sting your eyes at first Tam but quickly that will stop and then you can see the beautiful fish." Tam was excited. He had dreamed of seeing a real coral reef for most of his life.

They swam out a short distance and Tam watched the Saudi boys take a deep breath and dive under the water. He copied them. His eyes stung terribly and he could see nothing. He surfaced. He tried again. The fourth time he found the reaction had subsided. Suddenly he could see pink, white and purple coral, Yellow and black striped Tiger fish and delicate Angel fish. Abdul Aziz asked him to follow him. Under the water he pointed to a giant Clam, a huge shell with a fluorescent blue fish inside it. The boys regrouped on the surface.

"Follow us Tam and we will start catching our supper!"

Tam dived again and watched as the Saudi boys grabbed large conch shells and put them in a net that they had brought with them. Tam was delighted when he caught one. Soon the net was half full. They dragged it out of the water onto the beach.

"Now we collect wood and make the fire. We have done this many times in England."

The supper was delicious. Tam started laughing as Usman made black Egyptian tea in his kettle.

"This has become a new tradition with all of us who are lucky enough to know Usman in England. We do this every time we go to the beach."

In the cool of the night the boys played with their football. The week was spent in this manner. One morning Abdul Aziz took them desert driving, rallying over sand dunes, bouncing his passengers around until their heads ached. It was exhilarating! All too soon they were packing up to return to the city. The holiday was nearly over.

"Tam I am taking you for dinner tonight. Usman must talk to our parents. I have pushed him into it!"

Tam and Ali got into the Caprice. Ali was too young to have started driving in England so his experience of Jeddah had not been diluted and damaged as Usman's had been. Tam was in a constant state of shocked fear as the boy roared into heavy traffic flows at high speed and weaved frantically in and out of traffic lanes. They seemed to be heading out of town.

"First I will show you the business that your dad and mine are making together."

They stopped at a marina. Ali talked to the gate man in Arabic and gained entry. He led the way along a wooden jetty, to which were moored a wide selection of pleasure boats. At the end were two very new looking boats. Tam recognised one immediately as being of his fathers' design.

"Both are from your dad. My dad gets them built here and this is where they display the two models for sale. It was my dad's dream to do this. Your dad has given him an exciting new thing. Really it does seem that Allah wanted our families to become friends!"

They got back into the car and drove fast along the Corniche to the city centre. Ali pulled into a small shopping area.

"We used to come here after school. We could walk from school and it was fun for us. You will like Al Baik. It is special for Saudi and I know that Usman has always missed it. I do too!"

Tam sat at a table while Ali bought the food. He returned with two double portions of deep-fried shrimps with chips and garlic sauce, together with the inevitable Pepsi to drink. Tam found this meal delicious too. He was highly impressed by Saudi fast food.

When they returned to the house, everything was quiet. They went up to the top floor. Usman was sitting in their lounge, looking miserable.

"Hi! Did you like Al Baik?" He greeted Tam.

"Yes. How did it go for you?"

Usman shook his head wearily. "It was as bad as I thought it would be. Now my mother is crying and my father is furious. In the end I just told them that that was what I am going to do and that is the end of it."

Usman was driving with Tam to the new mall up near the Creek, on the Northern side of the city.

"I will buy an engagement ring for Jane. Maybe I will buy a wedding ring too. Gold is cheaper here than in UK."

"Maybe I should buy an engagement ring for when I officially get engaged to Sarah."

"You definitely should Tam. We can get a big discount if we buy two or three from the same shop."

They drove in silence for a while. Usman felt drained from the previous evening and his dad had already left for work before he had gone downstairs that morning. His mother had not spoken to him properly, merely giving him doleful looks muttering to herself about children who didn't respect their parents. He did feel guilty and a little ashamed but he was a man and it was his life. Whether he married Jane or not he knew that he could never settle happily back to life in Saudi Arabia. He had tried and tried to explain this but to no avail. He nearly missed the entrance to the carpark and had to swerve suddenly to the right to get in.

The friends started to explore the huge mall, with Its' multi domed roof, wide marble walkways and ostentatious shops all purveying top class luxury goods. As Abdul Aziz had said, there were a large number of gold shops. Having decided on a few shops that appealed to him for the style of rings that he could see in the window Usman went into the first one. He got the assistant to remove a selection of suitable rings from the display. He touched them, tried them on, talked to Tam. Eventually he asked the price of one. After some negotiation he appeared to have reached the "last best price." He repeated the process in four more shops. Tam was watching him quietly, fascinated by the lengthy Arab negotiating process.

"Have you seen any that you like Tam?"

"Yes, in the second and fourth shops."

"Then we will return to those and start again on the basis that we will buy two. You will see how the price changes!"

After three more visits to each shop, playing one off against another, they eventually secured a deal with which Usman was happy. His spirits thus lifted once more he led Tam off to have an Al Baik meal.

"I know you had it last night but I haven't had one yet and now the holiday is over."

As they ate Tam remembered the conversation of the night before.

"Maybe you should get a franchise to open these restaurants in England. I certainly find it delicious. It may do very well."

"I had thought about that once before. We could do it together Tam, become millionaires before we are thirty!"

When they returned the found that Ali had gone to his old school to meet some of his friends to have a meal together.

"We will go find Abdul Aziz. I need cheering up." The three had a great evening.

First thing in the morning they stuffed their things into their bags. They joined the family for a large farewell breakfast. Mr. and Mrs. Albad appeared to be in a good frame of mind once more and they sought promises from Tam that he would visit them again one day.

The driver loaded their luggage into the car and they bade their final farewells. The long return journey was underway.

Determination Required!

Tam returned to Hull almost a week after the term had officially started due to the heavy snow that had prevented either he or Usman from so much as leaving the house. He was concerned because he had to arrange for his dissertation to be typed up so that he could submit it before the end of January. He felt an urgent need to redouble his efforts at applying for any suitable job that he could find because he was beginning to feel that it was going to be very difficult indeed to secure a job for the Summer. He was starting to think about seeking a place on a post graduate course as a way of delaying the need to find a job rather than any burning desire to undertake more study. He loved being a student and dreaded going home with neither a job nor another course to attend.

"It's good to see you mate!" Dave greeted him at the Thursday training session. "Mohammed's far too tough on us all. We've missed our gentle friend."

Tam grinned. "I'm glad to be here. We need to get ready for the bumps and Head of River races. The first one is in three weeks' time. Maybe I won't be so gentle either."

After the crew unity meeting Kareem caught up with Tam as they headed to the car park.

"Assalamo alaikum! I've booked the doctor for next Thursday afternoon. Can you give me a lift?"

"Yeah sure. What's the matter?"

"Nothing yet. I have to get circumcised."

"Shit! Sorry mate, I wasn't thinking. I'll take care of you I know what it's like. It'll be a big relief when you've done it, and you do recover completely. I feel quite normal now. Haven't thought about it for ages, until this conversation."

"It's so good to have you as a friend, I know that you understand exactly the feelings I have. It helps to be able to talk about things knowing that I don't have to explain too much." They both laughed, sharing something very special.

Tam bought Kareem lunch on Thursday before driving him to the familiar and frightening surgery in the city centre. He sat patiently in the waiting room feeling uncomfortable in sympathy with the suffering of his friend. At last Kareem emerged, pale and visibly shaking.

"Let's get you home mate." Tam put a reassuring arm over his shoulder and helped him out to the car.

It had started to snow heavily and persistently. The clouds had that yellowish tinge that often heralds snow. Tam didn't bother trying to force conversation, he understood very well that Kareem would not be feeling much like it.

"I'm sorry Tam, I need to get this prescription from a chemist."

"No probs. You'll need those strong painkillers!"

Tam took him to his house because Kareem was living in a privately rented house with no heating in it.

"There you go, man, this is your bed for the next couple of days."

"I can't Tam, what about you?"

"I've got a spare mattress. I will be right here with you. Now strip and get into bed. You have to lie down on your back for the first four hours."

Tam sat with his friend until he slept. He returned after three hours to find him sitting up in bed.

"How you doing?"

I'm feeling ashamed and it's starting to hurt."

"You've nothing to be ashamed of. I'm going to get an ice pack. That will embarrass you but it really does help."

Tam took care to look at Kareem's face as he applied the ice between his legs. It is a horrible experience.

"Do you fancy a cup of sweet tea? Try to give you some energy." Tam handed him the steaming mug. "Take these aspirins too, ease the pain."

They sat talking for several hours. "I'd better get to training. Have to be a good leader. Will you be OK? I'll get us a pizza on the way back, cheer you up a bit."

Tam left the careers room after his customary once weekly visit, clutching the latest vacancy list together with half a dozen standard application forms. Every time he went there, he came away feeling despondent and frustrated. The truth was that he had no real idea about what he wanted to do in the world of work or how he could set about making a decision. He knew that he wanted a job that he would enjoy but he wasn't sure exactly what he would like doing. He did want a decent salary, he had seen that a fair starting salary for a new graduate appeared to be seven thousand pounds a year so he had set that as his minimum, not bothering to apply for any job that offered less.

He fancied a company car as well but they only came with sales jobs. He had been warned by several well-meaning people that he would not be a successful sales representative because of his sincerity and shyness but the lure of a new car caused him to ignore that advice.

What hurt him most was the length of time that he had to spend filling in application forms in his own hand writing and the way in which it was becoming clear that most companies never even had the courtesy of replying with a rejection letter. Simply nothing happened at all. Tam kept a detailed list of each company to which he applied with room to note interviews or replies. Most of these spaces remained resolutely empty.

Sometimes he felt like simply giving up but he knew that that was the wrong response. Years of suffering at school had made Tam very determined and self-sufficient and he would not allow himself to be ground down by difficult circumstances. He promised himself that, at the very least, he would never spend any of his money with any of the companies that treated him so rudely. He told Neil about his plan to punish these companies.

"The trouble with that idea is that, before either of us get a job, we'll probably have applied to most of the companies in this country so you'll never be able to buy anything when you do finally start earning a decent living."

Tam could see that this was true but he continued to cheer himself up with the thought of wielding some painful power over them in the future.

One evening he went to the house of the lady who he had paid to type up his dissertation to collect the typed and bound finished copy. He felt excited and proud to see and touch and then read his own hard work in a professional looking book. This was *his, with his name on it!* How much he wanted to send a copy to his old Head Master.

"This is the work of Tim Croy, who was never supposed to even get any "O" levels."

Tam hoped that he was not becoming full of hatred for so many institutions. He was, by nature, a cheerful kind of person and those kinds of thoughts did not fit well with his self- perception.

The Boat Club Elections came and went. Tam relinquished his position of captain and was replaced by Mohammed. The other positions were filled by new members, one of which was a girl. For the first time in two seasons the committee was no longer made up entirely of members of the First Men's Crew.

Tam felt strange. He was happy to hand the position to Mohammed because he certainly deserved it and would do it well but this kind of winding down of his responsibilities within the university emphasised his rapidly approaching and increasingly dreaded departure from student life into the adult world of work or unemployment. He simply didn't want to contemplate what was going to happen to him in July.

He began to pray for the help of Allah, to guide him as to what he should do and to open doors for him. He really wanted somebody to whom he could speak of his fears and dejection but he felt ashamed of his weakness and inadequacy and felt unable to talk about it. Why was it that so many people came to him with their problems but he felt that he couldn't go to anybody?

One evening, after filling in three long application forms with an increasing sense of hopelessness he simply lay on his bed and cried to himself. What was the point? What was so bad about him that nobody saw any value in employing him? What was he doing wrong? What was going to happen to him? Why was he so alone?

After almost an hour of destructive self-pity Tam could cry no more. He got up, washed his face in an effort to disguise the redness from tears, pulled on his jacket and went to post his application forms. The walk in the cold night air helped him. On an impulse he walked to the student village to seek the company of Mohammed. He found him writing an essay in his room.

"Assalamo alaikum! Can I disturb you for a few minutes? I need a friend." Tam hadn't intended to sound so pathetic but the words just seemed to come out of their own accord.

"Please do disturb me! Preferably for the rest of the night. I'm pissed off with this essay." Mohammed went to make tea and Tam followed him to the kitchen, feeling more optimistic already.

"What's happened to Tam?"

"How do you mean?"

"Well you said you needed a friend. You look like you're very upset. I am your friend and I intend to help."

Tam blushed, suddenly realising that he was humiliating himself and wasting Mohammed's time.

"I don't think there's anything you can do mate, and I don't think I can face going through it all again."

"Ok, tell me what you thought you wanted to talk about and then I'll decide if I can help or not." Mohammed was very good at getting what he wanted!

Tam told him everything, glad that he had cried it all out alone as that enabled him to stop himself from crying in front of his friend.

"That's enough to make anyone cry Tam. You should never feel like that all alone. Talking to a friend is much better for you."

"Who said I was crying?"

"Your eyes did! You don't need to be ashamed Tam. It's a huge fear for you and I understand how horrible you must be feeling. Will you promise me to come to talk to me every time you feel like this? I can't change the situation but I deffo can change your mood! Come on, let's go down the Lionheart and get something nice to eat."

Tam began to feel a bit better as Saturday and the first of the seasons' races approached. He had a great crew that had experienced nothing but success and they had every reason to believe that their success would continue. The crew assembled early at the boat house. Tam, who was now twenty-one and had held his driving licence for more than the mandatory three years was driving the Union minibus. He had had a one hour driving test in it a few days earlier and now felt quite confident. He was not so confident about towing the boat trailer, which more than doubled the length of his vehicle but it was a useful skill to develop. Dave was going to get tested too so that he would be able to share the duty with Tam. They loaded the trailer, locked the boat house and were on their way. Tam did feel unexpectedly nervous at first but, once out of the confines of the city he relaxed and was almost able to forget that he was driving anything other than his own car.

The race went well and Hull University were crowned Head of River for the third successive year. Tam was touched to hear Mohammed insisting that the crew should not throw him in because it was dangerously cold. In the pub that evening the celebration was as enthusiastic as it had ever been and Tam felt as comfortable and content as he had for the past two years. The fear of the future was banished for the day.

Tam sat in his room looking at the letter that he had found waiting for him on the hall table when he got in from campus that afternoon. He had been surprised to see the logo of a company to which he had sent a job application two weeks earlier on the envelope. Now he was almost in a state of medical shock as he read and reread the enclosed letter. He was invited to attend an interview in Bristol on the following Monday. They had booked a hotel for him on the Sunday night. A simple message but one so unexpected that Tam had given up hoping for any kind of reply from any company ever.

He wondered how he should prepare for this event. He suddenly felt very positive and hopeful and yet, simultaneously nervous and full of self- doubt. He busied himself by getting his largely unused suit out of his wardrobe together with his white shirt, blue tie and black shoes. Everything seemed to be as it should be. He would have to polish his shoes. That would mean buying some black polish. He also needed to get his hair cut. As his mother had been telling him for the past two years young men with long hair can't expect to be taken seriously. He looked out the advertisement to which he had applied to remind himself of exactly what he had applied for and what it was that they were looking for. He would need to practice a convincing talk about himself and his abilities. Tomorrow he would go to the careers office to seek some help. Now he needed a cup of tea!

The drive to Bristol was long and largely unfamiliar to Tam. When he arrived at the upmarket hotel, he felt rather embarrassed when a porter came out and asked to park his car for him. Tam imagined that he was more used to parking new Jaguars and Mercedes than seven year old Hillmans with rust showing through the wings. He followed another porter, who was carrying his bag for him, up to his large room in which was a king-sized bed and a luxury bathroom. He lay on his bed for a while and thought how nice it would be to have Sarah here with him now. Later he went down to reception where he was to meet with the five other candidates. The four young men and two women introduced themselves rather shyly and sat making small talk until they were ready to go into the dining room. The four men shared a table, the girls kept pointedly to themselves on another one.

"Do you think we can order anything from this?" One of them asked, looking at the leather-bound menu.

"I suppose so." Answered another.

They all agreed that it was a good move to choose whatever they fancied from each of the three courses so as to make the most of the company's hospitality. Talk turned to the quality of the rooms. Each boy wished that he had known that it was going to be so good so that they could have brought their girlfriend for a free break.

"I thought I might have to share a room!" confided a cheerful looking guy.

Tam laughed. "I was well ashamed when the guy asked for my car keys to park it for me. I don't expect he'd ever driven such an old rust bucket!"

After breakfast the four young men, dressed uncomfortably in suits and ties, set off on foot to find the head office of their potential employer. There had been no sign of either of the girls at breakfast.

"Obviously they need to get their hair and makeup right." Laughed a very tall man. Tam thought what a good oarsman he would make.

The morning was spent being given a presentation by senior managers and two of the previous years' Graduate Trainees, followed by a series of written aptitude tests.

There followed "lunch with the directors" during which the candidates were expected to stand, holding a plate and a glass of wine and eat scampi chips and peas politely with a knife and fork while making impressive conversation with the directors. This must be the biggest test of all, Tam thought to himself as he hoped the bald man to whom he was chatting had not noticed the avalanche of peas that he had just sent scattering off his plate and onto the floor. Couldn't they have chosen something easier to eat? Or was this all part of the trap?

In the afternoon each candidate had two individual interviews and was then free to depart. Tam felt that he had done well in the first interview and entered the second one in confident mood. The interviewer was a rather sullen looking middle- aged man who seemed to Tam to delight in trying to catch him out by asking similar questions to see if he would give the same or conflicting answers. He didn't *think* he'd made any terrible mistakes but he felt unnerved nevertheless. It was with much relief that he walked back to the hotel to retrieve his car and set off to the comfort of his familiar student house.

Two days before the end of term Tam received the "regret" letter. It would have been great to have ended the term with an offer of a job but he cheered himself up by reminding himself of how humiliated he would have felt having to drive around in a basic Mini Metro with the company name emblazoned on each side. There would be better opportunities waiting around the corner Tam hoped.

A Worry Shared

Tam felt tense, as if he was waiting for something important to happen. He couldn't concentrate or settle down to anything and, worse, he couldn't seem to relax. Since arriving home for the holidays two days earlier he had not been himself and he didn't understand why. He was tetchy and short tempered with Anabelle, noncommittal with his parents and he found it very difficult to show any interest in anything that anyone was doing or talking about. Usman was staying with Janes' parents for the first few days of the holiday to plan their forthcoming wedding and that also seemed to rattle Tam.

Mrs.Croy came and settled herself in the television room which she had seen her son slink into twenty minutes earlier. It was a strange place for him to go in the middle of the day.

"What's the matter Timothy? You've been like a cat on a hot tin roof ever since you got home. I don't think I've seen you smile once."

Tam sighed. He knew that what she said was true and he had also known that she would initiate this kind of conversation sooner or later. He wanted to talk, hoping that she could sort things out for him, as a mother is supposed to, however old her child may be. The problem was that he didn't understand what was wrong with him and he hadn't a clue how to verbalise his fears and worries. Now that he was having to contemplate what to say to her, he felt as if he might cry. Obviously, he couldn't do that so he struggled with his rising tide of emotions before he started to speak.

"I'm worried. It seems like it's impossible to get a job these days and I don't think my degree is going to help me at all. If I can't get a decent job the whole of the last three years will have been pointless. I don't want to just come home and be on the dole. I don't think I can bear leaving Hull and all my friends with nothing to go to next. I feel like the failure that Barforth always said I was going to be and I just feel helpless, hopeless and useless."

He didn't trust himself to talk any more. He swallowed hard, trying to eliminate the lump of hurt that had risen up his throat and was threatening to overwhelm him. He looked down, feeling ashamed and wishing that he hadn't said all that he had said.

His mother sat, composing her thoughts and feelings. She knew very well the political and economic situation in the country at the moment and she had seen several current affairs programs on television which had highlighted the plight of young people trying to start their careers. Her old friend Anne from school had a son who was two years older than Timothy and he had been unemployed for nearly two years now. One of his friends had committed suicide because of this problem. She was sure, and prayed, that Timothy was made of sterner stuff. For possibly the first time in her life Mrs. Croy could think of nothing to say. She knew that she *must* respond to poor Timothy but she didn't have any kind of magic solution to his problem or even any positive advice or cheering slant on the situation. Obviously, she must not appear patronising to him and he needed her to support him.

"Things are very difficult for everyone these days. I know it sounds trite but it is not in any way your fault Timothy and you *must* keep that in your mind always. I know it's not what you had hoped for and that you will feel lonely after the fun of university but this is your home dear and we are your family and we love you very much. It may not feel like it right now but this situation will appear to be just a difficult patch that you have to survive when you look back at it in the future. You are going to have to be very brave, as I know you are Timothy."

Mother and son sat in silence in the cool room. Neither had anything to say or any sensible suggestion to make.

"I'm going to go and check the cylinder mower. I think the front lawn ought to be mown while the grass is dry and the soil is wet enough for the roller to smooth the ground."

Tam got up and made for the refuge of the coach house.

With a deep sigh Mrs. Croy went to the kitchen. She felt a need to make some of Timothy's favourite foods in an effort to comfort him. How could this lovely country have become so difficult and hostile for young people to try to build their lives in? Was it something that her generation had done? Had they all behaved so selfishly that they had ruined the future for their own children? That was just too awful to contemplate.

"Timothy dear would you mind collecting Ali from school tomorrow? I know he'd rather chat to you than to an old woman like me!"

Tim set off dutifully to collect his friends' brother from his school. He was a nice enough lad and Tam knew how important it was to look after foreign visitors to the country well. He had assumed responsibility for Usman as soon as he had met him at Barforth and Ali had followed in due course. The youthful enthusiasm and joyous hopes for the holiday were infectious and, by the time they got home, Tam was feeling more cheerful. He helped Ali take his things out of the car and up to his bedroom and enjoyed listening to all his news as they had tea with his mother in the kitchen. Ali had been learning to row at school and he was keen to talk to Tam about his efforts. He was a tall and fit young man with a keen intelligence and he had learnt quickly and been moved rapidly up the ranks to find himself in the Second Eight.

Tam was genuinely impressed and quizzed him about the various head of river races that he had competed in. It was strange to hear about schools with which he had once competed. He told Ali of the several occasions when he had coxed against Somerton and won decisively. Ali resolved that he and his crew would beat Barforth if they ever found themselves racing against them. Tam laughed at the prospect.

"I'm going to hold you to that Ali!"

Later that evening Usman 'phoned to say that he would be coming back the next day. Tam felt a great joy and relief at the prospect of having someone to talk through his worries with. It would be easier to talk openly with his friend.

Usman arrived in high spirits just before lunch and spent the meal talking excitedly about his forthcoming wedding and how, now that preparations were in motion, he was feeling much more confident and positive in general. Mrs. Croy listened to all his news, commenting and suggesting at appropriate junctures. She still had some motherly concerns about two very young people marrying but she accepted that it had been their collective decision and they would have to make the best of it. She hoped that Usman would find the joy and love that he deserved.

While they were eating dinner that evening the 'phone rang. Tam went out to the hall to answer it.

"Good evening. May I speak to Tim please?"

Tam was sure he knew the voice but could not quite place it.

"I am Tim."

"Oh Tam! I didn't recognize you. It's Kareem here."

" Kareem mate! How's it hanging?"

"Could we meet up for a day sometime soon? I need a mate to talk things through with."

"Is it Islam?"

"Yeah, I'm hitting my first really tough time. Delayed shock maybe."

"Come and stay here for a couple of days, I've got my mate Usman and his brother here. They'll be able to help you too."

"Are you sure?"

"Yeah. Come down tomorrow if you want. Tell me what time your train gets in and I'll be there to meet you."

"Cheers mate. I feel better already!"

Tam had arrived at the station twenty minutes too early. He sat in his car in the small car park and tried to compose his feelings and thoughts. Kareem was an excellent friend and Tam had promised him that he would help him at any time that he needed support in his decision to become a Muslim, which he had made not long after Tam had done the same thing. It was very important that he should do so and he felt pleased that Kareem had wanted to turn to him for help.

The trouble was that Tam was feeling in need of help and support himself and he knew that he was sinking rapidly into some kind of lonely helplessness from which he could see no escape. Where was the person to whom he could turn? He trusted Allah and he believed whole heartedly in the teachings of Islam so he understood that Allah would never forsake him but somehow, lately, he couldn't *feel* it. He desperately needed a human being to whom he could talk freely and from whom he could seek help and reassurance. Tam prayed for exactly that as he sat in his car in the station car park. It made him feel slightly calmer and more peaceful immediately. "When you become a Muslim, you have grasped a hand hold that will never fail."

Tam locked the car and went to wait on platform three. The train rattled in moments after he got there.

"Tam!"

Kareem was hurrying towards him, smiling shyly. He was a quiet young man, if you didn't know him you would think that he was very serious, but it was just a kind of protective camouflage.

"Assalamo alaikum Kareem! Welcome to my neck of the woods!"

"It's so good to see you Tam, when you invited me yesterday, at once, without any fuss or questions, it made me realise exactly what a brilliant friend, no *brother*, you are. I started feeling better immediately. Now I feel like I'm on holiday so I feel like a fraud!"

Tam laughed, truly joyful for the first time in ages. "You're the least fraudulent guy I know. And you are on holiday anyway. I am too. We're going to have a great few days."

"Mum, meet Kareem. He became a Muslim soon after I did and I've been in his crew for the past two years so we're very special friends."

"Welcome Kareem. We so much enjoy meeting Timothy's friends."

"Thank you Mrs. Croy. This is a fantastic house."

"Well the best thing about it is that we can have lots of people to stay. It always feels much happier when it's full of friends!"

Tam took Kareem upstairs to find him a bedroom and give him a tour of the important parts of the house. They found Usman and Ali on the terrace, smoking. Tam made the introductions.

"Did you become Muslim like Tam did?" Usman was amazed to meet another person who had chosen his religion.

"I was thinking about doing it for a while but when Tam told us he had done it, that made me brave enough do it too."

"It was Usman who got me interested, then Mohammed that pushed me more."

Tam was keen to give credit to his valued friends. He went in to collect a tray of mugs of tea and a big cake on a plate. The young men sat eating and drinking and enjoying the Spring sunshine.

Tam suggested that he and Kareem should go for a walk. The Saudi brothers were watching football on television, a sport that held no interest for Tam. He wanted the opportunity to chat to his friend in private.

"What's been hassling you then mate?" Tam didn't beat about the bush.

"Nothing huge, just lots of little things that have added up to suddenly freak me really."

"I know the feeling Kareem. Are you going to tell me about them? When it happened to me, I found that saying everything out loud to Mohammed made me feel much better and then he helped me with a few of them."

"Well you know how I took Shahada in November. Obviously, that was exciting and I had loads of help from Mohammed and you, learning all the daily necessities. When I went home for the holidays it was Christmas so there wasn't much action beyond the family. That was fine. This holiday I started trying to meet up with old mates and seven different guys just don't want to know me anymore. It really hurt, hearing pathetic excuses from one of them after another. Then there is the career thing. You know I do pure maths and that kind of leads me towards banking or the stock market, great pay and still plenty of jobs in that sector. But then I realised that all that kind of work is haram because it all involves interest or selling things that either don't belong to you or don't exist at all."

"You mean selling futures and that kind of thing I'm guessing?"

"Exactly. So that makes it so much harder to find a job and I'm frightened of being unemployed."

"I'm suffering terribly from that fear too Kareem, but it isn't because of Islam in my case."

"The last thing is that I'm finding it more and more difficult not to chat up girls. You know how I was always chasing after them before!"

Tam knew that Kareem needed lots of confidence building, which could not be achieved in a trite five minute chat but he also knew that he needed to address each thing immediately to demonstrate that nothing is insurmountable.

"There will always be some people who don't like you becoming Muslim and drop you as a result. Do you remember how afraid I was when I told you guys in the crew what I had done? I really thought you might do that to me. But you've just found two new friends this afternoon! Usman and Ali are amazed by people like us who revert to Islam. The job thing is frightening and it must be even harder for you, thinking how, if you hadn't become Muslim, you might have been able to get a good job. But I think that that is just Satan trying to push you to renounce your faith. The facts are that there is no certainty that you would have got one of those glossy jobs and, knowing what a nice, honest guy you are, I don't think you'd be happy doing that sort of thing anyway. Girls? Well I stopped seeing my girlfriend Sarah, I was very upset when I had to tell her that I couldn't see her after I was Muslim, but, subhaanAllah! She said she loved me even more because of my decision and she is waiting for me until I can marry her. Usman split up with his girl because he was ashamed of himself after I started asking him about Islam and then she came back to him and asked him to marry her. They're getting married in July! So, Allah really does reward us for giving up something just for Him."

They were standing at the top of the hill now, looking out over the patchwork of fields in the river valley below.

"Thanks Tam. You always know how to make things seem simple. I knew you meant what you said about being there for me any time but I was afraid when I called you last night. I thought maybe you'd not like it in the holidays."

Tam looked his friend deeply in the eyes. "You're my mate. We've shared some tough times and loads and loads of great times and we've shared the greatest thing of all in becoming Muslims. I will always be here for you."

This discussion served only to make Tam feel more isolated and less able to seek help. He had hoped that Kareem would ask him about his worries but he didn't and he was not going to burden his friend with his feelings. That wouldn't be fair.

Tam suggested that they walk to the next village to enjoy a drink in a quiet country pub. He was keen that the brothers should get to know Kareem. Tam intercepted Usman as everyone was collecting coats and cash.

"Can you talk, gently, to Kareem about how difficult you found it when you suddenly started giving up things in the name of Islam? He's having his first jittery patch since he became Muslim and he needs lots of cheerful encouragement. Obviously don't let him find out that I've primed you, he'd be very embarrassed."

"Leave him to me! I want to get to know him better anyway."

As the evening progressed Usman and Ali quizzed Kareem about how he had learnt about Islam and what he had found easy or difficult about his new life. When they got back home everyone crowded into Tams' room and he and Ali went down to the kitchen to make tea and raid the cake tin for their bed time snack.

"It is so kind of exciting for us to know and talk to people like you and Kareem. You have to make so many difficult changes when you become Muslim. Somehow when I listen to your stories it makes me nearly cry."

Tam felt embarrassed at such a sincere comment from Ali. "It's because of people like you two that we find Islam. That is how important you are in your daily life here in England. Maybe some of your friends will see things in your life that make them want to take shahada. Then you will become responsible for them like Usman is responsible for me and now Kareem too."

As they entered Tams' room, they were surprised to find Usman and Kareem hugging. Kareem looked at Tam and he could see that there had been tears in his eyes.

"Are you OK Kareem?"

"I am now, yes. Usman makes everything seem easy."

"Usman is famous for being like that!"

Downhill to Distress

Tam drove back to Hull for the last time with a huge thunder cloud of impending doom filling his head. He wasn't worried about his "Finals", exams had never phased him before and he had no reason to fear these ones now. The dread that seemed to tinge and taint everything else was that he would be unable to secure a job, would return, alone, to live like a boy once more, controlled and curtailed by his parents and living on the dole with all the humiliating connotations of failure and inadequacy that that brought with it. Everyone would be pointing at him and laughing up their sleeves about this precocious boy who thought he was clever getting a degree and just look at him now, on the dole and sponging off his well to do parents. Tam didn't think he could bear that situation and the fear and dread of it had started to dominate his life.

After the first training and subsequent unity meeting Kareem walked with Tam to the car park.

"Thanks, so much for letting me come to see you. You and Usman really, really helped me through a terrible time."

"I'm glad we could."

Tam spoke with his voice choked with distress that he could no longer control.

"What's the matter Tam?"

"Nothing."

"That's not the right answer man!"

Kareem put his arm over Tam's shoulder and pulled him towards him. The warm, human contact of his caring friend tipped Tam over the edge.

"Shit Kareem! I just can't hack all the mess of not being able to get a job and leaving here with nothing to go to and……"

With a sob poor Tam dissolved into the tears that had been so close to the surface for the past month. Kareem pulled Tam close to him in a safe, reassuring, masculine bear hug. The two stood rooted to the spot in the empty car park as Tam soaked his friends T shirt with tears of self-pity.

"I think I need to come back with you Tam."

Kareem made clear from the tone of his voice that there was no room for negotiation.

"I'd like that." Tam spoke shakily, hoping that he would not cry again.

"How long have you been feeling like this Tam?"

"It's been building up for ages, I guess for the last month or so. Listen, you don't need to put up with my silly worries, it's the last thing that you need. I'm really sorry about earlier. I made a right idiot of myself. I feel well ashamed."

"Tam you told me that we were special friends. Brothers now we're both Muslims. Did you mean that?"

"Obviously."

"So why won't you let your friend and brother share something of yours?"

Tam smiled weakly. Kareem was right and had caught him well and truly. It would help to talk, he had known that for ages, and yet now he was trying to avoid doing so. He hoped that he wouldn't start to cry again but he felt as if he probably would.

"I think it's because I was so unhappy at school. I was never a success and I was always being put down, told I was no good, would never get to university. I was constantly being made to feel like I was useless and a failure. The three years here have rebuilt my confidence and my belief in myself. I've got great friends like you and life's been brilliant in every respect. I guess we will all be sad when it comes to an end. But if I leave without a job it will seem as if it was all a waste, everyone will see that the school were right about me. I'm a useless failure. I don't think I can live with that feeling again."

Tam's words trailed off. He couldn't talk any more. He could feel his grief overwhelming him again. He bit his lip and held his breath to try to regain control over his emotions.

"I thought you coxed the first eight at school?"

"Yes, I did."

"So how did they make you feel useless and a failure?"

"They hated me, I just didn't fit in. The Stroke of the first eight was always made captain of the boat club and a school prefect and given all sorts of awards. The cox was always just forgotten about. That's just the way it was."

"Just forget about such a crappy school."

"I thought I had but now that I can see that I'm going to be unemployed, a failure, all the hurt and pain from school is flooding back. Places like that never let you get away. I know it must sound crazy to you, but just talk to Mohammed about it and he'll confirm what I mean."

They sat in silence. Tam struggling to compose himself, Kareem struggling to comprehend something that was totally beyond his experience or understanding.

"I'm not going to pretend that I understand how a school can have such a powerful effect on you after you've left, because I don't. But I can see that you're very hurt and upset. You helped me a lot by making me talk about things so now I want you to talk to me. Tell me everything Tam, make me understand!"

Tam needed to talk. He told his friend everything about Barforth, the constant bullying, the abuse, the isolation, the oppressive weight of the demands of the school that Tim had never been able to fulfil and the constant fear, self-doubt and lack of confidence with which he still had to live.

"Shit! I'm so sorry mate. I always assumed that you'd been lucky in life, all that posh education, the privilege. I even wasn't sure that I could get on with someone like you at first. I know Kevin picked on you because of it too. And all the time you were suffering from all that hurt. Thinking how you've put up with all that and still come out of it as the great guy that we all know you are makes me feel really bad."

Kareem seemed to be thinking.

"Now I get why you never seemed to be very friendly with Richard. We often wondered how that could be."

Tam managed a smile.

"My heart sank when I was registering here on my first day at university and I met him. I felt as if the school had sent him to spy on me and keep control of me. I very nearly refused to come to cox you when you found me because I knew I'd have to deal with him. It scared me shitless to be honest."

"I'm going to make us some tea. I can't believe I've been so rude and not offered you anything. I won't be a minute."

Tam hurried downstairs to seek refuge in the kitchen. He felt very ashamed of his outburst and feared that he had said too much.

Tam's tearful evening with Kareem proved to be a considerable help. While he still maintained an all-encompassing dread of the rapidly approaching future, which made everything that he did seem kind of pointless and uninteresting, he began to feel focussed on his revision and found that he could even almost enjoy the boat club again. May, with its' two Bank Holidays and the first of the seasons' regattas, sped by and, almost before he was aware of it, Tim was setting off to sit the first of his six final exams. As always, he felt little of the dread and fear that afflicted so many of his peers.

The exams were over almost before anybody realised that they were underway. There was nothing left to do but wait for the results that would be published after two weeks.

The crew began to train even harder, all but Mohammed would soon be leaving Hull for the last time and none of them had secured a job to go to. The extra training served as a release from their growing fears and tension as well as being a way to try to ensure a continued unbroken season of wins, which would make three such seasons in a row. They all wanted to end their time at the club on a roll.

Tam went to collect Neil Blashford from the student village to go to find out the results of their Finals. As in the previous two years, they would be pinned on the department notice board by the secretary at two O'clock. The two young men went to get lunch in the Union refectory together, both resolutely radiating cheerful self confidence which neither, despite his best efforts, really felt.

"This is it Neil!"

"Yep. The culmination of three years of hard graft."

"Let's go get it!"

A crowd of their friends were milling around in the wide central hall at the top of the stairs. A buzz of nervous banter filled the air, everyone peeling their eyes for the first sight of the secretary opening her office door.

There she was! The crowd of students parted to let her get to the notice board. She pinned the two sheets of paper that would make or break so many futures to the board and returned the way she had come. Everyone surged forward, keen now to get the discovery over with.

Neil and Tam somehow found themselves near the back of the mass of students and it took a few minutes before they could get close enough to read the type written notice.

Tam located his name, near the top as always, thanks to his sir name. He clocked his result.

Tam looked again in shocked disbelief, just to be certain of what he had read.

His head filled with a strange kind of dizziness, a remoteness borne of total disbelief, unrecognition.

His eyes were not deceiving him. It was true. Written in black and white. Beside his name. There could be no mistake. And yet……How?

Tam pushed his way back through the thinning crowd. He had to get away. He could feel tears burning at the back of his eyes. He thought maybe he was going to be sick.

He hurried down the stairs and sought refuge in the gents.

Taking slow, deep breaths to calm himself he took stock of the situation. With relief he realised that he wasn't going to vomit. Glancing in the mirror above the wash basin in front of which he was standing Tam saw that he was crying. Streams of tears running down his cheeks. How pathetic!

Tam turned on the cold tap full pelt and began scooping handfuls of the icy water over his face, trying to stem his tears and clear his eyes. He started to splash water over his head, drenching his hair and, at last, bringing his emotions under shivering control.

He straightened up, took a few more deep breaths and smiled a dripping smile at his reflection. "Come on man. Be strong!"

"Tam! What are you doing mate? I've been looking for you everywhere!" Neil burst into the room. "Shit! Are you alright?"

"Yeah, 'course I am. It was just a shock. I wasn't expecting that. I just didn't know how to react. I'm really sorry."

"You're a strange man, sometimes Tam. Come on, the party's started and everyone's looking for you."

"I don't think I'm up for that now Neil."

"**What?** You get a first and you don't feel like coming to a party? I really don't get you mate."

Neil grasped Tam's wrist and propelled him out of the toilet, up the spiral stairs and into the departmental party.

Tam felt immediately shy as he became the focus of everyone's attention. He relaxed soon enough as he began to mix with his friends, tutors and lecturers.

"Tam! I've been trying to get to you all afternoon!" Chris Parker, one of Tams' Geography tutors eased him to one side.

"Congratulations! I think that result might have surprised you."

"Yes. I'm still shaking to be honest."

"It was your dissertation that did it. An academic paper of pure genius."

"Thanks!"

"This isn't the place to talk. Would you come to see me in my room at ten tomorrow morning? There's something I want to put past you."

"OK. I'll see you then. Thanks."

"Hi Mum! Yes, I'm fine. I got a first!"

Tam realised that that was the first time that he had said those words. Out loud, for the world to hear. Tim Croy, the boy who was unlikely to get any A levels, had achieved a First Class Honours Degree!

"Oh Timothy. That's fantastic. A *first!* Well done. Here's your father."

Tim could hear his mothers' whispered conversation with his father. He pictured them in the square, cool hall.

"Well done Tim! I won't say I knew you could do it because I didn't, but that is a big achievement."

"Thanks."

"Tam, that's very punctual. I sometimes think you've got an atomic clock in your brain. Let's get some coffee. You can come in to the staff office now you're no longer an undergraduate."

Settled into two easy chairs in Chris's room, Tam felt as if he was waiting to start one of his tutorials again. For the first time in nearly twenty-four hours his head filled momentarily with the feeling of gloom and sadness about his impending departure from the happy life of a student.

"Have you got a job to go to yet? I know that's probably a silly question in this climate but I have to ask, for reasons that will become clear."

Tim looked down. He felt humiliated having to answer. "No."

"You're all having a very tough time. I really feel for you all."

Both men took a swig of their overly hot coffee, as if by burning their mouth the pain of the economic situation might be abated.

"I'm going to come straight to the point Tam. Your dissertation was nothing short of inspiring. So much so that I felt certain that your ideas are worth further investigation. I've got a couple of friends in the industry with whom I took the liberty of discussing some of them. Both of them agreed with my analysis."

Tam was listening with interest. He had always liked Chris Parker and had found him inspiring in both lectures and tutorials. Something in what he was saying now was starting to ignite a feeling of hope and optimism within him. He bit his lip, not daring to let such feelings take hold within his head for fear of subsequent disappointment.

Chris laughed. "I was supposed to be coming directly to the point of this meeting and look at me. Reminiscing instead!"

Chris looked Tam in the eyes. "They want to offer you a fully funded, three year research studentship. I will supervise you, they will direct you and, if all goes to plan, you will gain a Phd at the end of it. I would expect that to lead to well paid and interesting employment with one or other of them."

Tam sat staring at his tutor. For the second time in less than one full day he could feel his emotions reacting inappropriately to wonderful news. He wondered if the worries of the recent past had pushed him into some kind of madness.

"You mean they want me to stay at the university?"

"Got it in one Tam!"

"But I don't know if I could do that. I've never thought of myself as being clever like that. Do you think I'd be able to manage?"

"If you were my son, I'd give you a good slap! I think it might constitute common assault if I did that to you so I won't. That dissertation has given you the basis for most of what you will need to do. The Ordnance Survey are going to sponsor you so all your costs will be covered and you'll have about a hundred a week living expenses. They wouldn't be making an offer like that if they didn't believe in you and your ability."

Tam drank some of his coffee. His brain was struggling to process the rapid change in his fortunes. The past day felt as if it had lasted a hundred years and he felt as if he no longer knew who he was. It reminded him of his feelings when he had become Muslim.

"You are going to accept, aren't you?"

Chris pulled him back to the here and now.

"Yes." He replied resolutely.

"Fantastic!" Chris reached across to shake his hand. "I'll get the guys to come up here very soon so that you can sign the paperwork and get to know each other. Work won't start until September. You clearly need a holiday. Oh, and I will talk to the university and get you a decent room in the student village and sort you out an office here too. You'll be doing some lectures and tutorials for the under graduates once you find your feet, you'll start to understand how over worked we all are now!"

After two hours of rowing that afternoon Tam was buying drinks in the Boat Club bar. Once his crew were settled with drinks and nuts, he told them of his sudden change in circumstance.

"That's fucking amazing mate!" Dave volunteered.

"You're the first guy I know who's got a first. I knew you were pretty brilliant but it's good to see that I was right!" Mark laughed

Kareem and Mohammad were more physical. Both stood, hoisted Tam from his seat and came close to asphyxiating him in a massive, two man, bear hug. "I think we should throw him in!"

Suddenly Tam was being carried out of the boat house, up the embankment and, with a massive splosh, into the River Hull.

As he took a much needed hot shower to clean himself of the sticky mud, Tam understood, for the first time, the reality of his new situation. It felt as if the fear and dread of the past three months were being washed away with the mud. When he joined his crew in the bar once more he felt as he should. It felt like the relief of recovery after a long illness or, at least, the lifting of a bad hangover!

"Does that mean that I've solved the problem of finding a cox for next year's First Four? Mohammad was seeing wider benefits of Tams' new situation.

"If you want it to, yes" laughed Tam. "Now look, it's you asking me to help you in the boat club. Allah really does make things balanced!"

Printed in Poland
by Amazon Fulfillment
Poland Sp. z o.o., Wrocław

54219498R00200